DAUGHTER
of the
SHADOWS

KERRY CHAPUT

Black Rose Writing | Texas

ISBN: 978-1-68513-167-8
PUBLISHED BY BLACK ROSE WRITING
www.blackrosewriting.com

Printed in the United States of America
Suggested Retail Price (SRP) $22.95

Daughter of the Shadows is printed in Abhaya Libre

*As a planet-friendly publisher, Black Rose Writing does its best to eliminate unnecessary waste to reduce paper usage and energy costs, while never compromising the reading experience. As a result, the final word count vs. page count may not meet common expectations.

Cover design Asya Blue http://asyablue.com/

DAUGHTER
of the
SHADOWS

CHAPTER ONE

Quebec City, 1667

Naira tells me that dreams are the language of the soul.

This seventeen-year-old Huron warrior's eyes seem to see into my depths. In the warmth of her longhouse, I welcome her guidance, the only one who understands this treacherous choice I've made to live a dual life. On the surface, I am Catholic. A supportive soldier's wife and a Daughter of the King. But these guises are nothing more than a front that hides the burning of my Protestant heart.

"Well," Naira asks. "What do your dreams say?"

My dreams are nothing but acidic memories of torture. The secret prayer that could have ended in boiling water poured down my throat. The beatings that left my people bloodied and broken. Dreams that remind me how I escaped and left so many to perish back in France.

"My dreams remind me I have much to atone for," I say.

"It is not your fault your people are tortured and killed."

"I betrayed them. I turned to Catholicism and fled to the colony while they're held as prisoners."

She stares at me over the fire, elbows rested on her knees. "The question, Isabelle, is not what you have done wrong, but what you will do with this opportunity."

"I'm trying. But the lies—they're growing difficult."

Nine months of brutal winter have kept me away from the Huron settlement. Shuttered in my home, I've listened for every bit of information that trickles from my husband. I pay close attention to his dealings with the king's military counsel.

But today, I'm here again with Naira, survivor of an Iroquois capture and whisperer to bears. Skilled hunter, she has saved my life more than once. She seems to have been created by something mystic— as if the moon and stars touched her before she was born, ensuring something magical exists on this corner of the earth.

"You have been practicing?"

I nod.

"Come," she says.

I follow her out of the longhouse as she swipes a caribou antler bow and a deer bone tomahawk from a hook on the wall. Her long black braid swooshes against her back and the painted edges of her deerskin dress ripple, like a beautiful snake hissing her warnings.

I follow her past the edge of the camp and into the trees, where my boots sink into wet earth. Moss blankets exposed tree roots and as wind gusts through the pines, the forest floor appears to breathe slow, emerald breaths. I'm eager to show Naira my progress, having spent hours secretly practicing in the woods behind my house.

Without warning, she drops everything and lunges for me, an arm across my chest. She yanks my hair to disarm me. I flail, trying to remember what she's taught, but it's too late. I'm already on the ground, arms pinned at my sides, tomahawk positioned at my neck.

"I even dropped the weapons for you," Naira says.

"I wasn't prepared."

"You should always be prepared." She hands me the tomahawk. "Do you think the Haudenosaunee give you a warning before they scalp you? Stand." She steps out of the way and waits for me to rise.

The blade is heavy in my hand, and my breath aches in my chest. I focus my eyes, widen my stance, and spot the tree fifty paces away, a circle of red bear grease painted on the bark.

"Now," Naira says.

Without thinking, I twist my body and throw my shoulder forward, my hand following the trajectory as she taught me. A thick white cloud breathes from my mouth, framing my view of the tomahawk as it spins through the trees.

Crack. The metal blade lands in the center of the circle, jutting out like a flag in a claimed territory.

"Do you feel that?" Naira whispers.

"Feel what?"

"Power."

My body vibrates, knowing that my hands can protect me in a way they've never been able to—until now.

"Yes." Her voice lifts. "You feel it." She hands me the next weapon. "Now, the arrow." She points to a passenger pigeon perched on the limb of a sugar maple.

"I'm better with a gun."

"A gun is loud, unpredictable. *French*," she scoffs.

"I can't get the draw right, and the wind…"

"Don't think. Just listen." She nods in encouragement and stands behind me.

As I position the arrow and tighten my elbow, Naira whispers, "Listen."

I draw with all my strength, steady my arm, and breathe. I release my grip and watch the arrow spin and thrash. The shaft slams into the bark then falls to the ground, the useless arrow not even close to the pigeon.

I drop the bow to my side and sigh.

"It is all right, Isabelle. Practice. Patience."

"I've been practicing, but archery doesn't come naturally to me."

Naira grazes her fingers over the hawk feathers on the ends of the arrows. "When I say listen, it's to the whispers of the world you know. The wind, the trees, your breath. When you let your mind rule, you cannot hear the call of the warrior."

"I'm not a warrior," I say. "I'm a soldier's wife."

"You may be both. And have been called to do so, yes?"

"I suppose I have." I stare at her fierce, dark eyes like black pearls. "In your time captured by the Iroquois, you worked with your enemies. How did you live with the people who killed your tribe?"

She turns to let the wind cool her face. The Iroquois, or Haudenosaunee as the Natives call them, dominated this land for hundreds of years before the French stole it as property of the king. The moose fur that dangles from her skirt flutters in the breeze. "I made a choice. Just as you have done."

"How did you ignore your hatred for them?"

"I focused on my greater purpose, and I learned to listen," she says. "The quieter I became, the more I heard."

"The things I hear only worsen my dreams," I say.

"It is not the memories that haunt you. It's the feeling of helplessness that still resides," she points to my heart, "right there."

"Is this the warrior speaking?"

She hands me another arrow. "No. It is the woman."

I drop the bow to the ground and lift the rifle. Barrel pointed at the trees, I aim and focus on the belly of the pigeon. With a twitch of my finger, a shot rings out and the bird plummets to the ground. "If I'm going to be a soldier's wife, I must be the kind who can kill."

•   •   •

Freshly skinned pigeon stew simmers over the fire as Naira's words play over and over in my mind. James knows nothing of my ability to hunt. He thinks I purchase all our food in town. The more he believes me to be defenseless, the better.

"More wine, Isabelle." James waves his goblet in my direction, eyes steady on the men across the table. Two royal soldiers drain their wine. They loosen cravats around their necks as their cheeks flush pink.

"Yes, dear." I lift the jug of wine that is now half empty.

As they glug, I chop squash at the end of the counter, ready to supply food and drink at their request.

"Paris promised us one hundred more soldiers. Where are they already?" one man says.

"They'll arrive next week," James says. "Not to worry. The king needs us as much as we need him."

Every time they mention the king, I make sure I'm hard at work to hide my attentive listening.

"I don't know, Lieutenant," the younger soldier says. "We're all the way out here in this God-forsaken colony. Why would he care what happens outside of Paris?"

"Young man, you underestimate Quebec. Our fur trade is very lucrative," James says.

"So, the king will protect us, then?" The young man nervously yanks on his collar. "No one will leave their homes without a weapon for fear of the Iroquois. I have a young bride to protect."

The older soldier slaps the young one on the back. "We've been fine here in town. Don't worry."

"I've heard they burn farms. Scalp the men and kidnap the women."

"We'll eliminate those savages soon enough," James says. "You and your young bride have nothing to worry about. Now please, go home and spend the evening with your wife. Isabelle, please see him out."

I hand the soldier a stewed apple cake wrapped in vellum. "Please take this to your wife." His eyes grow wide as a doe caught in front of a gun's barrel. "Madame Beaumont, you're not frightened here? It's so terribly different from France."

"No, Monsieur, nothing frightens me here." I bite my tongue to hold back what I want to say, which is that I swallowed my fear long ago. I now have a larger purpose, one only my soldier husband can help with—unknowing brute that he is.

"Oh, that's good," he says with shaky breath.

"Have a wonderful evening." I shut the door before he can release any tears. Poor child will find out soon enough that the stories of Iroquois are true.

We're all in a fight for our lives.

Back at the dinner table, I fill their goblets and offer them a tray of bread and freshly churned butter. Tender blisters line my palms from today's work, but I must never rest.

"How much money can the fur trade really supply?" the soldier asks.

James leans back and unbuttons his jacket. "Enough to fund the king's grand plans, I hope."

"Why do you care about his plans?" he asks.

"The Sun King is desperate for money," James says.

"He's the King of France. What need does he have for more money?"

"Versailles is not yet complete. He has intentions to rule the world, and this means wars fought on all fronts. Wars cost money."

The man drains the last of his wine. When I present the jug, he holds up his hand. "No, thank you. I'll be lucky to stay upright on my horse after all this." He raps his knuckles on the table. "Lieutenant Beaumont, I support your plans for a larger regiment. Once the Iroquois are no longer a threat, I care little what happens back in France. Good day."

James stumbles, but recovers with a bow, heels clicked together. After the door closes, James mutters, "Fool."

"He's naïve," I say. "Most of them are." I lead James to the chair by the fire and hand him a warm ale. I've found that once he's full of drink, James is much more likely to let his mind wander to his mouth.

"I don't need any of these men." He lifts his hand in a dismissive wave. "The king trusts me with his plans. Gather all the fur in the colonies and make him enough money to build his empire. I will not let him down."

"Of course you won't, James."

My husband has plans of his own. Living in the lower tier of the nobility has left him with a rather insatiable need to climb to the inner circle. One can buy his way in these days and James wants nothing more. My stomach turns at the idea of becoming French Nobility. I care for only one thing—secrets.

"The king must be doing well if he's ready to expand his reach," I say as I rub James's shoulders.

"Well enough, I suppose."

"What could possibly stand in his way?"

"The priests… they buy his favor." James yawns and rubs his eyes. "You don't care about these politics." He pulls me to his lap and clumsily unties my bodice.

"But I do care. You're important to France's future."

He kisses my breasts, then looks up at me and smiles. "The priests pay him, and in turn, he rules in favor of their requests."

Bare breasts and compliments are all this man needs to divulge his innermost thoughts, so I run my hands through his hair and let him get lost in my bare skin.

"What do the priests care about?" I ask.

"The Huguenots are a problem. They want to destroy them."

His voice is muffled in my chest, and I worry he can feel my heart jump. How quickly he forgets that we once were the hunted.

"Are there any left to torture by this point?" I ask with forced calm.

"Plenty." He pulls at my dress and runs his fingers along my torso. "The priests will not stop until every one of them has converted."

Everything in me tenses like an over-tightened strap.

I help him with my dress, as his drunken fingers seem incapable of managing clothing. I sit atop him naked, kiss his neck, and run his hands along my hips. "So much brutality."

He pulls my head back so I'm facing him. "Your Huguenot days are over, and our allegiance will always be with the Crown. Protestants will meet their fate."

By their fate, he means forced conversion, torture, or murder. If Protestants dare seek a better life out of France, they're captured and arrested. Anyone caught helping is sent to the galleys.

As I remove his clothes, he watches me. Stares at my body in wonder. I used to bristle at his stares, but now I derive strength from them. I've made my choices.

"The nobility has convinced the king to intervene," he says.

"Hasn't he already done that?" I pull off his breeches and slide the last of his clothing from his scarred body, reminders that years ago, James was imprisoned because of me.

"He's ordered the children to be taken away from their parents unless they convert." His eyes hang heavy, but his hands are eager.

I swallow the lump in my throat, as I push away the memories of burns and beatings, being forced to dance all night as my feet blistered and swelled. Secret prayer. Memories of the day they dragged our friend's corpse through the streets of La Rochelle, bound and naked. And now the unimaginable—children ripped from their parents' arms.

My face must have betrayed my thoughts because James brings his hand to my cheek, eyes suddenly alert. "Those days are behind you." He slides me closer and pushes inside me. No wine ever dulls that side of him.

A hot boil of rage bubbles deep in my belly. James did save me, but he also supports every death and every beating. He ignores the lives of my people, snuffed out by a selfish king and the evil people who allow it.

I push those thoughts aside and focus on him. "You deserve all the power, James."

James reaches for my hair and tucks it behind my ear. "Perhaps you will finally give me what I need."

Every intimate moment between us is a bargain.

My gold is secrets. His is taming my freedom. At the core of every fight, every touch, is his need for my ultimate loyalty.

I pull away. "Must we discuss this every time?"

"Until you agree to marry in the church, I will never fully trust you." He holds my hips and squeezes. A warning of his capabilities, and his restraint.

Our bodies don't stop moving together, and neither of us relents.

"A notary marriage is sufficient in Quebec," I say.

"How am I to gain power if my wife will not marry me in the eyes of God? What does that say about me?" He rolls his head back and moans.

I slam James's arms to the chair and hold them tight in my fists. James smiles and falls passive in my tightened embrace. Despite myself,

I've learned to enjoy the feel of him. A small solace for the life I've chosen.

"You'll have to trust me," I say.

"Trust is for fools."

As we move and rock together, I run my hands along his scars, reminders that we all make sacrifices and eventually, we all get burned.

• • •

James wakes the next morning, eyes bright red with a face to match. "Why do you let me drink so much?"

"You are your own man, James Beaumont. I'm merely a soldier's wife." I hand him a wet cloth so he may wipe his face and neck.

The late spring breeze is cool, with a hint of summer in the bright sun that shines through our morning window. I sometimes ache when I look at my surroundings. Warm furs, endless firewood, and a pantry full of food. Every luxury serves as a reminder that across the ocean, Huguenots starve and freeze, fighting for their right to exist.

James slides a slab of stale bread and cheese near me, his less than humble request that I prepare his plate. "Are you going to the abbey again today?" he asks.

"Yes. The new Daughters of the King have arrived from France."

James wraps his arms around me. "I've accepted that this is important to you. Since you've been unable to conceive, I'm sure it soothes your emptiness."

Behind my smile, my teeth press together so hard my temples ache. Three years I've been without child, and he assumes the strain from our first few months in Quebec has ruined my chance at motherhood.

I let him think it.

I kiss him on the cheek. "I'll have supper waiting for you when you return home tonight."

"I hope you will have more than that waiting for me," he says with a wink.

Part of me thinks he enjoys that my body will remain his. Grateful that a child hasn't stolen my breasts and my affection. He cares about image too much to ever fully accept a childless marriage but for the time being, it works for both of us.

"Goodbye, James."

He dons his hat and smiles as he leaves our home. I watch from the window as he mounts his horse and gallops through the thicket of balsam fir and white spruce toward town.

Once he's out of sight, I draw the curtains and light a candle. The loose board in the corner of our bedroom welcomes me yet again. I retrieve my hidden Geneva Bible, its worn leather binding as soft as a mother's touch. I hold it to my chest and breathe, but glimpse my rosary. Glass beads and a gold crucifix pendant dangle from the dresser, seeming to cast their displeasure.

On my knees, I open the Bible and hug the words. I remember those who sacrificed, and those who died for me. Tears gather in my eyes, and I sing a soft hymn in French as I think of the families ripped apart, spit at, beaten, and chained to walls. My past in La Rochelle never lies far from the surface. Visions live in my memory of sunlight bouncing off limestone buildings and waves beating a constant drum in the background. The brutal beauty of my hometown sits like a stone weight on my heart.

Every day I begin on my knees in secret prayer and mourn my losses. And every day I close my Bible, resolute in my purpose. This is the life I have chosen, and through heartache, I see survival. Not just for me, but for my people.

A last glimpse at my arm before I once again bury my secret. My branded H that once throbbed hot, now aches with power. My marriage affords me knowledge of the Sun King's plans—knowledge I can use. If I save even one Huguenot from torture, it will all have been worth it. I kiss my Bible and slide the board back into place.

"Until tomorrow, old friend."

I mount my horse and ride toward town, as the cool May air sharpens my focus. Faster and faster, I push my horse toward a gallop and then a run. I know these trees intimately and under the shady pines might be the only place I feel free. Sunlight flicks past me as the scent of dirt and moss fill my nose. Deep into the forest, I head toward the edge of the city. Past the legal territory and into a region that James has strictly forbidden.

By the time I arrive at the tiny shack in the trees, I'm breathless and bursting to tell my secrets. I throw open the door and find Henri reading by the fire.

He greets me with a wicked smile. "You aren't due for another three days. Do you have news, or have you just missed me?"

I remove my cape and pour myself an ale. "I think your time hidden in the woods has gone to your head, Henri."

"I'm not always alone." He stretches back in his chair. "Plenty of lonely women in Quebec who can keep a secret."

I shove his chest. "Don't be a fool. You'll get caught."

"They think I'm a reclusive hunter in need of a warm bed. What am I to do, live for weeks out here alone while I wait for your secrets?" He kicks his chair back and stands. "Speaking of, what do you know?"

"The nobility is coming up with new forms of torture. They want to steal their children unless they convert."

"Steal them?"

"Give them to Catholic families."

"Monsters." Henri snarls and looks up to the ceiling. "They'll all die if we don't do something."

"We need a plan, Henri."

He paces the tiny room as his face pulses red. "Geneva is distributing pamphlets that encourage Huguenots to flee to Helvetia. They're welcome in most every country outside of France.

"How do you know that?" I ask.

"Andre brought a message back last week."

My body tightens at the mention of his name. The man I walked away from, and the man I try so desperately to forget. I avoid him, as seeing him breaks my will to carry on with this dual life. Henri and

Andre travel to English-ruled Acadia, where they send and receive letters from the Protestants back in Europe.

"France will never let the Protestants leave," I say.

"Those bastards hate us but still hold us prisoner rather than let us flee." Henri throws his book at the crumbling bricks of the fireplace. "Of course, they need us. Every silk weaver and artisan is Huguenot. The country would fold without us."

I'm fully aware that my old friend's intentions are as aligned with the murder of Catholics as the rescue of Protestants, so I'm grateful he's on our side. Revenge seems to run through him like a lightning storm. I can't blame him. We've both spent our lives under the cruel hand of Catholic power.

"There's more."

"James has provided again. Good man." Henri snarls but focuses his attention.

"The priests own the king. They pay him to rule in their favor and without them, the monarchy would be in financial ruin."

"And the only thing the priests want," Henri says, "is to kill Huguenots."

"That's correct." I step up to warm my hands at the fire.

"But our people," Henri mutters. "They're so frightened, they won't leave their homes."

"So, we make them listen," I say.

"They know what will happen if the Catholics catch them escaping."

"Can you get your hands on some of those pamphlets?" I ask. "We need to distribute them."

"It's risky, but we can try," Henri says.

"We need to get word to the next ship to distribute them in France."

"I'll have Andre ask for them on his next trek into English territory."

His name once again sends my chest aching. I open the door and take in the morning sun to avoid Henri's stare. I think I've hidden my thoughts, but my old friend knows me too well.

"You have to let him go, Isabelle," Henri says.

"Yes, I do." I grip the doorway and take a deep breath. "It's been three long years since we said goodbye. You'd think the pain would fade by now."

Survival demands sacrifice, and my love was the first volunteer.

Henri wraps his arm around me, his scent like a familiar dream. Children of the shadows, we grew up in a secret church with a hidden fire in the depths of La Rochelle. Our fight started back then when we were hit and burned, branded, and intimidated. Everything we lived through brought us here, across the ocean to New France, where heartache swims a constant stream in our lives.

I force myself to remember the screams that ripped through La Rochelle from the prisoners chained to the tower wall. Maman's last breath in my arms. My backside lashed when I worked as a servant.

A broken heart is nothing I can't tolerate.

"We need you, Isabelle. Your secrets keep our operation alive."

We stare at the maple trees as their leaves flutter in the morning breeze. "I won't stop—ever. I'm in this until we get them all out. Every last one of them."

He squeezes me tight. "We're working on it, old friend."

The sun casts golden light over the forest. I step off the porch and into the fresh warmth, eyes closed and cheeks toward the sky.

"I must do more," I say. I turn to face Henri. "I'll finally have to swallow the burning need for freedom. James can move to the king's inner circle if he chooses carefully."

"So, now you won't just listen for secrets, you'll push James closer to the ones we're trying to fight."

"Of course, I see the irony of that, Henri. I'll help James become a monster."

"He was well on his way before you," he says.

"James can be manipulated, and I'm learning that for more secrets, he must get closer to the royal court. We both must."

"You're serious?"

I turn to look at Henri as his wild dark curls flutter in the wind. "Do not underestimate me."

"I would never," he says with a smile.

"Until next week, then."

Henri nods, rarely speechless. I mount my horse and sail through the trees as wind whips through my curls and snaps my cheeks with cool air. I kick my heel to the horse's side, and we fly through the Quebec forest toward home.

Here, every day is a new sacrifice.

CHAPTER TWO

The latest group of King's Daughters arrived yesterday, but my impromptu visit to Henri kept me away from the abbey. I was among the first dozen girls to land on the shore of the St. Lawrence River, and they arrive by the hundreds now. Promised a new life, these young women leave extreme poverty in France for the opportunity to choose their husbands in Quebec.

"Madame Beaumont." Sister Marguerite embraces me. This wise nun helped me through the difficult transition to Quebec life three years ago.

"Lovely day, isn't it, Sister?"

"That it is," she says. "The girls are restless. They're eager to choose their mate."

"Must we force them so quickly?"

"It's their choice, Isabelle. If they wish to marry today, it is my obligation to help them sign their contract."

"You've set a gathering for *today*?" They're expected to choose a husband before the seasickness wears off.

Sister Marguerite shrugs. "I'm doing as I'm told. Many settlers will arrive this afternoon, eager to impress our young ladies."

"Then let's make sure our young ladies understand that there is a tomorrow, and a tomorrow after that. There's no need to choose a husband right away."

Marguerite shakes her head and extends her arm toward the staircase. "Well go on, then. They're in their quarters."

"Perfect." I lift my skirts and march upstairs to the newly appointed sleeping quarters. With a quick knock, I slide open the door. "Hello, ladies."

The girls all turn to face me as their hopeful eyes glitter with promises of a family and food and a fresh start.

Twenty beds, each with a trousseau. Inside the chests will be clothing, sewing supplies, mirrors, combs, and, of course, money. The king gifted them each a dowry and a promise of a farm. They'll be paid more once they sign their contract, and again with each baby they bring to New France.

"Are you... the one that married a soldier?" one asks.

This is always their first question. Most Daughters marry settlers and fur trappers. I wish I could tell them that life with a soldier isn't all that it seems.

"Yes, I am," I say. "And I'm here to welcome you to Quebec. Today you'll learn how to write your name, and I'll teach you what goes into a marriage contract."

"Why would we need to learn that?" The voice comes from a beautiful young girl in the back of the room. Tall stature with big, round eyes. "I'm here for a husband, not an education," she says.

I wait for the room's attention to return to me. "You are here for both, my dear."

"What time will we meet the settlers?" another girl asks, her cheeks already pinked like a summer sunset.

I cross my hands in front of my hips. "Tell me, have you thought of what questions to ask these men?"

"Questions?" She shifts her weight from one foot to the other.

"Certainly, you don't intend to choose a man based on his facial hair?" I ask.

A few snickers bubble through the room.

"I..." she stutters, "I hadn't thought."

A girl steps forward from behind the others. "You should ask if they have a home, hunting privileges, an established farm, and what they want out of a wife."

I straighten my posture, pleased to hear that at least one young woman understands the weight of this opportunity. "Very good," I say. "Step forward."

The girl's blond curls fall unrestrained around her shoulders. Creamy vanilla skin with clear, bright blue eyes that stare me down like an eagle. I can tell right away she isn't from Paris. She's too wild.

"Where are you from, Mademoiselle?"

She hesitates. "The coast."

The ones who've been through hell back in France have earned a hardened skin that serves them well here in the colonies. This girl has something more than that.

"The others would do well to listen to you…" I tilt my head, not sure of her name.

"Charlotte."

"Yes. You should all listen to Charlotte's guidance. Now, everyone downstairs for a bite to eat and your first lesson."

The girls shuffle past as they look at their feet. Charlotte doesn't move.

"Is there something on your mind, Charlotte?"

She looks around to ensure everyone has left the room before squaring her shoulders. "I'm from La Rochelle."

A deep thump hammers my stomach. That city name breaks loose memories in my body.

"I've heard of you, Isabelle Colette," she says.

My breath catches. "I haven't been called that for many years."

"Because you are no longer a Colette. You are now a Beaumont. Part of the Catholic inner circle who tortures and kills innocent Huguenots."

I search her face for familiarity, but I can't place her. "I'm not sure what you're suggesting, mademoiselle."

She steps close. Uncomfortably close. "That you're a traitor."

If she were anyone else, and *I* anyone else, her cheek would sting from a slap. But I can't blame her for her harshness. Her life has taught her to fight and defend—to trust no one. I want to hug her, but I'm smarter than that. "I am not who you think."

"You are the girl who danced for the dragoons all night to save ten others. You are the girl who broke a man's spine because he threatened your mother during the exile. And you are the girl who found freedom in a new land, only to marry the handsome Catholic soldier who helped you escape."

Memories stab at my heart, like a fist with blades that squeeze until I bleed. "That was a long time ago."

"You are a loyal Catholic now, I see."

Words of truth want to escape my mouth, with reassurances that I haven't strayed from who I once was. But danger lurks in the truth. "As are you, Charlotte. A Catholic Daughter of the King."

"I didn't hesitate when they threatened my mother. I confessed to the crime of practicing Protestantism and converted right in the town square." Her shoulders soften, almost imperceptibly. "As I'm sixteen and did not put up a fight, they bestowed great kindness on me. They only whipped my mother three times instead of ten."

I turn away to control my reaction. Nightmares crawl underneath my skin all day and all night. Sounds haunt me. The searing flesh of a branding iron on my forearm and the whip of flesh from a lashing.

"What's wrong?" she asks. "Have you forgotten how terrible it is for us?"

I want to shake her, scream that I remember it every time I close my eyes. The way blood streams into ribbons when it catches water. The snap of bones cracked in two. It's all as clear and painful as it ever was.

I won't let her upset me. I'm now skilled at swallowing anger for a later day.

"I am no longer one of them, and neither are you. We converted and are here to fulfill our duty to France." I pretend to believe every word.

"You were someone to admire. Now look at you. A rosary in your hand and a soldier in your bed."

Her disrespect ignites my guilt, but I don't let her see it. "I don't know who you think you are, but you became just like me the moment you accepted their baptism."

She bites her bottom lip as her eyes redden with tears. "You saved my sister."

My tortured past floods back to me and I'm terrified to ask more. "Who is your sister?"

"Clémentine."

Her name knocks the breath from my chest. The girl I found shaking and bloody after a sailor had raped her. The night I danced for the dragoons was to save her from a lashing—or worse.

"Clémentine?" My voice shakes more than I intend.

"She died last year."

I have no time to adjust to the news. *Dead.*

"They caught a group of women praying in the forest," Charlotte says. "The Catholics chained them to the tower wall. You remember the screams, don't you? After her capture, I would hide and listen for her wails. She caught a cough and died shortly after. I'm told her last words were, *I tried to be brave.*"

Prisoner screams. I can summon that sound with no effort at all. The pain and torture, the freezing nights. The visions grip me so tight that the room grows small. "I'm so sorry to hear that."

"I've chosen the same path as you, Isabelle. But I do not plan to take a husband. I will live free and wild in the forest. I will sew my own clothes and hunt for food. What I will not do is give into the demands of a Catholic world that has burned us at every turn."

I focus on the bright red flames as they lick the giant fireplace. "You'd do well to keep that information to yourself."

"I'm not stupid." She examines me, running her blue eyes over my face. "Our people talk of you as if you were a Protestant Joan of Arc. A hero. I'm sad to discover that you are merely another disappointment."

I want to scream at her and throw her to the ground the way Naira showed me. Then I remember Clémentine. She died because I forced her to be brave. My people are chained to walls while I live protected and safe in Quebec. Charlotte is right, I am a traitor.

"Good day, Madame Beaumont. I look forward to your lessons." She lifts her skirts and makes her way out the door while I stare out the window at a teary view of the garden.

I curl my fingers into a claw and scratch at the chipped paint on the window frame. Deep brown flakes stab into the tender space under my fingernail.

Flashes return as if I'm still living the horror.

Blood drips from the limestone walls of La Rochelle and streams over the white marble steps from the bodies of impaled Huguenots. The way the crimson blood splatters. The way their shoes point to the sky. I focus on the shoes so I won't see their contorted faces.

My entire body trembles. First, my hands. Vibrations thunder up my arms to my neck, which now beads with sweat. Frozen, the only thing I can move is my fingers, which keep peeling the paint.

"Madame?"

The voice feels far away and garbled.

"Madame?" Someone turns me and I now face Sister Marguerite. "Are you all right?" She shakes my shoulders to pull me out of my trance.

I swallow and find my voice. "Yes, I… I just felt faint for a moment."

"Sit." She leads me to the nearest bed. "You're as pale as a sickly newborn. Perhaps I should call for Monsieur Beaumont."

"No." I take a deep breath to cleanse my shaking body. My chest crackles as it attempts to expand. "I'm fine. A bit of fresh air and I'll be ready for today's lesson."

She lifts my hands, palms up, and examines the underside of my fingernails. She plucks a flake of paint, which stings as it retracts from my tender skin. "Are you certain you feel all right?"

"It might be time to freshen up the paint here," I say. I stand but pause for my legs to feel their weight against the floor. "See you at lessons."

Down the stairs and into the garden, I pull the last sliver from under my nails, secretly enjoying the sting that drops blood when the sharp edges trail along my flesh.

• • •

I stand with the nuns at the entrance to the barn and watch the girls line up, only armed with today's lesson on contracts and dreams of a family. This is the very barn I stood in when I first arrived. The grassy field outside these doors is where I first met Andre. I've avoided Charlotte's eyes all day, focusing on the rest of the young women.

"I spent the entire two hours today encouraging them to make a wise choice," I say to a nun. "I can only hope they listened."

"If they find their mate today, would it be so terrible?" she asks.

"Of course not. I simply want them to understand that the power is in theirs. They should take their time and choose wisely. They will most likely be with these men for a lifetime."

Or until they catch a deadly cough from the impossible winters, or they're captured by the Iroquois. But I don't say these things. No one wants to hear about illness and scalping on the day of their marriage.

"Line up, ladies," a nun says.

The girls take their places while they pinch their cheeks and fluff their hair. Charlotte stares at me, uninterested in her appearance.

We let the settlers into the doors and form them into a line. The men beam with eager smiles as they work their way through potential brides. I walk beside them with an intense glare, so they understand we are here to protect the girls. I am the only Daughter who has returned to help the future wives of Quebec. All the others are busy having babies.

"I choose him," the first girl in line says.

"She's spoken to him for thirty seconds," I mutter. "Why don't they listen to me?"

The nun shrugs and leads the pair to the notary against the back wall, where she drapes a strip of lace over her head and hands her a quill to sign her marriage contract. The entire unromantic affair lasts less than a minute. Once she signs, she will retrieve her ox, chickens, seeds, and, of course, fifty livres. In a few hours, she will disrobe for him and share his bed, to begin the important task of bearing children.

I hear many of the girls ask important questions, and it fills me with pride. Charlotte smiles, but her coldness indicates she will not be choosing a husband today. After two hours of this show, five women have chosen husbands and the rest will wait until the next set of interviews.

"Another successful day, Madame Beaumont." Sister Marguerite loops her arm in mine as we escort the women back to the abbey.

"Yes, Sister."

"Madame, have you spoken to Madame LaMarche recently?"

I turn to face her. "I make a habit of avoiding Antoinette."

"Oh. Well, I wish her well."

"Yes," I mutter.

"I thought you might have rekindled your friendship," she says.

"I can't say we were ever friends." That wicked woman tortured me. Harassed me and set my hair on fire as a child.

"I assumed, since Monsieur Beaumont meets with Antoinette and her father, that perhaps you've mended the rift."

An uneasy sickness ripples through me. My lying husband is meeting with the LaMarches behind my back. Their families tried to push James and Antoinette together back in France, but James chose me, and we've been swatting Antoinette away like a fly ever since.

I force a smile. "No, Sister, Antoinette remains who she has always been."

LaMarche is the reason the town tore us from our homes and beat us as we fled the city. He is the reason my father lost his ships and died in a fight to claim them back. How James can look that man in the eye and not send a knife through his throat is beyond my understanding.

I force myself to walk slowly and unconcerned, but my body tightens, desperate to run into the forest and scream into the open air.

Charlotte glances back over her shoulder. Her piercing blue eyes shoot disapproval straight through me.

I leave Sister Marguerite at the abbey gates, the place where I said goodbye to Andre and chose James. Loyalty seemed like the only thing that mattered back then, but the past is one thing we cannot change.

I walk toward home, deep in the trees along a worn path. It's only when I near my house that I turn and hasten a fast trek toward the river. The sun will set in a mere two hours, and James will be furious if I stay out past dark again.

Thirty minutes into the cover of trees, my breath forms a soft white cloud. I think I hear footsteps in the marshy ground, so I stop to look, but see nothing.

Birds scatter from a tree and the wind brushes against my cheeks. I hold still and quiet, and I listen, but the only sound is my heart thumping against my chest. Not a sound more than ice melt as it drips into puddles.

I exhale and step forward.

An arrow spirals past me, narrowly missing my face, shot into the bark of a balsam fir. I crouch to the ground and scan my surroundings.

More birds fly above and I'm not sure which direction to turn. The Iroquois rarely come this close to Quebec in daylight. I scan the trees but still see nothing. Then, quiet feet patter through the forest. The sound bounces in all directions and I sit, frozen. Perhaps I'm already surrounded.

I decide to crawl. Another arrow flies over my head and I throw my body to the earth, my cheek landing in a partially frozen puddle of mud. I should run, but fear holds my bruised cheek against the ice patch.

Footsteps thump toward me and I close my eyes, arms over my head. I can only hope they're merciful.

Hands grab me.

I flinch as they roll me to my back. I look up at the treetops and hold my hands to my face as I prepare for a tomahawk to the eye.

"You didn't even try to run."

I lower my hands and blink to focus. "Naira?"

She looks down at me, arms crossed. "You are not listening."

She helps me up. Mud drips from my hair and face. "I did listen. I heard footsteps and noticed birds break from the tree."

"Where is your weapon?" she asks.

"I don't have one."

She raises her eyebrows and places an arrow back in her quiver. "And how are you going to defend yourself? Your sharp wit?"

"I think that was an attempt at humor, but it's difficult to tell."

"Come back to camp. You'll freeze if we don't get you dry."

I follow her through the trees to the Huron camp. Women tend to their maize and beans, life sprouting from the ground as the snow and ice disappear into the earth. In her birchbark longhouse, we warm ourselves by the fire. She hands me a deer hide to wipe my face and neck clean.

"What were you doing out there, anyway?" I ask.

"Sitting with nature. Listening to its whispers."

"And you thought you'd shoot my eye out in a fun game?"

She shrugs. "I missed on purpose. Your eye was never in any danger."

Naira's husband arrives with their baby girl. A woman hands me a bowl of warmed broth, which I gladly take. I sip, and watch Naira hold her daughter, who grabs at her braid and slaps her cheek.

The child seems to have softened her, but the warrior in her remains always on guard. "She's simply perfect, Naira."

"Yes, she is." She kisses the baby's temple and Naira's husband flashes a warm smile before carrying the child outside.

"She looks so much like you," I say.

"It is no surprise she doesn't look like my husband," she says.

"Why is that?"

"He is not her birth father." Naira hangs the deer hide to dry near the fire.

I choke on the broth. "I'm sorry?"

"I took many partners. Six, to be exact."

My naïveté bubbles to the surface. "Oh."

"It is customary." Naira watches the fire crackle and smoke. "Wyandot women may experience several men—any they choose. When I became pregnant, my lovers all claimed my child, and I chose my husband from potential fathers."

All this while the Daughters of the King must have priests sign for their purity. "Why did you choose him?"

"He has kind eyes, and he understands my needs." She smiles at him as he bounces their baby on his shoulders. "Now, you are struggling. I see it in your eyes."

I hesitate, not wanting to relive the conversation from today, nor the terrifying memories that attack me when I least expect them.

"I can't rid myself of visions. Memories grab hold and they seem to control me."

She examines my face, taking a moment to consider my concerns. "When I presented myself to the Haudenosaunee, they took me to the chief. Stripped me naked and tied a rope around my waist. I lifted my arms to make it easier for them to secure. It was then that the chief instructed them to mark me with red paint, a sign that I could be adopted."

"You could have also been scalped."

"That is accurate," she says with a nod. "A man was there with me. A Frenchman captured after he killed one of their family. They tied him to a scaffold while the children stabbed his feet with knives and the grieving family peeled his fingernails, leaving bloody stumps at his fingertips."

I feel my eyes widen, but I try not to react as Naira doesn't even twitch.

"They made me watch to see if I would cry out. If I would recoil."

"How could you not?"

"I accepted my situation, as warriors do. I stepped to the scaffold and held my hands out to the family and offered my fingers for their torture."

"What did they do?"

"They returned me to the hut and left me alone for twenty-four hours. Then they appeared with a hot meal and two women to brush and braid my hair."

"Did they ever torture you?"

"No. But the memory of that man's fingers stayed with me. I have seen so much worse. But those raw fingertips still hold a space in my mind."

"For me, it's the way the blood clung to buildings like a crawling spider."

She nods. "The images return to us when we question our place in the world."

I look around the longhouse, to the thick furs and bowls of fishbones. The settlement of birchbark houses has moved many times over the years. With each Iroquois attack and famine and burning, her people find the strength to move again.

"I sometimes wonder if I should have died with the rest of the Protestants during exile."

"But you are here, Isabelle." She seems to stare straight through to my fragile center.

"I try to fulfill my purpose with information that might save more Huguenots. But the lies... they wear me down."

"You must remember, you are stronger than your fears."

A child runs through the door. She ducks under the animal hides and squeals as she runs toward Naira. Footsteps cause my heart to stop. I feel his presence before he steps inside the longhouse. All the emotions I usually ignore flood out of me and pool at my feet.

Andre.

He freezes when he notices me but pulls his gaze away, only to make sure his little girl doesn't knock something over. Naira and I stand. My legs want to run, but I can't seem to move.

"Isabelle," he says.

His voice ruins me. I look in his eyes but hold myself back from touching his arms as I teeter on forgetting everything I've done to move on from him.

"Andre." I steady my voice. "You look well."

He nods without even a hint of a smile. After three years, he can still take my breath away. In the moment of silence where we stare uncomfortably at each other, I remind myself that I chose James and Andre chose Louise.

"Monsieur Boucher," Naira says. "Welcome, friend."

Andre rubs his neck, which has flushed red.

Naira cradles the child in her arms. "Little Elizabeth. Would you like to visit the baby?" The child claps and Naira glances at the two of us. "I will take the children to tend to the crops. Isabelle, we will continue your lessons soon." She stops and looks over her shoulder. "You have work to do."

She leaves Andre and I to stare at each other, neither of us wanting to speak.

Somewhere, in the smallest corner of my mind, rests sweet memories of Andre. I let myself crawl into that space only at my lowest moments. I remember his kiss, his touch, the way he looked at me. The freedom I felt. I suspect being close is as torturous for him as it is for me.

"I should go." I turn to leave, but he brushes my elbow. The world seems to tip sideways, as the whisper of what my life could have looked like rests in his touch.

His fingers linger on my arm. "Remember our prayers? Meeting in the hidden barns of Quebec, darkness lit by candlelight and Protestant hymns. An entire life of possibility before us?"

"How could I forget?" I focus on the fire and the smoke as it climbs to the opening in the center of the high ceiling.

His hand finally slides from my arm. He pauses, then steps next to me, his chest nearly pressed against my shoulder. "I miss those candlelit nights."

I close my eyes and let myself feel his body against mine and try to steady my weak legs. "Your daughter. She spends time with Naira?"

"This clan is my family. Louise doesn't approve, of course."

I've heard Louise complain of Andre. She seems barely able to tolerate him. I think of my own marriage and how little James and I truly know each other. "I'm sure she doesn't approve of the months you spend away on fur expeditions."

"Our secret Protestant world—she would never understand. Neither would James." He pulls away, seeming to realize that our bodies have drawn together.

I turn to face him, finally letting myself bask in his eyes. "I try to keep distance from you, but our common goal has kept us close."

"And now you will help James become the people we fight against." He shrugs. "Henri told me about your plans."

"I will never be one of them. I'll only pretend to." My inner voice screams for me to look away, but I hold my gaze.

Amber light flickers against his reddened cheeks. "James hasn't become a monster yet, but he's capable."

Something I remind myself of every day.

"He can forget about his Protestant past," I say. "But I never will."

"It isn't our past, Isabelle. It's our present. I haven't given up on our plan."

Just like Henri, Andre worries that I'll fall apart under my husband's twisted games. That I'll forget my promises and let the Protestant fight slip away from my heart. I won't. "I might have lost my way three years ago, but everything I do now is for them."

He nods and steps back.

"I'm going to save as many as I can, Andre."

He runs his hand through his thick honey hair. "We both will."

I allow myself one last intense stare, an image I can hold when the darkness envelops me. "It's nearly dark. I must go."

"Where is your horse?"

"I walked." I hurry outside and wave goodbye to Naira and the children.

"Wait," Andre says. "Take my knife."

When I grab the handle, his fingers trail over mine. "Thank you." Stormy clouds brew in the distance, bruising the deep cobalt sky. "It's hard to be near you," I manage to say.

"I hate being here with you as much as I hate being without you." He exhales as all his rough edges soften and blur, our hearts seeming to connect over faded memories.

I can no longer look into his eyes. It's too painful. I don't dare glance back as I run through the forest toward home. My fingers trace the engraved initials on his knife... AB.

I once was a girl who risked my life to forage food in the forest, blade tucked in the ankle of my boot. My neck beads with perspiration when I remember the fighter I used to be.

The fighter I'm desperate to become again.

CHAPTER THREE

Sunday Mass nauseates me, as usual, but I force myself to smile, arm in arm with my husband in the front pew. The cathedral sits between the seminary and the Jesuit Church, reminding everyone that the Catholic King has his hand in every aspect of Quebec life. The Catholics busy themselves with all this nonsense of Latin and incense. I often wonder if James feels his faith the way I do, in my heart and in my breath. He was once a Protestant too, a fact he spends his life trying to erase.

Gone are the light head and fidgeting hands when the priest carries on about faith and God and duty to our King. Every word settles into me as fuel now, an education in the people I need to outwit.

"That bruise is unsightly," James whispers in my ear.

When I arrived home last night after the sun fell, James looked at my mud-caked dress and bruised cheek and said, "I can only assume you've disobeyed me again."

I did the only thing I could—I lied. I told him I tripped on the way home from the abbey. He was not sympathetic. He carried on for ten minutes about my selfish whims. In the end, he believed me because what else would a childless soldier's wife do with her time?

I loosen a lock of hair so a curl hangs over the bruise. "I'm sorry, James. You deserve better."

I learned long ago how to make him happy. He knows nothing of my true self, the girl only Henri and Naira and Andre see. So, I smile and swallow the yearning to run out of this church and never look back.

After Mass, we stroll through the marketplace so James can greet each of the town's wealthiest merchants.

We pass Antoinette and her father as they berate the barrel maker.

"You promised me higher quality," Monsieur LaMarche says. "These won't hold in a sea voyage."

"Perhaps we should hire a barrel maker from France," Antoinette says. "These country merchants aren't very skilled."

"I'm sorry, Monsieur," the merchant says. "I will try again."

Antoinette catches my eye and scowls. I smile as big and wicked as I can manage and pull James away from the door.

"She hasn't changed, has she?" I ask.

"She will always be difficult," James says.

I hesitate, as James doesn't like to be questioned. "Sister Marguerite mentioned she's seen you at the tavern with the LaMarches. Do you have a new endeavor?"

He bites the side of his lip and shoots a glance sideways at me. "You have nothing to worry about, darling."

"I'm sure I don't, but you know how I feel about them." Holding in what I truly want to say feels akin to a mouthful of acid. The LaMarches are pure evil. Every time I believe Antoinette might have found light in her heart, her father darkens it once again.

James pulls me close. "He's powerful, Isabelle. I need his connections. He can convince the king to send even more soldiers to Quebec."

I place my hand firmly on his cheek and position our profile in Antoinette's view while I kiss him. "You're ten times the man LaMarche could ever be."

My words ring of truth. For all his misguided notions, James aims for honor and loyalty. But his arrow is easily swayed, and changes course with the direction of the wind.

"Your kisses have a hold over me, Madame Beaumont."

I pull James away and glance over my shoulder. A crimson-faced Antoinette pounds the barrel in front of her. "You'll make them again and take ten percent off the cost."

I burn to ask more, but I must let it go for now.

"How was your time at the abbey yesterday?" James asks.

"Oh, uneventful."

"As I'm sure it usually is," he says with a laugh.

Charlotte's conversation still bites at my heart. I converted to the religion that branded an H on my flesh and killed my entire family. I became a King's Daughter and married a Royal Soldier in a Catholic colony.

And now I watch as the man who ordered my torture crawls his way back into my life—because my husband has welcomed him in.

• • •

This morning's conversation leaves me uneasy. I told James I would spend the afternoon at the abbey—another lie. After two hours educating the girls on marriage contracts, I slipped out the back door to avoid another encounter with Charlotte.

As my boots crunch pine needles and broken twigs on the forest floor, my breath settles into a steady rhythm. I run my fingers along the emerald moss that clings to the bark of a white birch tree. Under a canopy of pine boughs and cypress shadows, the world feels safe.

James knows how important the tribe is to our success here, yet he can't accept one particular person's influence in my life. The one person I won't let him take from me.

I stand at the entrance to the settlement and watch Naira bury whole sturgeon in cornfields. Her long black hair reflects the sunlight, ribbon weaved through her braid that trails to her waist.

"Naira," I call.

She dries her hands on her dress and breaks a smile when she nears. "Isabelle. Are you ready to get to work?"

"Yes, I am." I look over her shoulder. "Why do you bury whole fish?"

"The fish release nutrients to the soil over time. It lends to a larger crop to feed our entire clan."

"If the French were in charge of food, we'd throw the entire basket of fish on the fire and devour them whole."

Naira smiles. "Ah, it is a good thing I am not French."

At the clearing in the center of the encampment, Naira beckons me. Uneasiness thumps through my chest and limbs.

"Here? Where everyone can watch?"

"There is no better place."

I step hesitantly to her, noting the eyes that surround me. The Huron all seem to know I will fail. I know I will too, but here I stand.

"What is your greatest fear?" Naira asks loudly.

"I... I don't know."

She circles me. "Yes, you do."

I blink to focus my blurred eyes and tighten my fists to slow my rapid heart. It's unclear if she'll attack from the side, front, back, or some other direction entirely.

"Don't think," she says. "Just speak. What do you fear?"

Her quiet feet as she pads around me upset my focus and her extended arms keep me on edge.

"I used to be threatened," I say. "Beaten."

"That is not a fear, that is a fact. Try again."

Naira weaves closer and farther, wielding her power over me. "I'm afraid that... I'll be back there again."

She flips my hair from behind and I whip around to face her, only to find she has moved again. The Huron observers move closer, stopping their tasks to encircle us with inquisitive eyes. "And what happens if you go back?" Naira asks. "What do you fear?"

My arm pulses and my heart thumps in my throat. She shoves me from behind. "What do you fear?" she shouts.

I regain my stance and turn, facing her now as she walks in a circle. Tears pool in my eyes. We step in unison, arms out, eyes focused on each other. She lunges. She shoves my hand behind me, between my shoulder blades, my shoulder pushed to the edge of its joint. I pull away, but she's too strong. She towers over me, much taller, leaner, and fiercer.

She whispers in my ear. "Fear breaks us. What would break you again?"

I buck and throw my shoulders, but she holds me tight until tears spill from my eyes. "I'm afraid of being helpless." When I stop fighting, she gingerly brings my arm to my side but still holds my hand.

"Step one," she says. "Master your mind."

"What is step two?" I ask.

She kicks her leg forward and swipes my feet out from under me. My back thuds to the ground, and seemingly in a split second, her knees crush my elbows as her hand wraps around my throat. "Master your body."

Crushed under her weight, my body aches and longs to go home… but my mind feels alive. Something has sparked to life. "Ouch," I say.

She smiles and releases me, her hand extended to help me up. "When you came to me last year and wanted to become a fighter, you were not ready."

"I was scared." Naira's clan has returned to their activities, unimpressed with me. "I still am."

"Tell me more," she says.

"I'm forced into Catholic Church, near my greatest tormentor as I steal secrets from my husband. I'm afraid I'll be discovered and tortured."

"They still own your mind, Isabelle." She leads me to the garden and hands me a slice of dried bear meat. "That is how they beat you in France. The Catholics made you believe you were helpless."

I tear off a bite of meat, trying not to let anger swallow me. "We didn't have a choice, Naira. I watched my people killed. Dragged through town, their tongues and ears sliced and bloody."

"And when you decide they will never have your mind, nothing will take control of you ever again."

"You said last year I wasn't ready. What about now?"

"Your movements need work, and you let your weakness take over, and I question your instincts."

"This doesn't sound promising."

She leans closer. "But I saw the look in your eye as you sent that tomahawk slicing through the forest. I saw a warrior."

I tighten my lips to control a smile.

"We start with defense," she says. "Come."

Back in the clearing, I take a deep breath and focus. Naira shows me the areas that can take a man to the ground. Neck. Groin. Eyes. She shows me how to throw my elbow, plant my feet. How to knee and stomp and maneuver out of a hold.

With every movement, my memories begin to fade. My body is weak, but I will grow stronger.

"You do not want to fight your way out of a man's grip, but you must know how. Much better to attack when he least expects it."

In a moment of inspiration, I throw my elbow to her face, but she grabs my bony limb and whips me around by the waist as she shoves me to the ground, face once again in the dirt.

"One step at a time, little mouse."

"How do you do that?" I mutter into the damp earth.

"I listen. Now, up. Back to work."

She shows me every direction I can attack. Below, above, sideways, elbow, punch, palm, she teaches me how to block them all. We repeat over and over and over until I can no longer hold up my arms. I fall to my knees.

"Enough for today," she says. "Come. We will share chokecherry tea."

She doesn't look back and I assume I am to follow. I pull myself to stand and drag my weary legs into the longhouse where Naira seems very pleased with herself.

"Did you enjoy that?" I ask.

"Why yes, I did." She smiles and hands me a bowl of tea warmed from the fire. "You might not see it yet, but I do."

"See what?"

"Your life is about to test you with a great journey, Isabelle. And through that, you will learn to be the woman you can see only in your dreams."

"This journey, will I save more Protestants?"

"That depends on how you respond to your teachings." She sips her tea, knowing I wait for her guidance. "If you can finally listen."

I look deep into her glassy eyes. "Naira, can you see the future?"

She shrugs. "I dreamt of a wolf last night."

The bittersweet aroma of the tea reminds me of warmed almonds. "Is that good?"

"Wolves put their pack above all else, even above their own interests."

"And you think this has to do with me?"

"Yes, I do. When you came the other day, I saw one in the forest. Chestnut fur, eyes the color of clover. And again, that same wolf came to my dream." She leans forward, elbows on her knees. "Your test of bravery is nearly upon you. We have much work to do."

I straighten my shoulders and remember the screams back in La Rochelle. "I'm ready."

.   .   .

By the time I reach home, the rain has soaked my hair and neck. I shiver through the biting cold, but I'm exhilarated by Naira's words. James greets me at the front porch. He still hobbles, his once broken hip a constant reminder of his time in captivity.

"Isabelle, get in here. You're soaking wet."

I remove my damp cloak and warm myself by the fire.

James slams the door harder than I expect. "Where were you?"

"I told you, the abbey."

"Lies are unbecoming of a soldier's wife." He throws a cloth at me, which I catch and use to dry my face. "I stopped at the abbey after my business today and a very helpful Sister Marguerite informed me you never came today. So, I ask again—where were you?"

I swallow my fear. There's no way out of this. "I went to see Naira."

He clasps his hands behind him and paces the room, a habit I've come to loathe. As if he is a father considering how to scold a child. "You lied to me, betrayed my wishes, and left the city walls alone."

Our entire marriage has been about one fight—my freedom. "I haven't seen her in almost a year."

"What do you need with her?"

"You seem quick to forget that she once saved your life."

He turns on his heels and releases his hands from behind him. "Her influence on you is what I worry about."

Thinly veiled jealousy that I look up to Naira. "She knows how important you are to me." It's not a lie. I need this twisted marriage we've built.

He cracks his knuckles. "I will not tolerate lies, Isabelle."

"Of course not." I reach for him, but he stops me.

"You've been fighting me long enough," he says, hands gripped around my wrists.

"I won't lie anymore. But I will continue to visit her."

His stare pierces through me. "I see no point in allowing you to trek through the forest alone to slurp maize by a fire."

"That is not why I visit her."

His grip tightens. "What is it then?"

"She's my friend. The only one I have."

James's eyes soften into pity. "You should try harder. Spend time with other soldiers' wives."

I'd sooner eat dirt. "They aren't like me."

He releases my wrists. "That is because you choose to be different." He leans on the mantel and sighs. As he lifts his head, he notices Andre's knife. My body freezes. I left it behind a copper pot as I warmed myself by the fire yesterday. How careless I've been.

He reaches for the knife, slow and exaggerated. He turns it in his palm. "AR?"

I exhale, realizing the B has faded and appears to be an R.

As far as James is concerned, I have not spoken a word to Andre in two years. Before he can put together the initials, I calmly say, "Naira stole it from a prisoner. She gave it to me when I ran home after dark. To protect myself."

"Another man's knife in your hand. I do not approve."

"It's a knife, James."

"I'll see that it goes to our collection of weapons in town."

I want to yank it from his hand, but I control myself. *Master my mind.*

He throws the blade onto the table and walks toward me as my heart thumps. He trails his finger along my neckline, grazing my skin with the softness of a whisper. "I have tried for years to tame you."

"You speak as if I'm a wild cat and not a woman."

"Sometimes it feels as if you are." His hand moves up my neck and tucks my loose curl behind my ear. He examines my bruised cheek.

"I simply need to breathe," I say.

"That is why you will not marry me in the church. So you can cancel our contract whenever you wish."

I believe he stays with me because he enjoys the chase, like a fox hunt for a prized animal.

I glance down at my arm, the hidden H under my sleeve that he used to kiss but now ignores. He turns his eyes from the branding when we're naked. "I have no intention of cancelling our contract."

He tightens his fists with eyes closed as anger threatens to burst. "I've indulged this fantasy of yours for too long."

"The choice isn't yours to make."

He trails his angry lips along my neck.

I can't tell what holds me back the most, my need for a taste of power, or my lingering distrust for his ambitions. I'll always wonder what he's capable of, and I fear I have yet to see his limits.

"I've been patient with you," he says. "I chose a spirited girl and I've been tolerant. Far more than any other man would be."

"Yes, you have."

He kisses me hard, which presses the back of my head into the wall. I try not to flinch as my body is still sore from Naira's lessons today, but I want him to rip my dress off with his teeth. I focus on the power that beats between us, so I don't have to pretend to be seductive. It's easier that way.

"That stops now," he says. "You're no longer a child, Isabelle. You're a soldier's wife, and you will act like it."

I kiss him hard and suck his bottom lip. "I attend Mass and host your regiment and gladly perform my wifely duties. What more do you want?"

He holds both arms in his tightened fists as the light from amber flames shadows his face. "I want you to need me."

All the heat between my legs has cooled to silence. His love has revealed itself over the years to be nothing more than a burning need for power. I truly wonder if he is even capable of love.

I've tried—as the naïve girl who needed someone to rescue her and as the scared young woman who chose loyalty over desires. As the hidden Protestant who prays in a Catholic church and the woman with a purpose larger than herself. I've given him everything I'm capable of... except that dark corner of my soul that died and blackened when I left Andre. That, I am powerless to erase.

I pierce my teeth into his firm chest until he groans. "I do need you, James."

It's terrifying how I'm able to find a version of the truth, a shaded hint of honesty among the lies I live. One needs to find that to survive in a prison of the heart.

His jaw remains tightened. "I need more," he says.

Naira's words float back to me. Choices and sacrifice. I swallow hard against the tightening in my throat. "All right. I'll consider marrying you in the church."

His eyes brighten, and he stares at me in disbelief.

"I need time to adjust to the idea, but I want to make you happy." I could spit the bitter words right out of my mouth, yet I don't reveal a hint of that.

He smiles, an unsettling look of triumph in his eyes. Poor man has no idea the only way I can tolerate his touch is if I claw my way over his body.

"You will not stop me from visiting Naira, nor will you stop my ventures into the forest. Show me you can do that, and I will marry you in the church in front of the entire town."

"What sort of woman bargains with her husband?" He pulls me in for a hard, rigid kiss.

And this seems to be the only thing that matters anymore, so I close my eyes and hold on to hope that I can save dozens or even hundreds of Huguenots from their torturous existence. I remember Clémentine and the fire I once held. The fight that James has tried to burn out of me, and the strength I must once again find.

I rip off James's breeches and doublet and admire his gorgeous form. His scars have only added to his physical appeal—reminders of how broken we both are. I kiss along his chest and bite his nipple just hard enough that he gasps.

For the girl from La Rochelle who started this journey years ago, and for every other Huguenot in France, I will become a new woman.

A perfect soldier's wife with a secret agenda and a Huron fighter by her side.

CHAPTER FOUR

For the past week, James hasn't questioned my every move. It appears I've bought myself time. After church, I indulge his need to stroll through the square, so the town sees our lovely clothes and wide smiles. It's strange to bask in attention, as I've spent a lifetime hiding in the shadows.

With a plastered smile, I wave to the town and engage with the wealthy merchants at their stalls. Antoinette scowls at us from the doorway of the dressmaker. No doubt her husband's murder by the Iroquois has only fed her hatred toward everyone in Quebec.

I stop waving and nod to her, very formal and cold. I'll never fully forget our childhood.

Antoinette sulks, but just as we turn out of her sight, the hint of a smirk. I turn to examine her expression, but she flings her skirts and disappears into the shop.

James raises my hand for a kiss. "Finally, a day similar to France. Lovely, isn't it?"

"Yes. It is." I hesitate, still uneasy. "Antoinette," I say. "What's happening with her?"

"How should I know? That woman probably spends her day kissing her father's boots and admiring her reflection in the mirror."

He does despise her, and that fills me with glee.

He smiles at a couple as they stroll past. "No more talk about her," he says.

"She's up to something and I want to know what it is."

His impatient sighs have become part of his language, breathed as often as he speaks thanks to my willful ways. He pulls me to the wall where no one can hear. "Monsieur LaMarche is working on a new venture. One that will make us invaluable to the king. He lets his pathetic daughter attend the meetings and I'm forced to play nice with that wench."

"That wench has an evil streak like fire and would like nothing more than to see me ruined."

James stops and stares across the courtyard, his face hardened in an instant.

"What?" I turn to see Andre and Louise gather vegetables from a bin. Louise's little girl looks just like her. Round cheeks and dark, unruly curls. Andre catches James's eyes and the men stare, their intense gaze locked on each other.

Louise notices us, bounding across the marketplace with a giant smile. "Isabelle!"

I force excitement and kiss her cheek. "Hello, Louise. You and your family are looking lovely today."

"Hello, Monsieur," she says to James, who can hardly muster a smile in return. "Andre is finally in town, and I just had to get him to the market with me. Heaven knows when he'll leave me again."

Andre forces an uncomfortable laugh while James scoffs. We all fall silent, each of us with our own secrets to hide.

"Lovely to see you." James directs his words at Louise. "Good day."

James drags me away. I avoid Andre's eyes but can't help myself near the edge of the marketplace, where I sneak a glance over my shoulder. Andre catches my gaze and time seems to hover, suspended for a moment.

"Poor Louise," James says as we enter our carriage.

"Why do you say that?"

"Her husband, obviously." James is so predictable. He sits tall and puffs out his chest as he speaks of Andre. "Gone for months at a time. He runs illegal fur trades and God knows what else."

I don't respond. I stare out the window as the town fades from view.

"At least *you* chose wisely." He clears his throat and watches for my response, which I keep locked behind a stoic expression. "Your life is better than you could have ever experienced with that ruffian."

There's no need to speak, so I nod and place my hand on his thigh.

Back at our house, I open the trunk of the carriage to retrieve our food and notice Andre's knife. James must have forgotten about it. I slip the blade in my pocket and gather the beans, sugar, and cornmeal.

"Let me help you with that." James collects the rest of the food and examines the trunk.

"What's wrong?" I ask.

"I left that knife here. Someone must have stolen it. Just as well. Cursed be any man who steals another's knife."

I barely set the sack of cornmeal on the table when James presses my stomach against the wall and lifts my skirts. My cheek presses into the wood as his hand slides under my skirt and up my thigh. I panic, afraid he'll feel the knife. I flip around, back to the wall, and rip his coat open.

James kisses my neck. "Tell me I'm strong."

"What?"

His kisses seem to suck on my skin. "I'm the strongest. And the bravest. Aren't I, Isabelle?"

His insecurities turn my stomach. "Don't be ridiculous."

I push him off me, but he returns, pressing me to the wall again. "Tell me you hate Andre."

"I don't hate him." His breath is hot on my cheek.

"I need to hear you say it," he says with a low growl.

In a swift movement, I lift my arms and crash my elbows down on his. When he recoils, I slip away and hold my arms out, so he knows not to near me again.

"Where did you learn to do that?"

"I was just scared." A little lie.

He rakes his fingers through his hair and exhales. "I saw the way he looked at you. He's still in love with you."

My response to this question can alter the entire course of my marriage. "I married you, James. I chose you."

He hesitates, checking his words before he says them. "Was it because you owed me?"

I think a man knows things in his heart, things like if a woman truly loves him. Maybe that's why he fights so hard to make me into his perfect wife.

I lay my hand on his cheek. "I knew you could give me what I need." Three years ago, it seemed like enough to protect my heart. Now I'm in a constant battle where my body either craves my husband or loathes him. My heart says nothing.

"Because you've locked yourself away from me," he says.

"I'm giving you everything I have, James."

"Find more."

I slap his cheek. Not as hard as I'm capable, but hard enough. What he means is *be* more. Be a different woman. I'm not sure I can.

He rubs the side of his face. "Be very careful, Isabelle."

"Is that a threat?"

"That is for you to decide."

I lower my arms and collect myself. "Don't treat me like a prisoner. I'm your wife and you will respect me."

James reaches for his hat. "Perhaps you should try to earn my respect." He stops at the door without turning around. "I won't be back for dinner."

"Where are you going?"

"I suppose we both have secrets." The jugs that line our shelves clatter together when he slams the door, the rattle matching my frantic heartbeat.

I pace the room and breathe through my nose so loudly it whistles. He's hiding something. I should stay here, sweep the floors and wash the bedding, so he returns to a lovely clean home.

I care little of what I *should* do.

I don my boots and cape and slip into the forest. The brilliant blue sky shines brightest just before the sun retreats.

Naira taught me how to track hoof imprints. I follow his steps along the forest trail, which is not difficult, as James never ventures off the path. As the sun pulls a shade over the evening, streaks of pink and red bleed into the darkened sky.

The trail disappears at the edge of town as the earth turns to cobblestone. Our spring and summer arrive and disappear in a flash, so couples mill about, willingly breaking the new law that requires us to stay inside after dark. That law has less to do with Iroquois attacks and much more to do with encouraging babies. That is what they sent us here to do, after all.

I head for the tavern, but I don't find his horse. The military offices are closed, so I tiptoe through town, cape over my head. The merchants' doors remain open as they share ale with friends and welcome the balmy June air.

The moon shines over the St. Lawrence River from high on the cliffs of Quebec. Tonight, everything reminds me of La Rochelle. The water, the warm air, hiding in the shadows against the town's walls. The rapid beat of my heart, the quiet of my footsteps. I once had Henri at my side, as we ducked under arches and behind carriages to hide from the Catholics.

Near the intendant's palace at the end of a row of wealthy homes, I see our horse tied to a post outside the LaMarche porch. Heat rises from my feet and pounds through my body. As I near their stately home, my mind conjures images of James eating and laughing with the man that tortured my family. Luckily, they have left a window open as most have tonight, to let the breeze cool their homes.

Thankful for the cobblestones and not dried branches, I creep along the wall and hide under their window. I'm too afraid to look in case they see me, so I crouch and listen, their voices easily heard in the still evening. The wealthy aren't in the streets, they're inside—plotting.

"Why must we go to all this trouble?" Antoinette asks. "Just take them all prisoner and torture them until they convert."

"It's not that simple," her father says.

James adds his knowledge on the subject. "Huguenots do not believe they can convert. They are God's chosen ones, and no mortal choice can change that."

A hard slap on the table causes me to flinch. "Nonsense," Monsieur LaMarche says. "We all have a choice. When they see their children ripped from their selfish arms, they'll change their mind."

I close my eyes and remind myself to control the hatred and the fury, the part of me that wishes to jab an elbow to LaMarche's face.

"No," James says, "this is better. The French East India Company is struggling. They need to compete with the Dutch and English."

"What better way to do that than collect my resources?" I can hear LaMarche sniff from here.

"You're certain you have the connections to create a new trade channel?" James asks.

"Do not question my father," Antoinette snaps. "We have more connections than the king."

"It's true," LaMarche says, "Many merchants owe me. We'll bring in domestic slaves to Quebec, sell them to the wealthy and powerful. Farm slaves will help us dominate the beaver trade. The king will revere us for all the money we'll hand off to France. He'll have no choice but to agree to our every demand."

"Yes," James says, "And we trade Huguenot goods for the African people, turning Protestants into slaves to France."

When the word *slave* escapes James's mouth, something in me snaps. I suddenly want to revolt. Let the anger explode out of me and fight everyone in that room.

"They'll think they've found a new opportunity to sell their pottery and silk and clocks," LaMarche says. "Once they earn a few livres, they'll do as we ask. They'll trust us."

"Then we turn them over as property to the king," Antoinette says. "Versailles can become a workhouse of French craftsmanship. For all their filthy, thieving ways, the Protestants do make the finest goods."

"Essentially," James says, "the king will own the slave trade into Quebec, the beaver trade out of Canada, and the Huguenot merchants, while diminishing the power of his enemies. He would promote us to the royal court. Senior nobility."

"And if the Huguenots fight you?" Antoinette asks.

James exhales. His exasperated sigh is all too familiar. "Then we take their children."

The air sludges thick and heavy through my lungs. My legs falter under the weight of what I've just heard. The bright night glows unnaturally bright, ominous in its silvery sheen. I stumble back along the city walls. My mind spins, wondering how I can be a part of this horrific scheme. Buying and selling *people* to gain the king's favor—all for status, money, greed.

Laughter bounces through the town square, but I can't hear or feel it. I run when I hit the edge of town, my trusty boots slamming against the bridge and along the path to home. Under the moonlight, I charge to our home, where I throw open the door and fall to my knees.

I cry into my hands for a few moments, sick with the idea of more prisoners, more torture, more death. Children ripped from their parents. And it will be my husband who's responsible.

I collect myself and walk upstairs, still numb to everything around me. I slide the rug to the side and reach in my pocket to retrieve Andre's knife. It's a miracle James didn't recognize the initials.

I place Andre's knife next to my Bible and slide the floorboard shut. My hands throb with an aching need to throw something. I remember James's grunts as he pressed me against the wall. He's fragile and weak, a dangerous combination for someone whose morality is as fickle as the Quebec wind.

Naira tells me to master my mind before my body, but I can't see clearly. My chest tightens like a clamp. I tromp down the stairs and throw the front door open again to feel the breeze, the balmy air long gone as night has crept in. Behind the house, an ax sticks into the air, ready for log splitting. I grab the handle and yank with all my might, but the blade won't budge. The ax seems to mock me.

Listen, Naira tells me.

I close my eyes, quiet my breath, and listen to my thumping heart. A gust of wind spreads over me and flutters a few curls loose. *Be smarter. Calmer.* I reach for the handle and gently rock forward and back to coax the blade from its position wedged into the wood. The metal loosens and glides easily away.

Play the nice, pious wife while James buys and sells and makes slaves. I cannot do it.

Feet positioned and body turned, I raise the ax behind me and launch the blade through the trees. It somersaults through the shadows into thumping gusts like butterfly wings. When the ax lands in the center of a white spruce, I exhale as a white cloud of warm breath escapes my mouth.

I must find another way.

I've listened, just as Naira instructed. My journey starts now, and it will not end until every Huguenot is free... or until the last breath leaves my body.

CHAPTER FIVE

Henri, Andre, and I meet every month on the first Friday, unless I have urgent secrets. Today is our Friday and after yesterday's news, it's not a moment too soon. Knowledge of James's plan settles on my heart and eats away at my insides.

This morning, I woke to a black room, unable to tolerate James next to me. He slept soundly, not a stitch of guilt to keep him awake as I stared at the fire and considered my options.

Pausing at the bottom step, he coughs and tightens his cravat. "Good morning, darling."

I swallow, unable to form words. My eyes stay steady on the fire. He walks up behind me. He kisses my neck, which might as well be poison for the way my body reacts.

"I'm sorry we fought," he says.

I don't move. Not one twitch.

"Isabelle, please look at me." He kisses the back of my hand to avoid even a grazed finger across my branded H. "I shouldn't have pushed you against the wall the other day. I know how you like to be in control when we make love."

He's right. Excitement thunders through me when I roll him to his back and slam his arms to the bed. For a moment, I can shove my own demons back down to feel the rush of power. "I forgive you." The words feel like pebbles stuck in my throat.

James sits at the table, gesturing for me to serve his breakfast. I tie my apron and prepare his tray. Bread with sliced onions and brandy for dipping, a side of curdled milk with sugar. An old loaf has turned rotten, so I trim the dried ends but keep a portion of the green center.

"How did you learn to fight like that?" he asks.

"I wasn't fighting."

"You used your elbows to shove me off you. I've never seen a woman do that."

I present his tray where the old bread soaks up the brandy. I could have given him the clean slice, but I think he deserves the green one.

"James, there's no limit to what a woman will do when she's threatened."

He nods with a hint of derision, and I imagine the other ways I might throw my elbow or foot into his body.

•   •   •

It's still early when I arrive at Henri's, the secret I learned yesterday burning inside me. Smoke twirls into the sky from his chimney as the smell of roast pork trails into the air. The door clicks open before I can knock. Henri greets me, surprised, his arm around a dark-skinned woman with tousled hair and a sleepy grin.

"Oh, hello," Henri says.

I stare at the woman, frozen and unsure if I should hide my face. She grabs Henri and kisses him with such passion I feel I should turn away… but I don't. Henri welcomes her kisses and pulls her in close. As they engage in their passionate goodbye, a horse clops through the trees. Andre arrives and joins me on the porch to watch the two devour each other.

"Sorry to interrupt," Andre says.

"I don't think they can hear us," I say. "Their tongues seem to have taken over."

I close my eyes to remember when Andre once kissed me like that. It leaves me lightheaded. The woman pulls away from Henri, but not before a bite on his lip.

"Ouch," Henri says as he slicks his hair back into place.

"It's so you won't forget me." She takes a deep breath and tightens her cape. "Madame Beaumont," she says as she saunters past me.

"Do I know you?"

She waves her hand. "I suppose not. I'm also married to a soldier."

My heart jumps, and I shoot Henri a stern look of disapproval.

"Don't worry, Madame," she says. "I'd say I need to keep our secret more than you do." She mounts her horse and blows Henri a kiss, then gallops through the clearing and into the trees.

I shove Henri back into the cabin, both hands on his chest. "What is wrong with you?"

"Hey, I'm a man with needs."

"You're a fool. Bedding a soldier's wife?" I move closer as he stumbles back to avoid another shove. "How long until one of their husbands shows up here with a rifle? And now she's seen me here with you and Andre. All because your cockerel seems to make your decisions for you."

Andre steps in. "All right, both of you sit. We'll figure this out."

Andre possesses an unnerving ability to disarm anyone with a smile and a calm voice. We agree to sit, but Henri and I shove each other once like the siblings we practically are.

"Henri," Andre says, "it truly is irresponsible of you to bring women here. I know it must be difficult, but you put all of us in danger and risk our mission."

Henri lowers his elbow to his knee. "What am I to do, Andre? I'm stuck alone in this wild land, with only the occasional visit from either of you. I'm lonely."

"Have you been to town?" Andre asks.

"Only at night. To the taverns."

I groan and bring my hand to my forehead. "Antoinette or James could have seen you. Monsieur LaMarche. Did they?"

"No," Henri says. "I made sure of it."

If anyone were to find Henri, a known Huguenot, our friend would be immediately arrested.

Andre rubs his chin and shoots me a glance. "We must find another way. Henri can't be left to his own devices. Sorry, my friend."

Henri shrugs. "You're probably right."

"This is a conversation for later." I wring my hands together. "I have news."

"James is full of helpful information these days," Henri says. He has never liked James. I should have listened to him, to my mother, to my instincts.

"He's planning something awful with the LaMarches." I pace the room and fidget with my dress, the nervous energy about to eat me alive.

Andre stands and nears me. Hand on my arm, he says, "Take your time. What do you know?"

I nod and exhale as the awful memories from last night bleed out of me. "Since the French East India Company is failing, they aim to provide an alternative. A company so powerful that the king will need their riches."

"And how are they going to do that?" Henri asks.

"They'll buy slaves from Africa. Ship them to the colony and sell them to stately homes as status symbols. Dress them in fine French clothes and show off their dark skin for all to admire."

"How will they buy slaves?" Andre asks.

"With Huguenot goods. Pottery, silks, silver. The LaMarches plan to own the beaver trade, the slave trade, and eventually, all the Protestant artisans. They'll take them as prisoners if they don't agree to work for the court. If they fight, they'll steal their children and adopt them to Catholic homes."

Knocked back by the news, the men stumble back to their chairs, grimaces wrinkling their faces.

"Henri, do you remember when we saw slaves in La Rochelle?" I ask.

"How could I forget? A line of terrified men shackled and nearly naked."

"Whipped if they didn't obey. Chained to the galleys to row the boat to their own prison."

We stare at each other, speechless.

"Huguenot artisans are the best in France," Andre says. "That's why they need us. If they let us flee, the country would fall apart. France would lose everything, and the king would be destitute."

"Families will be torn apart," I say. "Fathers captured, murdered, or forced into servitude. Children ripped from their parents and mothers tortured. It's too awful to comprehend."

"You heard this from James?" Andre asks.

"I overheard him planning with the LaMarches. My husband is the mastermind. He's planning all of this." I rock on my heels and back to my toes, trying to feel something other than the hate that sickens me. "I can't do this, Andre."

Andre holds my arms to steady me, but his touch only weakens my legs. I begin to cry, finally letting the tears flow. Andre wraps his arms around me, and I don't want to leave his embrace.

"I can't look at James, let alone stay married to him. I can't be a part of this."

Andre holds me until I calm down. "This has always been your choice. You stop whenever you want."

"What would I do if I left him?"

"You can move in with the nuns. That is what most women do when they break a contract."

Henri stands. "And James and the LaMarches will go right on with their evil plans."

Andre lifts his hand toward Henri's chest. "Don't push her."

Henri swats his hand away. "No, Andre. You look at Isabelle as this soft creature, this fragile woman who shouldn't be in danger."

"That's not true," Andre says. "She once trekked into the winter forest to save me from an Iroquois camp. She's anything but fragile."

"Here is the Isabelle I know." Henri yanks back my sleeve to reveal my branded H. "That black night when the dragoons held us down, they reached for me but Isabelle threw herself in front of the hot steel. An eight-year-old girl scorched her skin to save her terrified friend."

"They got to you anyway," I say.

"Yes." He pulls up his breeches to reveal his calf. His own H seared into his body as a reminder that we've always been prisoners. "But watching you try to save me was inspiring. You have the kind of bravery I could only ever dream of."

I reach for Henri and hug him tight, remembering all our terrifying days in La Rochelle.

"They threw our friend's severed tongue at our feet," Henri says. "They burned my father at the stake and made me watch." Henri's eyes fill with tears. He grabs my dress in his fist as if he might fall to his knees.

"How do I fix it, Henri? How do I stop them?"

"We kill them."

Andre steps forward. "I know we're all angry about what happened in France, but we can't become murderers. We can't be like them."

Andre, in a battle to justify his actions, always hesitates.

"They killed your entire family." Henri squares his shoulders. "The Catholics beat you bloody. How do you not want to slice them in half?"

"Because I'm a father now. I don't have room for that kind of hate."

Andre smiles when he speaks of his daughter. Pure and kind, his love for her is not conditional. It isn't dependent on secrets and power.

"I can work with James," I say.

"You want to reason with him?" Andre asks me.

Henri shakes his head. "Monsters can't be reasoned with."

"I know how to manipulate him. If I stay, we'll have a chance to stop him, but if I leave, we have nothing." I stare directly into Henri's eyes. "You trusted me at eight years old. I need you to trust me now."

"Fine." He pours himself an ale. "But we need to get word to the Huguenots before the LaMarches do. Convince them not to work with them."

"I'll set out tonight for Acadia," Andre says. "I just need to say goodbye to Elizabeth."

"And Louise?" Henri says with a grin.

Andre rolls his eyes. "You really can be disgusting, Henri."

"I'll prepare the notes," Henri says.

"I'll be on my way," I say. "And Henri, no more trips into town. We'll find you women if that's what you need. But no more soldier's wives."

"But it's more fun with them."

I shake my head. "You're hopeless."

Andre walks me outside. I take in the warm breeze and watch the treetops waver back and forth, their tips kissing each other under a cobalt sky. "How did we get here?" I ask.

"A lifetime of lies. But our world necessitates it."

"I feel helpless here. Right now, our friends in France hide in the forest to pray and hope the dragoons don't slash their necks."

"Your plan was to help James climb the king's ranks. I guess he's about to see that dream come true."

"Not like this, he won't." I turn to face him. "James just wants the title and the adoration. If I find him another way in, I'm certain he'll abandon the LaMarches."

"And how are you going to do that?" Andre asks.

"I don't know yet. But I'll figure it out."

Andre steps down from the porch. The sun shines on his cheek, lighting his dark eyes to a warm copper. One connected glance between us can expose all my weakness.

I reach for his hand but turn immediately to my horse, willing myself to walk away from him. Suddenly, his arm is around my waist, and he presses me against the cabin, the rough wood catching strands of my hair.

I let myself feel him and breathe in the scent of his skin and his golden hair. His touch seeps into me and fills the empty places I try so hard to ignore.

"I imagine a life where we live free. No more lies," he says.

"That's a lovely thought."

"Has there ever been anything more painful than to want something you know you can never have?" He swallows through a tightened neck.

"It does no good to dream of what could be. It makes what is real that much more painful."

He backs away, but his arms remain locked, hands pressed into the cabin wall on either side of my arms. "This life isn't easy," he says. "And sometimes it's impossible."

Pushing away from him feels as difficult as swimming through oil. My body wants him, but I must control my mind, just as Naira taught me, so I step away as his arms fall to his sides. I mount my horse and stare down at him. "Be safe, Andre."

Before he can respond, I gallop toward the trees, not daring to look back. When I'm safely out of sight, I let myself feel his touch, his words. I imagine living in freedom as a Protestant, safe in my world to pray in the sunlight without fear or punishment. The vision disappears to a watery memory and slides away from my heart.

CHAPTER SIX

My house has been cold for the past week.

I spend every day at the abbey teaching and helping the Sisters with cleaning, cooking, and sewing, avoiding my husband's sickening touch. Today, as I lower the pulley of the well near the garden, panic grips me. The slosh of water brings me back three years to the wine in Jacques's goblet when he lashed my backside. How the noble family's son would rub his body on me as I counted to three hundred.

My hands shake so hard I nearly lose the rope.

I was a powerless servant back then—until the day I broke Jacques's face with a wooden beam.

"Lovely day, isn't it?"

I turn to see Charlotte, cheeks pink and hair perfectly pinned. Her innocent looks are a successful cover for an angry young woman with deep wounds.

I pin my hands to my stomach to hide their trembling. "Yes, it is."

"I received a letter from home," she says. "My mother offers incredibly detailed accounts of the town happenings."

I quickly untie the rope. As I stand and lift my skirts to walk away, she steps in front of me.

"Kindly move out of my way, Charlotte."

"I will not. Not until you hear me. Put down the pail."

Her audacity impresses me. I place the pail down and stare at her. "What atrocities do you have to torture me with? Because I have lived it. I have seen it all and survived it all, so don't expect to shock me."

"You don't care to hear about the beatings in the town square? Women lashed in front of a cheering crowd, their children forced to watch?"

I shove past her, knocking her off balance, but then I remember that anger, and what helplessness does when you don't harness it. I walk back and whisper close to her, "If you want to change the world, then do it. Because standing here whining like a child gets you nothing."

I take two steps away when she says, "Why did you stop fighting?"

Much as I want to help her understand, I have no room for more lies. "We're all in a fight, Charlotte. Doesn't matter which side you're on. If you're breathing, you're fighting."

I hate that this girl unnerves me.

• • •

James appears this morning out of his military dress. Instead, he's wearing his pristine doublet and shining black boots.

"Where are you going?" I ask.

"The opportunity has arisen for a trip to Montreal. I'm leaving this morning and I should return within a week."

"What will you do there?"

"Business," he says.

I pull the chair in front of me and hope he won't come any closer.

He shifts his eyes around, obviously hesitant to tell me the truth. "I'll be traveling with the LaMarches. There are shipping contracts we wish to secure."

"Ah. You'll be spending the week with Antoinette, diving deeper into whatever scheme her father has convinced you to take part in."

Eyes bulging, he hurls a plate across the room. The silver bangs against the wall and clatters to the floor. "I hate that woman. I shouldn't have to prove myself to you after all this time. It's as if you look for ways to mistrust me."

"Then don't make choices that force me to mistrust you."

His fingers tighten into trembling fists. "This is an opportunity for us. Buy noble status and create a life neither of us could have ever dreamed of. Riches we will pass to our children. A legacy."

"We have no children."

"We will someday. I believe that." He reaches for me, but I jerk away.

He has never discovered the tea I drink to prevent pregnancy—and I hope he never will.

When I don't display sadness over our lack of children, he grabs my face and forces me to look at him. "You are my wife. I would do anything to make you look at me the way you used to." I fight to escape his grip, but the intensity in his eyes tells me I won't win.

I want to scream that he can never force me to love him. That I have given everything, and it still wasn't enough.

He grabs me tighter and forces his mouth against mine. He presses his lips hard and full of anger—as if he hates himself for loving me. Once he pulls away, he doesn't seem to care that tears line my eyes. "I decide what happens in this family."

As if he can force a child into my womb. The idea sickens me. "I know what you're part of."

His hands slide from my face and down my neck. "You know nothing."

"I know everything. I hear more than you think."

He tilts his head and runs his finger along my bodice, grazing the skin at the top of my breasts. "There are things you don't understand."

"Then explain them to me."

He rolls a lock of my hair in his fingers. "I miss the way you used to look at me." He pulls me in again, this time for a soft kiss. An attempt at intimacy. "We can have that again. But you must trust me."

I have no trust for him, only loathing.

He gathers himself and steps away. "Here is how I will prove myself to you." He exhales long and slow. "I know about Henri."

My breath catches and I can't move. "How?"

"I saw him one night at the tavern. I followed him, certain I was seeing things. I can only assume he's here to be close to you."

"He is."

"I know how much he means to you. Let this be a show of trust, Isabelle. Get him out of Quebec while I'm away with the LaMarches."

He shuts the door behind him, and I collapse in the chair. I claw at the tabletop, scraping my fingernails against the soft wood. He would save Henri but kill hundreds of others.

One evil at a time, Isabelle.

I stand so quickly that the chair topples to the floor. In my bedroom, I slide the floorboard to the side and retrieve Andre's knife. This time, I attach the blade to my thigh where its sheath can rest against my skin. Cape and gloves on, I mount my horse and ride at top speed through the forest, as urgency fills my every breath.

When I arrive at the tiny cabin in the forbidden territory, I'm breathless and eager to warm my hands by the fire. Henri meets me on the porch. "What are you doing here?"

"Get inside. We need to talk." I shove him back and step to the fire, noticing a woman's shift hanging from the post of his bed. "Henri, you need to find yourself another hobby."

He swipes the shift and stuffs it under the bed. "Never mind that."

"James knows you're here. He saw you in the tavern."

"Dammit." He paces the room.

"He's gone to Montreal for a week. He told me to get you out of town."

Henri raises his eyebrows. "James wants to save me. Why don't I believe that?"

"He wants to prove himself trustworthy, but he always has another motive."

"Hopefully, he thinks I'm a lost Protestant, searching for my childhood friend." He tosses his head to clear a curl from his eye. "And not that I'm hiding in the forest to collect secret information from his wife."

"And we must get you out of here before he finds out."

Henri lives simply, with only one change of clothes, his Bible hidden in the brick fireplace, his knife, and a rifle for hunting. We always knew he might need to leave in a moment's notice and today it's on my shoulders to keep him protected.

As we direct our horses south through the forest, the shadows from the treetops cast a cool cover of shade and protection over us. Henri's cheeks flush pink despite the light breeze that whistles through the pines.

When we arrive at the Huron settlement, Henri whispers, "Will they accept me?"

"Try not to offend them and yes, I'm sure they will." We dismount our horses and tie them to the stakes at the perimeter of the camp. The women tending the garden smile and greet me. Henri removes his hat and smiles at all the tall, beautiful Huron women with their sleek hair and skin that glimmers gold.

"They're all so beautiful." Henri says.

I grab his sleeve. "If you so much as breathe too close to any of them, I'll beat you myself."

"Understood."

Naira emerges from her longhouse. "Welcome, Isabelle."

"Naira, this is Henri. May he stay with you for a few nights? I need to get him out of Quebec."

Her untrusting gaze bores into him. "You're a friend of Isabelle and Andre's?"

Henri nods, shooting a glance toward me for reassurance.

"Then you may stay," she says. "You will help the men skin caribou."

Henri, for all his devious ways, has never been what I would call tough. I doubt he knows how to skin an animal.

"Oh, yes." Henri holds out his knife. "Show me the way."

"That is for tomorrow." Naira leads him to the men gathered behind the longhouse. "Today you catch a bear."

He digs his feet into the ground and pushes back against her hands. "Bear? You catch bear?"

"Yes," she says. "You run after him and scare him into the water where the men wait with nets."

"You want me to intimidate a bear?"

"Andre has done it many times. You'll do fine." She shoves him into the men with a nod and they wrap their arms around his elbows. He reminds me of a mouse picked up by an eagle, locked by talons.

"Naira, you'll kill him with fright."

"Ah." She waves her hand. "It is good for him. Perhaps he'll soil his breeches."

"How is that good?"

"Humility is something most Frenchmen lack." She crosses her arms and examines my eyes. "Now, you come with me to pick berries. I see you have much to tell me."

With a nod, I reach for a basket and follow close behind Naira, away from the settlement and deeper into the cool mist of the forest, over mossy ground and fallen larch branches.

I keep my eyes on Naira's back, prepared for a strike.

Without turning around, she says, "You look different. What's happened?"

"James. He's in Montreal to make connections with shipowners."

She maneuvers over the forest floor like a fox but says nothing.

"To buy and sell slaves," I add.

Naira halts, and I raise my arms, ready for her to throw me to the ground. "Slaves?" she asks.

"Yes." I search her body movements for signs of a swift attack. "He'll buy slaves with Huguenot wares, and eventually turn Protestants over to the king so they work as prisoners, funding the trade of people in chains."

"Very upsetting."

"My husband wants to imprison my people and shackle innocent men and women as if everyone is a commodity. Perhaps that is what I am, too."

"Your James is dangerous." She crouches low to look for signs of berries. "He cannot tell ambition from savagery."

"He's unpredictable," I say.

"Here." Naira steps deeper into the trees where low bushes hold clusters of black huckleberries. "Help me gather."

I pick the berries and place them in the woven basket. "What do I do?"

"You have been called to save your people. You do that any way you can."

The berries are plump and firm, and they plunk when I drop them into the basket. I release a deep sigh.

"Your answer will come, Isabelle."

I kneel to gather the low fruit hidden under the leaves and place my hand into what feels like slick mud. Black like oil with a shimmering float of thickened red. A drop falls to the pool right next to my hand. I turn slowly to look over my shoulder, and see two purple feet dangling, toes severed and dripping blood. The mangled flesh glides back and forth at my eye level, the only sound a creaking rope above. I'm too frightened to look any higher.

"Naira?" I choke out.

She drops her basket and reaches across my chest to pull me to the ground. Leaned against her, her arm around me, we both dare to follow our gaze from the bloody feet up to an unrecognizable man slowly spinning from a noose tied to a branch of a black spruce. His stomach has been carved out, leaving only a hollow cavity. His clothes are shredded thin and blackened by dirt as if he'd been dragged.

Naira whispers in my ear. "They've been watching us."

CHAPTER SEVEN

As night crawls into the sky, the air grows heavy, and unease fills every corner of the camp. Henri and I wait in Naira's longhouse and stare at the popping fire. Henri's eyes are like full moons. "There was a real bear. Just steps from me."

"They know what they're doing. I'm sure you were never in any real danger."

"Why is everyone acting so strange?" he asks.

"We saw something on our walk today—a Frenchman's mutilated body dangling from a tree."

Henri bites his bottom lip, no doubt reliving some of our past tortures. He escaped the galleys two years ago, where he watched men die all around him. "Iroquois?" he asks.

"Naira thinks they've been watching the camp."

Henri yanks at his cravat, loosening it from his neck. "Why?"

"I don't know."

A long, eerie silence descends on the longhouse. Naira returns an hour later with her family. She sends her husband to tend to her daughter while she joins us and stares into the center of the flames. "Two years ago, the Haudenosaunee released me with one condition. That my clan would not trade with the French. No goods or furs."

"Have you kept that promise?" I ask.

"Yes. We need little outside our settlement."

"Why did they kill that man?" Henri asks.

"To send a message." She rubs her neck, unusually nervous and pacing around the fire. "That man tried to trade with us. You should stay here for the night."

"All right." I hesitate and turn to face her. "Are you worried?"

She gazes at the smoke as it crawls through the opening in the longhouse toward the bright moon above. "We have lived with the threat of the Haudenosaunee long before your people arrived. This is nothing new for us."

She guides us to cots stacked along the wall near the fire. Henri takes the top and I the bottom. Wrapped in beaver fur, I'm warm and comfortable, but still filled with a feeling of dread. "Henri?"

He peers over the edge, his black wavy curls flopping over his face.

"Where do you want to go?" I ask.

"New York. The English welcome us. We should all start a new life there. Imagine it, we can attend church in the center of town. No more hiding in the shadows."

"And what about our purpose?" I ask. "All this time collecting information and sending it to France."

"We can still help the cause, Isabelle." With his arms under his chin, he looks just like he did as a child. His eye is always on the next opportunity. He looks around and leans lower to whisper. "There's a group of English that works with the Iroquois and supplies weapons. I can help them take down the French."

I throw the fur off me and grab Henri by the shirt, dragging him off the cot where he stumbles and grabs the frame to stay upright. I shove him against the wall and hold my forearm at his neck like Naira taught me. "Henri Reynard. You selfish child."

"What do you care what I do?" He tries to push me off him, but I'm too angry.

"You got me into this mess. I walked away from Andre and stayed married to James so we could save Huguenots. If you weren't sleeping with half the town, we'd still be able to. And now all you care about is Catholic bloodshed."

He stops struggling. "I'm tired of hiding. Aren't you?"

His big, dark eyes remind me with one look that we used to dream of a land where Protestants live free. "Now that I know what James is up to, I have to stop him. If you don't want to help me, I'll do it alone." I release my arm from his neck.

"Isabelle, I do want to help."

"Then stay with us."

"Those Catholic bastards need to pay. I want to shove my blade through the bellies of the dragoons. Chain them to walls and light their skin on fire like they did to us."

"I won't join forces with the Iroquois. I couldn't do that to Naira."

"For such a strong woman, your loyalty certainly gets in your way."

"What else do I have?"

Henri pulls me into a hug and holds me tight. "I'm sorry I let you down."

"You didn't. But I've started this and I'm going to see it through. I hope you'll join me."

He climbs back to his cot. "Goodnight, Isabelle."

. . .

When the sun breaks through the opening in the birchbark roof, I realize how long I've slept.

Everyone is up and has started on the day's work by the time I join. At the door to her longhouse, Naira bounces her daughter on her hip.

"Good morning," I say to them both.

"Your friend left before the sun rose. Where did he go?"

I sigh, disappointed but not surprised. "New York, probably."

"That young man will find himself in harm's way. He craves it." The baby grabs Naira's braid and smiles with her toothless grin. "The Haudenosaunee will continue to attack," Naira says. "You should prepare."

"I doubt they'll attack inside the town's walls."

"No, they don't want that fight. Watch the farms at the edge of town. The tortured Frenchman was a warning not to aid your people. They're preparing for an ambush."

"What can I do?"

"Not every fight is yours to take on," she says.

I smile at the baby, watching her squeeze her fist over my finger and wondering how this world is so cruel when there is joy like hers.

"I should go," I say.

Naira turns to me with head cocked to the side. "Have you had any dreams lately?"

"They're memories more than dreams."

"Keep listening, Isabelle. I'll be here."

I stay for another moment of baby squeezes and smiles and leave before my heart begins to hurt. "Thank you, Naira."

As I mount my horse, a flash of that man's dead body dangling over me sends chills up my spine. My hands grip the reins so hard that my palms ache. My arms and shoulders tremble, tight as a silk weave. The blood drips through my memory. Plop. Plop. Dead faces frozen mid-scream. Pools of blood in the muddy ground of La Rochelle.

Several long minutes take hold and I wait until I can breathe again before instructing the horse to trot toward town. The ache in my chest squeezes hard, even as my breath returns.

After a stop at the bakery, I continue to the outer edges of town, eyes secured on the trees. Every crack causes my heart to falter. By the time I arrive at the cabin, the afternoon sun hangs bright and low.

The door is open to let in the air. I knock twice. "Louise? It's me. Isabelle."

Louise appears from the kitchen, eyes heavy, and face covered in porridge. "Oh, Isabelle. Come in. Elizabeth's being difficult today, as you can see."

"I'm sorry if this is a bad time. I brought bread."

"Come in."

I step into their cabin. Warm and solid with two fireplaces, it strikes me how empty the room feels. Fur and sculpted furniture fill the home, yet a quiet solitude seems to sprinkle the air like a fine dust.

Louise removes her apron and checks her reflection in the mirror to fix her hair, but gives up. "What can I do for you?"

"I came to speak with Andre."

She puffs out her lips and stares at me, waiting for more.

"I need advice on a safe path through the illegal territory." A little lie won't hurt anyone.

"He's the one to ask." She collapses at the table. "He's gone so much." She wipes her daughter's cheeks as best she can and lowers her to the floor. "Go play."

Once Elizabeth is far enough away, she says, "I'm so lonely."

Louise thrives in town, around friends. Not out in the woods, with only the birds for company. "I know, Louise. We all are."

"Really? I've seen the way your husband looks at you. It's obvious he worships you."

Not something I particularly enjoy.

"He is gone a lot too," I say. "He's in Montreal on business right now."

"It's not the same." She stares out the window. "Andre doesn't look at me like that. He never has."

I want to say that she has never looked at him that way either, but none of that matters anymore. "Marriage is difficult, Louise."

"Much harder than I expected." She fiddles with her apron. "Andre won't talk to me."

"Is he good to you?"

"Yes. He's kind and a wonderful father. But I still dream of a different life." She turns the handle to rotate the ham smoking on the spit of the blackened fireplace. "Perhaps I should have married the man who looked at me that way."

"The man who hit you?" I wish I could make her understand that happiness isn't found only in a man's affections.

She wipes the sweat from her brow. "It was only a slap or two."

I grab both her hands and squeeze harder than I intend. "All of us married without being in love. We chose men out of a line based on who had a hunting license and a fireplace. If he is kind to you, cherish it."

"You talk like James is not a handsome soldier who would do anything for you."

"We're not perfect, and neither are you and Andre."

Elizabeth begins to cry, so Louise lifts the child to her hip and checks the progress of her pickling asparagus. "I hope another baby will make him happy."

I force a smile to cover the sick feeling in my stomach. "Are you expecting?"

"No." She places her hand over Elizabeth's ear. "But I'm working on it."

I stand and straighten my skirts before I let her words sink too far into me. "May I ask him about the territory?"

"He's chopping wood, as usual. Go on."

Out back I find Andre slicing an ax into a stump of wood. He stands next to a pile higher than the house behind him, all uniformly cut. Enough to last a lifetime. "Looks like you're trying to cut down the forest."

"Winter is coming. We need to keep the house warm." He continues to slice the blade through the wood without looking at me.

"It's June, Andre."

He stops and wipes the sweat from his brow. "What are you doing here?"

"I brought Louise a loaf of bread." I step forward, closer to where I can whisper. "And I need to speak with you. Henri is gone. To New York."

"Gone?"

"Yes. James found out he was in Quebec and threatened to report him to LaMarche."

"But he didn't report him," he says.

"No, he didn't." I notice an intricate carving, like a painting out of chiseled wood. A seascape with towers lining the shore. I bend down to examine the details. "This must have taken you months."

"That's what I remember from home," he says. He places the ax down and leans on the handle. After a glance over my shoulder, I turn away, so I don't stare at his glistening skin.

"Do you miss France?" I ask.

"No." He kneels next to me, close enough that his arm brushes against mine. He points to a narrow building on the shore. "That was my house. I woke to the sound of the ocean every morning. Until the day the Catholics killed my parents."

"Why do you want to remember this?"

He exhales, slow and soft. "I want to remember what I'll never be."

"You'll never be like the Catholics. You're too good."

"I'm no better than Henri with my resentment. I simply use it differently."

I stand, suddenly aware that my heart is fluttering. "James wants me to trust him."

He glances up with one eye squinted against the bright sun. "Do you?"

"You know the answer to that." Fifty paces from the house, the babbling creek flickers with silver light as a robin whistles from the grassy edge.

"She stays close," Andre says as he stands.

"The bird?"

"Come." He waves me to a tree near the back of the house. Andre props up his knee and pats his thigh, indicating for me to step up. I do and pull myself up to see a circular nest nestled in the low branches of the jack pine. Inside, a cluster of three bright turquoise eggs.

I lower back down and notice Andre's smile. "They're so blue," I say.

"They nest near people. The mother likes it here, despite Louise's constant yelling at her birdsong. She frolics in the stream and keeps me company while I work."

Andre has always loved birds, their distant connection to humans, their freedom in the world. I think he envies their ability to just do as their bird heart desires, without justification.

"While Henri flees without a goodbye, you stay here and protect these little blue eggs."

He stares deep into my eyes, enough that my chest tightens. "Two years ago, we made a promise. Despite our mistakes, we've trusted each other to carry out this plan. Henri is impulsive, but you and me? We have something deeper."

I turn to stare at the nest, though I can't see the eggs. I often wonder how he has turned our nightmares into righteousness because I have let them spit inside me like hot oil, burning a trail of regret.

"Isabelle, look at me."

Against the urge to run far, far away, I turn to face him.

As if he can read my mind, he says, "Your passion is the reason I've been able to live this secret life. Without you, I'd die full of regret, wondering how I didn't save more people."

"I won't give up, not ever."

The trees rattle in the wind, and Andre looks up to let the breeze cool his face. "Tell me how to help."

"Did you send word to France about James's new plan?"

"Yes, I did."

"Good." I look back to the house and see Louise watching us through the window. "She thinks I've come to ask you about a safe path through the illegal territory."

"Okay. I'll play along."

I lift my skirts and walk toward my horse but stop when I sense Louise's eyes still watching me. "Louise is lonely, Andre."

"Aren't we all?"

Louise deserves to be happy. They both do. "Please try. We must let go of the past."

He nods and rubs the back of his neck.

On my horse, I prepare to head back into the forest when Andre says, "You'll find a way to stop James. I know you will."

His belief in me strengthens my resolve. "Yes, I will."

With a kick to my horse's side, I gallop into the forest. I feel eyes everywhere, flickering their shiny orbs in the shadows of the ferns and leaves. At the path toward home, I veer upland into the whisper of the trees. I'm willing to risk Iroquois eyes because there is only one place I want to be.

I arrive at the camp and find Naira waiting for me at the entrance. "I knew you'd be back."

I step up to her. "Teach me everything."

"As you wish, Madame." She extends her hand to welcome me inside, latching the gate behind me. "You're certain?"

The man dangling from the tree reminded me that no one is safe. This time, I'm going to be prepared. "I'm ready."

CHAPTER EIGHT

"Again."

Naira believes in the power of patience. Outlasting your opponent with bravery and using your wits to listen for the right time to attack. Which is why she has me start the day with my nemesis—the bow and arrow.

As soon as I arrived last night, she began her teaching: instructions to listen to the sounds of the forest, the shift in wind and the rustle of trees. Today, we work.

"Tighter to your body." Naira gently presses into my shoulder. "Relax the bow arm but tighten here." She straightens my elbow. "Now breathe and aim."

A long exhale helps relax my shoulders and I squint to focus on the tree with the red circle. Release. I wait anxiously as the arrow spirals forward. My heart leaps when it nears the tree, only to have the arrow fly right past into the depths of the forest.

"It flew straight this time," Naira says flatly.

I cock my head to the side. "I think you're mocking me."

She plucks a waxy leaf from a bush and crushes the greenery in her hands. "You let your mind rule too much."

"What do we work on now?"

"Again." She hands me another arrow.

We carry on with twenty more attempts that all end the same—an untouched tree and arrows scattering the forest floor.

We sit against a tree trunk to eat our lunch of smoked eel and melon. "I doubt I'll ever need to use a bow and arrow to defend myself. Why must I learn it?"

"Because you are not good at it."

I scowl but can't offer a rebuttal. She's right.

"You must learn to conquer anything in your way. Discomfort and pain and disappointment all limit your ability to fight. Conquer the arrow and you will strengthen your will."

I savor the sweet orange melon as its juice drips down my hand. "Naira, I have to stop James."

"James pretends. He acts as though he wants power, but really what he wants is for someone else to come along and rule him."

"I doubt that."

"Trust me on this," she says. "You have more power over him than you've ever realized." She glances at the angle of the sunlight. "Now, are you ready to continue?"

My aching arms say no, but my mind is ready and willing. "Yes."

"Good." She hands me a canteen. "Fill your mouth with water, but do not drink it."

"Why?"

"Must you ask so many questions?"

"Yes."

"Do it." She shoves it toward me again.

Seems nonsensical, but I oblige. I take a swig of cool stream water and hold it in my mouth. I shrug as if to say *what now?*

Naira places the quiver over her shoulder and lifts her arrow. "Do not for any reason spit out the water," she says.

My face twists into an untrusting grimace.

Naira reaches behind her and lifts an arrow, positioning it forward as she aims for the trees.

I make a noise that sounds like a grunt.

"You must beat the arrow." When I widen my eyes, she says, "You better hope I have better aim than you. Run."

I turn to run into the forest. The sinew string creaks as Naira pulls against the birch bow. I turn to look back and see Naira's arrow pointed straight at me. I keep running, too terrified to stop. *Why can't I spit out the water?* An arrow whips through the air with a slight hiss as it speeds past my ear. The tip lands in the tamarack trunk just to my right.

"Do not spit," Naira yells. "Run again."

I pick myself up, gather my skirts and run at top speed over fallen branches and rocks, slippery with moss. Another arrow whistles past, into a black maple in front of me, just above my head.

Maybe she doesn't want me to yell. The urge to swallow is strong, yet I hold back. I still trust her... despite current circumstances. Three more arrows land in my path, far enough not to hurt me but close enough to cause my heart to lurch.

On my knees, hands in the dirt, I inhale rapidly through my nose, trying to catch my breath.

Naira approaches. "Up."

I stand, trying to slow my heartbeat but having little success.

"You may spit now," she says.

Releasing the water instantly fills my lungs with air. "Why the water?" I eke out between breaths.

"You need to learn to control your breathing. Not using your mouth teaches your nose to work harder." She plucks her arrows from the trees and places them in the quiver.

"And shooting arrows at me as I run?"

"Danger is everywhere, Isabelle. Learn the weapons. Respect them. This is how you win battles."

"All right." I rub my arms, sore from the hard thud to the ground.

"Now we work with the spear," she says. "Back to camp."

I follow closely behind, waiting for any movement, but none comes. At the entrance to the settlement, Naira opens the gate to let me in. She reaches for the spear against the fence and in a flash, she juts the shaft forward with both hands toward my chest. I catch it and shove her back with all the weight my arms can manage, but I don't let go. She rolls her body and sends me spinning into the air. By the time I land splayed on my back, she has the spear aimed at my chest.

"Always be prepared, little mouse."

I want to shove the spear off me, but I'm too tired and cannot catch my breath. I manage a grunt and shut my eyes.

"You may rest, and I will show you what a woman can do." She reaches for my hand to help me to standing.

My back tightens, but I shake my head. "I'm fine."

Naira clears the open space in the center of the camp. She whistles, and three men step forward to surround her. The first man attacks with a tomahawk, but she uses her arms as a fulcrum, leaning back to lock him in place. She steps on his thigh and launches her other foot into his stomach, sending him to the ground, his tomahawk still in her hand.

The second man stabs his spear toward her. Her movements are swift and purposeful. Grabbing his arm mid-strike above his head, Naira launches both legs around his waist. She throws her weight back, still holding his spear as they tumble together like a rolling snail shell. She jumps up, pointing the spear toward his throat.

In the commotion, the third man has disappeared. Naira turns in a circle, waiting for him to strike. He jumps from the top of a wagon, his foot on her chest, and Naira falls to her back. The man shoves a spear toward her, eliciting a shriek from me.

Just as his spear nears her shoulder, Naira rolls away. She whips her legs across his ankles and his face smacks into the dirt. Naira grabs his hair and spins him around as she lands his spear across his neck. She could crush his windpipe with one hard press.

The elders smile and return to their crafts. She bows slowly, no smile and no sign of fatigue. Wyandot women aren't usually fighters, but Naira's father saw her potential.

As Naira walks up to me, she retrieves her knife, flipping and twirling it in her hand. She hands me the handle. "Your turn."

Breathless, I stare at the blade and the men she took to the ground. "I'm not done for today?"

"You are just getting started, little mouse. We learn every tool today. Starting with this blade."

"I don't suppose you'll go easy on me?"

"Why go easy on warriors? They have a pure heart that begs to be challenged."

Her sleek black hair reflects the lowering sun, not a lock out of place from her perfectly tightened braid.

I don't feel like a warrior—not in the tiniest corner of my being. But knowing her eyes see me as such makes me want to try.

"We work until daybreak," she says.

My heart sinks, knowing little mouse is in for a very long night.

．　　　　．

Every part of my body hurts, from my hair to my toes. We fought in the dark all night, as she taught me to listen for movement and drop to the ground when danger approaches. When sunrise illuminated the forest with a bronze light, Naira dropped her hands and weapons and walked silently to her longhouse. The woman seems to need little rest, a unique creature who never seems to break.

Under the blaring light of the summer sun, I stretch my tightened joints that creak like rusted hinges.

"Pain is momentary." Naira appears with breakfast. Boiled maize and venison.

"Why don't you hurt like this?" I ask.

"I have been practicing these ways since I was a child. My body has adapted. Yours is French and soft."

I look down at my body and realize how little of it I've used. She's helped me discover what I'm capable of and that burning fire of hate in me seems to have cooled to a focused flame. "What happens today?"

"Bow and arrow."

"Again? Why must you torture me?"

Naira laughs, reminding me she isn't magic. She is an exceptional woman of the earth. A mother and wife. A friend. "You must overcome your fears," she says. "Resistance is merely a challenge."

"I made a mistake," I blurt out. "Converting to Catholicism and running from fear was a mistake." I don't know why I say this, but the moment seems to call for it.

"I am not convinced of mistakes, little mouse. Just choices."

The deadened eyes of Protestant mothers fill my mind. I recoil from the memories of their ashen skin, the dried blood on their blue lips. "If I had stayed, fought harder, convinced everyone to fight with me…"

"Choosing when to fight is one of the hardest things to learn," Naira says.

I think about James and the evil he has stepped into in Montreal. "I hope I'll never need to use the skills you're teaching me."

"Learning the ways of battle is not simply to save your life. It is to teach your mind how to stay calm, how to settle your restless heart. That, Isabelle, is your greatest challenge."

I sip from a bowl of water and push away images of the bloody tongue thrown at my feet in La Rochelle.

She stands and bows her head with the control of a bear stalking salmon. "To the forest," she says.

Another hour of poorly shooting arrows leaves me so frustrated that I break one in half over the flesh of my thigh. Her people have worked hard to create that tool, and I instantly regret my foolishness. "I'm sorry. I shouldn't have done that."

"Anger will not help." She pulls the two pieces of birch from me.

I slump to the dirt and bury my head in my hands.

"We will come back to this. Now, time for forest travel."

She lifts me to standing and smears dirt on my face and hands. She tucks greenery and moss into my dress and hands me a branch full of bright green leaves. "Staying hidden is every warrior's best chance."

I follow her into the forest, on alert for any movement or hidden Iroquois, which is fruitless, as they can outsmart me at every turn. When Naira crawls on her belly, I follow. When she climbs a hill like a spider, I attempt to mimic her movements. At a low-hanging branch, she lifts herself ten times then carries on with quiet feet. My attempt at this hardly lifts my soft French body from the ground.

I stop to catch my breath, and the weight of her kindness falls heavy on me. She's the only one who inspires me. "Naira, I'm going to help you save the farmers. I'm going to make you proud."

Naira drops to the ground, as sturdy as a cat's pounce. "That is enough for today," she says.

Through the forest, we pass the flickering sunlight that slices through the treetops in yellow triangles. I keep waiting for Naira to say something inspirational, but she remains silent.

Back in her longhouse, she hands me a bowl of water and deer hide to clean the dirt from my skin. Why hasn't she discussed a plan for the attack?

"Are you going to help me?" I finally ask.

"I will not intervene." She avoids my eyes, staring at her moccasins. "A condition of my release."

"You would let them kill innocent children?"

She pulls a deep, slow inhale. "I must think of my clan. If I step in, they will come for all of us. I cannot risk that."

I scrub my face with the hide, rubbing hard against my hairline and neck until my skin burns.

Naira senses my frustration. "You may try to stop them, but I cannot."

"Me?" I stifle a laugh. "I can't even lift myself off the ground. I can't shoot an arrow, and I still can't sense when you're about to attack me."

"You underestimate yourself."

"I've just begun to learn. I don't have the strength to fight the Iroquois."

"You have five days to find it. That's when they will attack."

I throw the hide down and stand, staring at Naira, who doesn't look up. I storm out of the longhouse and grab the bow and arrows as well as three tomahawks, and stomp into the forest. At the clearing, I stare down the red circle on the tree one hundred paces away. Hips squared, shoulders relaxed, straight arm. Hand drawn back to my chin, I listen to the wind and release.

The arrow flies past the tree, disappearing into the green of pine needles. I throw the contraption to the ground and walk a frantic circle, tightening and releasing my fists. The forest speaks through the quiet rustle of leaves. I grab a tomahawk handle as I prop one foot forward and spin a half turn and release the blade. The point lands with a thwack in a pine trunk. Another partial turn and another blade, and my body begins to wake.

I hear a crunch in the forest floor, a foot breaking a branch. My hand tightens on the last tomahawk handle, and I twist. I throw toward the sound. The blade tumbles through the air and lands exactly where I intend. Breathless, I look around to the trees, wondering where the sound came from.

From behind a tree, Naira steps forward. "You have been listening, little mouse."

"I understand this weapon. I can throw with anger. It's the arrow's demand for calm concentration that baffles me."

Naira crouches next to me. "I have a daughter now, Isabelle. I am still a warrior, but my purpose is to protect her. You'll have to fight this battle without me."

I look to my feet, feeling selfish that I didn't see that before. "Of course. I understand."

"Try again," she whispers.

"It's no use."

"Again."

I stand, positioning the arrow on the tendon string. I lift the bow.

"Now, let go of every bit of tension." Naira steps back. "Forget all your anger, all your pain. Think about that circle and imagine the arrow drawn to the center. Focus on your will."

I remember my will to live back in France. My fight to stay alive and how fear owned my every breath. How I still see the dragoon's yellow teeth through his smile as he burned my arm. How my dreams haunt me like spirits rising from the dead. Naira's breath cycles in and out. A bird chirps in the trees and the river rushes in the distance.

I imagine the circle.

Hand drawn back, I pull my hand to my jaw, string under my tightened knuckles. I wait until my heart rate settles. When it does, I release my grip.

The arrow flies silently, slicing so straight that it doesn't even ripple the air. When the chert tip lands in the painted red circle, I stare in disbelief. "I did it."

"Well done," Naira says.

"I did it!" I drop the bow and arrow and pull her in for a hug, bouncing and laughing like a child.

Naira can't help but laugh. "What felt different?"

"I put my fear aside, like you said. I focused on what I wanted to happen."

"Now you walk away. We feast, and tomorrow we move forward based on your dreams tonight."

To the Wyandot, dreams tell the story of what our soul aches for. Naira interprets the whispers between sleep and waking.

"I only have a few days before James returns. It doesn't seem like enough time, does it?"

"It is only the beginning." She smiles and turns to walk home, leaving me to gather the weapons. I clumsily carry them back to camp and help the women prepare food.

We sit on the ground around the fire, under the warmth of the summer evening. My body is fatigued and sore, but my heart seems to swell in my chest. Naira laughs with her daughter, feeding her slivers of squash and bear meat, as her husband wraps his legs and arms around Naira in a protective embrace.

After hours of laughter and food and drink, we retire to the longhouse where their little family settles into a huddle on their cot. I lie on mine and let the warmth of the fire spread over me. My body is too tired to feel restless.

I fall into an easy sleep, drifting to a dreamland that disappears when I wake in the middle of the night, Naira at my shoulder. She whispers, "Well?"

I blink a few times, confused by the fire's shadows and my aching limbs. "What?"

"Your dream. I heard you whisper in your sleep, and I sat here until you woke."

"I dreamt of a wolf," I say. "Deep copper fur and sparkling green eyes."

Naira leans closer. "What was she doing?"

"How did you know it was a she?"

She smiles. "Instinct."

"The wolf stood at the tip of a rock, looking down on the valley below," I say. "She saw me approach and turned to face me. I wasn't afraid. The snow crunched under her feet, and she puffed out a breath into the cold. A cloud of warm air settled around her as she glanced over the edge. I moved next to her, somehow knowing that she would not attack. In the valley, they were all dead. Her entire pack lay bloodied and unmoving."

"What did she do?" Naira asks.

"She looked to me as the sun caught her verdant eyes."

"The wolf is you, Isabelle."

"Me?"

"Copper hair and green eyes." She gestures to my face. "Standing at the edge, afraid your people will all die without you."

My jaw tightens, and I sit up. "I have to do anything necessary to save them."

She places her hands together and bows her head. "Tomorrow, we learn manipulation. How to convince people and how to intimidate them."

"Why not more weapon work?"

"Your foes are your fellow Frenchmen. You need words to control them."

Naira walks back toward her cot, and I whisper, "Naira, have I progressed? Am I now little wolf?"

"Goodnight, little mouse."

After a growl, I settle back under my warm fur, the wolf's green eyes on my mind. I now must save the farmers on the edge of town *and* the Huguenots.

CHAPTER NINE

James returns tonight. My body feels as if it needs a week's rest, but there's no time for that. I must spend the morning at the abbey, as I'm certain James will check on my whereabouts this week. My heart pounds hard and fast, knowing I must warn the farmers today.

"Your church marriage comes later, Mademoiselles," I say to the Daughters. "The king has granted you the power to marry under a notary, so you may break your marriage contract at any point you wish."

The girls gasp. "Break our contract?" one asks.

Their reaction is the same as mine when I heard that women in Quebec not only choose their husbands, but may leave them if they so choose.

"That's correct. And some already have. You are not to stay if the man hurts you, neglects you, or makes you feel unsafe."

"Would the community shun us?" a young Parisian asks.

"No. In fact, you will have a line of men wanting to meet you."

I notice Louise in the doorway, her daughter behind her plucking dandelions in the garden.

"Ladies, it's time to wash up. Then make your way to the kitchen for bread making lessons."

The girls move like a flock of birds, flapping and gliding in a group to their next task. Louise waits to speak with me, her eyes red and swollen.

"You didn't mention what to do if you have children," she says.

"What do you mean?"

"Yes, we can break our contracts, but once we have children, it becomes much more difficult." She wrings her hands and shoots a glance at Elizabeth.

"Are you thinking of breaking your contract?" I ask.

"I've thought about it many times. Andre and I are like strangers. But I cannot raise a child alone. And who would take me with a daughter who screams more than she's quiet?"

We watch Elizabeth scoop a handful of dirt dotted with yellow dandelion buds. She reaches for the moist dirt with her mouth just as her mother shoves it away.

"Your daughter is curious and spirited. It will serve her well in life." I can't help but smile at the twinkle in the little girl's eyes. The same as her father has.

"Isabelle, I'm so tired. And lonely."

I reach for her hand, putting my own feelings aside. "Marriage is an odd thing, isn't it? We promise our bodies and lives to another, knowing nothing about them. We share a bed and maybe have children with them, yet we know so little of our spouse's true selves."

"You feel that way too?" she asks.

"Sometimes." *Always*, I want to say.

"Maybe I'm too hard on Andre." Her shoulders soften. "I practically forced him to marry me and to have a child."

I pushed that memory out of my mind long ago. "Andre made his choices, Louise."

"No, he didn't. He wanted you. Sometimes I think he still does." Her eyes don't waver from mine.

"Louise, we've all moved on, and it's best that you do as well."

She wants to say more, but Elizabeth has stood and teeters toward the sunflowers, called to the bright yellow petals that tilt toward the sky. Louise runs off to catch her.

I slip out the back door to the other side of the garden before Louise catches me. At the gate to the stables, I hear, "Where are you off to?"

Leaning against the fence, her cheeks reddened by the sun, Charlotte cocks her head to the side.

"I don't believe I report to you, Charlotte."

She strolls toward me. "I don't need lessons on how to make bread and forage for mushrooms. We learned it all in France, didn't we? We learned to fend for ourselves, how to steal food and survive on moldy wine and mice. How if you dared leave the house, never to look someone in the eyes."

She's right, but I won't let her bring me back there.

"Charlotte, I understand your anger. What I cannot figure out is what you plan to do here. Will you live with the nuns, secretly plotting an attack while they sleep?"

"I wish them no ill will. Only those bastards back in La Rochelle." She reaches for me and slides my dress sleeve back to expose my arm.

I yank away from her touch.

"I'd heard they branded you. It's true."

"Holding onto the anger that threatens to ruin you does no good for anyone. Now be a good girl and return to your lessons." I step out of the gate and untie my horse from her post.

"Is that what you are now, a good girl?"

I mount my horse and instinctively feel for Andre's knife strapped to my leg. "I am what I need to be."

Trotting down the path that leads out of town, I refuse to look back at Charlotte. That girl is like a fly, pestering me with guilt—yet I can't swat her away.

Two farmers live on the edge of town. Unlike the fiefs in town with long, thin strips packed against the river, these families own wide sections of land. Living near the forest provides space, but it comes with risk.

When I arrive at the closest farm, an eerie quiet blankets the house and seems to warn me of danger. The wind flutters through an open window, flapping a curtain into the stillness. As I approach, guns appear from every window and a hole in the doorway. Six barrels point toward me, ready to fire.

I halt, palms facing the house. "My name is Madame Beaumont. I'd like to speak with you."

The guns don't move. Through the darkness I see eyes blink. "What do you want?" a voice asks.

"I have a message for you. I'm concerned about your safety. May I approach the door?"

After a pause, the guns retreat as coiled tension unwinds in my neck.

The wife opens the door without hesitation. Hand on her hip, she says, "What is it?"

Behind her, four boys and one girl stand with arms folded. Their ages range from ten to around eighteen. The daily toil of farm work while protecting your house in a dangerous land seems to have created their own kind of warrior.

"I've received word that the Iroquois will attack your house and your neighbors."

"There is always that threat," the mother says.

"This is certain. They will attack in two days. Probably at night." I step forward to limit what the children can hear. "They will kill you all. To make a statement to the French."

"Madame, we have lived here for years. We are prepared for such an attack."

"How? They'll surround you and outnumber you."

The woman smooths her gray hair from her face. "This is our home. We will defend it. Won't we, children?"

They all lift their chins and grunt. All but the girl. She watches.

"Madame, we have survived wolf attacks and blizzards. My children have lived off the land for the entirety of their childhood. We survive. It is what we do."

"If you'll just leave for a few days, you can save yourselves."

Her hand raises to stop me. "Thank you for your concern, but we do not need you. Good day."

She slams the door, and the guns return to their position in the windows. "Leave," a boy says.

Crushed, I step back and lead my horse along the path as it winds behind the house. If this family thinks they can outwit the Iroquois, they are wildly mistaken. A creaking noise catches my attention. I turn to see the girl climb out a second-story window and scamper down a tree.

She runs to me, skirt raised to her knees. "Madame," she says breathlessly, "I've seen the Iroquois watch us."

"Yet your parents still don't seem concerned," I say.

"My father believes he can win against anyone. He can't."

"You're a smart girl."

"I'm fourteen, but I think I'm the most sensible one in this house." She looks back. "Please keep trying. They won't listen to me."

Without waiting for a reply, she runs to her tree, climbs the branches, and slides back into her room. Back on the path, I walk my horse slowly, as I listen to the rustle of leaves, and the shift in wind. Something's off. Naira tells me to listen. I think I hear crunching, like shoes on dried branches. When I stop, the noise halts.

I slow my horse. Whoever's following me remains twenty paces behind. I can tell by the way the sound bounces. I lift my skirts and quietly slide my blade from its sheath.

I whip my horse around and run toward the sound. A flash slips behind a tree. I launch from the horse's back to a pine branch. Blade in hand, I swing off the branch with one hand and land over top of his slight frame, knife pressed to his neck.

When my eyes focus, I see it is not a man. I'm holding a knife to Charlotte's neck. Her eyes are wide, and her hands tremble in front of her face. "I'm sorry," she says. "I'm sorry I followed you."

Reckless child. I tighten my grip on the knife before releasing her. "I could have killed you," I snap.

Charlotte stands, leaning against the tree trunk. "How did you do that?"

"You consider yourself so resourceful and witty, don't you?" I lift my skirts and return the blade to the sheath against my thigh. "You have no idea the danger of following me." I whistle for my horse who trots back to me.

"I wanted to see what you're doing. You're hiding something."

"Why are you so concerned with me?"

"I spent years looking up to you—well, the idea of you. A girl who fights Catholics and saves Protestants. Clémentine spoke of you often and I dreamed of becoming a hero, just like you."

I push her against the tree. "I am no hero. Understand? I am a woman trying to survive. Just like you."

"What are you doing out here?" she asks.

I turn to walk away, the horse's rope rough in my palm. I don't answer and hope she'll disappear. Of course, she doesn't.

"Let me help you," she says.

As she scurries behind me, I suddenly understand why Naira has named me after a tiny creature. I keep walking and try to ignore her.

"Please, Isabelle. I want to do something more than choose a husband and populate New France."

Much as I hate it, Charlotte reminds me of myself before I understood how complicated people are. Back when my fight was clear and easy to understand. Before I had to learn how to fight my husband and my own heart.

I stop and turn to her. "You may come with me, but you say nothing. And for the last time, do not call me a hero."

She nods, eyes lit like a child on an adventure. I might regret this.

⋅ ⋅ ⋅

At the next farm, a young woman greets us on their porch. She rocks her baby in the afternoon warmth. "Afternoon," she says. "What can I do for you today?"

"I have news I would like to pass on."

She stands and opens the door, bouncing her baby on her chest. "Come in. Maple cake's warming over the fire." She hands me the baby. I try to push her away, but the mother insists.

The sleepy baby fusses and rubs her fists on her cheeks, obviously wondering who this stranger is holding her. The woman retrieves a pan from the fire and scoops cake into bowls. This little baby in my arms has decided that my chest is a suitable place to stay as she yawns and nestles her soft cheek onto my skin. I wonder if she can hear my heartbeat.

"Bounce her so she doesn't cry," the woman says.

I bend and straighten my knees, looking to the mother for encouragement. The baby groans and her weight grows heavy. Soft and sweet, the scent from her head bubbles a memory from the depths of me. My baby sisters had this smell. I used to hold them and rock them in the chair by the fire just like this. Until they died from fever. I have never again smelled a baby's skin until now.

"Here." I peel the baby from my chest and hand her to the mother, noting my cool skin where the tiny girl's face had warmed it.

The mother holds her as if she's part of her own body. "What did you need to tell me?"

I shake myself back to the moment. "Yes. the Iroquois. They're planning an attack on your farm. Two days from now."

She stops bouncing and watches Charlotte enjoy her treat. With a mouthful of cake, Charlotte looks back at me. "You told me not to speak."

"How do you know?" the woman asks.

"The Huron. They're certain."

"Why? We've done nothing to them." She cradles the baby's head and I realize suddenly why having children seems so frightening to me. How much harder it would be to fight when a piece of your heart is so soft and fragile.

"They don't care. They're angry about the fur trade and want the French to pay. Your farms are far enough out of town that you're vulnerable."

"What do we do?"

"You leave for a few days."

She looks around. "What will they do to our home?"

"They will burn it."

She swallows and wraps her arms tighter around the baby. "We've built this home. We cannot leave it to become ashes."

"They will kill your family without a thought."

Charlotte stops eating and watches our interaction.

"I will speak with my husband tonight," the woman says. "I don't understand why they hate us."

"We hate what we do not understand," Charlotte says.

Silence fills the room, the only sound is the sleeping baby's heavy breathing.

On our way out, I say, "This land will become a bloodbath in a few days' time. Force your husband to listen to you."

Charlotte races to keep up with me as we head to my horse. "Why do the Iroquois want to kill these people?"

"They want to frighten all of us. Show us what they're capable of." I untie and mount my horse.

"I want to help," she says.

"No."

"Please. I know I'm young, but I'm smart and I learn quickly."

"I have no time to teach you anything. Besides, I'm still learning myself." She stares down the long path to town, eyebrows furrowed. "Get up," I say. "I'll take you back."

She grabs my forearm right over my scar, flicks her eyes to me, then grasps harder.

"Hold on," I say.

She wraps her arms around my waist, and I send the horse flying as fast as she'll go, to both frighten and exhilarate Charlotte. She needs to learn patience. Again, I think of my younger self. I don't slow down until we reach the abbey gates, both of us out of breath and with wild, windblown hair. Charlotte stays holding me even after we've stopped, her cheek pressed to my shoulder blades.

"You can go home now, Charlotte."

She peels herself from my back and slides to the dirt. She looks up at me and takes a deep breath. "I was wrong. You're still in the fight."

"Huguenots will always be fighters."

I kick my horse to set her running wild and free again, leading me home where I must wait for my husband and decide how to stop him from becoming a murderer.

· · ·

At dinnertime, James opens the door. He lowers his satchel to the ground and examines my expression. "Isabelle, I've missed you."

I wait by the fire, my only response a hesitant step forward.

"Are you still angry with me?" He removes his hat and doublet and runs his fingers through his wavy hair.

I step closer, staring deep into his eyes. The time for silence is gone. The only way to stop him is to expose his lies. "I know what you're doing with LaMarche."

His eyes trail over my breasts. "Please, your mind has run away again. Come to bed with me."

I slap his hand from my chest. "You'll sell slaves to the colonies and turn Huguenots into prisoners."

His bravado drops just a hair. "How did you…"

"It doesn't matter how I found out."

He lifts his hand as if he wants to touch me, but then he takes a deep breath and drops his shoulders. "I didn't want this."

"Then stop."

"I can't." His voice booms through the still house. "Antoinette threatened to seize my father's ships and strip my family of all our money. She'd send my sister to servitude and report to the king that I'm a traitor."

"Antoinette doesn't have that kind of power."

"No, but Monsieur LaMarche does."

There's something he isn't saying. "Why does he need you?" He stiffens, but I lay my hand on his chest and widen my eyes.

"My father owns a trading company," he says.

"You've never told me that."

"Because he competes with the king. It's made my family a tremendous amount of money. LaMarche will turn us in as traitors if we don't work with them."

Amber light warms James's face. I stand close to him and run my hand along his cheek. "What about the Huguenots?"

He pulls away from my touch, as if he knows it's how I soften him. "You must let them go, Isabelle. The only way to keep the king from ruining us is to offer him something."

"You would imprison innocent people and rip children from their parents?"

His copper hair falls in his face when he turns toward me. "I have no choice."

"You're a monster." I turn from him, but he grabs my arm.

"Stop," he says.

"Let me go."

"I don't know how to get out of this, Isabelle."

"You're weak. Your sister warned me you could not stand up to your father and I should have listened. I should have listened when my mother told me you were not who you seemed." My skin burns as I try to move from his grip, but he grabs both my arms.

"I've proved myself in the Royal Army and by fighting the Iroquois. It's gotten me nowhere."

"We were fine. I need no more than what we have. I never wanted to be part of the nobility."

James looks down, his forehead pulled taut and jaw pulsating. His grip still has not lightened. "If I walk away, my family and I could be imprisoned or sentenced to death. And by extension, you would be guilty too."

"Why me?"

"You enjoy the riches we have made because of my family business. And besides, Antoinette wants to see us both burn."

A strong desire rises to throw my weight to his knees and take him to the floor. But I inhale a deep breath and focus. "We can figure this out," I say. "But you can't lie to me."

Charlotte flashes into my mind. That persistent girl desperate to take part in something bigger than her tiny world. I think of the farmers and how I have one more chance to save them. And I think of Naira, throwing me to the ground to teach me to become a wolf.

Slowly, I unwrap the silk cravat from around his neck, exposing his red-hued skin. With a yank on both ends, I pull him to me, his chest pressed to mine. Mouth nearly touching his, I whisper, "You can beat the LaMarches."

He shakes his head. "How?"

"Shh," I say. "We can outsmart them." I lay my lips on his and taste his smoky kiss.

James brings his hands to my hips and lets me move him, like softened clay waiting to be formed. I tilt my head and untie his hair, loosening his curls to his shoulders. Hands to his chest, I press him to the chair and let him watch me undress.

James spreads his legs, rubs his hands on his thighs.

Once I'm stripped down to bare skin and release my hair, I lower to his lap. I grab his shirt and pull it over his head, letting my fingers trail slowly down his chest, so muscular yet riddled with scars. I run my hands up his neck and pull him in to kiss my breasts.

"We have a chance here, don't we?" I whisper. "To become powerful?"

James muffles a sigh into the skin at my breastbone. "My father would love nothing more."

He grabs my hair with a little roughness, which excites me. "We make your father more powerful and push the LaMarches out."

"Okay," he says between kisses along my stomach and ribs, his hair brushing my skin.

He reaches to kiss me, but I grab a fistful of his soft curls and yank him back so he must look up at me. "If you so much as think about buying slaves or imprisoning Huguenots, I'll burn you myself."

James hesitates. I would expect no less.

"You won't leave me?" he asks.

"Not if you do the right thing."

James nods. I have not released his hair. He slides his hand between my legs, making my body pulse. "I can be powerful," he says. "If you stay by my side."

In between heaving breaths, I arch my back and let him take me to trembling. "Prove yourself to me."

His hand sends me moaning and I nearly cry out in ecstasy, still with a fistful of his red curls firmly gripped in my fist.

CHAPTER TEN

This morning, I tried once again to convince the farmers to leave, but both men refused. By the time I arrive at the Huron camp, nervousness has taken over my body.

"Isabelle," Naira says. "What shall we learn today?"

I drop from my horse. "The art of surviving an Iroquois raid."

She raises her eyebrows. "You've been busy." Arm around my shoulders, she leads me to the longhouse. "Sit. Drink this tea to settle your worry. And tell me what has happened."

"The farmers are so stubborn. They think they can fight off the Iroquois." I watch her inhale the steam from her tea. "What would you do if they were coming to attack your house?" I ask.

"I would gather our fiercest warriors, send the rest away, and scatter us hidden in the trees for a surprise attack."

"I don't have a band of warriors," I say. "I have me."

"You have not asked Andre for help? Or James?"

"No." I shake my head. "I've been too careless with Andre. He has a wife and child to attend to."

"And James?"

My neck stiffens when I remember our conversation last night. "I can't trust him."

"That is not an enviable trait in a husband."

James is testing me just as much as I'm testing him. "I need to do this myself."

"Drink up. I have something for you." Naira disappears and returns, beckoning me from the door.

She stands with a wagon covered with burlap.

"What is this?"

"The Haudenosaunee can identify our weapons. The way we feather our arrows and paint our tomahawks. I've been collecting from other tribes and castoffs from the forest. I've prepared for this for months."

"You knew I would need them?"

She shrugs. "All I do is listen to the dreams." She pulls back the burlap. "Here. A dozen tomahawks, two bows, and quiver full of arrows, three spears."

"Naira, this is incredible." I step back, suddenly aware that I'll be taking on a band of fierce fighters when I can't even shoot an arrow straight. "What am I doing this for?"

"You don't need to step into this battle. But if you do, it is because you've been called to."

"What if I die? What if I don't save anyone?"

"That is not the question you should be asking."

The way she dismisses death has always unnerved me. "I don't know or care about these men. Why should I do this?"

"It is not the strength of the warrior that matters, but her bravery."

I count the weapons. "Hide in the trees, you say?"

"Don't let them see you. Attack from afar and give the family enough time to run away." Naira reaches for my hand. "People will die tonight, but you will not be one of them."

"How do you know?"

"The wolf showed me. This is your test. Your true journey has just begun."

• • •

The sun has disappeared behind the pointed treetops and a bright full moon casts a sparkling glow over the farm. From the tree, the fields next to the farmhouse ripple like water. Midsummer, the sun holds to the sky for a few extra hours, until it finally exhales and allows the moon its space.

I'm thankful for the long day, as I needed the afternoon hours to prepare.

Below me are tomahawks hidden under leaves and spears leaned against trees that blend with the trunks. I've walked the path between the two farms at least four times, to practice where my weapons are and how fast I can run to my next post.

Rifle slung over my shoulder for emergency use only, I need to rely on these arrows, but I've shot only one accurately. It's almost comical how ill-prepared I am for this fight. But I suppose that's how I've always lived—engaged in hopeless fights that should have killed me.

A subtle shift in the dirt disrupts my thoughts. The soft sound of shuffling feet sends my heart to my throat. If they've been watching me, I'm finished before I even begin.

Crack.

They've stepped on a branch. I quietly remove my quiver and gun, knowing they will do me no good up close. I have one shot—the tomahawk. In the shadows below, movement approaches. This is it. Attack before they can launch a spear into my throat.

Hands secured on the branch, I land crouched, then launch to grab my tomahawk handle jutting up from the leaves. I swing out from the tree, arm lifted and tomahawk ready to slice, when someone falls to their knees.

"Charlotte?" I drop my tomahawk and grab her by the dress near her shoulder. "You stupid girl! What are you doing here?" I keep my voice stern but quiet.

"I've been watching you all day. I've been learning."

What chance do I have against the Iroquois if I can't sense a clumsy child following me? "Foolish." I pull her back to the tree. "Can you climb?"

"Yes."

She scurries up the trunk after me without a problem. I'm not surprised. All of us Huguenots were forest children, running like foxes through the fields to find food and protection from predators.

"I can help," she says.

"Can you shoot an arrow?"

"Yes?" She coughs and lowers her tone. "Yes."

I try not to roll my eyes. "This is a terrible idea." I have no choice but to let her stay. "The second bow is—"

"Fifty paces down the road, on the second branch of the Eastern white pine."

"You certainly have been paying attention. Go. But walk softly. Apparently, you can do that fine."

She disappears, and I steady myself in the tree where I have room to pull my arm back. I should position her at the other farm, but now I'm responsible for this imbecile. She returns quickly and situates herself next to me, breathless.

"I... I'm ready," she says. "What's the plan?"

"This isn't a game, Charlotte."

"I know it's not. I don't care if I die tonight. I've spent my life as a prisoner in the shadows. When I left France, I decided I would rather die fighting."

Every time I dismiss her as reckless and immature, she reminds me how brave we've all had to be.

"The young mother with the baby? She'll slip into the root cellar." I point toward the underground storage. "Hopefully, that will buy us time to protect someone from this farm before running to the next."

"How do we attack?" she asks.

"We shoot at every Iroquois we see. We only have a minute, maybe two. Then they'll follow the direction of the arrows, so we need to run to the root cellar to save the woman and baby and get out of here as fast as possible."

She nods, then settles into her branch and aims an arrow near the house.

We sit in the quiet night for hours. Fatigue sets in, but we stretch our legs as best we can and rub our eyes to stay focused.

"Maybe they aren't coming tonight?" she whispers.

"They'll come." The silver moon behind the treetops suggests it's after midnight, and fatigue rolls over me. A bat whips its wings and frogs gargle from deep in the earth.

Charlotte taps my arm. "There."

Across the field, through the tree line—movement. We sit at attention. My heart thrashes in my chest. "This is it," I say. "You ready?"

"No."

"Me either. But here we are."

The Iroquois trickle out of the trees like a slow bleed. Disturbingly calm, they quietly trot toward the farmhouse in a blur of shining brown horsehair and red feathers.

Suddenly, gunshots ring from every window of the house. Blood spurts from three Iroquois who topple from their horses and roll on the ground. Sparks of light blast from the gun barrels again. The first round of Iroquois is down, but another wave emerges from the trees, this time with flaming arrows pointed at the house.

"Guns can't fight a house fire," Charlotte says.

"As soon as they shoot, we attack." She nods in understanding.

The men draw back their arrows that they've doused in oil and set aflame. They shoot through the sky and crash into the roof and through the windows, fiery breath blown into every corner of the house.

"Now."

We draw back and send our first shots through the air. I don't stop to see if I've hit anyone. Stay calm. Reach back, position, draw, breathe, release.

The daughter climbs out her window and grabs the branch to steady herself as smoke billows out behind her. Around the corner, an Iroquois lurks.

I draw back another arrow and shoot, missing him by enough that he doesn't register anyone has shot at him. I shoot again, and I miss again. Fumbling for another arrow, my hands tremble. The man nears closer. I draw back—my last chance to save her. But I can't stop the shaking.

With a sharp whip through the air, an arrow lands in the eyeball of the Iroquois man. The girl gasps and falls back to the ground, lying frozen next to the dead man's face. I turn to Charlotte in awe.

"Archery is easy," she says. "Wait, another." She draws back, shoots, lands another arrow in the fleshy area of his neck. Another man, another arrow. They turn and face us, knowing where the attack came from.

I jump to the ground, reach my hands in the leaves and come up with two tomahawks. Charlotte shoots them down as they near, but two reach back for their arrows, eyes on the girl in the tree.

I firm my stance, draw back my tomahawk, and launch. The sharp blade lands in his chest just as he was positioning his arrow. The next man draws back, and I throw another, remembering what Naira taught me. Listen, aim, follow through. The bit slices through his stomach. He collapses to the ground, writhing in pain.

The farm girl regains her wits, and races for us as fast as she can manage.

Charlotte jumps down, bow in hand. We wait the five seconds it takes for the girl to join us. We grab her arms and run down the path, not caring about the quiet of our feet. The remaining men approach us from behind. They pound the ground behind us. Thump. Thump. An arrow flies past me. I tuck my head and run. "Go," I tell Charlotte. "Get the baby."

Charlotte runs forward, dragging the girl with her. I stop, turn around and reach for the tomahawk hidden at the tree base. Hiding behind the tree, I wait until they approach. Two men, one tomahawk. Their footsteps quicken.

I jump from behind the tree and launch my last tomahawk into the closest man. It lands in his skull, slicing his face down the center. The sound is like a split melon. It's nothing like hitting a tree. The next man nears. No weapons, arms out.

He hesitates, which I don't expect.

The world slows, and the air between me and this fighter feels thick as stew. He's young. Younger than me. Naira tells me to show bravery. Do not retreat.

I tighten my fists and step forward, eyes steady on his. I may not win, but I am ready. He drops his arms and I exhale, relieved that he doesn't want to fight any more than I do.

An arrow blasts past me and lands in his chest. After he stumbles to the ground, I step closer to examine his face.

He stares at me, coughing and sputtering for air.

"I'm sorry," I whisper. But he simply closes his eyes and drifts to death.

Charlotte grabs my arm. "Come on."

"Why did you kill him? He wasn't going to fight me."

"You can't trust anyone—especially not the enemy. How have you not learned that?"

We run to the second farmhouse to discover the roof already on fire. "You go to the cellar," she says. "I'll cover you from here."

"Why you?"

"Because I have better aim." She crouches, arrow drawn, and I wonder how I ever underestimated her.

The farm girl sits curled against a tree next to Charlotte, her knees tucked to her chest.

Crouched low, grateful for dark clothes and mud hiding my pale skin, I run past the flames as they lick the treetops. Animals howl as the Iroquois slaughter them. The cellar hides in the ground, a small entrance barely seen when right next to it. The baby whimpers.

I tuck my head in. "Hello?"

The mother lies on the ground, unnaturally twisted from what I can see through the dark.

"I'm... I'm here," she says.

I feel my way down the stairs toward the baby's cries.

"Here, take her," she says.

"You can't stay here. They'll find you. We only have a few minutes."

"I can't walk. Please. I just fed her, so she'll be calm for a while."

The baby girl begins to fuss, probably sensing the upheaval in her tiny world. I tear my skirt from one end to the other, ripping a long trail of material. As I've seen the Huron women do, I tie the strip around my waist, then over my shoulder. With shaking hands, I settle the baby into my chest and wrap the cloth around me twice, tying what's left at my hips.

"Come." I reach for her.

"I can't."

"You can. Your daughter needs you to try."

She cries out as she tries to stand, and I cover her mouth. "Quiet. Understand?"

I feel her nod yes.

I cradle the baby's soft head against my chest. "Sit on the steps," I tell the woman. "Scoot up backwards. Don't use your hurt foot."

I ascend from the root cellar, looking around at the fire and smoke. A man notices me and runs with a long blade in his hand. Charlotte makes quick work of him as he falls face first to his death a mere ten paces in front of us. The woman stifles her screams.

"Stand," I tell her. "Wrap your arm around my shoulders and hop."

She begins to cry.

"No. Not now. You cry when we get out of here safely."

One arm wrapped around her waist, the other cradling her baby's head, I move swiftly. She suddenly gasps and crumbles forward. I fall to the ground next to her, looking back to find an Iroquois drawing back for another shot. Charlotte resorts to gunfire.

A shot rings out as the bullet blasts the man's face into a bloody mess. I reach for the woman's hand but she's on her side, an arrow piercing her spine. She isn't moving.

I shake her. "No, get up. Your baby needs you."

She's gone.

"Isabelle, run," Charlotte shouts.

I don't want to pull away from this woman, but I must save this baby.

Holding back tears, I run for Charlotte as she shoots again and again behind me. The farm girl holds her hands over her ears and cries. At the tree line, Charlotte grabs the girl and forces her up, her limbs like a rag doll.

We run into the forest, deep under the protection of darkness. "There's another trail near here, but we have to hide," I say. "They'll follow us."

We search for protection and find a hollowed tree trunk. "Get in," Charlotte says.

The girl goes first, and we work to cover the top with moss and leaves and anything we can pull from the forest floor. Charlotte enters next, then me with the baby. We cover the opening with branches and leaves.

Curled in place, we fill the dark, wet space with hot air and racing heartbeats. The baby yawns and sucks her knuckle. She'll soon wail for food or comfort, or both. Please, baby, do not scream.

I don't even know her name—or her mother's.

Voices. They speak Iroquoian. I stroke the baby's head, afraid that movement might alert them to our location. Their voices surround us on both sides as footsteps thump forward. Charlotte grabs my hand. I hold my breath and search the shadows as they wave like water around us.

The steps close in, and through a sliver of worn trunk, I can see a tall man with red grease streaked across his cheeks. I wonder if they can smell us—if fear has a scent.

He mumbles something and turns to look in my direction. I close my eyes and pray.

When I crack open one eye, he stands over me but is looking at his fighters. He points and throws his head to the right. The footsteps move past us, shadows flickering, as they quietly disappear into the forest. We all seem to exhale together. Even the baby.

The girl whimpers, and I lean my head back to the softened wood, staring at this strong little baby. We wait for hours until the sun appears with its pale, yellow light and we emerge from the cramped tree trunk.

Although we are all worn raw with fear, we manage to trek through the forest toward town. The baby finally begins to cry.

We approach the abbey, Sister Marguerite and James waiting impatiently at the gate. While Sister looks relieved, James looks furious.

Mud smeared onto our faces, leaves stuck into our hair, and clothes torn to shreds, we glance at each other with closed-mouth smiles.

We survived.

James hobbles to me as best as he can with his painful hip. Marguerite reaches for Charlotte to inspect her face. "Oh dear, I called for the Beaumonts when we discovered you missing. Are you all right?"

Charlotte sneaks out a wicked smile. "I've never been better."

"And then I discovered you missing as well," James says against a tightened jaw.

The farm girl crosses her arms in front of her chest and cries. I untie the material and hand the baby to Marguerite, feeling as if a part of my body has been ripped away. "She's hungry."

"I'll find her some milk right away." She leads the girls to the abbey and James holds my face in his hands.

"What have you done?" he asks.

"I saved them."

He growls in frustration. "I can see that. But why?"

I wipe the sweat from my brow. "The Iroquois attacked them. I had to do something."

He grabs my arm. "You foolish girl. You must stop this."

James's voice sounds just like how I spoke to Charlotte. I yank away. "You will not place demands on me any longer. Accept me as I am, or I will break our contract."

"This is how it will be? You threaten our marriage to get what you want?"

I pull back my shoulders and stare him down until he flinches. "You need me to be strong. Stop asking me to be weak."

He pulls a branch from my hair. "I hate that I find you so beautiful when you're angry."

"You need me angry, James. It's how we've survived this long."

He closes his eyes and forces his anger down. "How do we fight the LaMarches?"

"One battle at a time."

Charlotte waits in the doorway, watching me with her shining blue eyes. She looks older than she did yesterday.

"I need to speak with her," I say.

James tightens his lips and impatiently gestures that he'll wait in our carriage.

When I approach, Charlotte smiles through exhausted eyes. "Where did you learn to shoot like that?" I ask.

"We were all taught how to fight. But we were also told not to. Be passive. Stay strong in your moment of torture."

I lean against the doorway next to her, looking out over the garden of summer flowers and herbs. "Doesn't seem right, does it?" I ask.

She turns to face me. "I can help you."

"I think you've proven that."

"With LaMarche," she says.

"What do you know about him?"

She crosses her arms. "Other than how he imprisoned our pastor back in La Rochelle? How he ordered the women beaten and raped and the men shackled in the town square?"

"That was back in France."

"I'm not certain what he has planned, but I heard him after Mass discussing Huguenots. How they will all be owned as the pigs they are."

I restrain a snarl. "How I would love to shove his face in pig manure."

"What do you need from me?"

I glance over my shoulder to ensure privacy, then lean to whisper. "We need to limit his trade, strengthen James's family business, and force LaMarche out."

She leans back and takes a deep breath. "I wish you would have trusted me sooner."

"We can't trust anyone, remember?"

"Yes, true." She snaps a petunia bloom from its stem and holds it up to the morning light. "That woman from Rouen, the one who beds every young man but her husband?"

I know exactly who she's referring to. The woman at Henri's who recognized me as a soldier's wife. "Yes."

"Her family owns land all over New France. She has more money than anyone here and rejoices in revealing that to everyone."

I pull the purple bloom from her hands. "We get her to invest."

"She's only here to discover new ways to grow her family's wealth."

"And we know her weakness."

Charlotte takes a deep breath. "I pity women who turn weak around a handsome man."

I glance at James, tapping his foot and waiting to swoop me back to our safe home. "It's much better to be the one in power, don't you think, Charlotte?"

Her upturned smile widens to a full grin. "Yes, I believe I do."

"Charlotte, thank you. I couldn't have done this without you."

Her chest swells with a deep inhale. "Until our next adventure, Madame."

I saunter back to James, ready for him to undress me and clean the dirt and fight off my body. Ready to prove to him that I am the one here with the power.

CHAPTER ELEVEN

Her name is Jacqueline Doré. I've asked around, and she claims to be an illegitimate daughter from the Royal House of Bourbon. Her skin is very dark, almost amber, and completely unlike the French nobility. If she is indeed related to the king, she has quite a story. What I can't understand is why she spends her time with men like Henri. Rumor has it she has them scattered around town, visiting her lovers without the slightest attempt to hide.

Today I found her shopping for pottery in the town square, unaffected by the chatter of an Iroquois attack. I follow her, waiting for the right moment to approach. I've sent James to the tavern as he is more a hindrance than a help.

"I'll take them all!" she says with a laugh. "Deliver them to my palace."

She lives near the intendant. Nothing in Quebec is a palace. Not like France, where she most likely lived in a royal home fit for the princess she sees herself as. She stops, something catching her eye. I follow her gaze to the hat shop where Antoinette prances through the door.

Madame Doré strikes me as a formidable match for Antoinette. She glides to the shop, and I position myself just outside the door to listen.

"Tell me, Madame LaMarche," she says. "Who are you terrorizing today?"

"Out of my way, hag."

Antoinette's rebuttal sounds like a child spitting insults. She must feel intimidated, and it brings me great joy.

They pretend to linger, waiting for the hatmaker to slip to the back.

"It's quite pathetic how you like to compete with me."

"I compete with no one," Antoinette says.

"You've been to visit a few of my friends, as if I wouldn't find out about it."

"You have friends?" Antoinette snaps. "I thought everyone hated you."

"These men want me. They adore me." I hear the crack of Madame Doré's feathered fan click open. "They pity you."

"I am far more beautiful," Antoinette says. "With you, they see money."

"Jean-Luc tells me you practically threw yourself at him," Madame Doré says. "How unladylike."

Something slams hard against the table, presumably Antoinette's fist. "I will not allow you to treat me this way. I am a LaMarche."

"And Francois says you seem lonely. It's no wonder with that black heart of yours."

"The only thing black here is your illegitimate skin," Antoinette snaps.

"Do not push me, girl."

Just as Antoinette storms toward the door, I slip into the alley and wait until she disappears behind the silversmith shop. A minute later, Madame Doré steps into the sunlight. She hands a new hat box to her servant. "Take this home, please."

She takes a deep breath, enjoying her moment of triumph, and I stride next to her.

"Nobody understands Antoinette LaMarche quite like I do," I say.

She turns, surprised to see me. "You." She leans close. "Our friend Henri. Where is he?" She bites her lip. "Oh, how I miss his black curls and perfect pout."

I get the feeling I need to pour cold water on this woman's face, lest she begin heavy breathing right in front of me.

"He had business to attend to."

"Pity. He was one of my favorites. His confidence." She shimmies her shoulders and smiles.

"How many do you have, Madame?" It feels improper, but I sense she wants to brag.

"At least six."

"Seems like a lot of work," I say.

She sputters a laugh, which leads to a large, rolling bellow. "Oh, Madame Beaumont. I do like you."

Questionable manners aside, I like her too. "Madame, I have a proposition for you."

Her eyes dance. "Come. Stroll with me." We walk arm in arm. Madame Doré does not hesitate. "The LaMarches already approached me for their little scheme involving your husband."

"Oh. I assure you, I want no part in that."

"I do not do business with scoundrels. And that wench is as awful as her father. But your husband? They must have something on him."

"I'm not sure of the details. But I don't agree with the practices they'll adopt to make their riches."

She nods. "Slaves."

"Among other things."

"I've seen men brought in chained and naked. I do not understand how people can be so cruel."

"I'm trying to stop my husband before he walks into something he cannot escape."

"Ah. You want to find another investor."

"Yes. I'm sure you are aware of his family's connections?"

"Yes. But I have no need for trade in the Indies. We do quite well with our goods sent between here and France."

"What *do* you want?"

"Besides that delicious friend of yours? I want power. More land. My royal allowance is meant to keep me quiet, but I have no interest in that." She winks.

An allowance from the king? Perhaps she is an illegitimate child. "And your husband, how do you keep your indiscretions from him?"

"Oh, I don't."

I shake my head, trying to understand.

"Our arrangement works splendidly. We both married into power, each of us on the periphery of nobility. Something to prove, you might say. His romantic interests lie elsewhere."

We stop walking at the bridge that leaves town. "Madame, I do not wish to invest with the Beaumonts. I make my own money, my own way. I'm sorry to disappoint you."

"I understand."

She removes her arm from mine and turns to face me. "But I can offer you something else."

"What might that be?"

"All the men LaMarche works with conceal their many, many lies—poorly, I might add. Men can be so transparent. All it takes is an observant woman to discover what they're hiding."

"You would tell me what you know?"

She shrugs. "Perhaps. I was a pest back in France. A desperate woman trying to infest the nobility. They did not see me as a threat, so they were very careless around me. I heard everything they tried to hide."

"Why haven't you used their secrets to help yourself?"

"Who says I haven't?" She smooths her skirt. "How do you think I secured our land?"

"Why would you help me?" I ask.

"I know how it feels to be cast aside. Dismissed by the LaMarches of the world. Women like us must find our own path to success."

She turns to walk away, and I say, "I've fought with Antoinette many times in my life. She hasn't beaten me yet."

Madame Doré doesn't turn around, but I can see she nods her head in agreement.

•   •   •

"Well?" James asks once I return home. "What have you discovered?"

"She won't invest with us. But she will help us in other ways. I need time to get her to trust me."

James runs two fingers in circles on each temple. "LaMarche is hard at work enticing investors. Soon it will be too late."

I place my hand on his chest. "You can do this."

He pulls me close, his arms tight around my waist. "What would I become without you?"

The question sits on my chest, heavy and crushing. Without me, my husband would buy and sell humans, break up families, and steal children.

"I'm going to Naira's."

He pulls me tighter. "But I need you."

His touch is unbearable. I find a way to wriggle from his grasp. "You promised me freedom."

"And you promised to stay with me."

His eyes twinkle, both fierce and childlike. Against the lump in my throat, I lean forward to kiss him softly on the lips. "When I return, you can have me all day and all night."

"Fine." He tosses my arm aside and will not look at me. "I suppose your husband's needs do not matter, Isabelle? Only your own."

Without responding, I don my cape and leave our house, galloping through the fresh air and solitude as if I've plunged through the surface from underwater. The tightness in my chest lifts and the stone in my throat shrivels to a pebble.

By the time I reach the camp, my heart is racing, and I'm ready to fight, to learn. "Little mouse is ready for the day," I tell Naira.

"You saved two children," she says. "Well done."

"I should have saved more. But I'm grateful the baby is alive." I find myself bouncing in place, eager and nervous. "Where do we begin today?"

"Arrows."

I hang my head. "Of course."

"One day, you will welcome the arrow and no longer fear it."

I look to the bright, blue sky. "That day is not today."

·

Four hours into today's work, I've shot hundreds of arrows and correctly landed precisely ten of them. Naira has taught me to use speed and how to lift the arrow, spin on my knee and have my hand drawn before I steady my eyes and my breath. How to shoot from every angle and how to draw another weapon before the arrow has landed on its target.

"You are stronger," she says.

"Stronger, yes. But my aim is still terrible."

"That will come," she says.

"I think you're right. It isn't about my body. I feel stronger up here." I point to my temple.

"Why?"

"I'm not sure. Perhaps I finally see the fear for what it is—a way to protect me. I don't care to be protected anymore. The stakes are too high, and Protestants are still dying."

Her hands engulf my shoulders, pressing my back into her chest before I can process what's happening. Her braid whips the side of my face as we arch together. I reach back with my right leg to kick her knee and send her off balance. Then I tuck my head to my shoulder and press her arms up as I slide out of her grasp, but not before grabbing her wrist to spin her off me.

She smiles, her cheeks lit into a rosy glow. "You are faster too."

Instead of softening into her compliment, I widen my stance, ready for more.

A Huron arrives with my horse's rope in hand. "It's Andre. He is not well. His family has come down with a fever."

I look to Naira for reassurance.

"I cannot help. Your sickness is unknown to us. I could bring it back and kill every one of my people."

"Madame Beaumont, it must be you who goes," the man says.

My knees weaken. "Me?"

"We need him. Andre is the only one we trust for trade."

"He is family," Naira says. "I believe you are the only one he will want to see."

I shake my head. "That isn't a good idea. Louise is fragile."

"Would you be able to forgive yourself if they die and you did not try to help?"

I recount my brushes with death—of which there have been many. But I survived the fever when my sisters did not. I did not fall sick on the ship from France, despite holding my friend as she took her last breath.

"Okay, I'll go."

We hurry back to the settlement. Naira hands me a deer hide pouch filled with bundles of herbs and roots, with instructions for each one.

I grab her wrist and hold tight. "I can't bear it if he dies, Naira."

"Do your best." She hands me the rope and I mount my horse. "I believe in you, little fox."

A thumping swells in my chest, and I hold back tears. Before they let loose from my eyes, I send my horse flying through the trees, toward Andre's house. I don't know what I'll find, only that my heart aches with the thought of losing him.

I gather strength, bolstered by Naira's belief in me—the little fox.

CHAPTER TWELVE

I knock on their door, but no one stirs. It's unlocked, so I press the door open to a still, creaking house. A fire crackles and the air smells musty. Andre is on his side on a pile of fur by the fire. He wears no shirt, and his arms glow red and patchy, like strawberries have been smashed into his skin. I approach, realizing he is unaware that I've entered. I kneel next to him, noting how his face and neck glisten with sweat. His golden hair looks the color of wet earth, soaked in moisture as his teeth chatter.

I place my hand on his cheek and whisper. "Andre?"

He opens his eyes, trying to focus. "Isabelle? You shouldn't be here."

"It's all right. I've been through this before."

He shoves my hand. "Go away. You'll get sick too."

I place both my hands on his cheeks and force him to look at me. "I'm here to help you. Please, let me." I push him back down and cover him with linen.

"Elizabeth," he mutters. "She's burning up. They're upstairs."

"I'll be right back."

Up the stairs, I can hear moans and heavy breathing. Hot, thick air fills their bedroom with a putrid stench. I push the door open to find Louise and Elizabeth curled together on the bed, their skin brighter than Andre's. Louise shakes and mumbles to herself, her hand dangling off the edge of the bed.

I reach for her shoulder and whisper. "Louise, I'm here."

She throws my hand away. "No. Don't take her."

"It's me. Isabelle. I'm here to help you."

"I can't." She shakes her head violently and mistakenly shoves Elizabeth, who then cries out in pain.

I reach for Elizabeth and carefully set her on my lap. The child's wet hair sticks to her neck and her shallow breathing fills me with worry. "It's all right, little one." I rock back and forth, whispering in her ear. "I'm here. I'm here."

The girl barely has enough strength to whimper, wincing in pain when she swallows. Her neck is thick and bumpy, her body limp in my arms. I carry her downstairs, thankful that Louise has fallen into a twitching sleep.

Trying to bounce and rock the child, I spread out the herbs. Soaking the large flat ones in a wet cloth releases their bitter scent. I place the wrap on Elizabeth's forehead, and run the wet cloth over her face, neck, and arms, just as Naira suggested. The well water is nearly gone, but the last few drops go to her. She drinks, but not without releasing a cry of pain.

I must calm myself. I look at her and Andre, and know Louise struggles upstairs. They all teeter on death. I place Elizabeth down on a layer of fur, undress her, and rub the cloth over her bumpy, scarlet chest. She feels like fire, heat radiating off her little body as she clings to life.

I run to fill the pail from the well out back, as every second away from them feels like an eternity. Thank goodness they're all in the same struggle when I return. I beg Louise to sip water, but she shoves me away, so I hold her chin and force her. "Please fight," I say, but she's too weak and simply lets me drop water in her mouth.

Back downstairs, Elizabeth shakes like a hummingbird in a storm. I rub the leaf wrap again, focusing on her swollen neck and face. After a weak cough, she settles into a sleepy trance.

I move my attention to Andre. He reaches across the room toward Elizabeth but doesn't have the strength to turn and look at her. I lift his head and place it on my lap. "Andre. She's very sick but holding on."

"Why..." His voice trembles. "Why did you come?"

I stroke the wet leaf wrap over his neck, face, and shoulders. My fingers scrape through his thick, wet hair, fingernails scratching his scalp as I glide. "I had to try."

"Help them," he whispers.

"I will." I run my hands over his chest, across the large scar from a whipping. We are all scarred, forever marked by our enemies.

He lifts his chin and looks up at me. I'm too afraid to meet his eyes and focus on rubbing the cloth over his hot skin. He grabs my hand to stop me and waits until I meet his gaze. "Let me die. Save them."

My hand floats of its own will to his mouth. He closes his eyes and kisses my fingertips as I bite back tears and fall to my knees, sickened that I could lose him. Behind his glassy eyes is a fighter. A man who taught my cold, angry heart how to love.

"I will save you both," I whisper.

Elizabeth releases a wailing cry and I roll Andre to his side so he cannot see her anguish. I lift the girl and hold her as she falls limp again in my arms.

Hours go by as I squeeze the cloth into their mouths for sips of water, taking turns between the three. The sun has set, and the night surrounds us. Something about the black sky and quiet forest makes the fevers seem more menacing. I boil juniper berries to form a tea and force them all to sip. They grimace every time they swallow, but they drink when they can.

Louise cries and screams, so I run upstairs to settle her. "Calm down, Louise. Everything is all right."

"Maman, is that you?" She thrashes side to side, kicking the fur off her.

I reach for her hand. "It's Isabelle." She kicks me in the stomach, sending me to the floor with a cramping middle, and I cough to catch my breath.

"Did you come for me?" Her face twists as if crying, but her eyes remain dry.

I stumble back to her, but not too close. She lies naked, body soft and round, the way a woman's body is after having a child. Her skin glows red and blotchy. Her face so pale she appears gray.

I hold her hands down, gripped to the bed. "Louise. Stop. I need you to drink."

She thrashes against me, too weak to fight. "Let me die."

"No. You will fight. Drink the tea." I raise it to her mouth, but she shoves it away. It hits the floor and spills, disappearing into the cracks between the wood.

Elizabeth cries, "Maman!"

When I arrive downstairs, Andre is crawling toward Elizabeth as she pulls her hair, scratching at her skin so hard she's bled. I swoop her in my arms and hold her head to my chest.

"I want Maman," she cries.

"I know, darling." I reach for the witch hazel. Naira told me the fever would turn to delusions and their skin would burn. As I rub the concoction over Elizabeth, she whispers, "I hurt."

"I'm here." I run my fingers along her forehead and rub her earlobe the way my Maman did to soothe me when I was a child. She yawns, and I cover her in linen.

"Isabelle." Andre's voice still trembles as he scratches at his neck.

I run the witch hazel cloth over his neck and shoulders. "Is that better?"

"Yes." His eyes stay closed. "How is Louise?"

I glance back to make sure Elizabeth can't hear me. "She's not well, Andre. I'm worried."

"Go to her." He reaches for my hand and when he squeezes, I smile. There's life in that squeeze.

Back with Louise, I find her with long, deep scratches across her trunk and abdomen. She claws at herself, but her face remains lifeless.

"Louise, this will help." I rub witch hazel over her feverish body. Her fingernails slide along her skin one last time, then come to rest at her sides.

"It's too hard," she mumbles.

"It will get easier. Just hang on." I note her slow movements and slurred words.

"No, life."

"You have a beautiful daughter. A husband. A home and a future."

"I'm sorry." Her voice drifts away, light and thready.

I keep rubbing with enough intensity that her body shakes. "Louise." I grab her shoulders, but she does not respond. "Louise."

She takes one last sputtering breath and when her chest falls, something in the room shifts. The air moves like a wind gust, and I step back, watching her unmoving body and her empty eyes stare at the ceiling.

I pull the sheet to cover her face. No time to mourn, as cries beckon me from downstairs.

When I reach Elizabeth, she's on her side whimpering, her cold, damp skin causing her to shiver. I place my hand on her forehead. The fever has broken, leaving clammy skin beaded with moisture. I wrap her trembling body in linen. We sit next to Andre, who still writhes in pain.

"Louise?" he whispers.

I couldn't save her, and the pain rips through me. I shake my head, diverting my eyes to the child. "Elizabeth will be fine. She's a fighter, aren't you, little duckling?"

She sips more water, but she's so weak that it exhausts her. Andre lifts his trembling hand to her cheek. How a man opens a space in his heart for his daughter feels like the most hopeful thing in the world.

Elizabeth wiggles and then falls into a deep sleep. As I lay her down under the soft and warm beaver fur, I exhale a breath of relief. She's going to live.

But Andre. It terrifies me how his teeth chatter and his legs twitch. I brew more tea and fetch more water and by the time I return, he's mumbling nonsense the way Louise did. I can't lose him.

I shake his shoulder. "Andre. Drink this."

He thrashes his head side to side with a grimace. "No."

I hold up my hands in case he acts out nightmares. "Please don't kick me." I lift his shoulders gently and lean him back on my chest. His limp body spits fire and my skin grows damp and hot. I press my cheek to his temple.

"It's me. Isabelle." No response. "I need you to live," I whisper. I place the cup to his mouth again. He doesn't move, but when I say, "Please," he parts his lips.

Twenty torturous minutes to swallow a few gulps. I lean against the rock on the fireplace and place his head in my lap. The cool linen soaks up the moisture on his neck and face and I scan his cheeks for any sign that the fever will break.

His eyes open. "What if I die?"

His sleepy caramel eyes search for a reason to fight.

I lace my fingers through his. A thread of life tugs back from him. "Then a part of me will die with you."

His fingers twitch and weakly graze my wrist before his lids fall heavy. Only the hours ahead will decide if the fever wins. I think of Naira, how she does not fight what she cannot change. I cradle his head in my lap and stroke his hair as tears gather in my eyes.

Hours roll by. I count his breaths as they grow shallow and weak. Elizabeth stirs but does not wake. Shadows move across the room, crawling like spiders over the floor and walls as darkness creeps in yet again. Andre has not returned my touch since daylight. I lay my palm to his chest to feel his heartbeat that's more like a ripple in water than a pounding heart. Hardly strong enough to keep him alive, yet I don't let go of hope.

In the middle of the night, I wake, startled by something on my face. I smack it away and recoil, certain death has crept its way through the house. I sit up and gasp, looking around at the shadows. It's Andre's hand. My eyes sharpen to see him sitting in front of me.

"Are you dead?" I whisper.

"I hope not." He lies back, droplets covering his forehead.

I reach for his face and move close to examine him. He looks up at me with a sleepy smile. "I couldn't leave just yet."

I dry his skin and wrap him in fur, tears streaming down my cheeks. At his side until morning, I wake to an empty space next to me and an open front door. Elizabeth has emptied her water and returned to sleep. "Good girl," I say with a smile. "You stay a fighter."

On the porch I find Andre staring at the pines, hair tousled and eyes glassy. "She's gone."

A crisp wind greets me as I lower next to him on the top step. "I'm sorry, Andre. I tried."

"Elizabeth no longer has a mother."

"Elizabeth is strong."

He leans forward, elbows on his knees. "I wasn't a good husband."

"Don't do that, Andre. You gave her everything you could."

"No, I didn't. I never gave her my heart. She wanted me to, desperately. But I could never let go of you. She died knowing I loved someone else."

He won't meet my eyes. "She knew you cared for her."

"You moved on long ago." His voice is stronger now. Fuller. Angrier. "Why couldn't I? Why couldn't I have tried harder?"

I want to reach for him, but I'm afraid he'll swat me away.

"I failed her." He places his face in his palms. "I'm sorry, Louise."

Chickadees chirp their melodic song from the pine trees. Sharp and clear, their calls fill the morning with life.

Andre turns to me. "You should leave."

There's nothing more I can do. I nod, holding back tears. "Of course." I retrieve my cape. "There's fresh water from the well. Continue to drink the berry tea for another day to help with cramps."

He simply stares at me.

I step down from the porch, heart aching, and look back at him once more.

"How wonderful it must be. Your heart is free and untethered to the memory of another," he says.

I swallow, terrified by the way he stares at me. "I fear my heart will never be free."

We stare at each other for a moment before I turn to mount my horse, angry at myself for getting close to him. Angry at him for not taking me in his arms. Angry at Louise for dying.

I gallop away from the house, leaving a piece of my heart cracked off the edge, hoping a scar grows over the hole and stitches it down stronger than before.

CHAPTER THIRTEEN

I scrub lye soap and warm water over my body, unable to get Andre's face out of my mind. The door downstairs slams.

"Isabelle." James throws his hat to the bed and rushes to me, holds my naked body close to him. "What happened to you?" Before I can respond, he says, "Stop running away."

I push away from his eager embrace. I don a clean shift and sit on the bed, head hung low. "I was at Andre's."

He breathes deeply, his face reddening. "What were you doing there?"

"They were all sick," I say. "I tried to help."

"I'm sure you did." His shirt rattles against his thumping heart.

I don't have the energy for his jealousy. "I did everything I could, but we lost Louise. She died." I remember how her face went pale. How she welcomed death from her unhappy life. How Andre nearly died in my arms. I rub my face hard to prevent tears from flooding my eyes.

"Only Louise?" Even at a time like this, he calls on his hate.

"The child will live," I say. "And so will Andre."

"You put me at risk." He steps back. "What if you brought sickness home?"

"I think it's what my sisters died from. The red patches on the skin, the bumps in their throat. The fever that lasts three days."

"Irresponsible!" He leans against the doorway, wiping his hands on his thighs. "I cannot fall sick."

"Louise died, James. Stop thinking of yourself."

"And it was Louise you were there for?"

I want to throw something at him. "I was there for all of them."

"I have ignored your past because I do not wish to be that weak man who succumbs to jealousy. But the way you carry on after him makes me think you're lying to me."

I stand and pull my hair back from my face. "They nearly died. His wife's body lies lifeless in their bed. And you dare question my loyalty? I left him and chose you, yet you still obsess over him. Andre, Andre, Andre."

He holds up his hand, begging me to stop saying his name. "I can't risk sickness. I will stay in the hotel for three days' time."

I want to scream. Call him a selfish bastard. But it's no use. "Go."

"You won't marry me in the church, and it seems you would rather spend the night with your dying ex-lover than with me."

"He was never my lover."

"No, just the one you refuse to forget." He waits, hopeful for words of devotion and love. I have neither.

When I don't respond, he reaches for his hat. "You are my wife, Isabelle. Forget him, or I will do something about it."

"Is that a threat?"

He hesitates. "Perhaps. I will do anything to make you return my love." He turns on his heels and disappears.

James's brand of love has always been control, and I shudder to think what he means. I think of Andre, how he could never give Louise the love she needed, and I am just as guilty with James.

Partial love is as lonely a thing as there ever was.

⋅　　　⋅　　　⋅

By the time I arrive at the abbey, the girls have completed their morning lessons and Sister Marguerite pulls me aside. "Madame Beaumont, will you speak to Charlotte? She doesn't participate in our activities and shows no interest in adjusting to her new life."

I wouldn't doubt if she's making a list of every Frenchman and how to ruin them. "Where is she?"

"In prayer."

"I bet she is," I mumble. "I'll take care of it. Thank you."

I walk through the long corridors with their chipped walls and heavy silence, remembering when I lived here. When I once exchanged pain for heartache and convinced myself it was a fair trade. Once in the chapel, an echo bounces off the vast, empty chamber. I see Charlotte sitting in the third pew, staring blankly at the altar.

I sit next to her, but she doesn't move. "Why don't I believe you're praying in here?"

"You're right, I'm not praying," she says. "I'm filling the room with defiance."

"Charlotte, you can't keep on like this. Someone will discover your lies."

"I don't understand you." She turns to face me. "You looked so strong when we fought those Iroquois. But here and in town, you practically bow to the Catholics. You serve them and marry them."

I grab her arm a little too tightly. "That's enough. You know nothing about me."

"I know you've turned on your people. On everything you claim to love." She yanks away, but I don't loosen my grip.

I gather my control. "You said the words, didn't you? You stood in the town square and accepted Catholicism and sailed the ocean to live with the nuns. Don't lecture me on choices. You're also a Daughter of the King."

She stops resisting. "And I hate myself for it."

Her eyes drop to her lap, and I release her arm, because I know that hate all too well.

"Why didn't you stay and fight?" I ask. "Be the brave girl you want me to be?"

She hesitates. "I was scared." She meets my eyes. "Why did you convert?"

"I was going to be punished. I'd already lost everything—my family, my home, and I started to question. People like James and the kind priest who saved my life. Not all Catholics are like the dragoons."

"Just because they don't brand your flesh doesn't make them kind. They allow our torture. James is no better than the rest of them."

My eyes well with tears. She's right.

Sensing my thoughts, she says, "You haven't lost your fight. I saw it at those farmhouses. But you've let them break you. You've forgotten who you used to be."

This child knows nothing of my truth or how complicated it all is. She can't imagine the lies and the guilt that rip through me like a serrated blade. "You're the one sitting in an abbey pretending to pray." I rise to walk away.

"Tell me how to do this," she says. Her voice bounces off the walls and we both look around for listeners. "I can't become one of them. *I can't.*"

"Come with me," I whisper.

She stands and hesitates. "Really?"

"I'll tell Sister Marguerite you'll spend the next few days with me."

Charlotte stumbles out behind me. I can hear the excitement in her stride. "Where are we going?"

"To learn from someone who is a far better teacher than I."

.   .   .

Charlotte and I gallop through the forest as the afternoon wind rattles the branches. We both breathe easy out here. She doesn't need to say it. We both feel it. All our years as forest children, praying and living in the dark changed how we view the world from the trees.

At the settlement, Charlotte peppers me with questions without waiting for any answers. "What is this place? Are these Iroquois? The women, what are they wearing? Are those their houses?"

"Take a breath, Charlotte."

Inside her longhouse, Naira bounces her child on her shoulders. They're both laughing. It's good to see this side of her.

"You brought another friend," Naira says.

"This is Charlotte. I knew her sister back in France. Can we stay for three days?"

She places her daughter down and directs her to play outside. "Three days?"

"James is away at the hotel, and I have much to learn."

"Ah. Sit." She directs us to the fire and examines Charlotte for a long while. "You must be a Daughter of the King. Have you chosen a husband yet?"

Charlotte laughs, then covers her mouth. "I can't imagine marrying any of these men. Brutes who expect me to forget who I once was." She flicks a glance at me, but I don't dare meet her gaze. Her words slither into me.

"She's having difficulty adjusting," I say. "She was a Protestant, just like me."

"I helped Isabelle kill the Iroquois." Her eyes grow wide and bright.

"She's smart," I say, "but impulsive. Sometimes reckless."

"But I can shoot an arrow better than any man."

Naira glances at me. "Keep her here with the women. She will help in the garden and prepare dinner."

"Where will you go?" Charlotte puffs out her bottom lip and Naira nods to the doorway.

"I'm learning to be a wolf," I say.

· · ·

I collapse on my cot, body sore and bruised. Today, Naira taught me to climb and slide and hide. To swing from a tree to attack with my feet and how to throw a man twice my size from over top of me.

"You look tired," Charlotte says.

"I'm exhausted." I yawn, noting how even my eyeballs feel sore.

"I picked beans and stirred maize." When I don't respond, she says, "While you learned to fight."

I close my eyes, trying not to smile. I understand Naira's ways. The eager mouse needs to learn patience.

Charlotte jumps from her cot and sits next to me. "Tell me about Madame Doré. Did she agree to help you?"

"In a way," I say, my eyes still closed.

Charlotte jabs her finger into my ribs. "I'm trying to help you. Now stop ignoring me."

I moan and sit up, propping myself to the bedside so I don't fall over.

"You can trust me," she says. "Haven't I proved that?"

I look at her eager eyes. "Yes, you have."

"Good. Can you stop the LaMarches?"

"Jacqueline Doré won't invest with us. But she will help me with secrets… when she trusts me."

"Secrets?" She crinkles her nose. "What good does that do?"

"Can we talk about this tomorrow? I'm so tired."

I recline, but she grabs my shoulders and forces me back to sitting. "How can you sleep? Don't you remember what they did to us?"

My fatigue slides away for a moment and in her eyes, I see the pain I've known since leaving France. The bitter bite into memories that my dreams take me to every night. "Yes."

"The dragoons," she says. "I remember their faces. Their snarls and their smiles as they beat us bloody."

I rub my fingers across my brow. "I think of Clémentine often."

"She adored you," she says. "She looked to you to teach her bravery."

"Antoinette LaMarche tortured me as a child. As you know, her father found amusement in harassing us. One of his ship workers fought my father after he stole his fleet. The man stabbed him." I steady myself with a long breath. "LaMarche is the reason I cannot rid myself of the seething hate in my heart. Now my husband threatens to enter business with him."

"I want to see them all tortured the way they tortured us."

"Sometimes, in a quiet moment, I let myself feel that too."

The fire flickers against her pale face. "Let me help you with Madame Doré. I can avenge my sister's death by hurting the LaMarches. He once stood by drinking ale as a man dragged me down the alley by my hair, ordered by him, no doubt. I was just a child. I'm grateful he doesn't remember me."

"There's something only Huguenots understand. A strength that comes from being threatened—always living on the edge of fear. It makes us uniquely capable of holding our own secrets and keeping a very long memory."

"It makes me want to save them all," she says.

I nod. "Goodnight, Charlotte."

"Goodnight."

• • •

Day three. I don't want to return home, but I must face James eventually. My entire marriage has been learning the art of promises. As Naira locks her arm around my neck, I reach for her knife and twist her off me. When she throws me to the ground, I roll over her and swipe her blade. Charlotte watches with intent eyes as Naira puts me in one difficult position after another.

Today, I can escape every one.

Naira hesitates, knees bent, head lowered. I prepare my footing, open my hands wide. She's taught me to lift the front of my skirt between my legs and tuck into the waist below my bodice, so my legs can move freely.

She stares and hovers so long I grow nervous. *Attack already.* My heart races, and she can tell because now she lunges. In a blink, my arm is behind my back and my face is pressed into the dirt.

"I can see when you fatigue," she whispers in my ear. "Never show your enemy."

She releases me and I wipe my mouth, noting a pair of boots at my eye level. My gaze trails up to the person standing in them. "Andre."

He looks down at me. He's holding Elizabeth's little hand. Neither of them smiles. I stand and wipe the dirt from my clothes, though it's no use.

"Come," Naira says as she catches her breath. "We will all gather by the fire."

Andre smiles at his daughter, who turns to look at me with wide eyes. I wonder if she realizes I was with her mother when she died. That I failed to keep her alive.

On the way into the longhouse, Charlotte grabs my sleeve. "Who is that?"

"Someone from my past."

"Past? With the way he stares at you, I don't believe that for one second."

Naira presents us all with water. "Elizabeth will stay with us for a little while, won't you, cricket?"

Elizabeth giggles. "They say I laugh like a cricket."

Afraid he won't look at me, I smile at Elizabeth. "Where are you going, Andre?"

"West." He rubs his hands together.

"We're happy to have her," Naira says. "And grateful for your help."

Andre is the only fur trader the Huron will trust. Now that the Iroquois have forbidden them to work with the French, their trade with other tribes is essential.

Andre looks around. "I'll prepare my horse."

As he ducks out of the longhouse, I step to follow him, but Naira grabs my arm. "Give him time."

A young woman from the tribe holds Elizabeth's hand and leads her to a circle of children outside. They're stacking stones into shapes of a village.

"Why does he seem angry with you?" Charlotte asks.

"His wife just died. They were all sick. I tried... but I couldn't save her." We watch him from the doorway, the way his body tenses and he leans his forehead against the horse.

"I remember when Papa fell ill." Charlotte's voice deepens. "I tried to steal food and wine to save him. A dragoon caught me begging a merchant for cheese. He slapped me hard enough that I fell to the ground. Then he kicked me." She raises her eyes to me. "I was twelve."

I remember it all so well. All the memories have bled under my skin and now they're part of me. It feels as if I would have to cut myself open to release them.

I hesitantly walk toward Andre. He sees me approach and stretches his neck. "I have nothing to say."

Careful not to stand too close to him, I consider my words carefully. "I'm so sorry. For everything."

He pauses, hand on his horse's neck. "Elizabeth loves it here. I couldn't get through this without Naira."

"I've thought the same thing about Naira many times."

"I'll be gone for a week," he says. "I think Elizabeth is better here than with me."

"You're her world. She loves you even when you're going through a difficult time."

He scratches the horse, smoothing her mane, avoiding my eyes.

"I didn't come here to make you uncomfortable," I say. "I need your help."

He drops his hand to his side and takes one step so he's now facing me. "What is it?"

Andre's compass of goodness never waivers. "That girl with me? Her name is Charlotte. She's a Huguenot from La Rochelle. I saved her sister many times, but ultimately, she died because of me. Chained to the tower wall because I told her to be brave."

His shoulders soften. "Does she know the truth about you?"

"Not fully. She thinks I've given up on my people. She wants to kill every Catholic that wronged her. And maybe even more."

"None of us will ever forget what they did," Andre says.

"But we had Henri. And each other."

He glances behind me at Charlotte, who watches us from the doorway. "Can you trust her?"

I shrug. "Can we really ever trust anybody?"

He nods. "All right."

I leave Andre and return to the longhouse. Without a word, I grab Charlotte's hand and lead her to a dark, shady corner of the forest where the air cools and the trees seem to wrap their arms around us in a protective embrace.

"Where are we going?" she asks.

"You'll see."

Being forced to pray in hiding all those years, the trees and the earth now hold special powers for us. Where God speaks and the wind has answers. Where we feel at home.

We dip under a tree branch where Andre waits. He bows his head. Charlotte hesitates, but she's too intrigued—I see it in her eyes. Andre reaches under his doublet and produces a Geneva Bible. Charlotte's mouth opens, but she remains silent. She reaches for the worn Bible, and runs her fingers along its softened cover, a symbol of our faith. I place my hand on hers and we enjoy yet another hidden moment, connected by our tortured past. and an almost impossible hope for our future.

We close our eyes and pray, whispers so soft the birds seem to stop and listen. The wind flutters through me, lifting my body light and free, while my chest expands so wide my heart feels giant.

When I open my eyes, Charlotte has tears streaming down her cheeks. She begins to sing. Psalms of David in French. Singing in our native tongue, not Latin, is an act of defiance, just like holding this banned Bible and gathering with heretics. Andre laces his fingers through mine, just as he once did in a barn on a snowy night three years ago. The night I knew my spirit could never be wholly Catholic. The night I knew I would love him forever.

CHAPTER FOURTEEN

I said goodbye to Andre this afternoon as I always do, praying for his safe travels and wishing I could rid my heart of him—rinse him like muddy clothing in a soapy bath. As I dropped Charlotte back at the abbey, she said one thing to me. "You're still the brave fighter I always thought you were."

As I wait for James to return, I think of Madame Doré and what our next move must be.

James throws opens the door, his face flushed ruby-red. "We need to talk," he says.

"No longer afraid I'll infest you with my sickness?"

"Enough of that." He drags me to the chair by the fire. "The LaMarches have already begun trade with Africa. They've sent three ships to purchase hundreds of slaves. They'll land on our shore by fall."

Hands gripped to the armchair, I launch to standing. "Have you taken part in this?"

"No. But they expect me to ask my father to route three ships of our own. They demand I send word tomorrow."

I pace the room. "And the Huguenots?"

He bites his lip and looks away from me. "They've already convinced dozens to provide them goods."

"Convinced?"

He diverts his eyes. "Threatened."

"How long until they imprison them? Take their children?"

The air is thick and hot, no air flow and no light.

"We only have a few months," he says.

Needles prickle my chest. "It's not enough time." I despise him for this entire situation. The man is too weak to find a way out of this mess.

"If I don't act, they'll ruin us. You'll spend the rest of your life in prison." His pleading eyes make me want to throw something at him.

"If Antoinette has anything to say about it, she'll have me executed for treason."

James grabs my arms. "I don't know how to get out of this."

What he means is he wants to fulfill his own needs, and keep me close, without repercussion from LaMarche. There is no such answer to this riddle.

"Madame Doré. She holds secrets over every noble in Paris, even the ones closest to the king. She despises the LaMarches, and I sense she'd love nothing more than to help us disrupt the nobility."

"What good are secrets?" he scoffs.

When James appears innocent, I find it hideous, because he is far from it. He withholds truth and never reveals all of himself, and something in me cannot rest until I expose it. "James, how did you find this out?"

He trails his fingers down my arms to my hands. "LaMarche demanded that I act now."

"When did you see him?"

"I met him at the tavern." His voice strains with agitation. "He asked to see me."

"And Antoinette?"

"She was there too," he says.

My stomach clenches like a protective wall around my body. "Why?"

James purses his lips and hesitates, deciding how much to reveal to me, no doubt. "She wants me to turn on you. She despises how wild and free you are, and says I deserve a wife who allows me to be a man."

I step back, trying to control the searing hot blood that rushes to my head. He reaches for my face, cupping my cheek in his hand. "Isabelle."

I slap his hand away. "If you listen to her, you're weaker than I imagined."

He grabs my wrists, forces me to look at him. "I let her think I listen. But I want one thing. You."

"So, she thinks she has your ear while I am the fox who runs free and should be put in a cage?"

He pulls me to his chest and tightens his arms. "Don't be stubborn. Do not let her come between us."

I wriggle in his grasp. "Like you've let Andre?"

He releases me and removes the tie from his hair, shaking his curls loose. With a deep breath, he unwraps his cravat and removes his doublet.

"What are you doing?"

"The closest we ever are is when we're naked and you get everything you need." He removes his shirt and steps toward me. "When we lie together, there is no Antoinette. No Andre. Only us." Slowly, he removes his breeches, sliding his hands along his thighs. "Move me as you wish."

I hesitate but can't pull away from his stare, his body. His need for me. "Why do we do this to each other? Fight before we love?"

"I do it for you," he says, standing naked. "You need to hate me."

"I don't hate you. You're my husband." A pulsing ache begins between my legs.

"Show me," he says.

I untie my bodice, remove my skirts, and stand before him in my shift. Stepping up to him, I first kiss his chest. "Undress me."

"Yes, Madame." He gathers the material along my thighs and lifts it over my head.

I need to keep space between us, to be in my body and out of my head. It's strange that it's the only way I know how to be close to him. "Lay me down."

He wraps his arms around me and kisses my neck. I need the fire to burn, the anger to stay hot. I bite his ear, small and precise with my front teeth. He lays me down and kisses along my stomach, my hips. I grab his curls in my hands and press him down to the aching and when he touches his tongue to me, the heat grows and burns, erasing all memories of who we are outside of each other.

• • •

I hear the snickers and gossip behind Madame Doré's back. I listened closely at Mass today to hear several women remark on her questionable morals. The way she visits different men around town, embarrassing herself.

Jaqueline Doré doesn't seem to hear the gossip, or perhaps she does not care. She has no friends, it seems, other than her favored men. Knocking on her massive door garners me a few stares from neighbors, and I wonder if her men ever come here.

A servant opens the door. "Do you have a delivery?"

"No. I'm here to see the lady of the house. Please tell her Madame Beaumont wishes to speak with her."

He blinks a few times and his mouth puckers in confusion.

"Is something wrong?"

"Madame rarely has visitors." He shakes his head and welcomes me in.

While not the palaces of France, her house is quite impressive for Quebec. Tapestries decorate the walls and furs drape the elegant furniture like a second skin. In the second-floor hall, Madame Doré sits in a chair large enough for a king.

As I approach, I notice an enormous window that looks out over the town. "You can see everything from up here, can't you?"

She smiles, as if she's been expecting me. "I pass the time watching lovers quarrel and men conduct business. The intendant's brewery will sit right there." She points. "I've invested. He will need the help of the women brewers. They're the ones who know what they're doing. Just like everything else in life."

I stand taller at the news. "We will have women beer makers?"

"If I have anything to say about it." She points to a chair opposite her. "Please, sit."

"You don't seem surprised to see me," I say.

"I'm not." She waves to her servant, to ask for something I can't understand. "You have come for my secrets, yes?"

"Are you willing to give them to me?"

"I haven't yet decided." She crosses her hands in her lap. She doesn't fidget or squirm like many women do. Her hands hold firm as stone. "What is your plan?"

"My plan?"

"Well, yes. What will you do with this information?"

I sit tall and gather my thoughts. "I'm not sure."

"Well, that wouldn't be very smart of me to hand you the power to destroy everyone without a clue how to do it."

The servant appears with a silver tray, two teacups and saucers painted with pink roses. A dark liquid fills the cup, an odd brown color, but the scent is heavenly.

"Go on, try it," she says.

I want to ask what this concoction is as it looks like the mud that washes up the river at the end of summer, but I'm careful not to offend her. I lift the saucer and bring the cup to my mouth. Bitter and sweet and decadent. Velvety smooth. Unlike anything I've ever tasted. My eyes grow big and Madame smiles.

"It's called chocolate. Brought to France by Spanish monks."

I notice how small she looks in this cavernous room. How perfectly dressed and how creamy smooth her golden skin is. "Madame, may I ask? You have such wonderful things. An incredible life. Are you happy?"

After a deep sigh, she places the teacup in her lap. "I have everything one could dream of. Riches, power, the company of handsome men whenever I choose."

"Do you have love?"

Her eyes shift to the window. I assume she watches the world from inside because she does not feel part of it outside these walls.

"I gave up on love long ago. I joined forces with my now husband and fled to the open spaces of New France, away from the memories of our past."

The server arrives again with a platter of sugared oranges and chestnuts.

I understand this woman, more than I should. She comes from privilege and status and freely flaunts her insatiable appetite for sex. But she's also been shunned. She's accepted her marriage because it serves her. She still seems to feel like the woman in the shadows, just like me.

"I want to stop the LaMarches from growing their power. They've already sent ships to Africa to buy slaves. I have to stop them."

She tilts her head. "Why?"

Naira has taught me to slow my stuttering thoughts and center myself. "I am against the practice of slaves."

"No, not a good enough reason. Try again."

Behind a stoic face, my heart thumps in my ears. "They've bribed my husband. They've threatened us if we don't join them."

"Almost." She sips her chocolate slowly. "There's more you aren't telling me." She waits. "I've become an expert at reading people. You have something closer to your heart. I can see it."

It's as if she can already see my truth—like I'm glass and she can peer inside. "I'm from La Rochelle. To become a Daughter of the King I had to convert."

Her teacup clangs against the saucer. "You were Protestant."

"Yes. And while I've started a new life, I cannot allow the LaMarches to make prisoners of my... of them. They will force them into servitude for the king and if they refuse, they'll take their children."

"You still hold sympathy for them?" she asks.

"What kind of monster would I be if I did not?"

She reaches for the tray and enjoys a candied orange, then dusts the sugar crumbs from her lips. I gather she's around forty but looks as youthful as a twenty-year-old. No children and a life of freedom seems to have kept her young.

"You understand the cruelties of France better than anyone," she says. "It is my circle of royals that tortured you, is it not?"

"Yes."

"The things I know could ruin me," she says. "You understand this?"

"I do."

She rolls her bottom lip in, letting it slowly puff back out. "You've noticed my dark skin."

"Yes, Madame."

"You don't think it odd, a royal member of the family with skin like mine?"

"I presumed you to be Spanish or Roman."

Her fingers tap against her lap. "My mother is the Queen of France. And my father..." She clears her throat and continues to fidget with her skirt. "My father was her Black servant. He is a court dwarf."

I don't move. And I don't dare speak. The Queen bedded an African dwarf and now the royalty's illegitimate daughter threatens to turn on them from another continent? Nothing seems out of the realm of possibility anymore.

"The court swept me away the moment I was born. Sent to a convent and raised in secrecy, as if I had any say in who made me or how I came into this world."

"Do you ever speak to your family?"

"The royal family sends an allowance, which I gladly accept. I began making my way into the noble circles. Men love to bed my enticing looks, but no one would dare marry me, except one man. Monsieur Doré had wealth beyond most everyone at court. We do not love each other, but we've developed an admiration. His preferences are not for me, or anyone like me." She flicks her eyes up to ensure that I understand.

She wants to trust me. She needs me to destroy the nobles to defend her honor, make them pay for how they treated her. "It's your turn," she says. "Prove to me you want them to bleed the way I do."

I stand and walk to her, staring down at her hopeful face. I pull back my sleeve to show her my forearm. "I'll never forget the way my skin seared against the burning metal. The way it smoked. I bit back a scream because I didn't want my mother to hear me cry."

She swallows, flicking her eyes between my face and my scar.

"A noble tried to rape me, but I fought him off and left him with a broken face," I say. "I'm capable of much more than secrets."

She extends her hand to invite me to sit. "You must know, you're entering a fight you cannot come back from."

"I entered that fight the day they branded me."

She pauses. Then the hint of a smile. "We'll start with the king's mistress. Her lady's maid isn't who she seems."

"How do you discover these things?"

She leans forward. "I've learned that men are easy to talk to. When you press your soft, naked skin to theirs, they lose all ability to think straight."

James has proven that truth many times over. "So, the lady's maid. What do we need to know about her?"

Her devilish smile tells me this is going to be exciting.

"She is much more than a lady's maid. She listens to conversations and hushed words, hiding behind a plain face and downcast eyes. Everything she hears goes back to her husband, an advisor to one of the wealthiest families in Spain."

"They're spying on the king?"

"Successfully, I might add."

I lean back in my chair, remembering the scared Protestant I once was, and how otherworldly and intangible the Catholics seemed to be. "That is deliciously good," I say. "I can use this."

"My dear, that's not even the most interesting thing happening at court."

We sip our chocolate, and I sharpen my attention. What Madame Doré is about to tell me will change the course of my future.

This little fox is about to become a wolf.

CHAPTER FIFTEEN

"She told you this today? They're spying on the royal family?" James asks as he paces the house. "We must get to the king before the LaMarches do."

"If you can offer something more valuable than trade, he won't listen to anything LaMarche says." I reach for the paper and quill.

"No," James says. "I can't trust a letter. Too many thieves who might intercept it. I have to do it."

"And how are you going to do that?"

He rubs his jaw. "I must go back to France."

Sailing back over the ocean to return to the land of persecution and poverty, but this time dressed as a soldier's wife? I'd sooner die. "I'm not returning there."

He pulls me into his chest and kisses my forehead. "I won't leave you."

My heart races with the thought. "I can't, James. The memories are too awful."

"So, I leave my wife to sail across the world? No, you need to come with me."

"No. You'll have to go on your own. Our future depends on it." And the future of every Huguenot and slave who will end up shackled.

He slides his fingers through my hair. "Tell me how you'll miss me."

His attempts at romance make me squirm, but I must find something to tether him to me. "When you return, I will marry you in the church." A heavy thud drops through my stomach.

A hesitant smile pulls at his lips. "You will?"

I place my hands on his chest. "I promise."

A strange test of loyalty and courage—holding our marriage prisoner until he can prove himself to me. I'm doubtful he'll pass.

"Antoinette awaits word of our ships. When she discovers I've left for France, she'll come for you."

"Let her."

"Please come with me," he begs.

"My home is in Quebec. So is yours."

"If I thought I could throw you over my shoulder and drag you on that ship with me, I would do it."

"You could, but I would hate you for it forever."

He kisses my neck and nibbles my earlobe as he undresses me. He'll take me right here on the table, where he'll suck every drop of our marriage bond before he sets sail for our homeland.

. . .

A strange energy courses through the town this morning. James has gone to secure passage on the next ship out of Quebec, careful to keep his plans quiet.

Madame Doré walks straight for me, her servant in tow. When she nears, she whispers, "What have you decided?"

"James will return to France. Use what he needs to secure his good favor with the king."

"Not good enough." She motions for her servant to fan her.

"I don't understand."

"It is you I trust and gave my secrets to. You're the one with the motive to rip the royal court apart."

I consider her proposition. I never dreamed I would need to return to France. Before I can answer, Madame tips her head close to me. "I'll be moving soon. I can't allow a scandal to follow us. So, I bid you farewell. I expect that my trust in you will not go to waste."

"Of course, Madame. I won't let you down."

"Good luck, Isabelle. You will need it."

She continues past me, head held high, and she feels like a dream. I continue around the corner of the bakery only to hear a familiar voice approach. "What are you up to, little swine?"

I turn on my heels and smile. "Your childish insults do little to hurt my feelings, Antoinette. Be on your way."

"You're up to something," she says.

"I am merely walking through town, enjoying a lovely summer day."

I walk away, but she steps next to me, walking as if we are friends on a stroll. "Your husband would be a fool to cross me."

"I don't believe my husband is any of your concern."

She releases a snide little laugh. "Oh, but he is my concern. I need him."

I stop and stare at her, willing my hand not to slap her cheek.

"For his ships, of course."

"Antoinette, why don't you speak with him yourself and leave me be?"

"Because you are always slinking around, about to cause trouble. Just like you always have, scurrying the streets of La Rochelle like a little rat searching for food crumbles."

"Every time I think you might have changed, your horrible screech of a voice returns to remind me you have not. You are a weak, spoiled child, a puppet, and your father holds your marionette strings."

"Your husband listens to me," she says. "He knows I'm part of his world. Nobility, class, money—I understand him in a way you never will."

"I think when he undresses me and makes my body shake, that is a way you'll never understand him."

She tightens her lips as her cheeks flush red. I leave her standing in the alley and carry on toward the bridge.

"Watch yourself, Isabelle."

I ignore her and continue into the trees where shade cools the air and stone turns to earth. Just as I approach the road toward the abbey, Andre appears, and my heart nearly drops to my feet.

"Andre," I manage, "you've returned."

"Yes."

"What are you doing standing here?"

He looks across the bridge. "Trying to build the courage to enter town."

"I can imagine how hard it's been since Louise passed."

He leans against a tree, one knee bent and foot on the trunk for balance. "I can't handle all the questions. How she died, what will I do, have I chosen another wife?"

"People do tend to pry."

He looks down, holding something back, it seems. "Isabelle, I'm sorry."

"You don't need to apologize."

"The way I treated you after you saved us. It was unforgivable."

I step closer, careful to keep space between us. "You had just lost your wife, Andre."

He shrugs. "I was angry at you."

"Because I couldn't save her?"

He rakes his fingers through his thick, golden hair. "Because I want you out of my mind."

My heartbeat quickens, and I must remind my legs to stay put.

He pushes himself off the tree and takes a step closer. "When I almost died, I was grateful it was in your arms."

A woodpecker drums a frantic rhythm near us, though I can't see him. Andre once told me that each type of woodpecker has his own tone and speed, like a musical instrument. "I nearly lost you." I want to say more, but I can't form words.

"But I'm still here. So is Elizabeth. Thanks to you."

I continue to scan the trees to find the woodpecker, as I cannot bear to look at Andre. I sealed that part of my heart long ago. If I dare let myself feel him, I'll break inside the prison of my marriage. I'm barely hanging on as it is.

"Isabelle, we've both made our choices, I understand. Our purpose is larger than marriage and loyalty."

"We're bonded by secrets," I say.

"Do you ever wonder if we're doing enough? If maybe... we could save them all ourselves?"

"Every second of every day, I think that same thought."

He smiles. "When you decide the next step in our Protestant plan, I'll fight alongside you."

"Until then."

"Until then." He rubs my arm and a rush of softness thrums through me. After James's harsh touch, soft certainly seems thrilling. Andre walks away and I'm left with the familiar ache in my chest that reminds me how painful life is when you let softness in.

•

I walked to Naira's today to enjoy the birds chatter and the sun warm my cheeks. At the settlement, she greets me at the gate.

"Isabelle, I've been expecting you," she says.

"I'm ready to work."

"Come." The day starts as it always does. She lifts the bow and quiver full of arrows, and I follow her to our clearing. Except this time, she lays the quiver at my feet. "Wait."

"What is it?"

"The wolf came to me again this morning. You have news."

"James leaves for France soon. He's going to warn the king of his enemies, and hopefully save us from LaMarche's grip." I know I should go, but I can't tolerate the thought. "All is as it should be."

Naira lowers to the ground, sits cross-legged and extends her hand, gesturing for me to join. I sit opposite her, feeling like a child playing in the dirt.

"What is your purpose?" she asks.

"To help my people."

She waves a string of beads in front of me. "Do not lose sight of that."

I sit taller, trying not to feel slighted. "I did all this to save them from becoming prisoners to the LaMarches and the king."

"A warrior does not simply prevent her family from falling off the cliff. She clears the path for them to escape the danger that forced them there."

"I don't understand."

"You are capable of more."

I look to the treetops, unable to tolerate her deep stare. "I'm doing everything I can."

"The wolf tells me otherwise."

My hands ache as I press them into the ground. I steal and trade secrets. I force myself into Mass when all I want is to run free in the forest. What more does she want from me?

"You told me you are afraid of being powerless."

"That is why I come here and learn from you." I exhale, trying to control my frustration.

"Your future whispers to you. Can you hear it?"

I shake my head. "No, I hear nothing but wind and birdsong."

She stands and hands me the bow. I position the arrow and stretch my arm firm and take a slow, deep breath. Naira steps back and I pause. I sense movement in the corner of my eye. When I break my focus, I see a rust-colored wolf with green eyes standing between two trees, watching me.

The wolf doesn't frighten me, though her intense stare makes my heart rattle against my chest. Powerless. How I lived and how I fought. How I never want to feel again. My anger doesn't spit this time. It rolls and drips, feeding my desire to stare the way the wolf does.

Repositioning my arrow, I hold all that tension in my core and remember my Maman. My lost family, our friends that were killed and tortured. I release my fingers, watching the arrow spiral a shot through the air, landing in the center of the red circle as easy as breathing.

"Again," she says.

I reach behind and grab another. I shoot the next tree. Then the next. Then the next. All with precision and control. When I stop to look for the wolf's reaction, she is gone.

I drop my bow and stare at the arrows all perfectly burrowed into the trees, and I smile. Then my feet are swiped from under me. My hands hit the ground and I roll to my back, using my bent knee to take Naira to the ground. She hooks her legs against mine like a buck's horns and pulls herself by grabbing my dress. I slide my hand under her body and arch my back to throw her off me. By the time she launches for me again, I have steadied my feet and twist her arm to turn her and throw her to the ground. I swipe her blade from her holster and hold it over her neck.

Through our deep breaths, I suddenly realize what I've done. I didn't think, I didn't fear, I just listened. I release her and stand, turning the blade around to give her the handle.

"You are ready, Isabelle."

"Ready for what, I don't know."

"Your journey." She wraps her arms around me, and I let my cheek fall to her shoulder. I want to cry for all she's done, for how deeply I care for her.

She pulls back and looks at me, the slightest sheen of tears over her eyes. "You are now the wolf."

·   ·   ·

My body is a mix of excitement, hesitation, and wonder. The walk back home feels clear and quiet, a focus I haven't felt before. I try to understand my journey, what I will do once James leaves, and how I can keep my promise to Madame Doré from here in Quebec.

When I approach our house, something feels strange. Unsettling. A roaring fire warms the house with a glow against the darkened night. I open the door to find the house turned upside down—tables upturned, jars broken, food strewn on the floor. Nothing is in place. I swallow and look around, wondering if someone has stolen something.

The wood floor creaks under the weight of my boots. At the foot of the stairs, I see James's cravat, thrown in a heap. More creaking as I ascend each step. Once I reach our bedroom, it feels as if the blood has drained from my body, leaving me empty and weak.

James sits on the bedside, floorboard slid open at his feet. My Geneva Bible in one hand, Andre's knife in the other.

"I should have seen it," he says. "AB. Andre Boucher." He stands, so intense with controlled rage that I consider running. "How do you blind me, Isabelle?"

"Nothing has happened between us. I promise you."

"Antoinette saw you with him. Outside of town today, close enough to kiss." He turns his head and snarls with closed eyes. "I believed you'd eventually love me."

My hands begin to tingle like rising secrets. "Andre and I have history, but that is all. I've done nothing to betray you."

He holds up my Bible. "Except for this."

Seeing it in his hands makes my stomach turn. "You've always known who I am."

"I believed you to be Catholic, Isabelle!" He thunders past me, down the stairs, Bible and knife in hand.

"What are you doing?" I follow him.

He paces the room like the bear held at the Huron camp. "You've been lying to me this entire time. That's fine, because I've been lying to you too."

I can't pull away from the hate in his eyes. "What are you talking about?"

"I sent for my father's ships. They're on their way to buy slaves right now."

Bastard. Though I know he's capable of evil, like a fool I continue to hope he'll change. "How could you?"

"Don't look at me like that. It's a way out if Madame Doré fails us."

"If our plan falls apart, you'll still imprison and torture innocent people?"

"I don't want to, but I'll have no choice." He leans his hands against the mantel. "Tell me, do you picture *him* when we lie together?"

"James, don't do this."

He drops his arms, hands clutching the items at his side. "When I touch you, do you wish it were him?"

"Stop."

"You were never the woman I thought you were." He throws my Bible in the fireplace.

"No." I slide to the fire on my knees, but the Bible has already gone up in flames. Its worn pages burn and smoke as James stands behind me, watching.

I gather my tears and screams, and fight to catch my breath. I turn to him, biting back my hatred. "I've tried to make you the man I know you could be. But you keep failing, miserably."

He lifts his hand and smacks his open palm to my cheek, sending me stumbling. I could have stopped him, but I didn't. He's right, I have lied—about everything.

When I look at him through the loose curls that shade my eyes, he's biting his lip, shaking his head. "I… I've never hit a woman."

I regain my composure and stare at him, wondering when he will leave so I can be free of this horrendous pain ripping through me.

"I'm sorry," he whispers.

He steps toward me, but I lift my hand to tell him to stop. "You promised you would never hurt me."

He stutters to find words, moving closer as he does. "You make me feel like a madman, Isabelle. I love you so much. The thought of losing you to that man makes me sick."

"You didn't lose me to him. If anything will make me leave, it will be your lies."

He slouches against the wall. "I leave tomorrow."

"You let Antoinette come between us."

"She told me you're hiding something and that I can never trust you." He stares at the fire, my Bible now nothing but fuel. "We both lied. Why do we do this to each other?"

I can't trust him. He'll leave tomorrow, and I'll have no idea what he's doing in France. No idea who he has betrayed and what sort of monster will return. When I look into his eyes, I no longer see the hope for a good person. I see a traitor.

He touches my cheek. "I'm so sorry. I can be better."

A knock at the door startles us both. My heart pounds and James straightens his doublet before opening the door.

"Charlotte?" I step forward. "What are you doing here?"

"May I speak with you for a moment?" she asks.

James doesn't take his eyes off me. I can't be near him for one more second. "Perhaps you should clean up your mess," I say to James as Charlotte and I hurry outside.

Charlotte grabs my arm and motions with her head toward the trees.

"What is it?"

"Come." We walk down the path and hidden in a thicket of tamarack... is Andre.

"What are you doing here?" I ask. "James found my Bible and your knife. He knows I've been lying. He'll kill you if he finds you here."

"They have Henri," he says.

"What? Who?"

"The French. They captured a group of Protestants in New York and sent the French ones back to Paris to be dealt with by the royal army."

I grab the tree to steady myself. "They didn't kill him. Why?"

"They want to take over the English colony as part of New France. They'll torture him until he reveals what he knows. And then they'll kill him."

"I sent him away to save him but pushed him right into the hands of our enemies."

"I found Charlotte at the abbey and asked her to come here so I can get word to you. What do we do?"

I rub my forehead. "He's in Paris?"

"I hear he is at the Bastille until they decide what to do with them."

Charlotte places her hand on my arm. "You have a plan, don't you?"

I glance back at the house. No sign of James yet. "Charlotte, can you play the part of a lady's maid?"

Her eyes light up. "Absolutely."

"Then prepare for a journey."

I look at Andre, something inside me crushing to dust at the thought that I might never see him again. "I'll send word as soon as I can. I'm going to get him back."

Andre nods and looks at the house. "Isabelle, don't trust James."

"I'm not sure I ever have."

Andre pulls me close and stares into my eyes. His breath warms my cheek. "Will you return?"

"I hope so."

"I think maybe... you were born to do this." He lingers close, neither of us wanting to let go. Alas, that's all we ever do—let go. As we step away, I refuse to allow my emotions to take hold, so I force a smile and nod.

I pull Charlotte with me to the house and whisper, "Play along."

Once inside, I find James cleaning the mess he's made.

"James, this is Charlotte. She's coming with us."

"Where?"

Unable to believe what I'm about to say, I close my eyes. "To Paris."

CHAPTER SIXTEEN

Standing on the deck of Le Brézé, all James can speak of are the five companies of military that this ship carried to Quebec, the ship that now carries me away from my home. Again.

James practically glows as he talks of these military men, how they will demolish the Iroquois, and prove his importance to the king. Now our focus is to survive the next two months, arrive safely in Paris, and fulfill our promises.

As the ship drifts softly over the deep, never-ending ocean, James and Charlotte move underground, Charlotte to rest, and James to befriend the captain. I stay on the deck to watch the sun set behind us into a bleeding orange sky.

"I remember the last time we stood on a deck together, watching the sea."

My palms curl around the railing, fingernails digging into the shining wood. Of course she's here.

Without turning, I say, "Antoinette, I spared your hair from my blade once. If given the opportunity to do it over, I won't be so kind."

She steps next to me, and we watch the burst of sunlight fade to dull gray. "I no longer look up to you like I used to," she says.

"Why is that?"

"You can't even keep your husband happy."

"At least I have a husband to disappoint."

I shouldn't have said it, and I can't look at her. She lost James to me, then married the most disgusting man whom she let burn at the hands of the Iroquois. "I suppose you're here to ensure James follows your direction?" I ask.

"Yes. My father is with him and the captain. I believe they're discussing shipping routes and charting courses between France and Africa. Just think of those ships, full of silk and pottery and clocks, made by Huguenots... and traded for human slaves."

I grip the railing harder to stop myself from flinging her overboard. "You don't need James's ships. You have plenty to make this little plan of yours happen. Why the obsession with him, Antoinette?"

"Like I told you, families like ours need to stick together. My father had plans for him. Until your needy, frightened eyes manipulated him."

"Do you not remember that your own father sent you to the colonies because he didn't want to be bothered by you?"

Neither of us bristles, having long ago realized that we will always hate each other.

"Isabelle, we are here to ensure James fulfills his promise. For if he doesn't, we will send him to the stretcher, where he'll be pulled by a crank until his joints split in two."

"You wouldn't do that. You've always loved him."

"Shows how little you understand me. I am capable of the darkest things when someone wrongs me. Watch your back, old friend. I'm not the weak girl I once was."

"Neither am I."

We don't look at each other, but as her footsteps fade into silence, I imagine what joints sound like when they split open.

•   •   •

James has secured us a private room next to the captain's quarters. Charlotte is in a room below with other servants. The ship creaks in the subtle rocking of the water as candlelight flickers shadows around us.

"Antoinette will have you sent you to the rack if you defy her," I say to James.

"She has no power over me."

"It seems her father does."

He glances sideways as he unwraps his cravat. "You question me more than any woman should question her husband."

"I'm here to stop them—and you, if I must. I answer to a higher call than the rules of a civil union."

He grabs my arm, harder than usual. "You will tread lightly, Isabelle. You're lucky I tolerate your insolence."

"Perhaps you should have left me in France," I say with a smirk.

He pushes me against the wall, back pressed hard against the ridges of the wood. "Perhaps you should respect me."

"Would you like to hit me again? Go ahead."

I can't tell if he wants to hit me or kiss me. Probably both.

A knock at the door. "Aye, Captain wants you to join him."

James shakes a loose curl from his face, hands still tight around my arms. "Of course." He looks at me, an anger in his eyes that warns of his potential. "You act as though you haven't hidden another man's knife next to a Geneva Bible under our floorboards. As though you aren't dripping with lies and deceit."

It takes everything in me to withhold a slap. "The captain is waiting, Lieutenant Beaumont."

He releases his grip and straightens his doublet. Tightens the tie in his hair. "You're coming with me."

I can't get more than a squeak out before he drags me into the captain's quarters. He pinches the back of my arm to remind me to play along.

"Lieutenant and Madame Beaumont. Welcome."

The captain is tall, with broad shoulders, and clean fingernails. I suppose he doesn't touch any ropes or carry any crates. He sits in his room, directing others and reading maps.

"Yes, welcome…"

I turn to follow the voice, and find Monsieur LaMarche behind me, grinning like the wily fox that he is. "Can I offer you a drink, Madame?"

"No, thank you."

"Fine." He hands James a jug of wine. "We're all friends here."

The men take turns drinking as I look around the room at the captain's pile of furs, his candle chandelier, and the wall of windows framing the black night.

"The captain has been enlightening us with information on trade routes," LaMarche says. "Isn't that right, Monsieur?"

"Aye," the captain says. "The slave trade is growing. Plenty of men to be sold to wealthy families."

I turn my head to hide my disgust.

"He wants to help our little endeavor grow," LaMarche says. "Be a part of something that will make us a tremendous amount of money and power."

Everything Naira taught me was about control. I turn and face LaMarche, shoulders back. "The king has no idea what value you will bring to him, does he? He knows nothing of your endeavor."

LaMarche's eye twitches, but I don't falter.

"We have much to offer him," James says. "And now, we have another ally here on the seas."

The captain nods and takes a giant glug of swill. "Now we feast."

The captain summons trays of food. As the men set up a table, LaMarche leans uncomfortably close, pressing his chest into my shoulder. "You've been naughty, I hear."

Of course, Antoinette told him I spoke to Andre. Nothing happened, and she knows it. "I've been nothing of the sort, Monsieur."

"It's all right," he whispers in my ear, "We've all been a little naughty."

On instinct, I shift closer to James, who wraps his hand around my waist. His touch feels secure and soft, so different from earlier when he shoved me against the wall. LaMarche laughs to himself, and it sends shivers up my back.

"Please, sit," the captain says. "Enjoy."

The four of us sit at the table piled with bread, candied fruit, nuts, cold sliced beef, and ale as the lower decks eat nothing more than dried biscuits and spoiled wine.

"Tell me, Madame," LaMarche says as he tears into a loaf of bread. "Are you excited to return to your homeland?"

He knows full well I want nothing to do with my homeland. "Of course, Monsieur."

"We all knew each other back in La Rochelle," he tells the captain. "I knew Madame's father."

My body tenses at the mention of my father but I settle myself, think of Naira, and how I could bring each of these men to the ground if I had to.

"After La Rochelle, you left for… Rouen, was it?"

"When I was exiled, yes."

James's eyes widen, a warning to be careful.

"Exiled?" The captain sounds intrigued.

"Yes, our dear Isabelle used to be a Protestant—a heretic."

I slice my meat slow and controlled. "Once I converted and renounced the errors I had made, the church welcomed me with open arms. As did Quebec and the king."

The captain seems very amused by this. "Once shunned and exiled, and now you are a Daughter of the King? Returning to France to meet with the monarch himself. That is quite the story, Madame."

James can't tolerate the tense conversation. "Captain, two months it will take to reach Dieppe?"

"Perhaps faster, if the winds are in our favor."

"I'm eager to impress the royal court," James says. "Tell them of our grand plans to save the empire."

The captain leans back, glugs again from the jug that he appears to no longer share with the men. "I'm grateful to be part of this. We can make buckets of gold." The captain devours his food, then burps loudly, his face flushed bright red. He slaps his palm on the table. "I have a little collection of things taken from slaves and prisoners in the galleys. Would you like to see?"

"I believe my wife is quite tired," James says. "I think I'll retire with her to our bedroom."

"Nonsense!" the captain says. "This is my ship, and you do as I say." He pauses, then releases a laugh so deep it causes him to cough. "Come."

He leads James to a room down the hall and James looks back at me over his shoulder. I nod him on, knowing I can't avoid LaMarche forever.

"So, Madame Beaumont." He runs his eyes over my breasts and smiles. "We find ourselves alone. After all these years."

"Don't think I have forgotten the role you played in my family's demise."

"Your ships did very well for me. Besides, Huguenots can't own property. I was following a direct order from the king."

"And now my father is dead and the child you tried to ruin has found her way back into your world. What should I do with this opportunity?"

"I must say, Isabelle, you've grown to be quite the brave girl. Or, woman, I should say." The glimmer in his eye makes me want to find a blade and stab it straight through his skull.

"I think I'll retire now," I say. "Good night."

I rush to the door, but not before he races behind me to close it. His breath on my neck, he says, "You must know how desperately my daughter wants your husband."

I turn, place my hand on his chest, and push him back with force. "Do not disrespect us, Monsieur."

"I wouldn't dream of it." He widens his stance, hands on his hips. "No, I need your help."

I don't respond, but I ready myself for an attack.

"You see, James is under your spell. He always has been, poor boy. His father couldn't talk sense into him. He wanted me to return him to France, and I've done that. But James is weak. He's trying to disobey my wishes. I can't tell why, but I presume it has something to do with you."

"James is his own man."

"I don't believe that for one second." He steps closer. "Don't be frightened. I won't hurt you," he says.

Little does he know I could slice his neck clean to the bone and wouldn't regret it.

"You see, I need James to follow along. He won't listen to my daughter. He won't even listen to me. But you hold some sort of power over him. I need you to control him. Make him follow my lead."

"Why would I do that, Monsieur?"

"Because I will take you back to Rouen. I will place you on trial in front of Jacques Dupre for attempted murder."

The day I took a beam to Jacques's face showed me I could fight. When he held me down and pressed his cockerel against my thigh, something in me broke. I smashed his face into a bloody mess.

"I see that gives you pause," he says. "Would be a shame to see such a beautiful woman sent to the stretcher."

He steps closer still and runs his fat finger along my collarbone.

I grab his finger and twist back so far it snaps. When he doubles over, I slam my knee into his groin hard enough to bring him to the floor. As he writhes and groans, in too much pain to scream, I lower next to his face. "I'll help you. But if you ever lay a hand on me again, your finger won't be the only thing I break."

James rushes in, concern in his eyes. "Are you all right? I heard a crash."

"Oh, Monsieur LaMarche here caught his finger in the door. Poor man. Monsieur, you should wrap your hand and get some rest," I say. "We have plans to make, don't we?"

He squirms on the floor like a wounded animal.

"James," I say sweetly, "take me to bed?"

He wraps his arm around my waist and leads me back to our room. As soon as he shuts the door, he whispers, "What's going on?"

Unable to control this fire inside me, I throw James to the bed. Rip open his doublet and yank loose his cravat.

"I'm still angry with you, Isabelle."

Removing his breeches with my teeth, I can't help but bite the flesh on his stomach. "I'm so angry I can hardly look at you."

He grabs my hair and forces me to kiss him. "You lied to me."

My hand gripped to his neck, I pull him to sitting. "So did you." I scratch my nails down his back while I stare into his eyes and watch him wince.

Naked, tangled, and full of fire, we tear into each other's bodies because we can't stand each other's souls.

• • •

I slipped from James's arms this morning when he was still sleeping off the ale. His hand brushed my hip as I slithered away, and he released an easy grunt as he settled back into sleep. I froze, staring at his scars and his subtle curls decorating the pillow. And then I dressed, hoping to avoid him for the rest of the day.

Down in the lower rooms, the odors are intense. Human waste, sweat, and wet wood, stronger now than it was to me three years ago when I arrived. Charlotte's door is open, and she fixes her hair as her bunkmates snicker.

Charlotte hurries over. "Isabelle, thank goodness. Two days and I've already gone mad. It's nothing but church gossip."

"Come. I've snuck something for you," I say.

"Ooh, something exciting! Finally."

I lead her into a storage room and close the door. "Here. A proper breakfast."

The captain's feast from last night sat on his table, unnecessary waste while the rest of the ship listens to their stomachs growl. I yank the cork from the jug of wine.

"Sliced beef, bread, cheese!" She swigs from the jug and smiles. "Won't you join me?"

Happy to avoid my husband, I agree.

"Isabelle, what's our plan?" she asks.

"I know things, Charlotte. Secrets that could ruin everyone at court, including the king. I must be very careful."

She leans forward, elbow on the table. "What kind of secrets?"

"The kind that could get you killed."

She takes a bite of hard cheese, chewing slowly and thinking. "You would have told James enough to keep him loyal, but held enough to protect yourself."

"You're a sharp girl, Charlotte—very sharp."

She cocks her head to the side. "So, who will protect you?"

"I have to assume that no one will," I say.

"You're on this ship to get Henri back, yes?"

Another glug of wine to cleanse my dry throat. "Yes. And to stop James and the LaMarches."

"You're conspiring to take down the liars at court, outsmart your husband, stop slave ships, and rescue your best friend from the largest prison in France."

"You make it sound difficult."

Charlotte laughs, her cheeks warming to a rosy hue. She looks so childlike when she smiles. Until her laugh fades and the hardened young woman comes back into focus. "I'm here for anything you need. I'll risk my life every second of every day to avenge my sister's death. Let's ruin those bastards."

I roll the cork in my fingers. "What I know is so powerful and so dangerous, it could ruin everyone."

CHAPTER SEVENTEEN

Three weeks at sea. The captain assures we're making excellent time. The secrets I carry burn a hole through me as I bide my time near James and the LaMarches. Antoinette and her father lurk near us constantly.

On this cloudless morning, I watch the passengers soak up the sunshine on the deck. I'm certain there has never been a colder place on earth than Quebec, where ice patches remain until summer, and this slice of full body warmth feels like a gift.

Charlotte elbows me, but I ignore her. "Isabelle, let me help. I know things too."

I release an elongated sigh. I still don't trust her impulsivity. "Go on, tell me."

She tips her chin down and lowers her voice. "James will have you followed in Paris. He doesn't trust you."

This is not a surprise. "What else?"

"I… I can't tell you."

I square my shoulders at her. "What? You don't keep information from me. That's not how this works."

"I want to tell you." She glances behind her. "I don't like keeping things from you."

"Isabelle." We turn to see James tapping his foot. "You're requested in Monsieur LaMarche's room. Please come with me."

His anger hasn't softened since we left Quebec. At night, our bed is full of fire, and in the day, he can hardly look at me.

We pass Antoinette in the hallway who winks at James. Something understood between them and hidden from me. James wraps his arm around my waist, avoiding her shoulder as she passes. Before I have time to process what hidden conversation just occurred between my husband and my sworn enemy, Monsieur LaMarche has welcomed us by shutting his door.

"Good afternoon, Madame Beaumont." He offers me a drink, but I pass.

James's hand remains on my hip with a tightened grip.

"I told your husband about our conversation the other night," La Marche says. "How you are very supportive of our mission."

Naira whispers in my ear. *Breathe, listen.*

"Did you?" I turn to James, but he reveals nothing.

"How much we all want to see the Beaumont ships join ours in our quest for power."

Rolled out on the table is a scroll. A list of names. I don't dare show my worry.

"I hope your hand is healing nicely, Monsieur," I say. "Wouldn't it be a shame to find another finger in a slammed door?"

His eyes narrow, but he quickly recovers with a smirk. "Please, come look at what we have."

I walk slowly around the table to examine the scroll. It takes a moment to understand, but when I do, my neck breaks out in a cold sweat. The names—they're all Huguenot families.

"These are our list of merchants," he says, too close to my ear. "We will start in La Rochelle, but this is just the beginning. We'll gather them from all over France. Turn them all into prisoners."

Naira lived among the Iroquois after they scalped members of her tribe. I can do this. "It appears you have it all figured out. I'll return to the deck to enjoy the sun."

As I step away, LaMarche slams his knife flat on the table. James's breathing speeds up but still, no glances toward me.

"We aren't done." LaMarche coughs, waiting for me to turn back to him. I do, and I wait. "You choose," he says.

"I choose what?"

"Who we start with. These are the men with families. You may decide who will have their children taken away. We will place the children in Catholic homes and lock the merchants up in factories as they churn out goods for trade." He steps closer, heaves his stale breath toward my face. "I'll even let you have first pick of the slaves we bring from Africa. Strong, male specimens to perform any household duties you desire."

Again, James says nothing. LaMarche has something on him. I need to find out what it is. "Certainly, you aren't suggesting any man enter my home other than my husband? Perhaps you have forgotten what a satisfied woman looks like."

LaMarche slams his palms on the table. James pulls me away and whispers in my ear, "Stop. Do as he asks."

The names on the scroll bite at my heart. The family I left in the misery of La Rochelle. "Your weakness put us in this situation, James."

"Now, now. Don't quarrel," LaMarche says. "I'm simply looking for reassurance. Collateral that you both are people of your word." He points to the scroll. "Now, choose."

"No," I say.

"No one says no to me, Madame."

"I just did." I lift his scroll, place it in my hands, and rip it in two.

"I believe Jacques Dupre would love to hear of your arrival, Madame."

"James?" I stare, begging him to overcome his cowardice. "Our promise?"

There is nothing he wants more than for me to marry him in a grand Catholic church.

"Monsieur LaMarche," James says. "That is quite enough. My wife will be safe with me, and you will not harass her. I've sent for my family's ships and this theater is now merely to prove your power. If you hurt her, I will call it all off."

LaMarche's top lip twitches. He hadn't expected James to find his chivalry. Frankly, neither did I. James grabs my arm and drags me outside. "Stay away from her, Monsieur. Or you will have me to deal with."

James leads me to our room, his grip tight. Once he closes the door, he stands still, eyes closed, fingers digging into my arm.

"What is wrong with you?" I pull away, but he holds tight.

"You fool," he says through gritted teeth. "All you had to do was choose some names."

"Decide who of my people would have their children stolen?"

"Yes!"

I keep pulling, but he won't budge. I hide how strong I've become. "*You* are the fool. He knows I would never turn on my friends. He wants you to see that I will always be Protestant, a filthy heretic. He wants you to hate me for it."

"You are a filthy heretic."

The disgust in his eyes—it's been there this whole time—under the surface, waiting to explode. I try one last time to peel his fingers from my arm and when they don't budge, I lift my other elbow and slam it down on the bend in his arm. When he recoils, I shove my palm into his nose. As blood trickles from his nostril, fire explodes through me, my anger matching his hate.

He wipes his nose with the back of his hand. "You are not the person I thought you were," he says.

"Likewise, Monsieur Beaumont."

He grabs a linen sheet and wipes his bloody lip, examining the crimson red stain as if it's the proof he needs.

"LaMarche has something on you," I say. "Tell me what it is."

"I owe you nothing, you lying little traitor."

He's never spoken to me like this. Never looked at me with such disdain.

He dabs his gums to catch the ruby-red saliva. "When we arrive in France, you will accompany me to the palace. I need my wife by my side to make this plan work."

"You still want to stop them?"

"I want out of all of it, but I can't have my father's money, so I'll need to find my own. Help me land a position in the court and we'll save the Huguenots."

My wrist aches from how it bent back when my hand crushed his nose. "You'll take the help of a dirty traitor?"

He steps closer, but when I lift my hands to fight, he stops moving. "I've worked so hard to love you. But you never work with me, only against me with secrets and lies. What else am I to do?"

"You want me to trust you now, after all this?" I say.

"I could say the same of you."

I want to scream, but it's no use. "I'll stay with Charlotte tonight."

He straightens his doublet. "You'll stay here, with me."

The idea of being near him makes my skin crawl. "You asked me to betray my people."

He sniffs loudly, the last of the blood beginning to dry. "They are not your people. We are *Catholic*."

If he says it enough, perhaps he believes it will become truth.

"Force me to stay and see what I do."

As I open the door to walk away, he says, "I can't make myself hate you, much as I've tried."

"You shouldn't hate your wife."

I close the door, sick with every emotion rolling inside of me like pebbles down a hill. When I arrive at Charlotte's room, she doesn't question me, but simply hands me her pillow. I settle into her tiny bunk, her feet near my head, and I wonder how I can manage all that I've taken on.

. . .

I wake in the night, realizing that Charlotte's stockinged feet are no longer at my ears. I feel around to find she's gone. Heavy breathing mixes with the creaks and moans of the ship, and I step out to the hallway, into darkness. She could be anywhere. I walk the hall, listening at every door. Nothing.

I remember there's another floor below for storage. Whatever she's hiding from me, that would be a prime place to do it. Perhaps she's working with the LaMarches too.

Down into the darkness, I sneak past barrels that leak wine and water onto the floor to spoil what little food is left for the journey. The air is wet and musty. Pockets of green float on the puddles of wine that have probably gathered for weeks.

Whispers. I hide behind a set of barrels fastened to the wall, and I wait. Charlotte appears, candle in hand, and lifts her skirts to step out of the storage room and into the hallway. I want to grab her, force her to tell me the truth, but I need to discover what she's hiding, so I wait for her light to disappear into the stairwell.

I step into the storage room, listening for movement. Footsteps. A grunt.

Whoever is here hasn't left yet, which means they've heard me. It could be anyone. I step over an unraveled rope and note the filtered moonlight that pours through the holes in the wall. The movement stops, matching my steps.

Behind a stack of crates, I see a shoe. A man's shoe. If this is LaMarche, I might have to kill him. I lunge past the crates, arms out, ready to fight to the death.

My heart stops.

"Andre?"

Hair combed back and cheeks flushed, he's only grown more handsome in hiding—like the wild in him is too strong to break. "Shh," he says. "No one can know I'm here."

My heart thumps like the wingbeat of a hummingbird. "What were you thinking, getting on this ship?"

"I didn't want you to do this alone."

"How very kind of you." I shove him with both hands. "You fool! You've put us both in danger."

He leans back against a barrel, not trying to fight back. "I know something. I came here to tell you and knew I couldn't let you have all the fun in Paris." His slight smile instantly softens me.

"This complicates things." I rake my fingers through my hair, trying to focus.

"I have to tell you what I've discovered. James, he's—"

I shove him again. "He's going to kill you if he finds you." Andre continues to smile, presumably finding my anger charming. The fire in me suddenly turns to a smoldering heat. "You're really here."

He steps closer. "I left Elizabeth with Naira. I couldn't tolerate you being on the other side of the world from me."

His stare can find the one part of me I've never been able to control. That soft, fragile center I must keep locked away for fear that once I expose it, I'll lose any courage I've built.

With a step back, I shake my head. How am I to tolerate being near James with this disarming man staring in my eyes? "I'm glad you're safe. I'll see you in Paris."

I pull up my skirts, navigate away from the mildewy wine.

"I wasn't finished," he says.

He's never forceful, and the firmness of his voice gives me pause.

"I have information that can help Henri and you, and all the families who will be destroyed because of James and the LaMarches. Be as angry as you like. But I'm still following you to Paris. I'll remain close, for whenever you need me."

I need to hear how James has betrayed me this time, but I can't tolerate being near Andre for one more second. Without the will to fight, I walk away, tears in my eyes, and return to Charlotte's bunk. We both pretend to sleep, not a word passed between us.

• • •

"Why are you mad at me?" Charlotte finally asks after a week of me sleeping in her bunk. We sit cross-legged together on her bed as the servants braid each other's hair.

"You lied to me," I whisper.

She tightens her shoulders. "You know about…"

I place my finger to my lips, motioning for her not to finish that sentence.

"I wanted to tell you, but he made me promise." The girls laugh and ignore our conversation. "Is it so bad?" she asks. "You could use another ally."

"He complicates everything, he always has. I just want to get to Paris, destroy the ring of nobles, and save Henri. I have no time to let my heart have a say in anything."

"You aren't sleeping with your husband, so I'd say your heart has a few things to say."

A girl dabs perfume on everyone's necks and the air seems to thicken. "I need to think. Just stay here."

It isn't her fault, but I can't focus. So much is at stake. Down the corridor, near the staircase to the upper deck, a hand on my arm. I turn but know who it is.

"LaMarche, don't forget what I did to your hand. Don't make me do it to your face."

"I have something to show you," he says.

"I'm not interested."

"Oh, I think you are." I reluctantly follow him to his room. "You can leave the door open if you prefer. I merely want to help you understand you are in over your head."

"You don't intimidate me, LaMarche."

He looks out his porthole of blown glass and stares at the blue water. "I wanted your help, but I fear you aren't able," he says.

I step closer, looking past him to the sea. Afraid I might find Andre floating dead in the water, I hesitate. Then I hear something. Someone.

I look again at the water over his shoulder.

"Not there." He turns to a hole in the wall. "Here."

I peer through the break between the boards. Antoinette's room. I blink hard, trying to focus. There she is—bent over the bed, a man's hand gripping her blond curls, her breasts shaking against her torso with every thrust. I follow back to see James, entering her from behind. He's angry, excited, and when he pulls her hair back, she groans in pleasure. She looks straight at the opening and smiles at me.

I gasp, pulling away from the wall, the shock still sawing its way through me. My heart thumps so loud, it drowns out any chance of attacking LaMarche.

"You've lost him, Isabelle. He's ours now."

LaMarche's teeth gleam yellow from the sunshine. I stumble back, desperate to move away from the view of their naked bodies thrusting in unison.

No words. I force myself out the door but can't face anyone. I find a storage nook and let myself sit in the anger of it all. He touched her naked flesh and grabbed her hair. Flashes of their bodies sear my brain hard enough to force a fresh wave of fury through me.

Crouched and shaking, I remember the blood streaming down the walls of La Rochelle. The scent of burning flesh when they took a torch to Henri's father. Somehow, James's betrayal has opened the cavern of horrific memories I've buried deep in my mind. My vision narrows and my breath tightens. That coward will never be anything but broken. When I finally gather myself, the sun has lowered in the sky. Against all judgment, I climb down the ladder to the belly of the ship.

When I step between the crates, Andre is there, hands behind his head, daydreaming.

"Andre."

He looks at me in disbelief and stands somewhat clumsily.

I begin to cry, not from sadness, but from rage. "Have you ever needed anger like you need air and water?" Tears sting my eyes as I let myself feel how much it would have hurt to be away from him for so long.

He holds me, tight but still tender. He doesn't caress me or touch my hair, but he holds me. Exactly as I need to be held. "What happened?" he asks.

Flashes again of James's hand on Antoinette's bare backside make me cringe, and I grit my teeth. "It doesn't matter."

"Yes, it does." He pulls away and holds my shoulders as he stares into my eyes.

"James. I saw him with Antoinette. LaMarche forced me to watch them through the wall. They were naked."

Andre brushes the hair from my eye, tucks it behind my ear. "I don't need to hear the details."

"I feel nothing but anger toward him. But I've survived on it for years, let it bleed into me and fill me with everything I needed to live these lies. Now, how am I to keep up this charade?"

"Is this a surprise?" he asks.

"He ruined what we had—mutual loathing that served us both."

"I suppose all things end, Isabelle. Good and bad."

I let myself look deep into his eyes. "James called me a dirty little traitor."

"Well, we all are, aren't we?" He forces a smile, and I can't help but soften. "We can do this without him. When we get to Paris, we'll get Henri back on our own."

"I need to get to the king. It's the only way to stop everyone—including my husband."

"What I came to tell you, can I share it now?" he asks.

I nod.

"The tavern owner is a friend. He hears everything the soldiers discuss over pints of ale." He hesitates. "James gave the order to capture Protestants in New York. He's the reason the French captured Henri. And he's just getting started."

"Bastard. Him and Antoinette are perfect for each other."

Andre's shoulders—there's always been something about them. Broad and strong, but they seem to hold all his softness, like a bottled-up embrace. The reality of what James has become is too awful to think about, so I stare at Andre's neck and shoulders.

"Isabelle?"

I shake myself back to focus.

"Are you hurt by his betrayal?" he asks.

"No, I think I finally feel free to use him the way he's used me."

"Good." One side of his smile lifts and his eyes sparkle. "We'll be in Dieppe in two days. How do you want to do this?"

I've always been able to trust Andre, and I can't do this alone. It's time to tell him what I know. "Can I tell you a secret?"

"Always."

"Some women of the court aren't who they seem."

"Aren't all royals lying about something?" he asks.

"Not like this." The ship hits a rolling patch of rough water. Swells and drops remind me this ship is nothing more than planks nailed together. We grab the wall support to steady us as the ship rattles. "I need to expose them, but I'm not sure what to do after that."

"If you threaten them, they'll probably do anything you ask. We can force them to help us, and we could use their power. Are these secrets really that dangerous?"

Madame Doré spent years collecting dirty secrets from her lovers. The royal family pays for her silence, but she has patiently listened and prodded and collected secrets that could ruin every person at court—including the king.

"James may have ships and slaves and Huguenot goods," I say, "but we have the dark, ugly world of Parisian witchcraft."

"Witchcraft?" His cheeks glow red.

"Black magic, to be precise." Warmth spreads through me at the thought of these powerful secrets. "They make and distribute poison and kill members of the court who cross them."

His eyes grow wide. "That sounds exactly like the kind of women we need on our side."

The ship rises like a horse rearing on its hind legs. The bow crashes down, sending us into the wall behind the barrels. Unlike the scared girl from years ago, rough seas no longer scare me. I hug the support tight and remember the pride in Naira's eyes when I last fought her.

"Arsenic and black magic. Now that's power."

"Question is, Isabelle, how will you use it?" Andre asks.

"How will *we* use it."

Andre and I stare at each other for a long while. We ride out the hourlong area of choppy sea braced to the support beams and plotting for our future. When the sea calms, I step away, still furious from James's betrayal, but ready for the fight I can no longer turn from.

Andre winks. "See you in Dieppe, Madame."

As I walk away, gratitude overcomes me when I think of all that Andre has risked over the years. All that we have both sacrificed. I run back to him and wrap him in a hug.

My cheek resting on the strong mound of his shoulder, I say, "Thank you for following me."

His arms pull me into a warm, soft, perfect embrace. "You can thank me by breaking Henri from the Bastille. I don't know how exactly, it's nearly impossible."

"Except when you have magic poisons and dark secrets on your side—and women willing to risk everything."

CHAPTER EIGHTEEN

It took everything in me to return to James's room last night, the final evening on the ship before we land in Dieppe. He pulled me inside, held me tight, and cried. Not the reaction I expected. He doesn't know that I watched him through a peephole or that LaMarche encouraged it. But his regret is clear by the way he grovels for me to return to his bed.

I couldn't lie naked with him, but I let him hold me all night as he begged me to never leave him again. He whispered *I'm sorry* so many times it lost meaning. "I'll pretend I don't know about your lies," he said, as if he can ignore the Huguenot next to him and see only the Catholic he wants to see.

Let him see as he wishes. Honesty is no longer my concern.

This morning, hand in hand, we watch the shore of France approach. "I never thought I'd be back here," I mumble.

"You are French, darling," James says. "We belong here."

The LaMarches sneer at us from the other side of the ship. My skin itches when James touches me, but I conceal my disgust.

"Will we rest in Dieppe or move straight away to Paris?" Charlotte asks.

"Paris, of course," James says.

"Where will we stay?" I ask.

"Palais Royale. The Cardinal offered me housing whenever I returned."

Charlotte squeezes my hand, a sign that she will relay the message to Andre. She excuses herself to attend to my things.

"Perhaps this is a new start for us, Isabelle," he says.

"That depends." I look over my shoulder, ensuring we won't be overheard. "What have you decided? Offer the king secrets to save his court, or offer him slaves and broken families to appease LaMarche?"

He leans to my ear, stopping to taste my neck before he speaks. "I've been a fool. I will never lie to you again."

I smile, more to the approaching Dieppe than to him, knowing I will use him until the last drop of information has run dry.

The moment the ship docks, a familiar feeling settles into me, one of anger and purpose. Approaching my homeland, standing in the same place I once was a practicing Protestant, stirs up joy and anger and deep resentment, like the ocean floor in a storm.

James and I make our way to land, ignoring the watchful eyes of the LaMarches. We meet with Charlotte, who nods to the crates and barrels being carried off the ship. Assisting with stacking, I see Andre, hat low over his eyes. Knowing he made it and how close we are to our goal sends a thrill from my toes to the base of my head.

James wraps my hand around his arm. I want to pull away from his touch, shove him off me, but I swallow that need and I smile.

"We have plans to make, my dear," James says.

"I suppose we do." I turn to Charlotte. "Are my things taken care of?"

"Yes, Madame," she says with a smile.

James extends his arm. "A carriage awaits."

We set out on the bumpy road, and the coast disappears in our past. Hours pass but we don't speak, which is just as well, as I prefer to take in the rolling golden hills of the country I never thought I'd see again.

I remember the tattered clothes I wore in Rouen, the freezing nights I traveled with Maman before she died on a lonely hilltop. The bruised and battered body that carried me to the ship that would take me to a new life.

And suddenly, Paris comes alive around me.

We pass through the city walls over a bridge, and into the enclosed city of chaos. People and horses and carts fill every cobblestone in the streets. Hooves clack against stone and men yell at the market. Prostitutes hang from doorways like creeping plants.

"The manure." Charlotte holds her hand to her mouth.

"Yes," James says. "At one time, the monarchs used perfumed water to cover the scent of horses. They even covered the buildings in tapestries and filled the fountains with milk and wine."

"And now?" I lean out the window and notice the river of vermillion mud around us. Our wheels splash the sulfurous-scented stew as we roll through the thickness.

"Now slaughterhouses discard blood right into the streets. It thickens with the mud and these people have no choice but to wade through it."

"That smell." Charlotte nearly chokes.

"Ah, yes. Emptied chamber pots and animal blood. It's a river of waste. Disgusting." He grimaces and keeps his eyes forward, unwilling to look out to the street's filth.

"Why do royalty live here?" Charlotte asks.

"Oh, royalty live in Le Marais, a lovely neighborhood over the Seine. There, people care about cleanliness. The king lives across from the Palais Royale," James says. "At the Louvre. I will request an audience with him as soon as we're settled."

"And he will allow it?" I ask.

"I still know important people, Isabelle."

I release a controlled smile and withhold the eye roll that begs to be set free. Besides, I'm too shocked by the filth that covers such grand architecture. Romanesque bell towers and stone archways that roll like waves. Domed palaces and stone facades that reflect the sunlight. I don't suppose I will ever understand a man who is capable of such beauty but chooses to fight wars and murder Protestants.

"Here we are." James waits for the driver to open the door and he helps me to the ground. "I presume you will want a rest after our long journey."

"That would be lovely," I say.

He ignores Charlotte, who huffs before lowering herself next to me. James didn't ask why I brought her. I assume he likes the status of his wife having a lady's maid.

Palais Royale welcomes us with arched walkways and a courtyard filled with meandering women in silk brocade gowns with spangled bodices and metallic lace. A man greets us and bows his head. "Pleasure to meet the beautiful Madame Beaumont," he says.

James smiles proudly, as if he hasn't recently held the bare bottom of my sworn enemy in his lying, cheating hands. We follow him to our quarters.

James waits for me to settle into the lavish room with a view of the king's palace. He paces, glancing at me as he moves.

"What is wrong?" I ask.

"The ships have been sent. Our plan is in motion. I'm not sure how we can stop it."

It somehow feels worse to let myself loathe him. Like I've opened a well of hate that is about to overflow. "James, we have something more important than a trading company. We have secrets that could ruin the empire."

"If the LaMarches find out we're working against them, they'll ruin us. He'll send you to Rouen for sentencing."

"If Monsieur LaMarche wanted me imprisoned, he would have already done it."

"This could turn on us," James says.

"Yes, it could. But I will save those slaves and Huguenots, or I will die trying." I force myself to touch his chest, but my palm feels like fire. "Go inquire about an audience with the king."

He smiles, with a hopeful, needy glance. "With you, I feel I could be someone else." His hands slide from my arms, and he bows before departing for the Louvre. I restrain a grimace until the door slams shut.

Charlotte steps in from her servant's quarters, eyes bright. "Are you ready?"

"Yes. We must be quick."

It's a thirty-minute walk along the Seine. Andre follows close behind.

Vile muck gathers in static pools under our feet. Stone buildings are stained black from years of filth and waste, while breezeless air worsens the suffocating stench. At first, we cough and gag, but settle once we enter a section of street that has been mopped of its excrement, blood, and offal.

"Have you and James spoken about…?" Charlotte asks.

"No."

"Why haven't you told him you know? You can completely control him."

I keep walking, trying to ignore the oppressive heat crushing my chest. "Not yet."

"He's weak," Charlotte says. "I don't see why we need him."

"He's Isabelle's only way into the royal circle," Andre whispers.

"Enough of this. We're here to get Henri back." We halt, stare up at the imposing fortress with its turrets and impossibly thick walls and the empty moat that envelops the bastion.

Charlotte gasps. "How will we get him out of *there*?"

"I asked around," Andre says. "This building has been here for three hundred years. It's crumbling in places. There are about forty prisoners, people they want to question, or anyone who displeases the king."

"Eight towers," I say. "Connected walls as tall as the turrets. Armories and guards." I turn to face Andre. "It's not possible to get him out."

"Everything is possible," Andre says. "We just need to be creative."

"First, we find out if he's alive," I say. "If he's truly here."

"What do you want to do," Charlotte asks, "just walk in and ask to see Henri Reynard, known Huguenot detained for heresy?"

I remember Naira's teachings. To control the minds of others, I must stay calm in my own. "That is exactly what we will do."

We cross the bridge over the emptied moat, toward the arch at the entrance. "I overheard LaMarche speak of the Bastille," I say. "Political prisoners, mostly the aristocracy. They're well cared for, their release at the discretion of His Royal Majesty."

"Well cared for?" Charlotte says. "A Huguenot sent back to Paris to be interrogated. Why don't I believe they are treating him with kindness?"

"Follow along."

Through the arched gates, past women and men gathered in the courtyard as if a party were about to commence. Visitors carry trays of food and books. One servant balances an exotic bird on his shoulder that twitches and shakes his red feathers in the man's ear.

"What is this place?" Charlotte asks.

"This is unlike any prison I've seen," Andre says.

Through the giant gates, we enter the cooled air inside the thick stone walls. I expect to smell rotting flesh and hear screams from tortured men, but all I smell is wine as a man wheels a barrel past us, sloshing red liquid over its edge.

A military man stands at the entrance, guiding the barrel to the Liberty Tower. Guards flank the entrance, seemingly uninterested in the three Protestants that just crossed their threshold.

"Pardon, we are here to inquire about a man," I say. "A Huguenot sent here from the English colony."

"Monsieur Reynard. What about him?"

"Yes, that's him," I say. "Might we visit him?"

The man examines us, narrows his eyes at Andre. "He has no approved visitors."

"What a shame. My husband has not submitted the proper request, but he's tied up at the Louvre at the moment. My lady's maid could run to fetch him if she doesn't faint in this heat."

Charlotte, never missing a thing, fans herself with her hand.

"Your husband is at the Louvre?" the man asks.

"Yes. Requesting an audience with the king." I let him sit with that. "He works with Monsieur LaMarche, and this Reynard scoundrel has stolen from me. I wish to question him. Perhaps discover where the thief has hidden our family's silver."

I elbow Charlotte, and she forces tears to well in her eyes. A talent useful for every woman. *Well done, Charlotte.*

"Oh," the man says. "I see no reason you can't have a moment with him. Bastard probably has secrets hidden all over France, Huguenot liar that he is."

I snarl, mirroring the man's disgust. "He will meet his fate, I assume. My husband will be furious if I return without answers." I turn to Andre. "He has sent his brother to ensure our safety."

Andre nods.

"All right then, come along."

We follow him down the long passageways, dimly lit from the sunshine that streams through the small windows high near the ceiling. Andre hesitates and rubs the back of his neck nervously.

"You aren't helping," I say.

"I know how to trap animals and fight off Iroquois, but Catholic prison guards still frighten the life right out of me."

We pass the towers to find surprisingly lavish rooms. Not the prison cells I had envisioned. Decorated with tapestries and upholstered armchairs. One prisoner plays the violin as the guards applaud his stirring performance. In another, a member of royalty undresses a prostitute, unbothered by our shocked stares.

"This can't be real," Andre says.

At the end of the hall, we descend a staircase where the air shifts from wine to sweat and waste. A rat scurries across the floor and the guard kicks him away. "Here we are." He points to a small cell tucked into the corner of the circular tower, nothing but a bed and a chamber pot, and the depressing air of hopelessness.

"Thank you, Monsieur. I will ensure that my husband hears of your kindness."

The man clicks his heels. "The guard at the staircase can see you out when you're done."

Henri stumbles to the narrow opening as his bony, pale fingers wrap around the bars. He stares at me in confusion.

"Henri, we're here," I say.

He blinks as tears pool in his eyes. "Isabelle? Is it really you?"

"Yes, my friend." I reach my hands through the opening, and he grabs them in his icy fists. His eyes are wild, his black curls a flattened mess, and his cheekbones have grown jagged and sharp.

"They know I've been passing secrets. There are other Protestants here too. I've heard things."

"Henri, slow down," I say. "Breathe. We're going to find a way out of here."

"How?" He glances at Andre and Charlotte. "Who's she?"

"This is Charlotte. Clémentine's baby sister."

He raises his eyebrows and his breath catches. "Clémentine? From home?"

"She died," Charlotte whispers.

Henri shakes the hair from his eyes but does not let go of my hands. "The king hasn't summoned me yet. When he does, I won't talk. I won't tell him anything, even if they torture me."

Andre steps forward, grabs the rails and peers through his hands. "We have a plan. We're going to rescue you. I promise I won't rest until we can all run free—together."

Henri trembles. His sinewy forearms twitch as he rocks back and forth. "Let me go. Save the rest of them."

I shake his hands to force his attention. "Your friend, Jacqueline Doré. She told me things. Important secrets that could ruin everyone at court. Not only are we going to save you, but I'm going to take out LaMarche, his wretched daughter, and everyone we can from the royal court."

He pulls me close. "I can't believe you're here."

"We started this together the moment they held us down and seared our flesh. That day, they branded our lives and our hearts. I think we've always been on this path. Only now, we have the power to do something about it."

"Well, you do. I'm stuck in this damp, dark cellar, dreaming of climbing the hills to Helvetia."

"Helvetia?" Charlotte asks.

"That's what I've heard. Protestants travel the mountains at night to escape. Mountain people protect them and steer them from the villages where Catholics thirst for their blood. The king has heard rumblings, but he doesn't know how they escape."

A voice rises from the darkness. "Ships take them in secret to England too."

A young man slides out of the shadows into the shaded sliver of light in the front of his cell. Andre steps closer. "How do you know that?"

"I... I help them. Well, I did before I landed in here. You're all Huguenot?"

Andre looks at Henri, who nods in approval, indicating we can trust him. "Yes, we are," Andre says.

"They arrested me last week on suspicion of treason. They're right. I hide Protestants on ships and under cargo. In carriage trunks and in trees if I have to. I get them out of France."

"Who's working for them now?" Andre asks.

The young man presses his cheeks to the bars. "There's a group here in Paris. We work together but separate, you understand?"

Andre nods.

"There's a family. They're expecting me to meet them in the corner of the Place Dauphine tonight. I can't let them down. Please help."

"What do you want us to do?" Andre asks.

"This man has been hiding. He refused to be sent to the Palace workhouses. A six-year-old girl needs him."

I shake my head. "This is LaMarche's doing. It must be."

"They've made quick work of this plan," Charlotte says.

The man grabs Andre. "All you have to do is meet them. Take them to the next hiding place. You'll be given another name and another point."

Andre leans closer to the bars. "Now you want me to run the Protestant resistance?"

"Just help them, then you can walk away. Please. That little girl? She's mine. I left her with my brother when my life grew dangerous. He can't die for protecting her. She has nothing left."

I turn to Henri. "You're certain we can trust him?"

"He's one of us, Isabelle. He's been out there fighting, just like we have."

A door bangs shut in the distance.

"Where do we take them?" Andre asks.

"Well... I don't know exactly. Someone in a red cap will tell you."

Andre closes his hand into a fist. "That doesn't help me."

Footsteps approach.

"I can't say any more than that. Please help."

I run to Henri. "We'll get you out, I promise." He nods, but I can tell his smile is for my benefit. He's losing hope. I kiss the back of his hand in the narrow slit between the bars and back away just as the guard approaches.

"Have you gotten what you need?" he asks.

"No, this man won't reveal a thing." I flip my skirts away from my shoes and nod to the guard. "Perhaps I will try again another day... if you haven't sent him to the stretcher by then."

All that training from Naira, all that teaching of how to bring a man to his knees, steal his knife, and protect myself, the most useful tool of all has been to control my emotions. I feign gratitude and smile at the man until he blushes. "See that I get on the approved list of visitors. I'm not done with him yet."

"Of course, Madame."

We follow him away from the corner cell where Henri and his young friend will die here if we don't save them. I glance over my shoulder to see Charlotte frozen, staring at Henri. I snap my finger and she turns to me, tears in her eyes. "We're just going to leave him?"

"I know," I whisper. "I know."

She catches up to us and we follow the guard back upstairs, where the nobility feasts and plays music and laughs as if they are at Versailles.

Andre leans to my ear. "Looks like I'll be at the Palace Dauphine tonight."

"You won't be there alone. Tonight, we save a Huguenot family. Tomorrow, we find the women with poisons."

CHAPTER NINETEEN

Under the dark, cloudless sky we are to find a man and his six-year-old niece, take them to an unknown location on the advice of someone in a red cap. With no idea what time this transfer is to occur. I know one thing—I would risk everything to save them. My plan is to stall until James goes to sleep so I may slip into the shadows under the moon and cross the Pont Neuf to Place Dauphine.

"His Majesty can't meet with us for an entire week." James throws his cravat on the table.

"I'm sure he's busy," I say. "He is the king."

"LaMarche sent notice to my father yesterday, demanding that he increase pressure on the merchants. He's organizing travel for them to Paris."

"Prisoners, you mean. Those merchants are now Huguenot prisoners."

He slides his fingers through his hair, exhaling his frustration. "I'm trying here, Isabelle."

"Are you?"

"Why would you say that?"

Because you stuffed your cockerel inside my sworn enemy. "You've lied to me so many times. What makes this any different?"

His jaw twitches, but he restrains his anger. "Sometimes it seems I can do no right with you."

"You met with LaMarche behind my back. You ordered slave ships when you promised you wouldn't. You called me a filthy traitor, and you let that hideous woman come between us."

James's eyes widen. He wonders if I know. I can see it in his eyes. He steps closer but does not touch me. "You practiced Protestantism in secret, hid your Bible in floorboards and kept a knife from the man you wish you would have married. You're not innocent."

Silence hovers between us as the sky dims toward night. James's face drops. He leans forward as if he wants to embrace me, but I don't budge. "I've made mistakes," he says. "But since the day they threw me in that Spanish prison, I've fought for you. I only wish you would try."

He's right—I've never fought for him. I've spent years ignoring who I am to be the wife he needs me to be.

The sky has turned to ink as darkness blankets the city. A six-year-old girl waits out there somewhere, hoping someone will save her.

"Come to bed with me," he says.

I turn from the window, staring at his vulnerable face, his open chest. "I will spend the night with Charlotte in the servant's room. If I stay with you, we will tangle our naked bodies up in tension and anger and ignore the very real truth that we despise each other."

"I haven't given up on you, Isabelle. I never will."

"Good night, James." I walk past him toward the servant's door.

He grabs my arm, pulls me close, and whispers in my ear. "When I convince the king to stop LaMarche, you'll see. I've tried to be a better man for you."

"Until then, James."

He releases his grip and tears crest his eyes. As I close the door to Charlotte's quarters, I wonder if he will stay here or go find another woman to get lost in.

"We must hurry," Charlotte whispers. "It's already night."

"I'm sorry, Charlotte, you need to stay here."

"No!" She tightens her lips like a pouting little girl.

"I'm sorry. I need you to watch James. He can't find out about Henri."

She thumps into the chair with arms crossed. "I came so I could help, not to sit in this lavish apartment and spy on your husband."

"I know, but you will help. I promise."

"Fine. I'll watch him. You better hurry."

I squeeze her hand. It must be torture for her. Our people suffer while she watches for my husband's mistress. I don't want her to disrupt our plan this evening, and I secretly want to know just how deep James's lies run.

I slip into the hallway with light feet, past the windows into the courtyard where couples dance and laugh. Through the south doors, into the empty courtyard, and under the arches, I make my way through the gardens toward Rue St.-Honoré.

Andre appears from the corner of the garden, motioning for me to join him. My heart thumps deep and hard, knowing we're taking a tremendous risk in a strange city.

We hide under the dark shadow of a manicured bush. "How are things inside?" he asks.

"James thinks I'm sleeping with Charlotte in the servant's quarters. She's watching him while we're out."

"Good. So, I've walked the Place Dauphine. There are two entrances. The west entrance exits to Pont Neuf, and the east entrance through the Île de la Cité."

"Why would they choose an island surrounded by the Seine?"

"The best way to hide someone is in plain sight. Besides, there are plenty of places to hide in dark corners."

"Shall we?"

His eyes flicker like shining gems. "A little girl's freedom awaits."

It's a short walk across the water. The arched bridge holds bastions, domed areas for passengers to step out of the way of carriages. But here, in the dark of night, they're filled with dubious vendors. Women slither along the bridge with their breasts exposed, tongues hanging from their mouths. Men in black hats hold signs offering everything from tobacco to tooth pulling. A man steps toward me, asking through a toothless grin if I would like to watch him touch the prostitute. Andre pulls me away and shoves the man to the ground as we carry on.

"Paris is nothing like Quebec," I mutter.

"Paris is nothing like anywhere."

In the middle of the bridge, we face the narrow point of a triangle. Two tall buildings create an entrance, a statue of Henry IV on a horse. "They do love their monuments."

"Come on." He places one hand softly on the small of my back and lowers his hat over his eyes with the other. We duck into a shaded corner and watch. People mill about while music and laughter seem to bounce out of the windows that line the triangle.

"There are so many people that live here, and all look down on the garden. I can't understand why they would meet here," I say.

Andre shrugs and we scan the courtyard. Nothing. No red cap, no little girl.

After nearly an hour, Andre breaks the silence. "Isabelle, what will happen after this?"

"I hope we'll see them sail away to England."

"No, after we stop the LaMarches and the slave ships. After we release Henri and fight to keep the Huguenots in their homes. What then?"

I consider that, not having spent any time thinking about what comes next. "I suppose we return to Quebec."

"My daughter is there. So is our Huron family. But you're meant for more. You always have been."

Moonlight slices through the black sky, shining a grainy illumination over Andre's eyes. "Maybe I don't want more."

"What do you want?" he asks.

I lean against the building and run my fingers over the rough stones. "I want this. To save them all one by one."

"And you can do that as James's wife?"

"When you can't have what you truly want, your heart finds a way to beat. It shrinks and expands in strange ways until it resembles something like comfort."

Andre's brow furrows, almost like he's in pain. He leans against the wall next to me. "Something like comfort." I know he's remembering Louise right now, and that his own twisted and stretched heart understands fully what I mean.

Suddenly, through the darkness, a slight figure in a red cap. Hands in the pockets of his loosened breeches, he strolls past, barely glancing over his shoulder.

"Is that him?" I ask.

"Sure looks like it."

We step in line behind this slim figure and follow him to the widened end of the triangle, into the arched arcade under the residences. He disappears and Andre and I spin in circles, wondering where to turn next.

Suddenly, Andre is thrown face first into the wall, hand behind his back. Without a moment to react, I knock my leg into the back of the man's knee and throw him to the ground. He's so slight, I can turn him to his back and hold his hands at his sides, while my body weight easily holds him in place. Except, he's not a man. He's a young girl whose blond hair has fallen out from under her cap.

"What were you thinking?" I say as I help her up.

"I wasn't sure I could trust you." She tucks her hair back in and straightens her clothing. "They never send two people."

"Who are *they*?" Andre says.

She looks around, checking the corners. "You know who."

"We are here to help a girl and her uncle. Her father is in the Bastille. He sent us in his place," I say.

"The Bastille?" She rubs her cheek and begins pacing. "Who are you?"

"We're friends," Andre says. "From La Rochelle."

She looks at me. "Not with those clothes you aren't."

"I'm married to a soldier in the Royal Army. But I assure you we are *friends*."

She paces, pulling at her doublet to ensure her breasts stay hidden. "I have no choice but to trust you."

I pull back my sleeve, show her my burned H. "We will do everything in our power to save this girl."

Her wide eyes resemble blown glass in the moonlight. She rolls them back and forth between Andre and me. "Can you fight?"

I launch toward her just fast enough to watch her flinch. "What do you think?"

"Fine. You need to get them out of the city walls." She sneers toward the east entrance. "The view from my residence looks into the court and the authorities have no idea that this wild artist hides heretics on their way to the next hiding spot."

"Why do you risk it? Are you Protestant?"

"No. The king and his royal pigs commission me to sculpt for them. My parents resisted during his takeover of the Parlement. They were exiled while this spoiled King revokes Parisians' rights. They all think me mad, and that works just fine for me."

"We'll get them safely to their next destination," Andre says.

"The right bank has fourteen gates with drawbridges over the moat. They're kept closed until six in the morning when the sun rises, but you must arrive early. A friend will lower one bridge two minutes earlier than the rest. Find him, escort the girl and her uncle to a wagon that waits in the field outside the gate. They will take them on to cross the channel to England."

"Sunrise?" I ask. "It's barely midnight. What are we to do with them for six hours?"

"That is now your problem. Another family arrives tonight. Stay out of sight and avoid the chained-off streets."

Before I can ask what that means, the girl disappears into the dark and returns with a tall man, holding the outstretched arm of a little girl who limps next to him. She looks closer to three than six.

"Be on your way," the artist says before being sucked into the dark shadows.

"Hello," I say to the girl.

She looks at her uncle. He nods. "Where are we going next?" she asks.

Andre straightens his jacket. "We must find somewhere safe to hide until the drawbridge opens. Come along."

We move slowly to accommodate the girl as she drags her right foot. The outside sole of her shoe has worn thin, and her right hand curls into a fist toward her chest.

We snake through the maze of narrow, winding streets, a few lit by flickering oil lamps. Tall wooden houses block out the moonlight, crowded together like stacks of books. The night is quiet and eerie, a thin mist hovering motionless in the air. The only sounds are meowing cats that blend into the dark, pattering feet, and one long slide from the girl's worn shoe.

We wander, not sure which direction to go. The walled city reminds me of La Rochelle, and all the nights Henri and I hugged the walls in the dark, hiding from the dragoons. I always felt like a rat, scurrying between shadows. Now I feel like a wolf, tracking its kill.

"Wait," the girl whispers. Her leg turns rigid, sending her body into tremors. Even her hair shakes, and she bites her bottom lip. The man lifts her, her body like a wooden plank.

"Is she all right?" Andre asks.

"She's had this since birth. We do our best to keep her comfortable but..." His voice trails off.

Footsteps approach. Heels click on the stones around the corner. A chain blocks the street to our right, so we guide them to an alley where chamber pot contents steam into the night. Everyone chokes on the smell, but we cover our mouths until the men pass. We watch the girl, waiting until her body calms.

"They patrol the neighborhoods and take names of visitors," the man says as he motions to the guards inside the chained streets.

Creeping out of the darkened alley, Andre and I glance at each other. The man situates the girl's limp body over his shoulder. Her sleepy eyes stare at me hopelessly.

"Where can we take them?" I whisper.

"We'll find somewhere," Andre says. He must see the worry in my eyes because he reaches for my fingers, brushes them so lightly I hardly know he's touched me.

We walk slowly, snaking in and out of moonlight shadows, listening only to our drumming footsteps.

I lean to the man's ear. "If we cross paths with someone, will they recognize you?"

"I am one of the more prominent weavers in Paris. And I killed a man."

He didn't need to say anything more.

"We met your brother," I say.

"In the Bastille?"

I nod. "He's with a friend of ours. What will happen to them?"

He glances over his shoulder and scans the windows for wandering eyes. "They're Protestants. What do you think will happen to them?"

My stomach compresses, tight and coiled.

"Here," Andre says.

We stop in front of a tall gate. I gaze down the curved wall to see another gate barely visible in the darkness. "There are fourteen of these. How do we find the one we need?"

Andre searches the empty street. "We have several hours to figure that out." He motions to the man. "Come on."

The houses are all shuttered, their peaked roofs casting slivers of darkness onto the cobblestones. Andre leads us to a stone structure tucked between two rows of houses. Inside, a large floor to ceiling fireplace smells of burnt wood.

"This is a communal oven," the man says as he pulls the girl tight. "The feudal lord will have us arrested if he finds us here."

"Then we must leave before he finds us," Andre says. "The city will stir soon enough, but for now, we can stay out of sight here." Andre finds an old blanket next to baskets in the corner and lays it gently over the girl. The man settles into a curved wall as Andre watches the little girl drift to sleep on her uncle's shoulder.

He sits next to me on the opposite wall.

"You miss Elizabeth," I say.

"I always miss her in the quiet of the morning. My life is not suited to being a father."

"Yet you are one."

He smiles, leans his head against the stone. "If it weren't for Naira, I don't know what I would do."

"You left your daughter and slept in puddles of spoiled wine to travel back to a country that didn't want you."

He picks up a stick and peels away layers. "I did."

The room smells of roasted wheat and yeast, a strangely comforting scent that reminds me of my childhood.

"I'm glad you're here with me," I say. My chest aches as I wait for his reaction.

He takes a deep breath and stares at the low, angled wooden roof, then back at me. "I'd like to tell you I feel the same, but I'm afraid you might pull away from me again."

I nibble on my bottom lip to restrain a smile. "The only thing I want to run from is the mistakes of my past."

"I understand," he says. "Part of me hopes that by helping you save those that didn't get the chance to flee, I can sleep again."

Dreams are the language of the soul. Our past haunts us through images and memories too dark and deep to forget. "You have trouble sleeping too?"

"It started when Elizabeth was born. I would watch her sleep and think about all the babies in France who'll be tortured, and their parents killed, all because of our faith." He tries to shake away the emotion, but I can see it stays heavy on his heart. "I guess her eyes make me feel like I see the eyes of every Protestant child, like they're all mine."

I want to cry, but I hold back the tears, not wanting to frighten the girl who still flutters her eyes open to watch us. "They *are* all yours. And mine. They are our past and our future, our hope for freedom. They are our murdered parents and tortured friends."

He turns sideways, leans his shoulder and head against the wall, and looks into my eyes. "Why do you trust James?"

"I never said I trust him."

"You're still with him."

"I need his power," I say. "The only way to stop an enemy is to keep them very, very close."

"So, your husband is your enemy?"

"Sometimes, yes." We're so close, I can smell the leather of his coat, and the remnant of green Quebec forests that still lingers on his skin. "I wonder if maybe I can't let go of the girl I used to be. If I conquer James, maybe I can find the strength to face my past."

"Will you stay with him? After all his betrayal?"

I want to say that I will run, that I will leave him and become the leader of the Protestant revolt. But I don't say that. Part of me thrives on the hate that James supplies. "No, I won't."

When I don't respond, Andre smiles. "You are a good person, Isabelle."

"Sometimes I wonder. I want to save them all for the right reasons, but it scares me… the things I'm willing to do." I stare at his stubbled jaw and red lips. "And my heart never fully recovered from you."

Andre's eyes move from my mouth to my eyes. "You don't need to justify a thing." He runs his hand along my cheek, moves a wayward curl from my brow. "You simply need to be the fierce fighter you were always meant to be."

I don't know why, but I lay my head in Andre's lap. Maybe I need to feel him close but cannot look into his eyes. Maybe I need to say I'm sorry for making the wrong choice three years ago. Or maybe, I want a break from fighting. Just for a few moments.

He strokes my hair and twists the curls around his fingers as I slip into a quiet slumber.

Andre wakes me as the birds chirp outside, the dark morning giving the slightest hint of sunrise to come. "It's time," he whispers. He lifts me to standing and smiles before waking the man. Andre lifts the girl from his arms. "He needs a rest."

The girl curls into Andre's neck, wraps her arm around his shoulder and Andre leans his cheek to her hair.

A few people mill about under the grainy black morning. The man lowers his head, pulls his hat down to cover his face.

"You stay with them," I say to Andre. "I'll find the gate."

I walk at a brisk pace along the wall, listening for any sign of chains or a crank of one gate ahead of the others. Men stare at me, unsure about a woman who isn't a prostitute lingering around the walls of the city.

I keep walking, faster and faster as the city stirs to life. A man approaches and I watch for eye contact. He looks over his shoulder, sees me, and turns to face me. "What are you doing out this early, fancy thing such as yourself?"

"Are you here to lower the bridge?"

"It's still a few minutes early. I'm under strict orders to wait until sunrise."

I glance back, estimating it would take five minutes to get them here. "I'm here to cross, if you'd lower the bridge a bit early."

He steps forward. "Are you asking me to break orders? Or are you just some rich wench who thinks she can tell the commoners what to do?"

I step back, realizing he is not our man. "Sorry to trouble you, monsieur."

I keep walking and listening. It could take an hour to find the right one. I decide to run back and grab the group. It's nearly time and I don't know what else to do. "Come on, we will have to do this together."

The man lifts the girl, still sleepy on his shoulder. Andre and I walk in front of them, our eyes scanning for trouble.

"Hey, what are you doing out here this early?" a man yells.

"Simply visiting family, monsieur," I say. We speed up, ducking into an alley when we see two men about to cross our path.

I close my eyes and listen. I hear nothing. No metal, no creaking drawbridge. Suddenly, a noise. "I think that's it," I say. "Come on."

We rush to the wall, only to hear another bridge lower. Then another. It must be time for all of them to open.

"We missed it," Andre mutters. "Every one of these men will be on the lookout for our well-known weaver and the little girl who drags her foot."

"So, we find another way." Without time to question myself, I lead them to the closest bridge, manned by a stocky worker in threadbare clothes with a dirty face and tired eyes. "Wait here and cross when I have him distracted," I tell them.

"Good day, monsieur," I say with a smile.

The man nods, too sleepy to respond.

"Might you help me?" I ask. "I'm in search of a farm."

He completes his job, lowers the bridge until it clicks into place, working far too close to the man and his sleeping niece on the edge of the wall. He grunts and rubs his eyes. "I have another three bridges to open."

"Please, monsieur, I hate to be out here by myself in the dark."

He glances at me and steps forward. "What farm?"

"I'm not sure. My husband requests fresh eggs in the morning. He's an important man, you see." Andre steps from behind the wall, the man and girl in stride behind him. I turn the man to face me. "He works for the king, my husband. You understand? I need fresh eggs and I don't have any. Where can I purchase some?"

"All right," the man snaps. "Just cross the moat and go straight for ten minutes. There are a dozen farms that can help you. Now, let me return to work." He pulls from me just as Andre crosses behind. I yank the man's doublet to turn his back to our group. "You're kind, sir. Perhaps I will repay you with an egg or two."

"Fine. Now release me." He shakes himself free. The group has crossed, walking away on the path toward the green hills.

The bridge creaks underfoot as I hasten toward them. "That wasn't so hard."

"The artist told us to find a wagon," Andre says.

"We should walk then." I start ahead, noting the man fatiguing already, but we have no choice but to press on. The sun has appeared from behind the horizon, a deep orange glow bright enough to cause me to squint.

Through the glare, a shadow forms. "You. You aren't that Huguenot they're looking for, are you?"

The man's voice was not unkind. Still, my body tenses.

"You must be mistaken, monsieur," Andre says as he leads him away.

"No, I'm not." He turns to follow us, yanking on the man's sleeve. "I know it's you. The weaver."

"Be on your way, monsieur," Andre says.

The man produces a knife. "No, I'm going to turn this man in and get the reward. We don't want any filthy Huguenots roaming around, do we?"

The girl stirs, lifting her head to stare at the man with a knife.

"You can get the stretcher," he says, "And that invalid girl can rot in prison for all I care."

Andre steps forward, arms out. "Go," he tells the silk weaver.

"I can fight with the best of them," the man says, tightening his hand around the handle of his knife. "There's too much money in this criminal." He walks sideways, toward the girl.

I rush to help, but the man with the knife slashes his blade through the air near me. "Leave them, woman."

I pretend to shrink away, fearful of his pathetic blade. He has no idea I once threw a tomahawk into the eye of a white-tailed deer. The man launches himself at Andre, narrowly missing his stomach. Andre hovers, waiting for the man's next move. He lunges again, grabbing Andre's wrist. Andre reaches for the hand with the blade while sending his knee into the man's thigh. He's strong though, and writhes his arm free, taking a slash through Andre's coat. The leather stops it some, but the blade contacts his chest and bright red blood seeps through the fabric.

The man makes the mistake of turning his back to me.

As he grabs Andre's doublet, I slide low, slicing my foot across his, sending him to his knees. My hand on his hair, I throw my body weight forward, sending his face to the dirt. I jab my knee into his back, both hands on his shoulders, pulling until I hear his spine pop. Andre launches for his knife while he's distracted. I lock my knees over his wrists and my legs over the back of his knees.

With a mouth full of dirt, he mutters, "Filthy whore."

I grab the blade from Andre and crash the handle into the man's forehead, careful to avoid his temple. I cracked his skull just hard enough that he'll still live but wake with one wicked headache.

I stand and dust off my skirt, swipe my curls from my face. They all stare at me, mouths agape.

"Who's going to help me find a wagon?" I ask.

And we do find the wagon just as it's about to leave. The man and his niece crawl into the back and wave goodbye. I hope they will make it to England safely, but I can't stop thinking of the girl's father in the Bastille. How unfair it is that some live and some die.

As Andre and I walk back to the Palais Royale, daybreak rises around us with people and laughter and hurried movement. My hands still tingle with the rush of fighting.

"Naira taught you well," Andre says.

"She did."

"I'm grateful to have you on my side, little wolf."

I can't contain my smile, remembering his hand brushing through my hair, his connection to Naira, how he sees the woman I wish to be.

"I'm merely getting started." I unbutton his doublet and run my finger along his bloody shirt.

"It's nothing," he says.

"It's not nothing. You're bleeding." I press my hand against his chest.

"Barely a scratch," he says with a smile. "And what's next for us, madame?"

"Three women hide a poisonous secret. We use them to help rescue Henri."

"And what about the king?"

Beyond the city wall is a girl in a wagon, fighting for a chance to live free as her father withers away in a prison cell to give her that opportunity. "The court will see a pious soldier's wife. A Daughter of the King. Underneath these lies lives an angry Protestant who will never forget. A Huguenot who will risk her life to save another girl and another uncle and father."

"I do believe on the other side of the world, Naira is smiling," Andre says.

"She was right. It's best to attack a man when he least expects it."

CHAPTER TWENTY

With Andre tucked away in a basement room to catch up on sleep, I creep back into Charlotte's quarters. She grabs me by the arm and drags me through the door.

"You were gone all night," she says. "James was furious."

"You let me deal with him."

Charlotte steps closer, hands cradled together. "Did you save them?"

"We got them out of the city. The rest is out of our hands." I stop to examine her perfectly coiffed hair. "You're dressed lovely today."

"I'm prepared for anything."

I face the door to gather my strength and focus.

"Be careful with your words," Charlotte whispers. "He secured a party tonight and expects you to accompany him."

I nod, grateful for her help.

Through the door, I find James examining documents and maps. He doesn't look up, but his voice conveys a warning. "Where were you?" he barks.

"I think you have lost the right to know my every move."

He closes his eyes, tightens his lips. "I am your husband. You cannot allow your childish insecurities to come between us."

Childish. He still doesn't know I watched him bed Antoinette. I could tell him. Prove that I'm justified in my hate. But it would change everything. He would turn weak, allow his emotions to take over. He'd become unpredictable. No, I need him where I've always needed him. Angry, with me just out of reach.

"I was searching for someone who can help us," I say.

"I don't want my wife crawling around Paris at night."

I've forced myself closer, every step painful. He should think I need him. "I was searching for the women Madame Doré told me about." A little lie to keep him from questioning me.

"Mistresses? Why would you be on the Paris streets looking for them?" The magnifying glass cracks against the wood when he slams it on the table.

"Not just mistresses," I say. "Some have other secrets."

James straightens his spine, eyes narrowed. "What do you know?"

"They run an apothecary… where a woman might be treated."

It's obvious he's growing impatient. "I don't understand. Why did you hide this from me?"

Only way to keep him satisfied is to make him think I've protected him. "It's quite unsavory. A secret apothecary where women go to rid themselves of an unwanted pregnancy. Surely you want nothing to do with that."

He softens, leans his shoulders to me. "You still should not be running around in the dark."

"Like I did in Quebec?"

"This isn't the colony. The nobility live here. If anyone sees you…"

I place my hands on his chest, lean my body into his. "You secured an invitation for tonight, I hear."

"Yes." He looks down at me, hungry, and hating himself for it. "We can discover who in the nobility is weakest."

While he busies himself with nobles and vying for his way into the ranks of Parisian nobility, I'll be searching for my own secrets. I remind myself that James's ambition can only help us. As long as he doesn't discover Andre or our secret Huguenot resistance.

Lying is easy once you have justification for it.

James wraps his hand around my waist and pulls me close. "I know you don't trust me."

I glance behind him at the documents on the table. "What are those?"

He motions for me to read them. "LaMarche obtained them. Accounts of the king's dealings in the East Indies."

"How did LaMarche get these?"

"A noble of the Treasury owes him a favor."

I trail my finger over the papers and pretend to act bored. "I'm quite tired," I say. "I think I'll rest."

"Fine." James wraps his documents in a leather folder and pulls the leather to his chest.

"You are doing all this to stop LaMarche?" I ask.

"I give him the loyalty he demands, but secretly, I plan to become a marquis or a baron, and he will bow to my power."

James's confidence is his greatest charm—and his greatest weakness.

"I will see you tonight then," I say.

"Yes. I've ordered new clothing for you. The seamstress will arrive at noon. We mustn't look like wild things from Canada."

I think of Naira and want to slap the words right off his tongue.

After James leaves, I collapse on the bed, thinking of ways to save Henri, when sleep takes over and I fall into slumber in the bright morning sun.

. . . . .

The seamstress spent hours here, working until her fingers cramped, but she nearly cried when she stared at her finished product. My dress is so large I wonder how to remain upright. Royal blue silk hugs my waist and cascades to the floor, gold stitching catching the light. The neckline scoops so low I wonder if it's indecent, but she crowned the edge with a gold bow. Every woman in Paris seems to expose her décolleté.

The seamstress points to the bow. "To bring attention." The only three words she has spoken all afternoon.

I stare into the mirror built into the wall of the dressing room. The Huguenot who wore scratchy gray wool would despise the liar I've become. I must continually remind myself that this is not me. I am and will always be the girl in the shadows.

Charlotte opens the door and inhales a sharp breath. "Isabelle?"

"I know. It's unnecessary."

She walks up behind me, examining my reflection. "You're stunning."

The silk gown and rigid stomacher weigh so much I grow lightheaded. "It's no wonder women of the court hardly speak. It's difficult to draw a breath against all this."

"You will charm them all, I'm sure. You were made for this."

I turn to face her, about to say that I would rather learn to fight from Naira in the muddy earth of Quebec. I suddenly realize she's been gone all day. "Where have you been?"

"Oh." She runs her hands along her waist.

She blushes like summer fruit. "Well?"

"I went to visit Henri."

"You went to the Bastille unaccompanied?"

She leads me away from the window and unpins her hair. Her long blond locks fall away to reveal a miniature book. "I hide our Bible in my hair."

The worn book is so small I wonder how she can read the words. "You read from the Geneva Bible in a royal prison?"

She nods. "I remember you and Henri running through the streets of La Rochelle. My sister would tell me how brave you both were. I once saw Henri steal salted meat, and he winked before handing me a piece. I felt a thrill that made my neck tingle and I watched for him everywhere. After they burned his father and Henri disappeared, I couldn't bear it."

"That's why you were eager to come to Paris."

"Yes. That and the obvious. I came to help you. We can make a difference. I know we can."

"Did Henri enjoy your visit?" I ask.

Charlotte beams and I consider telling the poor girl to control her affections, but I can see it is too late.

"I believe he did," she says.

I place my hand on hers. "Hide that Bible. James will return any moment."

She tucks the Bible in the lining of her underskirt. "I will dress quickly." She walks to her door but stops. "James left last night around midnight."

"Oh?"

"I followed him. He went one floor up. To Antoinette's apartment."

A strange rush of excitement pounds through me. I've become dependent on my anger for him. "Thank you, Charlotte."

I spend the next hour staring out the window, fussing with this ridiculous gown, considering my situation. I've used the heat between James and I, drank it like oil to feed a flame. How difficult it might be to fight without it.

The door latches open, and I turn slowly, forcing a stoic face.

James takes a deep breath. "Stunning."

"It's merely fabric, James."

He approaches, dressed in an intricately stitched doublet and breeches elaborate enough to pass as a skirt. Ribbons hang from his waist and sleeves. He examines me, runs his hand along my cheek. "You are the most beautiful woman in the world."

The incredibly sad thing is that he means those words. Beauty blinds him. With all the lies between us, all I see is his exposed, blackened soul.

"Enough of that." I pull from him. "Are we ready?"

"I have something for you." He reaches into his pocket and pulls out a string of pearls. "All the noble women wear them." He turns me to face the mirror and lowers the strand over my neck. The cool stones sit on my flushed skin.

"You will waste all our money on clothing and jewels."

"It's required here." He lowers his lips to my neck, kisses the curve as he slides his other hand around my stomach to hold me against him in a suffocating embrace. "I need you."

How true those words are. I remind myself that the only way into the royal circle is through him. "Shall we?"

"Yes, my darling." He wraps his arm around mine and I call for Charlotte, who steps in behind us, straightening my skirts.

As we exit the Palais Royale, I lean to whisper to Charlotte. "Have you seen Andre?"

"He went to talk to the artist. To find another family to save."

My heart thumps deep in my chest when I think of Andre. James is unaware of my secret life, just as his remains hidden. Perhaps this suits us fine.

Only a few streets away, brightly lit by oil lamps, we arrive at a manor house so grand, I wonder if there are several houses in one. "Where are we?"

"Le Marais," James says. "Where we will live someday." I stifle a groan as he winks at me. "The duke is on the king's royal counsel. His wife entertains every influential person in Paris."

We enter the foyer. Painted walls drip with gold and crystal sconces. Oil paintings trimmed in metallic frames glitter with amber candlelight. A servant bows and offers us champagne, but I need to keep my wits, and politely pass. James leads us past the grand staircase to the ballroom. Floor to ceiling mirrors framed with gold scroll make the room look like it never ends.

"The people," Charlotte says. "They're all so beautiful. Too bad they're also monsters."

I warn her with a stern look.

"Come." James leads me to a circle of nobility who all smile politely. The men wear wigs of buoyant curls. Many women have drawn beauty marks on their upper lip and wear black moons and stars on their cheeks. "Good evening," James says. "May I introduce you all to my lovely wife, Madame Beaumont."

They smile, but just barely. As if they can tell I'll never be one of them. James, however, blends in like the damask drapes. He joins the men by the fire and Charlotte fans me as she whispers, "Who are we looking for?"

"I'll know when I see her."

I scan the room, through women with ringlet curls and dresses so large they cannot sit. Madame Doré told me everything I need to know. "Patience." I say it for Charlotte's benefit, but I also need the reminder.

Hours go by as we busy ourselves with music and food. We admire the elaborate sculptures that line the hallways. James returns, face red and happy. "So much power in this room, Isabelle. I'm learning how a man may buy his way into the king's circle."

"Wonderful, James."

"Are you staying busy?" he asks.

Poor, simple man has no idea I have my own purpose here tonight. "Yes. Now go."

Just as hope begins to slide away, I glimpse a woman—the one I've been looking for. Her hair shines light red, so blushed it appears pink. As she ducks into the parlor, I grab Charlotte's arm. "Her."

We pretend to admire the vases and tapestries as we approach the room where this woman seems to entertain a multitude of men, and a few women. She tells jokes and laughs loudly. Unrestrained.

Jacqueline prepared me for this. I know too much about this woman. Charlotte and I near, watching how she holds the attention of everyone in the room. Her pale skin practically glows, a kiss of freckles on her nose and cheeks making her appear more youthful than she is.

"Please, enjoy your evening," the woman says. "And leave me be!" She feigns fatigue, and the room erupts in laughter but still backs away, giving her space to be fanned by her lady's maid.

We approach and the woman stares at us, confused. "I don't believe we've met. I would remember a woman with those stunning auburn curls and green eyes." She instructs her lady to stop fanning. "So green they look like glass reflecting the leaves."

"Thank you, Mademoiselle Boulais."

Her hand to her chest, she says, "You know my name?"

"A friend sent me. Madame Doré."

She freezes, her bright face washed of all its color. "Madame Doré? Why, no one has heard from her in years. Rumors say she disappeared to live in the mountains with the goats."

"No," I say. "She lives quite well in the colonies. She asked me to relay a message."

Mademoiselle Boulais stands and fluffs her dress. "Come with me."

We follow her up the stairs and through a door to a long, dark hallway. I nod to a hesitant Charlotte to reassure her I can protect us both. Mademoiselle opens a door and pulls us inside. A small but lovely room, with a window overlooking the Seine.

"What did she tell you?" she asks.

"That you are the woman to see if we need something soft and white. Inheritance powder, I believe you call it."

She searches our faces. "Perhaps I might know of such a thing."

"Inheritance powder?" Charlotte repeats.

"So called because women use it to kill their husbands. Or fathers, or anyone else they may choose, so they may inherit their fortune," I say.

"There are many versions of arsenic floating around the city. Half the women downstairs in the ballroom have it hidden in their perfume bottles, dreaming of the day they may send their husbands to the grave."

"But you," I say, "you have grand plans, don't you? Have you begun poisoning the royal court yet?"

She tightens her lips and takes a steady breath. "I've done nothing of the sort. Perhaps I will have you thrown out of here."

"Where are we?" I look around. "Whose room is this?"

"It's mine. I'm the duke's mistress and sometimes I stay here where he can access me any time of the day and night."

"You live under his roof? While he sleeps in bed with his wife?" I ask.

"Madame, you obviously have not been in Paris long. Every powerful man keeps mistresses as a symbol of wealth and status."

"I suppose I don't belong in this world, then."

Music from the ballroom downstairs vibrates a soft rhythm in the floorboards.

"What did you say your name was?" mademoiselle asks.

"I didn't." I eye a perfume bottle on her vanity and wonder if poison fills the glass. "Madame Beaumont. My husband is a Royal Soldier."

"I could have you killed." She unrolls a fan and waves it to her neck. "You know that, I'm sure."

"But you won't. I know too much. And you don't know who else I've told."

She runs her hand along her chest, twirling a curl at her shoulders. "Madame Doré is a known liar."

"Then why do you look so frightened?"

"What is it you want? I have many houses like this. With my own room, and exclusive access to the men I desire. You want money? Power?"

"No," I say. "I want your help."

"You want to kill someone?" She doesn't whisper and intrigue rings in her voice.

"I know the king's mistress dabbles in magic and sorcery," I say. "He would have her sent to the rack if he knew."

Mademoiselle Boulais stares at Charlotte. "You aren't a normal lady's maid. What are you doing here?"

"Let's just say I have a purpose. My own list of names I would like to eliminate with one of your powders."

Charlotte's intensity is unsettling—as is her ability to jump into this conversation without hesitation.

"We know the mistress has considered poisoning the king," I say. "We don't want to ruin her... or you, but we need your help."

"What do you want?"

"You have relations with the royal treasurer, yes?"

"Yes."

"The LaMarches, a father and daughter, are trying to undermine the king's trade. They have begun their own company, bringing in slaves from Africa and sending out goods for export. I need him to stop them."

"Why?"

"When you offer a patron arsenic or belladonna, do you ask why?"

"Usually, the women are covered in bruises and scratches. You, I can see, have another agenda."

Moonlight twinkles on the Seine, which shines as bright as polished silver out her tiny window. "It's for a good reason, I assure you."

"The LaMarches are pests," Mademoiselle Boulais says. "She's desperate for attention and him, well, he would slice off his own finger for a bucket of gold."

"That's them."

"If I report this to the treasurer, and he can find cause to arrest the LaMarches for treason, you will leave me alone?"

"You'll never see me again."

Her pale skin has turned to pink circles on her cheeks and chin. "I need assurance."

Charlotte steps forward. "Give me your fastest acting poison. Now I will be one of your customers and you can report me if we don't stay true to our word."

Does this girl understand what she's walking into? "Charlotte, careful."

"No." She defiantly shakes me off. "You are too careful. Too loyal to people who wrong you. I want revenge."

Mademoiselle Boulais smiles. "Meet me at my house tomorrow. The narrow home next to the pâtissier in Faubourg Saint-Antoine. I will see what I can do for you."

"Good evening, Mademoiselle." I lead Charlotte away, down the hall and stairway, and pull her into the dark corner beneath the stairs.

"What was that?" I ask.

"She'll want to work with us if we are just as naughty as her. She wants nothing to do with piousness."

I pull back and realize she's right. "You certainly can read people."

"Besides, poison might be our only way to release Henri," she says.

"What are you planning to do, poison a guard?"

She shrugs. "Perhaps. And I wouldn't lose a wink of sleep over it."

"If you aren't careful, you'll soon be carrying hemlock in your hair instead of that Bible."

"I'm sure whoever I carried it for would deserve it."

James appears. "There you are. What are you doing under the stairs?"

"Nothing." I pull Charlotte into the foyer. "Was your night successful?"

"Very." He smiles and raises his eyebrows. "I might have found a way to gain the king's good graces. And you?"

I glance at Charlotte, noting her stern eyes. "Nothing to report, I'm afraid."

"Well then, I have more to discuss with the duke. Apparently, His Majesty takes financial advice from his mistress. What a foolish mistake."

"That's understating it," Charlotte mutters.

I knock my hips to hers hard enough to send her off-balance. "We'll return home to rest and let you conquer the nobility."

James swoops me into his arms and plants a kiss on me. He doesn't seem to care that I've pulled away, cringing. "This is going to work, Isabelle. We can be more powerful than the LaMarches. More powerful than any man or woman in that ballroom. It will all be worth the sacrifice."

I suddenly realize what he's inferring. He's sleeping with Antoinette as a means to our end. He thinks he can satisfy the LaMarches while furthering his own ambitions, believing that I will be there at the end, willing to forget all he did on his quest for power.

The heat between us worked... until it didn't.

"Good night, James."

He smiles like a schoolboy and struts back to the party.

Charlotte glances at me. "When will you tell him that his touch is akin to kissing a toad?"

"When I no longer need him."

We settle back into our apartment, and I require Charlotte's assistance to disrobe me. I used to think servants were so the rich wouldn't have to lift a finger. Now I realize that it's impossible to remove one's body from these unnecessary clothes. She hands me a nightdress, but I reach for my simplest gown.

"Another night of shadow hopping?" she asks with a smile.

I kiss her cheek. "Charlotte, someday you will make a man very happy—or very terrified. Choose wisely."

Back down the hall and stairwell, toward the basement. In the storage room, I find Andre leaned against the wall, foot propped up behind him. His tousled hair looks wild, like his eyes.

"Who are we saving tonight?" I ask.

"A sixteen-year-old who can save her parents if she converts and marries the Catholic that threatens their family. We must get her outside of Paris and on her way to Geneva."

"The night is young." I lace my fingers through his and stare deep into his eyes as my stomach thumps with anticipation. "We can be back here before anyone is the wiser."

"Or..." He looks down at our hands clasped together. "We can search the city. I'm sure there is more trouble to be had."

"It seems Paris is full of women with dark secrets," I say.

"Does that mean you've found the woman you came here to meet?"

"It does. And with any luck, I'll beat James and the LaMarches before they understand just how far I'm willing to go."

"Never underestimate a quiet woman," Andre says.

"It's the quiet ones who listen the best."

Andre's eyes meet mine and his smile nearly knocks the breath straight from my chest.

CHAPTER TWENTY-ONE

The narrow house next to the pâtissier's kitchen leans to the right. People walk past, not seeming to realize that hidden inside are poisons and powders capable of stopping a man's heart. A clever sign that reads "Palm Reader" hangs from a nail by the side door. Once I gain her favor, my plan will come to life, and I'll be free to shuttle as many Huguenots as I wish through the shadows, and into the freedom that waits outside of France.

Mademoiselle Boulais opens the door with a smile. She wears a black robe that covers her arms and neck, with a linen apron over top. "Come in, my darlings."

She seems quite casual for a woman whose secrets could kill.

"Welcome to my home. Well, I do not live here, only brew potions and the like. My home is all over Paris." She wiggles her fingers in our direction.

"I can't believe that you trust us already," I say.

"Oh, I do not trust *you*. I trust her." She nods at Charlotte. "Anger boils inside of her. I can see why she wants my poisons. I understand her."

"You need not understand me, Mademoiselle Boulais."

"You force me into a high-risk game by threatening me. I think I understand you well enough."

"The last thing I want is to reveal your secrets," I say. "I don't wish to save any of those men at court." It's true, though I don't have the seething need for revenge Charlotte and Henri do.

"If I can't brew my potions," she says, "women will suffer. Beaten by their husbands and kept from their own money. Left with nothing when the husband dies."

We stare at each other for a long moment, neither of us breaking eye contact.

"Show me your options?" Charlotte asks.

Mademoiselle cocks her head and examines Charlotte. "You want to know about black magic?"

"Very much."

"Come with me." She leads us through a door, into a dark room with shaded windows. The air is thick and smoky, with an acidic bite.

"What is that smell?" Charlotte asks.

"Arsenic. When heated, it releases a sweet, garlic smell."

Shelves line the discolored walls, holding glass jars of powders and roots, liquids, and teas. "Where did you learn all this?" Charlotte asks.

"One of my lovers was a chemist. A brilliant man who isn't part of the court or even the nobility. He taught me everything."

"Was?" Charlotte asks.

"He died in an experiment gone wrong. Such a sad loss."

I examine the jars, filled with oddities I can't quite understand. Nail clippings. Dried flies. Something powdered and red like clay dust.

"Dried menstrual blood," she says. "We think the body excretes toxins and waste, but the blood from a woman's womb is incredibly powerful."

"What are you brewing here?" Charlotte points to a cauldron over simmering water.

"Savon noir. It's an arsenic paste you rub on your husband's clothing. It causes weeping blisters on his skin that lead to a fever."

"How can that be useful?" Charlotte asks, with a little too much interest.

"The poisoner can tend to her husband's ailments to avoid suspicion. She can play the caring, concerned wife… while she slowly feeds him arsenic powder in his food and wine."

"Why are you showing us this?" I ask.

"I want you to see that I do something awful, but for the best of reasons. Women have nothing in this world. We are merely owned by the men in our life, with no way to earn money. They dress us up in fancy clothing and strip us naked when it suits them. They also bruise and break us at their will."

"Most of your clients are these types of women?" I ask.

"Among others. I do not question their motives."

"What are all these?" Charlotte points to vials that hang from hooks.

"Toad poison. Witch's thimble. Hemlock." She runs her hand along the glass tubes, pointing to each one. "Blobs of hanged-man's fat. Belladonna. Excrement, urine, and semen."

"I do not wish to know how you obtained those," I say.

"Don't act as though you are better than me, Madame Beaumont. I know you have secrets." She leans toward me. "We all do."

There's something unsettling about a woman who keeps blood and nail clippings within arm's reach. "All we ask is that you request the Treasurer of France seize their ships that buy slaves and compete with the king's trade."

"I'll do it," she says. "Mostly because I despise LaMarche. He's known for being rough with his mistresses."

"That doesn't surprise me."

"We all hate Monsieur LaMarche," Charlotte says. "He made our lives miserable in La Rochelle."

"Well, ladies, this is Paris. Where women perform dark deeds to keep alive. Once you have worked with me, you are one of us. No running because we now know your dark truths."

"We've killed no one," I say.

She hands Charlotte a velvet bag. "Not yet. But perhaps you might find a use for my special kind of favor."

Charlotte opens the bag and removes a perfume bottle.

"I do more than make poisons, Madame Beaumont. I'm an alchemist and a fortune teller. Perhaps you might need a poison in your travels."

"I'm certain I will not."

Charlotte closes the bag and tucks it under her arm.

"Charlotte," I warn, "we don't want to be caught up in this."

"Isabelle, we're threatening the aristocracy. We need protection."

Black ash gathers in the fireplace as the logs crackle and burn. Orange flames lick the cauldron's sides and send smoke curling into the chimney.

"Bring that if you must, Charlotte, but I want nothing to do with it."

Mademoiselle opens a drawer and hands me a round pewter case smaller than my palm. "Keep it close. It's sleeping powder. I have a feeling this will suit your needs."

"How do I know this isn't arsenic?"

"Oh, you don't," she says with a smirk. "You will just have to trust me."

I grab Charlotte's arm and drag her out of that dark room. She looks over her shoulder, eyeing Boulais with admiration.

Once outside, I ensure Charlotte has hidden her bag. "I can't believe you took that."

"What?" she asks. "You're the one with a palm full of sleeping powder."

The cold, delicate pewter presses against my hand and I convince myself that it can't hurt to have a little black magic on our side.

⋅ • ⋅

As Charlotte and I approach the gardens, a hand reaches from the trees and pulls us into the shade. We gasp, but exhale when we realize it's Andre.

"A maid found me in the storage room and threatened to call the authorities. She thought I was a beggar."

"They can ask for your papers and banish you from the city if you aren't from Paris," Charlotte says. "I heard another lady's maid talking about it."

"Even the poor hold rank here," Andre says.

"We made an acquaintance this morning." I open my hand to show him the hidden powder.

"Well done," he says.

"And you?" I ask.

"I came across another family that needs our help. They must flee to Geneva."

"That could take weeks."

"There's no one else to help. This artist says the network isn't strong."

"Not yet," Charlotte says.

For all her wild ways, I do admire her optimism. Mine has dulled over time, worn down by circumstance. It's not the setbacks that tear at my hope, but the distance I seem to drift from where I started. Charlotte has shown me that my fighting spirit has been chipped away over the years, like a narrow chisel through a slab of oak. Each shave is small, but over time, grooves and depressions have left me altered forever.

"We can't escort them to Geneva," I say. "We need to get Henri out."

"About that," Charlotte says. "I've been watching. There's a shortage of guards. I heard them talking and from midnight to two, there are only two guards for the entire prison. We could use the sleeping powder and steal the key."

My stomach coils with the thought of poisoning a guard, but then I remember the wolf—her green eyes, the intensity of her stare. My pack has called on me to fight.

"Tonight?" Charlotte asks.

"We need somewhere to keep him," I say. "We can't break him out of prison without a plan."

"I can ask Mademoiselle Boulais to house him," Charlotte says.

"I don't think we want another favor from her."

Charlotte bites her lip. "Well, we must figure something out. Henri will face the royal interviewers by the end of the week."

"Why haven't you told us about that until now?" I ask.

"I was trying to find a way to help. I want to do more than watch your husband sneak into his mistress's bed."

Andre's eyes go wide, but my expression remains still as stone.

"I'm sorry, Isabelle." Charlotte reaches for my arm. "I shouldn't have said that."

"Never mind. Andre, you will stay with us."

"You?" he asks. "I don't suppose your husband would appreciate my presence."

"We'll keep you hidden. We need you close, out of sight, and ready to act when we say."

"Yes, madame."

His smile once again has the power to bend the iron cage around my heart.

Andre tucks behind the two of us as we enter the Palais Royale. Among the residents are exiled English royalty, and the king's official mistress, Madame de Montagne, who's been working hard to gain all his attention, aided by master alchemist Mademoiselle Boulais.

We stay under cover of arches, skirting the open gardens and courtyards, and slip one by one through the door near the theater.

Andre joins Charlotte in her room while I search for James. He appears to be gone for the day. I return to Charlotte's and ensure the door is locked. "We need a plan."

"Geneva?" Andre asks.

"But Henri," Charlotte says.

"Let me think." I pace the room, stopping to stare out the window to the courtyard. "If we can break Henri free, we need to get him out of the city immediately."

"He can come with us to Helvetia," Andre says.

"Andre, we can't travel for weeks just to get this girl to Geneva."

"Why not?" He steps close, shoulders leaned toward me eagerly. "We came here to save Huguenots, and that is what I plan to do."

"I *am* trying to save them." I push the window open for fresh air, to help myself think.

"By attending parties and playing royalty with James?" Andre says. "That's unfair."

Charlotte tucks her Bible in her skirt. "I think I'll go visit Henri, get some more information. It appears you two need a moment."

She ducks out of the room, glancing at me as she closes the door.

"What happened to the woman who galloped through a dark, snowy forest with me?" he asks. "The one who traveled into Iroquois territory to save me?"

"She's gone." As soon as the words leave my mouth, I can't believe I've said them. I can't believe I feel them.

His voice softens. "No, she isn't." He holds my arms and looks into my eyes. "You can dress up in layers of silk and strings of pearls, but you will always be a fighter."

I don't pull away from his touch. "I want to save more than just Henri and this girl. I'm trying to stop them from turning all of us into slaves."

He slides one hand down my arm. "Can't we do both?"

"It's too much. I don't know how to do it all."

"Isabelle." He places his finger under my chin and turns my face to his. "Naira prepared you for this. All she did was show you who you already are."

His touch weakens any resistance I have. He makes me want to save them all and face the LaMarches and defy the king. He leans toward me, our breaths heavy, the room hot. His hand slides from my chin to my cheek, cupping my face in his strong hand. I lean into the pressure, remembering our passionate kisses from a lifetime ago. How his lips took me somewhere James never could.

A door opens and shuts.

"James." I pull away, grab Andre's hands. "Hurry. Under the bed."

Andre throws himself to the floor and slides under the bed, tucking his feet in just as James steps inside. "There you are. What are you doing in here?"

"Looking for Charlotte. It appears she's taking some fresh air."

"Good. I have you alone." He rushes to me, takes my hands in his. I can hear Andre's breathing and I wonder if James can too.

"What is it?" I ask.

"We have an audience with the king." His cheeks are flushed crimson and his eyes glisten with excitement. "He's returned from Versailles early and wishes to meet with us."

I try to turn him so his back is to the bed, but he won't budge. "That's wonderful."

"We're so close, Isabelle. I've secured knowledge on every noble in this town. I know who is lying, who is cheating. Who we need to destroy."

In James's world, only the men have worthy secrets. This is how Mademoiselle Boulais has remained successful. No one thinks to question the women.

"And once you gain your noble status, what about everything else?"

"What everything else?"

I want to slap him. He knows exactly what we promised. "Don't play games with me." I yank my hands from his and rub them together, turning to walk back to our apartment.

"Don't walk away from me."

I throw the door open with a shove. "What will you tell the king tomorrow?"

James doesn't move and stays in Charlotte's room. "That the LaMarches are trying to compete with his trade. I'll offer money and secrets and ask for noble status."

"You will stop making Huguenots prisoners? Stop the slave trade?"

"I have no need for either of those once I gain my title."

The bed creaks when Andre shifts. James glances back, but I grab his hands. "Come, let's have wine and discuss tomorrow."

He pulls me into him, arms around my waist. "We can live the life we've always wanted. Nobles here in Paris."

I have never wanted either of those things.

"Don't you want to forget all those years of pain and enjoy the power of being close to the Crown?" he asks.

All I want is to save my people. Once I'm assured James can keep his word, I'll be using Mademoiselle Boulais's sleeping powder to break Henri from the Bastille and running through the countryside of France toward the Rhône-Alpes. My plan hinges on trusting James—something I have never been able to do.

I kiss him on the cheek and swallow my anger. "Nobles in Paris. We can do it together."

My voice breaks. James doesn't seem to hear me falter, or he doesn't care.

He pulls me in tight, kissing me with such intensity that all my joints stiffen. I must kiss him back, but it turns my stomach. Andre is mere steps away, watching me.

I think of his lips on Antoinette, and I remind myself of Naira's teachings. Attack him when he least expects it.

"James, we have much to discuss. Our power, our future. How we will secure your rightful position among the king's people."

He smiles so brightly, I nearly squint.

"Now," I say, "tell me everything about the slave trade. I need to know about the ships."

James leads me to our apartment, and I turn to shut the door, noticing Andre's eyes peering from the shadows. I nod, to remind him I won't betray him. Not now, not ever. He returns the nod, and I close the door, prepared to siphon every drop of power from my dishonest husband.

CHAPTER TWENTY-TWO

Through the grand entrance to the Louvre and into the three-walled courtyard, I don't focus on the Italian painted ceiling or the detailed stonework, but on my husband's face. A young man with so much to prove and who stands at the precipice of nobility. I absorb his power, as I've learned to do over the years. Tonight, the ultimate test of who he is—who we all are.

Servants welcome us into a sitting room with frescoed walls and gilded mirrors. We sit with the courtiers ready and willing to charm the king. James looks taller, with confident eyes.

"Why do they all have one frighteningly long fingernail?" I whisper.

"Knocking is forbidden," James says. "They are only permitted to scratch at a door."

Marble sculptures and gold bookcases decorate every corner of the room. Dangling chandeliers reflect a constellation of light on the parquet floor. I wonder whether one grows accustomed to all this metallic light, making the rest of the world appear dull.

"I will speak," James says. "You merely need to keep your eyes down and look pretty."

I force a smile, remembering the sleeping powder in my pocket.

"His Majesty will see you now." An unsmiling servant walks past us and it's obvious we are to follow. James's cheeks are flushed, his chest puffed like warm bread dough.

We walk arm in arm through the grand doors to the royal sitting room. The windows are open, filling the room with a light wind and an off-putting odor of sweat. King Louis XIV, draped in a velvet robe, sits on a ridiculously large gold-rimmed brocade chair. Red stockings cling to his feminine legs and his rings nearly blind me when the sunlight reflects off the gems.

All these years, I have envisioned the king to be the center of my suffering. An all-powerful being larger than even the Catholic Church. He is the Church, and everything it represents—murder and torture and the suffering of innocent people. As I stand before him, I do not see a devil spewing fire. I see a young man playing dress up.

The king waves his jewel-encrusted hand and James bows as I curtsy. I keep my eyes down yet glance at James's face. I watch him step into the moment he has dreamt of for a lifetime.

"Your Majesty." He bows his head slowly. "What an honor to be in the presence of the great Sun King."

"Monsieur…" He looks to one of his servants who whispers in his ear. "Ah, Lieutenant Beaumont. I understand you have been instrumental in our fight against the Iroquois."

He places his hand to his chest. "All for the glory of your France, Your Majesty."

I fear James might fall to the man's feet and kiss his high-heeled shoes. They have bows.

"May I introduce Madame Beaumont. A Fille du Roi."

"Ah!" His voice lifts. "I have yet to meet one of our young pioneers. This must be quite a treat for you to be in such a grand palace."

How I wish I could throw him to the floor by his ostentatious periwig. "It is an honor." I curtsy again and dare to raise my eyes. His nose is the size of his forearm. I think of my branding—my burned flesh at the hands of his monsters. My webbed skin hides beneath a glorious gown, burning hot like I haven't felt in years.

The doors behind us open as another servant announces, "Monsieur LaMarche and his daughter, the widow of Lieutenant Leroux."

All those names send shocks through my body, yet I hold steady, drawing power from my rage. Naira's voice whispers in my ear, *master your mind.* We turn to watch them approach. Antoinette glides into the room in her enormous gown, her blond curls pinned in a crown and adorned with pearls.

Monsieur LaMarche, a Noble of the Robe, gained his status through his role in the Parlement. The king bought his favor, leaving him with no title beyond *Monsieur*, and hated among the established aristocracy of Paris. He does not hold the respect of old noble families or the Nobles of the Sword.

"Welcome, Monsieur LaMarche," the king says. He waits for LaMarche's lengthy bow. "Monsieur Beaumont, I understand you have formed an alliance of sorts with our mutual friend."

James tilts his head, sweat beading on his forehead. "It is why I came to speak with you today."

"Do not worry, Monsieur," LaMarche says, "I've already informed Our Majesty of the details of our venture."

I stare at His majesty's flushed, damp hairline as his servant dabs his skin dry. He doesn't look angry as I envisioned he would. LaMarche has undermined his power, created a competing trade company. What isn't he telling us?

"Yes," the king says. "I understand you have an interest in handing over your trade to us. Wise move, as I do not take kindly to anyone competing with my efforts."

"We believe you can prosper from our connections," James says.

"We took a chance starting this company without your consent, Your Majesty," LaMarche says. "We wanted to have a working trade. Something solid we could offer you. And now we do."

The king stands and waits as two servants fluff his robe and dab more of his wet skin. He steps forward and LaMarche pushes his daughter closer. She smiles and lifts one shoulder.

"Your Royal Highness," she says with an extra dose of breath.

She's vying for a spot as one of his mistresses. In front of my husband, whom she bedded to please her father. Every time I find sympathy for her, she reminds me what a vile creature she is.

The king is taken with her beauty, as most men are. He smiles back, stares at her blushed face. "How are you finding New France,

Madame?" He curls his fingers over his thumb to display his array of rings.

"I miss France, Your Majesty. I especially love Paris, and all its grandeur. All its... beauty."

"Perhaps you will need to stay here. All of you." He gestures to the room. "Our trade company will finally be profitable by purchasing slaves with fine French goods."

Made from the hands of Huguenot prisoners.

James reaches for my hand, and I surprise myself by not recoiling. *Master your mind.*

"The Huguenots are unruly," LaMarche says. "Their clocks and silks and pottery are the finest in the world, yet they fight their purpose in helping France."

The king sniffs. "I care little about Huguenots, only that they stand with France... with me."

"We've taken the Protestants by force in La Rochelle. We send them to workhouses and take away their children if they resist," Antoinette says.

The words leave me lightheaded. I tug on James's arm, widen my eyes, and plead for him to stop this.

"Monsieur Beaumont has been instrumental," LaMarche says. "His family has supplied ships and money to sustain the workhouses. We're pushing out more goods every day."

James will not look at me. "Yes, Your Majesty. I want nothing more than to be part of your supreme reign and support you in every capacity. I will do as you wish, and hope, ever so humbly, that you might reward me with your trust."

The king continues to bead with sweat, drenching his clothing and permeating the air with body odor. "Ah, you wish for noble status."

"I bring as many livres as you desire, His Most Christian Majesty."

James is sure to use every title the man possesses. Like an unwed woman vying for a bachelor's attention.

"I will consider it," the king says.

LaMarche leers but still manages a wink. James instinctually wraps his arm around mine. "Thank you for your consideration." He bows again as the king dismisses him.

On our way to the door, Antoinette's eyes remain on me. I stop to whisper to her. "Careful, Antoinette. You're playing with the wolves now."

"Wolves are for the wilds of Quebec. I'm a Parisian."

"Yes, and so are the women who will love to eat you for breakfast." I nod to LaMarche as we approach the door.

"One more thing, madame," LaMarche says. "I've assured the king that you will participate," he says to me. "With your knowledge of the Protestant life you turned from, you may be of excellent service."

I turn to stare at the king.

"I care little of your past, Madame. In fact, your willingness to further our trade makes you all the more worthy of a noble title."

"It would be my honor, Your Majesty." My words make my stomach turn.

"Good," LaMarche says. "You can start by attending the questioning of a Huguenot prisoner retained at the Bastille. Monsieur Reynard. Perhaps you might enjoy observing his torture as we demand details of the Huguenot resistance."

I picture myself in the woods, bow and arrow at my feet. A red circle across the clearing on a tamarack tree. Naira whispers in my ear. Listen. Breathe. "I would want nothing more than to watch secrets pried from the ones who have wronged me. Whether it be by a blade through the gut, or a poison hidden in one's wine. Yes, I would enjoy that very much."

A final bow and curtsy, and we exit the Louvre. My breathing is tight. My arms are heavy. The Parisian summer air weighs on my chest and I feel faint.

"Come, let's get you back to rest."

I don't speak to James until we are back in our apartment. As soon as the door shuts, James lifts his hands in an apology. "Please, you must believe me. I didn't know he would be there."

"You agreed to everything, James." I prop my hands on my knees, my vision growing dark. "They want me to watch Henri's torture."

"Of course." James stands, looks down at me. "You came here for him, not me."

I swallow the fear that threatens to devour me. "It's true. I'll never let anyone hurt Henri. I came to ensure that you do as you promised. And so far, you have failed."

James lifts a glass goblet and throws it against the wall, raining shards on the wood floor. "I have no choice in any of this. What was I to say to the king? I cannot join in trade with you because my wife is still a Protestant? She puts us at risk every day and yet I still love her?" His eyes bulge red and wide.

I stand, despite my legs faltering. "You will be responsible for the death of hundreds of my people. And hundreds of slaves torn from their home. What kind of monster does that?"

He grabs my arm, pulls me to him. "You have never respected me."

"I've tried everything to be who you need me to be. I hid Bibles in floorboards and curtsied to the king when he asked me to help kill Protestants. All for your needs."

I pull away but cringe when he digs his fingers into my arm.

"Why do I still love you? After all your lies, all I want is for you to look at me the way you used to."

I stop writhing and stare at his hand. "I know."

"You know what?"

I look up at him, take my time to stare into his icy blue eyes. "I know you keep Antoinette as a mistress."

James's face falls into something close to sorrow, his anger lost. He lets go of my arm. "How did you…"

"LaMarche made certain I knew of your indiscretions. Going so far as to make me watch you."

James rubs his face, stumbles back to a chair. "I didn't know what to do. She has tried so many times to seduce me, and I fought it every time. I hate her, Isabelle. I truly hate her."

"That did not stop you from rolling naked with her and pretending to want me."

He looks as if he might be sick. "I do want you. So much it turns me into a monster."

"Antoinette is about to enter a fight she will not win. A dangerous woman will take care of her. LaMarche, I can finally face. But you, you still hold some strange power over me. A symbol of the lost girl I once was."

"I should've never given into LaMarche's pressure," he says. "He convinced me I had to be part of their empire. But I could never let you go, Isabelle."

He looks shriveled and weak, but I feel no empathy. "You want me to forgive you?"

"It was a mistake. I knew you would find out, and you'd be mad with jealousy. I needed you to want me."

I kneel to face him. "So, you put your hands on Antoinette's naked body?"

"That snowy winter day it first happened, you had left me alone, again. I thought of you the entire time."

An icy shiver skitters through my body. Winter. His affair started back in Quebec. "Which winter day?"

"You were waiting for Andre, I presume. He left his wife even though she was expecting their baby girl. Coward."

Elizabeth is not yet three-years-old. "You've been bedding Antoinette for over two years?"

He presses my shoulders into the wall. "I fought it. Believe me, I hate myself for it. But you never loved me. Not like you did that pathetic fur trader."

I stare at him, tears in my eyes. "I want to forgive you."

He buries his head in my neck and cries into my skin. "I want this life with you, Isabelle. Us together in a grand palace in Paris."

I pull away and pour myself a goblet of wine. I drink an entire glass and fill the goblet again. *Master your mind.*

James gives me space while I stare at the wine for a long moment. "Do you still want this life?" he asks.

I turn to face him, fingers cramping against the goblet's handle. "What about the Huguenots?"

"It can be stopped. The plans are all there." He points to the desk. "But LaMarche still stands in our way."

I move closer, hating myself for every step.

James drinks from the goblet, gulping as much wine as I did. "Just promise to love me," he says. "I will fix this. I will. Please."

I place my hands on his chest. "It's too late, James. I am not the girl you followed to Quebec. I'm stronger."

His eyes grow heavy and fill with tears.

I run my fingers through his hair. "Dreams plague my every sleep. I've never told you that, have I?"

He grabs my waist, pulls me close as his legs wobble.

"I still smell the burning flesh of Henri's father and hear the gurgle from when they sliced off Etienne's tongue. I still feel the bleeding flesh from the lashings to my backside."

James legs give way. He falls to his knees. "Something's wrong."

I lower him to the floor and rub his cheek. "It's your turn for haunting dreams. I hope the screams of every child you hurt burn their way through your soul."

His body writhes as he reaches for me but cannot control his limbs. Andre opens the door and walks toward us. James tries to lunge for him, but he hardly moves.

"I do not want this life with you, James," I say. "I want to destroy you. Just as I will destroy LaMarche."

Andre lowers beside him. "Only time will tell if your wife gave you sleeping powder... or arsenic."

CHAPTER TWENTY-THREE

Paris nights are heavy and thick, luring the restless from their beds. The dark and wicked seem to rise from the earth and walk among mortal feet that creep through the night. Mortal feet like ours, approaching a house of poisons.

Charlotte knocks once, and Mademoiselle Boulais opens the door with a casual smile. "I knew you would return."

"We need your help. We haven't much time," I say.

"Have you brought money?"

"Yes, although I think we can offer you something more valuable," I say. "I have secrets."

She glances at Charlotte and pauses when she sees Andre. "Who are you?"

"I take orders from the ladies."

"You may stay," Boulais says. She pulls us into her laboratory. Potions boil away in various cauldrons around the room. The sweet garlic scent of arsenic seems to have settled in the walls and floor, with a new, herbaceous smell rising to the front. Like when the sun warms the forest floor after a rain.

"Wolfsbane," Boulais says. "It tastes foul, so you cannot hide the potion in food or drink. You can, however, add it to an open wound to cause death within hours."

"The sleeping powder. It won't kill, will it?" I ask.

"No. But it is very potent. How much did you give?"

"Half the container in a glass of wine."

"You do not hold back. Well done, Madame Beaumont. You dosed your husband, I presume."

"Yes, and he'll be furious when he wakes."

"My trust in you just doubled."

By the time Charlotte arrived at the apartment, we had moved James to bed. While he slept, we pored over the documents on the slave trade and discovered James's lies. Information we can use.

"You have fifteen hours before he stirs, several more before he can speak." Mademoiselle Boulais says. "What havoc do we need to spread before the sun rises, madame?"

"Your friend, the treasurer. Have you spoken to him?"

"You left my house less than twenty-four hours ago. Do you think I am your witch servant?" She fiddles with her instruments, lifting the vials to the light.

"I need you to host a party," I say.

She drops the vial to its holder. "A party, did you say?"

"It must be tonight."

"I love a party." Her hair shines like strawberries when the moonlight finds her. "Are we meant to poison someone?"

"No," I say.

"Although you never know how the night will go," Charlotte says.

"The guest list must include the treasurer, Monsieur LaMarche and his daughter, and Madame de Montagne."

"Interesting cast of characters," she says.

"We must be out of Paris by midnight," Andre says. "A young woman needs our help."

In the scrolls on the LaMarche slave trade are lists of Huguenot families, their goods and prices, names of ships and their captains, and the pirate ships that are most likely to attack them. In a surprising twist of fate, the financier to many of the pirate ships lives in Geneva. Right where we're meant to take the young Huguenot.

Mademoiselle Boulais wipes her hands on her apron. "I am an alchemist, not a philanthropist. I have a fee."

"Certainly." I hand her a bag of coins that I stole from James's chest. "Although you might be interested to know that LaMarche's daughter has aspirations to become the king's newest mistress."

"They all do, Madame Beaumont."

"But not all have the power she does. She controls shipping from La Rochelle to Quebec, which means she controls the fur trade."

Her eyes light with understanding. "The fur trade keeps the monarchy in riches."

"That's correct. And I believe you need Madame de Montagne in her position of power, yes? To protect your alliance and influence the king."

Jacqueline's secrets have proven increasingly helpful.

"So," Charlotte says. "It benefits both of us to eliminate the LaMarches."

"How does it benefit you?" she asks.

"Antoinette is my husband's mistress. The LaMarches have caused all our suffering as far back as our childhoods in La Rochelle."

Charlotte steps forward. "I want to watch them burn."

Mademoiselle Boulais swirls a beaker of brown sludge. "Yes. I will arrange it." She retrieves a book, or so it appears. She opens it to reveal tiny drawers and a glass jar. It's a hidden chest of poisons. "This is called the assassin's toolkit. Quite a clever name, I should say."

"Why is she so flippant about murder?" Andre whispers to me.

"Here." She hands me a small leather pouch. "Antimony cup. Place wine in it at your husband's bedside. The wine will act with the acid and cause him to vomit. It will buy you time and keep him in bed."

"Will it kill him?"

"It might. But a little purge is good for the soul."

She wraps her arm around Charlotte and leads her to the tiny chest of drawers, discussing how opium poppy and water hemlock can either increase a man's virility or send him to his deathbed. "Dosage is everything, my dear."

Andre turns to me. "I heard your fight with James."

I tuck the leather pouch in my pocket. "Two years, Andre. What a fool I've been."

"We've made so many mistakes, Isabelle." He tucks a curl behind my ear. The same wild curl that refuses to stay in place, regardless of how strongly I pin it back. "This is our chance to make it right."

"Can we do this, Andre? Save Henri and get them all to Geneva, and keep James sick long enough to ruin LaMarche?"

"I think of Naira in these times, when it all seems impossible. She remains calm and listens to the voices only she can hear."

"I miss her guidance."

"She's taught you everything you need. You are strong here," he points to my head, "and here." He points a finger to the center of my chest. "You're a fighter. It's who you are."

"You think too highly of me."

"Maybe when we cross the mountains into Helvetia, you will believe it too."

Steam coils through the air from the cauldron over the fire like bony, twisted fingers grabbing for something wicked.

Charlotte returns with a collection of vials. "Mademoiselle Boulais has prepared us for everything we might need."

"We don't need to kill every man in the court," I say.

"Don't be too sure of that," Boulais says. "Most of them deserve it."

"Thank you, Mademoiselle." I tuck the vials in my pocket.

"I will attend with you tonight," she says. "I have something special planned."

She dons a black cape. "Our friend the treasurer hides a secret, and you need to understand what you're up against. It's for assurance, so none of you turn on me."

Andre leans forward. "Are we about to perform murder?"

"Monsieur, we do not speak such words. No, no. It involves a hidden room and midnight mass."

"You're going to make us attend Catholic mass?" Charlotte asks.

"No," Mademoiselle Boulais says. "Black mass."

• • •

We planned through the evening hours. Madame Boulais is a wealth of information, holding the dark secrets of nearly every noble in Paris. She is driven by a thirst for power and, she believes, the ghosts of women scorned.

Andre secured a carriage and positioned it outside the southeast corner of the city. Charlotte returned to the Bastille to gain any last-minute information on Henri, and I returned to the Palais Royale.

As I enter the apartment, I can't help but fear what I might find. Has the sleeping powder killed him? Stopped his breathing? I stand at the door to the bedroom, vial in hand, wishing there was another way. A satin sheet covers his unmoving body, just as we left him last night. The scrolls are with Andre, wrapped to his chest under his doublet.

We will all meet in the garden behind the Palais and set our plan in motion. But first, I must poison my husband.

I approach his bed, noting his pale, damp forehead, his gaping mouth and dry lips. The antimony cup shakes in my hand, rippling the wine that I set at his bedside. I sit down and run the back of my hand along his cheek. So handsome. So weak.

I pace the room for what must be two hours, staring out the window and dreaming of a life of my own choosing. Paris rooftops glow silver in the moonlight. Blackness seems to have washed away the happenings of the day and now welcomes the evil deeds of night.

James stirs, groaning and licking his lips. I watch him, the man who could never find the answers in himself. He needed his father, the LaMarches, the king, me. I need him to stay in bed until midnight, when we will carry Henri and the girl to safety. This will be my goodbye.

He clenches his stomach as his eyes creak open, the whites gleaming a blood-red. "Isabelle?"

"I'm here, James." I wait, hands in my lap.

His face twists into a painful grimace. "What happened?"

He doesn't yet remember the sleeping powder, or Andre, or my promise to ruin him. "You fell. A bit of a blow to the head, it seems." I place my hand on his forehead.

"I'm so thirsty," he says.

"Here." I hand him the cup, almost hesitating. But then I remind myself that he will wrong me again. He will lie and kill hundreds of innocent people. "You'll feel better soon."

I know this might kill him, but I have no choice. I have put my trust in a woman of witchcraft, a woman who poisons men to help women access money and revenge. James's black pupils begin to tighten as the shining blue returns.

He glugs the wine and rubs his forehead. "I was on the floor, looking up at you."

"That was after you fell." I hand him the cup and watch him drink to the last drop.

He growls. "Andre. He was here. Wasn't he?"

I don't know how long I have until the poison takes over. "Yes."

He sits up, arms locked. "What?"

I stare in the eyes. "Charlotte and I came to save Henri from the Bastille because you gave the order to attack Protestants in New York. Andre followed us."

He heaves and turns pale. "He was here. In my house."

"I invited him."

The antimony flowing through his body is the only reason I can be this brazen, this *honest*. "I cannot stay married to you, James. Not after you lied. Not after you convinced me that my wild ways were unbecoming while you were bending Antoinette over a bed."

I stand and shake my head of any misgivings that might linger. All those years I ignored my heart to satisfy James, while all he thought about were his own needs.

"Don't lie to me, Isabelle." He stands, a little unsteady, holding the bedpost. "I loved you with everything. Antoinette was my weakness, yes. She let me feel powerful. You never did."

"I suppose it is my visits to Naira that sent you into Antoinette's arms?"

"Please." He laughs. "She was never in my arms. I could never look at her while we…" He pauses, looks at me and softens. "I despise her."

"You ruined our marriage to bed a woman you couldn't even look at?"

His stomach groans like a rusted hinge. "As if you are innocent. I realize now why you stayed with me. The secrets you hoped to find."

I snap my shoulder back as he reaches for me. He's right, I used him. For secrets, for comfort, for sex and power. "I tried to stay with you. I wanted to give you what you needed."

"Now you'll run off into the countryside with your Huguenot love? You are a fool."

"This has nothing to do with Andre. You knew how much I love my people. How could you imprison them, steal their children?"

James lunges for me, but weakness settles in as he stumbles and throws me to the bed. He pins my arms to my side. His hair falls in soft, copper curls around his face.

I once felt safe in his arms.

"I was trying to survive," he says. "To protect you! It's all I've ever done."

I don't throw him off me like I know I can. Not yet. "Your documents are gone. I'm going to stop your ships and the Huguenot workhouses. I'm going to stop it all because you were too much of a coward to do it yourself."

His fingers tighten into my arms, digging hard enough to bruise. "No. I won't let you leave. Not after all this. After everything I sacrificed for you."

"You don't have a choice. I no longer wish to be married to you."

His torso tightens and his neck muscles pull taut.

"Something wrong?" I ask calmly.

He fights the pain I know builds in his stomach. Sweat forms on his brow in fat beads like raindrops. "What did you do to me?"

"I'm no longer afraid of your disappointment or of your judgment. I am no longer afraid to fight."

I lean to his arm and bite as hard as my jaw can manage. Blood gathers in my mouth. He screams and yanks one arm away. I grab his wrist and bend it back with force over my other hand. I hear a snap, and he recoils with another scream.

I kick him off me and stand to gather myself. My breathing is not rapid, and my heartbeat is steady. "I didn't want to hurt you, James. But I will do anything to save these people."

He braces his wrist against his chest, bent over with stomach pain. "You will never beat LaMarche."

"You were the fool, James. You let evil in our lives." I step closer, unafraid. "You wanted to kill that Protestant girl you met. Finally conquer her because you hate yourself and your past so very much. You want to force me into a Catholic life that could bring us riches and power and status. Because then you could parade me around and say, 'Look how powerful I am. I washed her clean of heresy.'"

He grabs my dress with his good hand, pulls me close. His breath is sickly sweet as he coughs, his face dripping with sweat. "Why couldn't you just be a wife, a mother, a woman who does not run like a wild animal through the forest?"

"Because I am of the forest, the trees, the hills and mountains, and of the wolves. I used to pray in the dark of night under French oaks, smelling the moss that clung to their trunks in the mist, ignoring the fear that your people instilled in us. I might have sailed the ocean and married one of you, but I never stopped being that girl."

He collapses, clawing at my dress. "Help me."

I lower him to the bed, lift his legs, and cover him with the blanket. "The stomach pains will grow in intensity, as will your cough. You'll begin retching and filling your breeches with bloody diarrhea. It will not be pleasant, but you are strong."

He pulls his arm to his stomach and writhes. "Did you kill me?"

I lift his cravat from the bedside and wrap his arm tight enough to stabilize the damaged wrist. "No, James, I could never kill. But I need you out of my way."

"You are not this person, Isabelle." He heaves, hand to his mouth, but nothing releases—not yet. "Stay with me."

"I can't," I whisper. "I have people to rescue."

He reaches for my hair with a trembling hand. "Save me."

"After tonight, you will have nothing. No ships, no title. No wife. You'll be ostracized by the king you're so desperate to impress. But you'll always have Antoinette."

I stand and wipe my hands on my dress, take a deep breath, and turn toward the door.

"I won't let you go," James says.

"You don't have a choice."

"I'll find you." His teeth begin to chatter.

I ignore his pleas and his threats. I open the door to leave and turn to see him sitting up, staring at me with evil, bloodshot eyes. He holds back the vomit that will soon heave from his body, and he focuses on his rage. His defiance. "Run," he says. "Before I capture you."

The contents spew from his mouth, spraying the blanket over his legs and dripping down his chin, but he never diverts his gaze. His evil, knowing eyes stare straight through me.

CHAPTER TWENTY-FOUR

We will have two hours to break Henri from the Bastille. Two hours to poison the guards and wind through the dark alleys of Paris, evading the powers the LaMarches will no doubt send after us. But first, we have a party to attend.

Mademoiselle Boulais greets us at the steps to the treasurer's private mansion. In Le Marais just a few minutes from Palais Royale, this section of Paris holds more wealth than thousands of French families combined.

Andre stays at Mademoiselle Boulais's to plan our path through the city as Charlotte and I attend to the matter of the LaMarches. They wouldn't turn down an invitation from the king's treasurer.

A servant opens the door and welcomes us inside. Solid silver glitters from mirrors, balustrades, torch lamps, chandeliers and candelabras. Thick, carved moldings edge the hall over life-sized bronze sculptures.

"Do you think the treasurer knows most Frenchmen live with splintered floors and dozens of other people?" Charlotte whispers.

I run my fingers along a glittering tortoiseshell and brass clock, curious to touch its smooth contours. "He either couldn't fathom it or knows and does not care."

Charlotte retires to the kitchen with the other lady's maids. In the salon, Mademoiselle Boulais greets me with a welcoming smile. She introduces us to the treasurer, Monsieur Léon, and the king's mistress, Madame de Montagne.

"Pleasure to meet you, Madame Beaumont," Monsieur Léon says. "Where is your husband this evening?"

"I'm afraid he isn't feeling well." I cringe at the thought of the room covered in vomit as James teeters on death. This life requires me to do awful things, I remind myself.

"Good evening," Monsieur LaMarche bellows from the doorway.

Antoinette struts into the room until she notices Madame de Montagne and her confidence turns to disgust.

Madame de Montagne pulls her shoulders back and approaches them. "Pleasure to meet you. His majesty begged me to dine with him tonight, but I just love a dinner party with new friends."

Antoinette forces a pained smile with flared nostrils. Servants arrive with silver platters of wine, as the guests peer at one another with forced smiles and twinkling eyes.

"Madame Beaumont," Monsieur Léon says, "you are a Daughter of the King, I hear?"

"Yes. I left for New France four years ago."

"Wonderful." He smiles, rocking onto his heels and glaring at LaMarche until he squirms. "Monsieur LaMarche, you're from La Rochelle, yes?"

"Monsieur LaMarche is a powerful ship owner, aren't you?" I force a smile.

"Yes," LaMarche mutters. "We send ships to New France and Spain." He waits for Monsieur Léon to smile or nod, but he only scowls.

"And the East Indies, I hear," the treasurer says.

LaMarche sneaks a sideways glance at me. "Yes. We are very excited about this new venture."

Antoinette steps forward. "I spoke to His Majesty myself. He is quite pleased with our contribution to his fleet, and he has invited us to Versailles."

Oh, poor, misguided Antoinette has no idea what she's up against.

Madame de Montagne pulls a deep inhale, loud enough to turn the room's attention to her. "Child, you must purchase more impressive clothing if you wish to enjoy the company of our King." She runs her eyes down Antoinette's gown and purses her lips.

LaMarche clears his throat. "Of course, a new wardrobe it is."

Antoinette's bottom lip quivers slightly, but she regains her composure, as she always does.

"Life at court is nothing like the simple seaside town of La Rochelle," Madame de Montagne says.

Mademoiselle Boulais pulls me away to admire a painting, looking down at the decanters and goblets shining on silver trays on the credenza. "Go ahead," she whispers. "Just a pinch of arsenic powder will do the trick. Kill them both."

The purple wine glitters under candlelight. "No, I couldn't."

"Monsieur Léon is one of us. You can trust him to keep your secrets."

"I don't want that kind of secret weighing on my heart."

"What a shame. I would quite enjoy watching her froth at the mouth." She stares at the painting and sighs. "Madame de Montagne is growing impatient. Make your move, and I'll make mine."

I take one more glance at the wine and think for a moment about how easy it would be to kill them both, to watch them writhe and cry their way to death. Naira taught me to use my wits but keep the warrior ready to strike.

"Monsieur Léon, please tell us of your new program," I say.

"Ah, yes. I believe you might be very interested, Monsieur LaMarche."

Mademoiselle Boulais wraps her arm through Antoinette's. "Come, let me show you the palace. You will need a home like this if you wish to impress the royal court." Antoinette swallows but joins her and admires the floor to ceiling oil portrait, painted by the king's artist, no doubt. Madame de Montagne follows, with a wide, easy grin.

In other circles, it would be improper for me to drink alone with these men. But tonight, in this circle, it is just as we planned.

"Monsieur LaMarche," Léon says, "I understand you manage the beaver trade?"

"Among other things." He narrows his black eyes at me. "Shouldn't you be with the women? Leave the business to the men?"

"No, monsieur, I'd like to hear all about the new program."

"We received some unsettling information recently," Léon says as he paces back and forth. "Your family started a slave trade."

"The king is part of this. This is nothing new."

"Ah, yes. The East Indies. What the king does not know is that you have been secretly pilfering gold and slaves from his company. You've been working with the Dutch."

His face reveals nothing, but LaMarche's cheeks flush pink. "Nonsense. Where have you heard that?"

"Madame Beaumont possesses documents that show your contracts. You formed an alliance with the Dutch and stole money and goods from the king so you may keep your own connections as you make them."

He glares at me, knowing I have stolen documents from my husband. He turns to Léon and considers his options. "Unless you can produce those documents, you have nothing on me. I will deny it."

"They are in a secure place," I say. "My husband trusted me a little too much."

"Ah, let's talk about your husband. So much potential. It's a shame he's so weak. We needed his ambition, his military status, and his father's fleet. Getting him to bed my daughter was just for fun."

I hold back the desire to slap him—the deep need to punish him for all he has put me through. And then I narrow my eyes in an icy stare.

"Your documents provided me with the contacts and means to fund a new branch of the king's trade," Léon says. "I especially appreciate the storage locations of your gold and weapons."

LaMarche releases a sharp inhale. "I didn't have that in my documents."

"No," I say as I step forward. "James wronged you too. He kept his own records. Ones that show where he had them stored, away from you."

LaMarche's round face blushes, then glows red with rage.

"If you'll excuse me, I have something to attend to. Are you all right, Madame?" Léon asks me.

"Yes, thank you. I can handle him from here."

Monsieur Léon clicks his heels together and disappears down the hall.

"You think you're quite clever, don't you?" he asks.

I smooth my stray curl back from my brow. "If that is what you call using secrets to exploit people like you and your daughter, then I suppose I am."

He steps closer, trying to intimidate me, but I don't budge. "All I have to do is get the documents and find where that traitorous husband of yours hid our money. I'll find my way out of this. I always do."

"You underestimated me once. Are you certain you want to do it again?"

He slams me against the wall, hard enough to make the back of my head sting. "You wench." He leans so close his breath burns my cheek. "Maybe I should bed you, show you what a real man feels like."

I push him away, the hard mirror pressing into my shoulders. Memories wash over me. His taunting and sneering. My family and friends brutalized at his hand. *Fight*, I tell myself. *Fight him and ruin him. You know you can.* But his hands are so strong. His nails dig into my flesh through layers of silk.

"Do you like to be held down?" His voice is harsh. Angry. No control. This is good—let him think I'm afraid, then attack. Just like Naira taught me.

He presses his hips into mine, and I nearly vomit on his face.

"You are a beautiful specimen, even if you are a dirty Huguenot." He reaches for my breast, but I twist his wrist hard and shove his elbow sideways until he softens his grip. But he pins me against the wall again.

Why can't I do this? This man is everything I hate. Everything I fight for is because of his evil. *Do it.*

"I will have you. Right here in this salon if I need to. And I will make you hurt, just like I have other heretics, because you filthy bitches deserve it."

You are no longer powerless.

LaMarche opens his mouth wide and presses his fat tongue to my chin as he glides it up my cheek, wet and thick. Just as his slobber nears my temple, I hear Naira.

Now.

I grab his tongue and pierce my nails into the dense mass of purple flesh to grab hold. I twist and yank, shoving my shoe to his chest to keep the tongue extended so he doesn't bite my hand.

"You will pay for everything you've put us through." I twist again, my fingernails drawing blood as I pull hard enough that he chokes. I shove my foot into his chest and watch him fall to the wood floor with a loud thud.

He brings his hand to his mouth, wiping the blood that seeps from his ruby teeth. "No little girl will treat me like this." He yanks my feet out from under me. I fall to my backside, wrists stinging from the blow. He draws me forward, slides me toward him. I throw my elbow to his cheek, but he returns with a hard slap.

My cheek stings and my stomach churns with disgust. He climbs atop me and lifts my skirt. As his hand slides up my thigh, I dig my fingers into his eye sockets and press like I'm squeezing a snail from its shell.

LaMarche recoils, hands to his face, his body still over mine. I move and push to get out from under him, but his knees squeeze hard enough against my hips that I scream.

He lifts his hand to punch me, but his eyes struggle to focus, giving me time to catch his fist. I twist and bend his arm until his trunk softens. Elbow to his other forearm like an ax through a slab of wood. I grab his shirt and slam his forehead onto the floor next to my shoulder.

No one will come to help me. I must do this myself.

He grunts, rolling me to my stomach, his weight still on me. "Stop!" He yells. He's growing agitated, impatient. *Good. Outlast him.*

I buck and roll, distracting him until his hands move back to my legs again. I throw my knee to the back of his thigh, allowing room to maneuver to my back. Palm to his face, I yank his hair until he relents, then I kick him off me.

I'm fatigued and sore, but angrier than I've ever been.

"Where's the money?" He stands over me, hands out, ready to attack.

"Find your way to hell." I kick both of my boots into his shins, wiping his feet out from under him. His face smacks the wood floor with a deafening crack. I jump up and kick his fleshy side, but he grabs my foot.

He's stronger than I thought.

Calm. Listen.

I bend my knee against his grip and lower it to his face. Already bleeding, the crack of his skull against the floor causes him to slow.

I could yell, but I know they cannot hear me. The kitchen is one floor down, under a thick layer of stone and wood.

He grabs my hair and throws me into the credenza. A glass goblet shatters onto my hand, sending blood between my fingers and down my palm. My fighting hand.

He slithers toward me, his bleeding, swollen face ready for battle. "I took your mother in an alleyway, covering her mouth while she screamed."

The air stills. All I hear is my heartbeat.

"That is why she never left the house again. I broke her. To pay back your father. That bastard deserved it."

Blood gushes from my hand and onto the floor. Drip. Drip.

The hate in me breaks open like an oyster shell cracking at the joints. Something rancid oozes out. Something full of hate and bile. All the horridness of my life that I have refused to let inside of me has just leaked into every part of my being.

Helpless no more.

I grab the pewter tray through bleeding hands and scream as I throw the heavy metal into LaMarche's face. A clank reverberates when it contacts his cheek. His facial bones crackle like an animal's teeth crushing a bone for its marrow. He falls to the ground and lies there, stunned, but still awake, his black, round eyes staring straight ahead.

Breathe cycles in and out. Drip, drip goes the blood. My head and chest throb. I want to kill him. Right here and now. Throw the tip of my shoe to his fragile face and kill him.

But I don't.

I back away and slide down the wall to watch him twitch and bleed.

"Isabelle?" Charlotte runs in. "I heard a crash when I snuck up here to check on you." She stares at LaMarche. "Did you do that?"

"Yes."

She helps me up. I stop at my knees and lean my cheek to her arm, eyes closed. She waits. Once standing, she holds my bleeding hand in hers.

"I'm fine, Charlotte."

"Mademoiselle Boulais requests we join her."

"Where?" I ask.

"Underground."

•

We follow Mademoiselle Boulais down a spiral stone staircase, a lone candle lighting our way. The sounds of a nearby kitchen disappear as we descend into the depths of the stone underground. We come to a door, pointed at the top, and she knocks with two quick raps.

The door creaks open and she steps into the blackness. We follow, one by one, into Léon's lair. Candlesticks as tall as me line the walkway to an altar, lit with dripping black candles. A layer of black velvet hangs from a rod as if a show is about to begin.

Mademoiselle guides us to the steps, and we wait, listening to the heavy stillness of breathing in a silent stone cellar. Through a side door, Monsieur Léon escorts in Antoinette. Her face turns angry when she sees us, and then terrified when she sees the room. She turns to leave, but uselessly shakes the locked door handle.

"Come, my dear." Léon leads her to the center of our semicircle.

"I don't belong here," she says, her voice piercing. He places a finger to her lips and holds it there.

"You are right where you should be," Boulais says.

Antoinette hesitates, looking at me with pleading eyes. I turn from her, my hand finally beginning to throb in pain.

Monsieur Léon dons a robe, similar to a priest's, pristine white with gold stitching. He holds a black book, its binding frayed. "Welcome, friends."

He lifts his hand to the air and forms the shape of the cross. Antoinette gasps and steps back. "No, this isn't… what I think it is?"

The mysterious Léon ascends the three steps to the velvet curtain, gathers the material, and slides the curtain to the side. On the altar lies Madame de Montagne, naked, arms outstretched, chalice on her abdomen and a black candle burning in each hand.

Antoinette creaks out a whimper, realizing that they are here to call on dark spirits from the underworld. "No, I can't be a part of this," she says. "His Majesty rules the Catholic Church, and this blasphemy has no part in his kingdom." Antoinette shakes the door, but it doesn't budge. "I will make sure he knows of your evil deeds. All of you!"

"Shh," Mademoiselle Boulais says. "You cannot escape."

Antoinette covers her ears and winces.

Charlotte leans to my ear. "Never underestimate the power of black magic to instill fear in a Catholic."

Léon reads from a black book, with instructions to invoke power from some supernatural entity into the wine of the chalice. Madame de Montagne's vanilla skin shines bright in the shadows of darkness, a ghostly figure with only her eyes covered.

Mademoiselle joins Monsieur Léon, and they worship over her body.

"We ask you, in the name of the spirit, to lay your powers on this woman, so she may know the king's love forever and always. Above all others, and without hesitation, this body will entice and lure His Majesty into her magic."

The woman's full breasts and bare stomach glow bright white. I wonder how the king's mistress can pray to a Catholic God during the day, and something darker and evil in the night.

"All be the power to you," he says to the sky. "This woman's body shall hold the king's affections, aided by this magic potion."

I turn to Antoinette, who is so frozen with fear she cannot scream.

Mademoiselle Boulais descends the steps and faces Antoinette. "This is what you have to compete with, Madame. This woman is the favored mistress, and we have magic powers to keep her there. Back away, before we call on something sinister for your soul."

"You all are evil," Antoinette says. "Pure, black evil."

"What is evil?" Mademoiselle Boulais says. "The king adores this woman. We hold monthly rituals where the powers of a secret world bring her body alive. It turns the wine into a powerful love potion, only activated when she releases her body to its full power."

"I could make the king powerful without dark spells and evil rituals." Antoinette's voice sounds thready, shrill. "Isabelle, don't be part of this."

"I'm not part of it, but you are now. You've entered a new world. One you cannot come back from."

Mademoiselle Boulais stands next to Antoinette, staring at the naked woman on the altar. "You can't pull your eyes away, can you? The power of a woman in possession of sexual power is intoxicating."

Monsieur Léon lifts the chalice and carries it to Mademoiselle Boulais.

"Would you like a touch of magic?" she asks Antoinette.

"Never."

"You're fighting something far larger than competition for the king's bed. You're fighting ancient magic and powerful people who call on dark arts to ruin their enemies."

Antoinette backs up and knocks into me. She turns, breathless. "Have you fallen so far from the days of La Rochelle? Strayed so far from God that you would take part in something like this?"

"Who are you to speak of God!" I shove her with both hands until she stumbles against the wall, my bloody hand soiling her gown.

"Stop," she begs.

"I will not stop. I had hope for you, that someday you would learn goodness. That you all would. But you aren't capable. You, and your father, and James. I know everything, Antoinette."

She straightens her shoulders, trying not to stare at the naked woman on the altar. "He was always supposed to be mine," she cries. "We should have married back in La Rochelle, but he was weak. Distracted by your helplessness. It took me years, but I finally lured him back to where he belongs."

"You're correct about that. He certainly belongs with you. But now, we've witnessed your presence at a Black mass, and if you report to the king, so will we. And they will cast a wicked spell over you for all eternity."

She presses her back into the wall as I approach. Her breathing is rapid, her blond curls quivering in the candlelight. "Leave," she says. "Leave Paris and forget the Huguenots. We own them now. And I have stolen your husband's affections. There's nothing left for you."

I slap her, smearing thick crimson blood over her cheek. She falls to the stone floor, where she cowers in the corner, whimpering.

I kneel to face her. "I was afraid for so long. Because of people like you. Afraid to live and breathe and fight." I lift her face to look at me, my hand gently resting on her chin. "I will leave. But you will never be free of me. I will fight you until my last breath. Until every Huguenot is free."

"You have no power." She sounds strained. A little girl pretending, just as she's always been.

"I have more power than you ever will, you pathetic weakling," Madame de Montagne says.

The naked woman stands, removes her blindfold, and steps down, moving her legs like water as they glide across the dark stones. She looks at Antoinette and releases a deep, monstrous laugh. She slides her hands along her curves, forcing Antoinette to look away in disgust.

"The king will always be mine. Stay away from him or I'll have you poisoned in your sleep. You will choke on your own vomit, your heart racing so fast it suddenly stops from fatigue and shock."

Antoinette pushes up, holding my arm for stability. "You wouldn't let her, would you?" she asks me.

"Even if I could stop her, I wouldn't."

The naked woman looks at us. "An enemy of my enemy is my closest ally." Léon hands her a red robe stitched with eagles. She covers herself and stares at Antoinette. "We've steered the pirate ships toward your slave vessels. We will ruin you, madame."

"No, you can't."

I peel her hands from my arm. "We have." I lean to whisper in her ear. "Never get too comfortable. I'll always be watching."

Mademoiselle Boulais smiles, nodding at me with admiration, and I return the nod. She unlocks the door for us. Monsieur Léon tries to escort Antoinette, but she runs up the stairs, crying.

"We'll make sure she stays away from the king," Boulais says. "And we'll dump her father in the filthy streets to sleep off his injuries."

"Thank you."

"Off with you now. The night is young."

Charlotte and I ascend the stairs, neither of us speaking of what we just witnessed. We leave through the kitchen and slip into a dark alley, where she wipes a drop of blood from my cheek. "You're more of a fighter than I imagined."

"I'm just getting started."

CHAPTER TWENTY-FIVE

A black, heavy night has descended over Paris. The Bastille stands tall above the Parisian rooftops, surrounded by locked gates and stone walls impossible to scale. James is fighting for his life and the LaMarches have retreated to lick their wounds. All is calm, but for how long? The Huguenot girl waits in her home six streets from here. Everything teeters on the outcome of the next hour.

Andre met us outside the mansion. He wrapped my hand and Charlotte cleaned my face. At the doorway, Andre held my arm. "Are you all right?" he asked.

I wiped my swollen lip. "Better than ever."

Now we wait across the square, crouched against a tree trunk, staring at the giant fortress with its round, stone turrets. "There are only two doors in," Charlotte whispers. "One front and one back. They're both locked."

"Maybe we can stack barrels and find a low portion of the wall to climb?" I ask.

"The armory," Charlotte says. "The building is old. I snuck in there earlier today and shoved slivers of wood in the lock."

Andre and I stare at her, wide-eyed.

"I told you I was capable of more." She creeps across the courtyard. We follow her, our silhouettes dancing shadows across the stones. A subtle wind whistles through the buildings, brushing my neck like a whisper.

The armory, a long, low building, hugs the front wall of the Bastille. Windows frame either end, and the rest is a stone fortress, just like the prison. "This way," Charlotte says. We follow her to a row of trees leading up to the armory. She scurries along the branches as nimble as a forest sprite and shoves open the window. She leans out, hand cupped around her mouth. "No one ever checks the windows."

"How does she know all this?" Andre asks.

"The girl is sneaky. I'm glad she's on our side."

The door to the armory creaks open and she waves us in. We pass locked cells with weapons, and a main room for storage. I duck to avoid a spiderweb and hold back a cough from the air that's heavy with dust.

We creak the back door open, and we are in the courtyard.

Andre looks at me, brow furrowed. "That was too easy, right?"

"Some fortress," I say.

Our bravado is quickly checked when we hear footsteps. We jump the railing of the footbridge that leads to the front door. The once water-filled moat is now a dry and dusty hole in the ground. We slide down the hill and take cover under the bridge's arches.

A man whistles, an eerie lone call into the night. He stops directly above us. So does the whistle. His boots crunch on gravel and pebbles as he spins in a slow circle. We huddle together, staring at the black eves under the bridge. Two orbs shine in the dark, the outline of an owl coming to focus. He blinks and stares at us silently.

The man slides along the gravel, resuming his stroll through the grounds. The owl twitches his neck, blinking faster. Suddenly something flies through the middle of us, stuck in Charlotte's hair.

"Bat," she whispers. "It's a bat! Get it out."

She yanks at the offensive creature, but its wing is wound up in a mess of blond hair high enough to hide her Bible. Andre grabs the bat by one hand and untangles him. He thumps his wings to fly away from us, but not before Charlotte releases a yelp as it grazes her face.

We freeze, Charlotte closing her eyes, squeezing her face tight. "Damn," she whispers.

We wait, looking up as dirt drops from the eves, dusting our hair and faces. The footsteps return.

"Hide." I point to the recesses and we each find a black shadow to protect us. I climb uncomfortably close to the owl, who tilts his head back and forth, continuing to blink as he watches me.

"Hello?" the man whispers, almost playful, like this is a game. "Come out, come out."

I can make out their outlines across the empty moat. Andre crouches low, leaned against the stone supports. Charlotte is near him, eyes so wide I can see the white glare from here. The man walks slowly, deciding where he wants to descend.

I look left and right, but there's nowhere to run, just an empty, open moat on both sides. We'd be trapped. I glance at the turret where Henri waits, and I wonder if he can sense that we're close.

The guard slides down, landing with a thud into the dirt. "No peasants welcome," he yells into the darkness. "I'll give you a reason not to come back here again." He slaps a stick in his hands. Thwap. Thwap. He saunters, lowering his head to find the beggars he thinks only want shelter or food.

We want blood.

I can sense Charlotte's desire, her hunger to throw him to the ground and beat him senseless. Andre holds up his hand in the dark to encourage us to remain still.

The guard moves closer, walks the dirt path through the emptied moat, then halts and reaches for his knife at his hip. The owl fluffs his feathers.

As the guard steps closer, Andre shifts forward, but Charlotte holds him back. She steps forward sheepishly. "Hello?"

He drops his knife to his side. "A girl?"

"I'm so sorry. I shouldn't have come here." She steps closer, shoulders rounded. "A man was following me, and I was frightened." She steps closer still. "A window in the armory was open. I hoped to hide out until daybreak."

He releases a loud exhale. "This is a prison, Mademoiselle. Go back the way you came. I don't need any children causing a problem."

Charlotte cocks her head to the side.

"Oh no," I mutter to the owl.

"I am not a child," Charlotte says.

"I said go." He tugs at her arm, but she resists. "I don't have time to waste on you. Now, move."

Charlotte throws her arm back and steadies her feet. "Hands off me."

He grabs her with both hands and yanks far too hard. She stumbles to her knees. "Get up," he says.

Charlotte tries to use her legs to take him to the ground like she's seen me do, but he barely steps backward. "What was that?" He grabs her hair and pulls her to standing. Andre swiftly jumps to the next shadow, only steps from them. Distracted, the guard lifts his hand to slap her, but Andre has already launched himself. He stops the guard from striking Charlotte with one hand and punches him in the gut with the other.

Charlotte falls back, free from his grip. Andre and the man trade punches, grunts, and groans. The guard reaches for his knife, but Andre holds his arms, slamming his shoulder into the man's chest. The guard wriggles out of his grip and throws him off. They face each other, the guard's back to me.

I step from the shadows, high on the dirt hill near the top of the arch. Just as I learned in Quebec, surprise from behind is a powerful weapon. I bend my knees, pull up my skirt, and launch into the air, winding my knee up as I fall. Descending to earth, I shoot my leg forward so my foot lands hard in the man's ribs.

He falls, face first into the dirt, stunned and breathless. I stumble, but recover in a moment, which is all I have as the man gulps a large inhale, finding his breath. I swipe his knife and smash the wood handle into his forehead.

The man crumples, unmoving.

Charlotte grabs the knife from me and stares at the guard. "Is he dead?"

"Probably not," I say.

Charlotte kicks his arm out and waits for his response. When there is none, she slams the knife through the man's hand, slicing through his knuckles until the tip has gone through his flesh and lodged into the dirt. He moans but does not fight.

My instinct is to scream at her. But I remember what fear does. I once broke a man's spine with five blows to his back, when one would have been enough. "Come on." I wrap my arm around her rigid body until her breathing slows. "Don't let go of that anger, Charlotte. It will serve you once you learn to control it."

"I will never let it go," she mutters.

"Good, now let's get Henri."

Andre grabs the ring of keys from the man's breast pocket and whispers in my ear. "Did you just save me again?"

"Just doing as Naira taught me."

Andre flashes a smile. "I like this new warrior."

We sneak up the dirt moat and approach the giant door at the entrance to the Bastille. Andre tries a few different keys as we grow anxious. "What if he wakes?" Charlotte asks.

"We'll be out of here before then," I say.

"There it is." Andre unlocks the wood door and slides the massive slab open with a moan. No one is visible through the dark, cavernous entryway.

We slip inside but leave the door ajar. Charlotte motions to an alcove in the first turret where we can watch the guard's station. Our fight set us back and we now only have about thirty minutes for this plan to come together.

"He always keeps wine at the guard station," Charlotte whispers. "The duke in the biggest cell buys his favor and keeps him supplied." Charlotte reaches in her pocket and pulls out a vial. "Sleeping powder."

"Want me to do it?" I ask.

"No, I will." She hesitates but creeps across the entryway. Keys jangle and footsteps thud down the hall. Light bounces from a collection of candles in the alcove. Charlotte looks around the desk. No wine. She shrugs, then realizes he is almost near and slips into a curvature cut from the stone to let in light. If she crouches, she can remain under the sliver of moonlight and in the darkness.

The guard returns and exhales as he balances a lantern. In his other hand, a goblet. "What if he drinks it all?" Andre says.

"We'll have to find more."

"We don't have time, Isabelle." Andre rubs his neck. "We must get that girl out of Paris. The family is expected to convert tomorrow."

"You're just telling me that now?"

He shrugs. "Her parents were buying time to get her out. They will present themselves to the authorities and refuse conversion, but their daughter will be long gone."

"They'll be executed," I say.

"I would do the same for Elizabeth. Without a second thought."

I realize how much he must miss her. How painful it must be to love someone that much. Andre tucks my wild curl behind my ear, his thumb grazing my chin. "You're almost free, Isabelle."

"I'm not free until they all are."

He raises my hand to his mouth and places a soft kiss on my wrist. His lips linger long enough that my chest tightens and my heart flutters. "You've begun a journey that you'll never come back from," he says.

"I'm right where I'm meant to be."

We hold each other's gaze, outlines and shadows in the dark, but our hands still touch.

The guard grumbles and stands, ducking into a stone cutout near his desk. As he bends forward under the half stone wall, Charlotte moves quiet as a spider, pouring the vial into his goblet and swirling it a few times to dissolve the powder. The guard exhales and Charlotte has no choice but to fall back into the darkness out of the candlelight directly behind his desk.

We watch Charlotte. Her body pressed to the wall, she holds an intense stare at the back of his head. He should be grateful it's just sleeping powder. Charlotte has enough anger to slice his head clean off.

"How long will it take?" Andre asks.

The man sips his wine, releasing a loud burp that bellows into the night. "A few minutes," I say.

After ten of the slowest minutes imaginable, the man's head wobbles. He blinks feverishly and grasps his chest. When he tries to stand, his arms slide off the table and he crashes to the ground, where he writhes and groans.

"Come on," Charlotte says. She grabs his keys, and he looks up at her, his eyes fighting sleep. Charlotte stops and leans close. She slaps him hard across the face but doesn't elicit even one more groan. "Everything looks good here."

We follow her down the dark, cold, stone walkway that smells of wet earth, past the turrets, as a prisoner's bird squawks at us. "Help me," a man in his nightshirt says from a cell. His fat fingers curled around the bars display rubies and emeralds and gold adornments.

"You want us to help you?" Charlotte asks.

Andre tries to lead her away, but she resists, and leans closer to the prisoner. "Look at your jewels. Your exotic bird. Your barrels of wine."

"I am still a prisoner," he says.

"You know nothing about being a prisoner." She grabs a finger and pulls back until the man screams.

Andre and I grab an arm each and drag her away as the man wails. "Charlotte, there's another guard here and he'll hear that man screaming. Don't be reckless!"

"I've finally earned a chance to hurt them like they hurt us," she says.

"And how will that feel when you're in a prison cell next to Henri?"

She doesn't speak but follows us down the stairs to Henri's cell. The smell is worse here—human waste and rot.

Henri grips the bars with his thin fingers. His voice crackles as he bites back tears. "You came." Gray light shoots down from a sliver in the wall, casting shadows over his ashen face.

Charlotte lays her hand on his. "Of course we did."

Andre tries every key. Enough that I begin to panic that he hasn't found it yet.

"Where's the other guard," I ask?

"Either asleep in his quarters or checking out the screaming man with the broken finger," Charlotte says without remorse.

Andre finally finds the correct key. I creak open the door and throw my arms around Henri. His slight frame and protruding bones are shocking, but his embrace softens all his sharp edges.

"Let's go," Andre says.

I stop to stare at the man in the stall next to Henri. I forgot about him. He appears from the shadows but doesn't say a word.

"Your daughter and brother made it out of the city," I say.

He nods. Wipes away his tears.

"Andre, the keys."

"They'll lock this place down when they find the guard on the floor and a prisoner screaming."

"We can't leave him." I extend my hand.

"I'll do it." He starts with the same key from Henri's cell. Then the next, and the next. "Go," he says.

We help Henri up the stairs. He's weak but smiles when Charlotte wraps her arm around his waist. I hold them back and creak the door open. In the dark hallway, I close my eyes and listen to the faint sound of footsteps. "Hurry." I lead them to the main floor and back into the darkness of a black, curved wall. I place my hand on Charlotte's arm. When I have her attention, I raise my hand, indicating to stay still.

The guard approaches with furious steps. I widen my stance and breathe. Blocking them with my body, I prepare to fight.

When the man approaches, he doesn't see us. He opens the door and stares at the figures before him. Andre and the unknown Huguenot man, staring with wide eyes. For a moment, everyone is silent. The guard reaches to strike the prisoner, but Andre blocks him and quickly punches the guard in the nose. His head flies back, hand to his face.

I raise my arm and slam my elbow with force between his shoulder blades. By the time he falls to his knees, I've already grabbed his hair and slammed my foot into his back, holding his face to the stones. He fights, smearing his bloody nose all over the floor.

I don't want to kill him. But I look at my friends and realize how little time we have to escape the city. I freeze.

Charlotte reaches into her pocket. Pops a cork on a vial and throws a liquid in the man's eyes. He screams, and his body stops resisting my foot. His eyes bulge, frothy and swollen.

"Go," I yell.

We scramble down the dark hallway but stop at the entrance. "Okay, we have a plan," Andre says. "Once we're outside, we need to move fast. I have a path carved out of the alleyways, with one stop on the way. There's one gate out to the countryside that remains open. I broke it before nightfall, but overheard the guard say they'll have it fixed shortly."

A gulping sound catches our attention, and we all turn to find Henri has finished the last of the guard's goblet of wine. He makes an "ah" sound, wipes his mouth with the back of his hand, and places the goblet down with a clank. "I've wanted some of this bastard's wine for months." He sees us stare at him. "What?" he shrugs.

"We put sleeping powder in that wine," I say.

"Isabelle?" Charlotte whispers.

I turn to her, sensing we have a big problem. She points to the guard, pale white, eyes open, mouth agape, and *dead*.

"I used the arsenic powder," she says.

Definitely a big problem.

CHAPTER TWENTY-SIX

Henri can still move, but he's begun to sweat. We run out the doors of the Bastille, down the bridge, and out through the armory. I'm trying not to count the minutes ticking down before the bridge will be fixed and shut tight. Before James recovers, before LaMarche has time to track us down.

Henri coughs, with obvious difficulty clearing his throat. "It's happening," he says.

Charlotte looks at me with such regret. Her impulsivity has consequences. Never a harsher lesson learned than to poison the man you desire. It's like something from a Greek tragedy.

"We now have two stops to make on our way from the city." I loop my arm through Henri's. "I won't let you die."

He wants to say something witty, but he's unable to form words.

A man approaches and sees a shackle on the Huguenot's ankle. "What's this?" he says.

"Nothing, old man," Andre barks. "Go back home."

The man scoffs, but when two more men step forward from the dark alley, we stumble back. "Get out. Before we slice your fingers off." The man produces a knife, and the other two slap sticks in their hands.

"We're going," Andre says.

We make our way back through the courtyard and head to the north side of Le Marais.

"There's an intricate system in the streets," the prisoner says. "The slums are called the Court of Miracles. A hierarchy of beggars and thieves, each with their own territory. Their own leader and language."

"We don't know your name," I say.

"Antoine."

"That was my father's name." I smile, despite the painful memories.

Henri grabs at his throat and stumbles to his knees. We lift him as a group, dragging his feet as they barely take weight.

"Just one more block, Henri. You can do it," I say.

The site of Mademoiselle Boulais's door is a welcome one. But when she doesn't answer, we look at each other in panic. "She must be with one of her men," I say. "We don't have time to find her."

Andre picks the lock with his knife. "So poorly made," he mumbles.

We drag Henri inside, his eyes red and legs twitching. The muscles in his neck are taut and protruding. We bring him into the laboratory and lay him on the table. Charlotte stares at the shelves of powders and animal parts.

"You can do this, Charlotte," I say. "Just think."

"There's an antidote, I think it's called. I remember the jar. I just don't know where it is." She looks around, about to cry.

"No." I shake her shoulders. "You are brave and fearless, and all you have to do is stay calm."

Her eyes focus. "The assassin's toolkit. Maybe it was there."

"Perfect." I find the box hidden inside a book, open the covers and show her the drawers. Henri vomits and shakes. Andre rolls him to his side and rubs his back. "Which is it?" I ask.

"I... What if I choose wrong? Poison him further? He could die a painful death."

"He already is," I say. "Just breathe." I keep my voice calm. Touch her shoulder with a soft hand. Panic does us no good.

With a trembling hand, she reaches for a jar, then changes her mind. She runs her fingers along the tiny drawers and touches the knobs, I assume trying to see if something activates her memory. She swallows. Henri vomits with such intensity that it sprays across the wall, splattering against Mademoiselle's jars of bird feet and frog lungs.

Charlotte rubs her eyes then pauses, a flash of hope. She opens a drawer, pops a vial and runs to Henri. We prop him up and Charlotte holds the clear liquid in front of his face. "Drink this, Henri."

He shakes his head, clutches his throat.

"Yes," she says. "You can. It will hurt, but this is the only way to help you. You must." Tears gather in her eyes. "For me," she says.

He parts his blue lips as she pours the liquid into his mouth. I close his jaw and force the antidote down his throat. His body turns rigid, his throat gurgling.

"Please, try to swallow," Charlotte says.

He does, though it's obvious the pain is excruciating. She leans his head back to her hands and rubs his forehead. He remains tight, almost convulsing.

"What do we do now?" Charlotte asks.

My voice trembles, but I keep my gaze steady. "You'll need to stay here with him," I say. "We can help the Huguenot girl out of the city and come back for you."

"We don't have time," Andre says. "The gate."

"We'll have to find another way out. We can't carry him." Henri's ashen skin turns my stomach, but I won't let myself imagine this life without him.

"The thief system," Antoine says. "I know one of the ragots, a king of the beggars. He owes me a favor."

"Can you find him tonight?" I ask.

"Yes, but I will need to present you to him. All of you. He will only help us if he deems us worthy."

"And if he doesn't?" I ask.

"His lieutenants will beat us bloody." He looks to Andre, then down at Henri.

"We can do it ourselves," I say.

"Madame," Antoine says, "no you can't. They rule these streets at night and will attack anyone they wish with no consequences."

"You trust this man?" Andre asks.

"Not at all," Antoine says. "But he's our only choice. Otherwise, we'll be here until sunrise when they open the gates."

"Everyone will be after us," I say. "Andre," I place my hand to his chest, feeling the stiffness from the documents. "LaMarche will come for these. It has the location of his money."

"Looks like we'll be joining the Court of Miracles tonight," Andre says.

Henri vomits again over the side of the table. "Damn," he mutters.

Charlotte smiles, delighting that his sharp tongue has returned.

"Stay here with him and don't go anywhere. We'll be back as soon as we get the girl," I say.

"Let's go." Andre leads me to the door, and Antoine follows.

Charlotte nods confidently to me then resumes stroking Henri's hair.

Back in the city alleyways, into the black and gray shadows that turn static gargoyles into mythical creatures that seem to pounce and roar. We pass a man on his knees, his face under a prostitute's skirt. She smiles, all her teeth gone, waving seductively at Andre. He pulls me close and pretends not to notice the debauchery.

We creep past a boy sharpening his knife, crouched against a doorway with elbows propped on his knees. He mumbles, "Not wise."

"Stay clear of the streets west of here," Antoine says. "The worst and filthiest beggars live there. They use children and the elderly. Train them to perform for handouts, pretending to be crippled and blind."

"More sympathy?" I ask.

"Exactly. Then they return to their social circle, miraculously returned to a state of health. Hence the name."

"Up ahead," Andre says. "This house."

Houses here are nothing like Le Marais. Here in Saint-Marcel, the homes look like wood piles, crammed and stacked together with rotting holes for pests and insects to burrow into. We approach a narrow house smashed between two crumbling structures.

Andre knocks twice on the door. A man creaks it ajar, peers at Andre, and hurries us inside. "They'll be here in a few hours to take us to the square," the man says. "To admit our wrongdoing and accept Catholicism." His face turns serious. "Which we will never do."

"Of course not, monsieur." Andre rests his hand on the man's elbow. "We haven't much time."

The man holds his chin high, then nods, tightening his lips into a thin line. "Of course." He motions to the doorway as his wife with red, puffy eyes pulls their daughter forward. Maybe fourteen, with giant blue eyes and golden hair. She hugs her parents and sobs.

I turn my head as their sorrow burrows a hole into my heart.

"Please don't make me go, Papa."

"Josephine," the mother says. "This is the only way you can be free." Her voice catches on the final word, but she coughs and pushes her daughter toward the door. "Go now."

The father kisses Josephine's forehead. "Be good. Be strong."

The girl shuffles toward me, panic in her eyes.

I turn to the parents. "Why aren't you coming?"

"We can't. We are old and slow," the man says. "My wife has a painful leg."

Antoine leans to my ear. "We can't manage two more. Especially if they're slow."

"Besides," the man says, "we only had enough money for Josephine."

I let her words settle. "You… you paid to save her?"

"Of course," the woman says. "That is how these things are done."

"They shouldn't be." We should fight for each other every minute of every day. We should scale walls and poison guards and drag ourselves through slums to save each other.

The woman pushes us out the door. "Hurry, please. Before someone sees you."

Andre looks at me. "Isabelle, don't be foolish."

"They'll never see each other again. We'll break up this family and leave the parents to die, all over money. I can't allow it."

The father blows a kiss to his daughter as tears spring to his eyes. He retreats into the house, but I shove my foot in the doorway to stop it from closing. "Wait."

"Madame, please. It's dangerous."

"What is your name?" I ask.

"Perrin."

"Monsieur Perrin, come with us. Right now."

The wife steps forward, cracks the door open. "Us?"

"We don't require payment. We are just like you, and we want to help. Please. Right now."

"We simply cannot," the man says. "My business is here."

"Do you understand what they will do to you when you don't convert?" I ask. "Paris still needs their Protestant merchants, but soon enough they'll turn you into prisoners. The Catholic leaders will burn you, beat you, and break your bones."

"Isabelle, please." Andre pulls at my waist.

"Pour boiling water down your throat and bounce you against the ground. They made me dance all night and burned my flesh with a branding iron."

The woman covers her hand to her mouth.

"Get out while you can," I say.

"Enough," Antoine says. "Gangs lurk the streets at night. Someone will be here any minute." He pulls Josephine forward, followed by Andre.

I stumble back. "Please," I say. "Don't let them tear you apart."

Andre drags me, tears streaming down my cheeks as I twist to see the doorway, begging the father to step out of the house. My heart sinks when the door clicks shut. I shove Andre off me and run back inside. They stare at me, shocked and crying.

"If I have to carry you over that mountain myself, we will get you to Geneva."

The woman grabs the man's hand. "Please." Her voice is strong, more of a demand than a request. The man nods, runs to the fireplace and retrieves a small bag from behind a stone. "I am ready."

We catch up to the group. Josephine wraps her arms around her parents and weeps.

"Silence please," I say. "I need all of you to tread carefully. We have many obstacles ahead of us tonight."

"Yes, madame," the man says.

The broken bridge is only a few streets away, chosen for its location nearest the Huguenot household. The city wall comes into focus, revealing a fully locked gate.

"They repaired it already," Andre says.

Andre and I exchange a knowing glance with Antoine, who raises his eyebrows. "There is only one other way," he says.

Back through the alleys, toward Le Marais. Past the men crumpled in the streets like lumps of castoff clothing. Andre and Antoine lead the way. Around a curved building, they bump into a large woman dressed in black, holding a deck of cards to her chest.

"Night crawlers, seeking an escape," the fortune teller says, her voice deep and crackly. She steps in front of us, stares with her giant brown eyes. "I can offer your fortune."

"Out of our way, madame," Antoine says.

"As you wish." She flutters her fingers in the air as we walk past, stopping when she comes to me. She gasps and recoils. "You."

I ignore her and follow the Perrins, protecting them from behind.

"You are a warrior," the woman says.

I stop walking.

"You have a wolf," she says as she creeps toward me. "A wolf with green eyes walks with you."

Chills climb my body and I'm unable to speak.

"You are meant to walk a trail. The same trail many times. Through sweltering heat and frigid snow. You will continue to climb."

"I don't know what that means," I say.

"You will. But be warned," she wags a finger at me, "an arrow will puncture your heart."

My throat tightens.

"Unless you stop to listen. Listen. Listen."

Andre grabs my hand and pulls me away from this mysterious woman. "Isabelle, we have no time," he says.

I follow him, looking back over my shoulder to see that the fortune teller has disappeared. A white mist drifts away to darkness.

An arrow through my heart, a path, and the same message Naira gave me. I shake off her words and return to my position behind the Perrins. We pad through the alleys with soft feet. Madame Perrin limps but manages to keep up. All I hear is a patter of feet and our rapid breathing.

Back to Le Marais. We must have crossed the Right bank three times by now. The night grows darker still, but soon enough, the morning light will creep in. Back at Mademoiselle Boulais's house, we find Charlotte waiting inside the door. Henri sleeps in a wheelbarrow. Like a child's doll, his limbs spill out the sides. Charlotte has tucked a jug of wine near his hip and rolled a black cape under his head for support.

"We're ready," she says.

"Is he…" I pause.

Henri cracks open his eyes. "You aren't rid of me yet," he says.

Relief.

"He can't walk yet. We've tried," Charlotte says. "He can barely stay awake. But his breathing is steady, and he takes sips of wine when I ask him to."

"I can't imagine how this group will look suspicious," Andre says with a smile.

"A family of Huguenots, a prisoner with a shackle around his ankle, a soldier's wife in bloody clothing, and a newly poisoned man in a wheelbarrow. Should be simple enough," I say.

Back into the dark alleys and the suffocating, windless night. Our group seems to grow by the minute. I can only hope I don't encounter a child that begs for my help. I want to throw them all on my back and march them out of this filthy city.

As we near a courtyard tucked in the far northwest corner of Paris, boys appear like droplets on a dewy morning. Scattered along the walls, they stare at us with ragged clothes and filthy faces.

"Stay behind me," Antoine says.

An older boy, maybe fifteen, approaches Antoine. "Get out."

"I've come to see your ragot."

He eyes him, then the rest of us. "All of you?"

"We're a group," Antoine says.

"If I take you to him, I'm not responsible for what happens to any of you in there." He throws a warning glance at Josephine.

I lean toward Andre. "Are we certain this is the only way?"

He holds my waist. "Stay close. All of you."

We gather in a close circle, taking small steps toward the stone archway into the courtyard, the Perrins in the middle, surrounded by those tasked with protecting them. The courtyard, open to the sky, crawls with people of all ages. Women bounce crying babies, as grandmothers spoon bowls of soup from dented pots over fires along the perimeter. Prostitutes decorate the stairs like candlesticks. Tall and lean, their clothes seem to drip off them. They kiss the air at the men and twirl their hair.

A boy runs up to Charlotte, yanks on her dress. "That man is dead?" he asks. As he points to Henri, he reaches into her pocket. I grab his wrist and stare in his eyes. "Nothing. See?" He opens his empty hand and smiles.

We pass a decimated house filled to the brim with mud and stone and splintered wood. Multiple families cram inside, huddled under the decrepit roof.

A boy rams his shoulder into Henri, and another shoves Antoine. We move closer to Josephine and her vulnerable parents. Charlotte stands in front of Henri's wheelbarrow. The crowd of beggars and thieves moves toward us like bodies risen from the grave, with dead eyes and tattered, dirty clothes. A young, sinewy man circles us as the group watches on.

He stops at me, tilts his head and smiles. "You look like the tough one of the group." A scar mars his cheek from the corner of his eye to his mouth. Clean, straight, it looks as if someone has cut him slowly, purposefully.

I turn away, focusing on the terrified Huguenots in front of me.

"Come on," he says. "Madame wants to fight, does she?" He flips my hair and laughs. He looks at Andre and registers his tightened jaw. "Are you going to protect her, monsieur?"

"I do not need his protection," I say.

"I rarely fight women." He continues pacing, sauntering. "But I can see it in your eyes. You're street trash, just like us."

The Perrins tremble, holding each other and crying. "It's all right. We'll be fine," I mutter.

The scarred man reaches for Josephine, and she screams, shrill and frantic. I take hold of his wrist and bend back until he releases her. I don't let go. I shove his hand into his own face and knee him in the groin.

"I told you I sensed a fighter." He raises his fists and I widen my feet. Andre and Antoine jump him from either side as another man, younger and weaker, grabs my hair. Grunts and screams echo through the courtyard as we fight these feral young men. I hold both of this boy's skinny arms and twist out of his grip, yank his hands down as my knee lands in his stomach. I roll him to his back and shove my foot onto his chest when a cowbell jangles. The fighters retreat with hungry, deprived eyes.

Andre and Antoine keep the scarred man on the ground, and my foot balances on the boy's neck.

A rugged young man descends the stairs from an apartment. His skin is clean but thinned fur drapes over his shoulders. Newly shined black boots adorn his feet, but his breeches are so stained I cannot discern the color. As he descends, the courtyard becomes a quiet hush. He taps the stone ground with a scepter, whittled to create a circle on top.

"We have visitors, I see."

Antoine steps forward. "Monsieur." He bows to this strange street king, not yet thirty.

The ragot emulates the king's posture. Expanded chest and chin high. One foot positioned forward as he extends his arm to his scepter. "Monsieur. We do not have business. I paid my debt to you."

"You did, kind King. I've come for a favor."

The man searches our group. "Release them."

Andre lets the scarred man free, and I lift my shoe from the boy's neck.

"You're an interesting group," the ragot says. "You look to belong in a quiet house somewhere, sleeping the night away. Not here, in our lair."

"We need to escape the city," Antoine says. "Quickly."

"So, you came to me?" His voice lifts. "Because I have the power to decide who will live and who will be handed over to the mercy of our esteemed king? Who will escape in the night, and who will be eaten by the dark?"

"Yes, monsieur," Antoine says.

The ragot's face lights, welcoming the adoration. "I will help you. Under one condition."

Antoine pulls a deep inhale. "What is it?"

"You let me keep her." He points to me.

"She's a soldier's wife," Antoine says. "He'll be searching the streets for her any moment."

"She's a fighter. I saw it." He walks toward me. "You're unexpected, Madame. Beautiful, with your bright green eyes and luscious hair. You will garner sympathy from the masses when we blindfold you and teach you to limp."

"I do not beg," I say.

"Too good for us?" His lip twitches into a snarl. "You're running from your husband and have nowhere to go." He turns to Charlotte. "She is also pristine and pretty. But she doesn't have your strength. I want those who can fight, who won't be bullied."

"I will not stay here," I say.

He slams his scepter into the stones. "That is my offer. You may agree and I will assist you out of Paris before sunup, or you must leave through this crowd of street beggars who will strip you and beat you until you can no longer scream."

I turn to watch the group of boys, girls, adults, and grandparents prepared to attack us, prepared to follow this man's every command. I squeeze my eyes shut and breathe. Andre's hand gently touches my arm. "You won't do it," he says.

"I have to," I say. I step forward, past Josephine and her ailing parents. Past Charlotte and a barely conscious Henri in a wheelbarrow. "What choice do we have?"

Antoine looks at his ankle. "Perhaps I'm meant to remain in shackles. But you belong out there, saving the rest of our people."

"Antoine, don't."

He steps away from the group. "Take me."

The ragot laughs. "I don't want you. You escaped from the Bastille. Because of her." He points to me. "I want the cunning one."

Andre slips his hand into mine.

"I will be your personal artist. I can craft you more scepters and a throne fit for a king."

The man hesitates. He's skeptical but considers his offer.

"I envision a bust of your likeness, right here in the center of the courtyard."

"If you are to supply the materials, you have a deal."

Antoine shakes his head. "I have none, monsieur. They took everything when they threw me in the Bastille."

"Then my original offer stands. Madame, what will it be?"

Andre squeezes my hand tighter, leans into my ear. "No." I feel a pull, a tearing in my heart like a sheet of silk ripped in two. If I don't comply, I must watch these innocent people brutalized in front of me. I cannot take more of what already haunts my dreams. I open my mouth to agree, but a hand rests on my shoulder.

Josephine's father steps next to Antoine. He hands him the pouch from his fireplace. "It is yours."

Antoine opens the pouch. The light from the fires reflects off the gold. "I have the funding, monsieur." He offers the bag.

The ragot examines the money and hands it off to his lieutenant. "Very well." He calls a man forward. "See that they make it safely outside the city walls. I will see our new artist to his quarters." The ragot releases a deep, menacing laugh, and the crowd follows.

"Antoine," I say, "You can't do this."

"I just did. Now please, go."

"They'll just arrest you again, and maybe kill you this time."

He smiles. "They won't find me here."

"But your daughter, your brother. Don't you want to go to England and find them? That was the plan."

"Yes, madame, I do. But I cannot rest knowing I could have saved you all."

The lieutenant nods for us to follow. I search my mind for another way out of this mess, but nothing comes. Andre shakes Antoine's hand and pulls me away as I mouth, *Merci*.

Through a dark tunnel, we hold each other's hands to form a chain. We follow our breaths and thumping heartbeats as we descend lower and deeper beneath the city. The darkness eats away at my resolve like rats feasting on breadcrumbs. The dark closes in, squeezing at my throat. It's difficult to breathe. Someone panics, resists backward and whimpers.

"Don't... let go," I say. "No one let go."

My knees grow weak, and I squeeze Andre's hand over and over to remind myself I'm still here. We're still here. I am about to fall to the ground when light appears in the distance, gray and vaguely yellow.

The early morning light at the tunnel's end feels like life again. I tremble, releasing the fear that nearly overtook me in the dark. The man creaks open a grate, and we follow him to the stairs that lead to a room—no—a barn. Once standing on the earth again instead of underneath it, tears spring to my eyes. I count the group. The father and Charlotte drag Henri up the stairs, his legs helping some. The mother, Josephine, and Andre still hold hands.

"We're all here," I say.

"You are outside the city walls," the man says. He turns to me. "You made an impression on our ragot."

"Madame Beaumont makes an impression on everyone," Charlotte says.

"Where are you going?" the man asks.

"Away," Andre says. "Far away from here."

"I dream of running away," he says. "This life, it's not what I want. They beat me if I don't make enough money, or if I don't hurt the others."

"Come with us," Charlotte says. "You could have a new life in Geneva."

"Geneva?" He laughs. "That isn't possible."

"Yes, it is." I reach for her, but she ignores me. "Come with us," she says. "We will walk the hills to Helvetia together."

"No, thank you for the offer. I cannot leave. Best of luck to you all." He disappears back into the dark tunnel of the Paris underground.

"Charlotte, what were you thinking?" I ask.

"I was being like you. We can save people."

"Lesson for today, Charlotte. Do not allow your need for power to overtake your senses. We save Huguenots. We can trust them."

She bites her lip, looking like a chastised child.

"Henri, how are you?" I ask.

"Weak as a lamb. But I can try to walk."

"Good." I open the barn door to the faintest hint of daybreak. Yellow and gold warm the morning, lighting a path forward into the hills and out of Paris. I look at our broken group of hopefuls. "Ready?"

They nod, stepping hesitantly out of our Paris cage. The empty, unknown of the French countryside holds new dangers, but also, new possibilities. All we must do is travel south to the Rhône-Alps and over the mountains to Geneva, where we can all breathe free.

We take the first steps of another difficult journey. I think of the documents that hide securely against Andre's chest, reminding me that James and LaMarche won't allow me to slip away without a fight. I focus on my friends' smiles, and their hopeful hearts, and I swallow the tightness that circles my throat like a poisonous snake.

I sense our next fight has just begun.

CHAPTER TWENTY-SEVEN

August sun in the countryside of France beats your skin like batons. Heat descends on us in waves, our bodies slick with sweat and slow from fatigue. Andre's wagon and ailing horse barely carried us to Melun, where Andre handed them off to a farmer, who thanked him by offering us a night in his barn.

"Didn't you steal the horse?" I ask.

"And add to the number of people who want us dead?" He shakes his head. "No, I found a young farmer who needed his wagon sent back to his father in Melun, but couldn't leave his farm unattended."

"You're quite resourceful," I say with a smile.

Other than the uncomfortable heat and barely working wheels, the first stretch of travel was easy enough. If we walk ten hours a day, we could arrive in Helvetia in two weeks. But our group cannot sustain that. Josephine holds her parents as they stumble, and Henri is walking again, but we can't move more than a few hours per day.

Under the shade of a French oak, I express my worry to Andre. "We won't make it, not with this heat."

"I know," he says. "Henri and the parents might fall to their knees at any moment."

"We need a better plan."

"Perhaps we stay in the countryside for a while? Forget about Geneva."

"No," I say. "We can't stay in France. We know what will happen to us." I gaze across our group, knowing the wave of hate from La Rochelle will only grow and spread through France.

Monsieur Perrin approaches. "I have friends in Lyon. Huguenots. They will house and protect us, I know they will."

"That's still days away," I say.

He looks back at his family. "Leave us. Carry on and we will find our way."

"No. What we started, we finish together. Even if it takes months, we will get to Geneva."

He smiles and nods. "They would have thrown us in prison by now. Or worse." He pauses, brow furrowed. "Thank you."

He returns to his wife and daughter, who clasp hands and pray. Charlotte helps Henri drink from a stream.

"James and LaMarche will come for us," I say to Andre.

Andre crosses his arms over his knees. "How will they find us?"

"I don't know, but they will. I feel it."

"I'll have to steal a wagon this time," he says. "They can't carry on like this."

We shouldn't bring more attention to ourselves, but I see we have no choice. I nod and he places his hand on my shoulder. "We can do this."

My arm around Henri's waist, we carry on into the rolling hills. My dry, cracked cheeks burn under the unrelenting heat. We search for a farm—the kind near town with money enough to own a wagon, yet small enough to avoid workers.

We walk, and stumble, and even crawl at one point, but three days in, we find the perfect farm. Andre spots a wagon through the open door of a barn and three horses graze near the stone house.

We wait in a copse of alders, grateful for the reprieve, as our faces still glow red under the filtered light of the towering branches. Andre crawls to the edge of the trees near the barn. Smoke trails from the farmhouse chimney, carrying the yeasty scent of baked bread.

Hours pass, but Andre decides not to make a move. As the sun lowers, a featherlight breeze brushes our faces and our weary legs soak up the rest.

Andre returns and sits close to me, shoulder to shoulder. "I'm not sure I can steal that without someone chasing after us. It might be too dangerous."

"We can't carry on." I stare at our fatigued, ragged group as they lay scattered on the earth like rabbits sleeping in a burrow.

Andre wraps his arm around me. I lean my cheek against his strong shoulder and close my eyes. *A warrior needs rest*, Naira would tell me.

I teeter on sleep, softening into Andre's embrace, when I feel something against my arm. I creak my eyes open to find a tall, slender man. He nudges me with the barrel of his rifle. "Get up."

Andre has woken already, and he pulls me closer.

"All of you," the man says. "Get up."

We rise and huddle together as the man nudges his rifle toward his barn. I consider attacking, but something in his eyes makes me hesitate. We gather in the barn, Henri falling to the ground in fatigue.

The man slides the door closed and drops his rifle. "Well, if you're here to steal from me, you aren't very good at it."

Andre steps forward. "I'm sorry, Monsieur, we're hurt and tired, and we're trying to get to Lyon."

He examines Andre. "You wanted my wagon, I assume."

No one responds.

"What do you want in Lyon?" he asks.

"A friend can take us in," Monsieur Perrin says.

Charlotte steps forward and reaches into the lining of her skirt. She pulls out her Bible and I want to launch across the barn and throw her to the ground. Stupid child.

She walks closer, stringy hair framing her face, her giant blue eyes begging him for mercy. She hands him her tiny Geneva Bible. "We need help."

My heart races. The man places his hand on Charlotte's and closes his eyes. They bow their heads in silent prayer. The rest of us join in an unspoken language of trust and understanding.

"You may stay here for the night. My wife will bring you food and wine, and blankets for you to sleep on."

"Did you know we are like you?" I ask.

"I presumed. You all look like Paris castoffs without a livre to your name."

"That's exactly what we are," I say.

He steps out of the barn. I turn to Charlotte. "How did you know he was one of us?"

"It's in the eyes," she says. She's right. It's more than just our light coloring—even Andre's brown eyes shine amber in the light. Protestant eyes share a long-held suffering, hidden from the world, but clear as glass when one of our own looks back.

. . .

After washing our tired bodies with lye, we fill our bellies with boar stew. The man has agreed to take us to our destination, stating that he will do anything to save us from the hands of the Catholics.

Outside of Lyon stands a large stone farmhouse sheltered by olive trees. Two front doors glow a crisp white, framed by pale blue shutters.

"Here we are," Monsieur Perrin says.

We ask our new friend if he will stay, but he simply smiles and says, "Keep saving our people. You've got work to do." His wagon kicks up a dust cloud as his horse clops down the road.

Monsieur Perrin knocks on the door. An older woman creaks the door open and wipes her hands on her apron.

"Can it be?" she says.

Monsieur smiles and reaches for her in an embrace. "Lovely to see you," the woman says. "It's been years, old friend."

Monsieur turns to us. "My friends need a place to stay. We're a tired lot, just trying to make it to Geneva."

She lifts her chin and crosses her arms. "Well, you all look to be hungry and in need of a rest." She cusps Josephine's cheek. "Please, come in."

Low beams darken the rooms, but the stone keeps the house cool. A fire crackles in the kitchen, the windows open to release the smoke.

I note a Bible like ours displayed on the table in the center of the room. I nearly gasp, but the woman places her hand on my arm. "No need for alarm." She lifts the Bible and opens to the first page. Torn at the seams, the first few pages have been ripped out.

"The Catholic soldiers cannot read. They're taught to search for the title page, and if they can't see it, they assume it to be Catholic."

"Smart," I say with a smile.

"Everyone needs a rest before supper," she says. She directs the Perrins to a room near the kitchen, and Charlotte and Henri take the spare room at the opposite end of the house. She assumes Andre and I to be married, and points to a guest house across a path lined with lilacs.

The one-room guest house is as charming as a house has ever been. Picture windows that look over blooming vineyards. A poster bed with chipped paint dominates the room, with a narrow fireplace next to a round table and two dainty chairs. Madame has left a vase of lavender on the table, which fills the room with a woodsy scent.

"I think I might stay here forever," I say.

"Have you missed France?" Andre asks.

"I suppose. I haven't had time to think about it. But being here, in the sunshine, walking under the shade of olive trees…" I lean against the window, watching the sun lower to the hills. "I do."

"Quebec is home for me," Andre says with a sigh. "Beaver furs and trading with the Natives. The freedom of the wild, that has become home." He stares at me in the light of fading day and grazes my cheek with the back of his hand.

My stomach tightens, and I pull away.

"I'm sorry," he says. "I understand this is overwhelming."

"It isn't," I say. I open the window to allow the breeze to move the still air and cool our skin. "I never felt I deserved you."

He tilts his head. "How could you possibly think that?"

"The day I met you in Quebec, my heart cracked open. When you took me to the birch trees with their beautiful golden leaves, I was falling in love with you."

"Then why?" He gazes off behind me, and back, new strength in his voice. "Why choose James?"

"I was free, but Charlotte wasn't. Henri wasn't. I should have saved my people, but I was a coward."

His eyes widen. "You are the bravest person I know."

"Being with you felt like a reward I didn't deserve. I was afraid."

He turns his chest toward me. "And you punished yourself by staying with James?"

"I always knew he would betray me. Maybe I wanted him to."

"Isabelle, you don't need to save people to prove anything." He leans forward, wanting to kiss me, but stops.

I stare at his full lips as my heart races with anticipation. "Nightmares plague me," I say. "Terrible memories from La Rochelle. If I can save even one Huguenot from death or torture, maybe they'll stop."

"France will only get worse for them."

"Which is why I must be their hero, just like Charlotte said. I was too afraid, but I'm not anymore."

Andre's eyes lower to my lips and lift back to my eyes. "You can be whatever you wish to be."

I'm drawn to him, pulled like my body needs his, like I might faint without his touch. Andre hesitates. "I've always wanted you," he says, his mouth just near mine. "From the moment I saw you, I wanted you."

"And now we're here. And I'm almost free."

"Almost?"

"I'm still married, Andre."

He pulls away and catches his breath. "Wait here."

He leaves for the main house, and I try to calm my racing heart. Andre returns with a basket. "Here." He reaches into the basket and places a goose-quill pen and parchment in front of me. "You have the power to break your marriage contract." He nods his head and exhales. "If that's what you want."

"It is." I grab the pen and begin with the date. I address it to the notary who performed my marriage, as well as the intendant of New

France. I inform them of my wish to cancel my marriage contract to Monsieur James Beaumont. I release my house and its contents, and request that effective immediately, our union be dissolved. Signed, Isabelle Colette.

A deep warmth spreads through me at the sight of my last name. The return to my Protestant title, to my true self.

"There," Andre says. "Consider yourself unmarried. I will ask the lady of the house to send this to New France immediately."

"Thank you."

"I also brought food." He pulls from the basket a bottle of wine and a bowl of grapes. I sit in front of the fireplace and watch him build a fire, more for light than warmth. He lifts thick wood logs without effort, and I watch his hands rub together, wishing they were on me.

We sit by the light of the fire, sharing swigs from the bottle of wine. I pop grapes in my mouth, clusters of tiny green fruit that remind me of my childhood.

We discuss Elizabeth and Naira. Andre flicks an intense gaze at me when he talks of how Charlotte and Henri look at each other. We dream of depositing everyone into safety in Geneva, where they welcome Protestants with open arms.

"James always wanted to tame me," I say. "Mold me into a quiet woman with no fight left."

"And that is how he lost you."

"You've never made me feel that way," I say.

"How have I made you feel?" he asks.

"Like my wild heart is just perfect."

His smile turns serious, and he nods. "Because I have one too."

I stand, my legs soft but my heart pounding into my chest. I reach my hand for him. He steps close but does not kiss me. After all this time, we want to savor every moment.

I lean close, bring my chest to his, and lift his hand to my cheek. "The last time you kissed me on that snowy winter night on horseback, under the bright moon?" I exhale to soften my tightened shoulders. "I've thought about it every day since."

He tilts his head, leans near my lips. He runs his fingers through my hair and down my neck. Tension rolls through my body, as need and want and desire rip through me.

"Everything about you is perfect," he whispers.

Our lips find each other—a soft, sweet kiss shared with heavy breaths. My body lights from the inside as his lips and tongue tangle with mine. His touch is everything I remember, but more. So real, I can forget everything and be everything all at once.

I softly graze my fingers along his cheeks and neck, tasting his sweet lips. His hands slide along my waist, and I pull a sharp inhale, closing my eyes and letting my hands feel the way. He kisses my neck, his rough chin against the tender skin behind my ear.

I remove the pin in my hair and shake my curls to fall free over my back and shoulders, then untie the sides of my stay. My body warms as I lower my skirt to the ground, the shift soft against my skin.

I run soft fingers along his stomach, my eyes on his. He reaches back to remove his shirt. As he pulls it forward, his arms tense and I bring my lips to his chest, his neck, and his shoulders. I taste every part of his skin.

He removes his breeches and reaches to untie my shift. I feel no shyness, no hesitancy. Only need. Deep, unbridled desire I didn't know was possible. I slide away my shift and when it falls to the floor, Andre steps back to look at me.

His eyes tighten and he gasps. "You're more beautiful than I ever imagined."

Burning for him, I place his hand on my breast and press my hips to his. I'm about to whisper, *don't be gentle*, but somehow, he senses my need. He wraps his arms around me and lifts my legs around his waist, presses my back against the wall with just the right amount of heat. He kisses me deep and hard, until I ache for him to be inside me.

He kisses my neck as he sits on the edge of the bed. One hand firmly on the back of my head, he lowers me onto him. My body instantly pulses, like a heartbeat between my legs and into my mind. I lean my head back and moan.

He pulls my forehead to his and moves me up and down, rocking my hips so all I must do is fall into his power, his touch that knows exactly what I need. When he sends me to a near scream, his eyes remain on mine and we release in unison, every bit of our bodies tense, close, breathless.

I can't look away, even as my body relaxes and my heartbeat slows. I want to cry. But not for sadness—for complete and utter joy. I've spent my life always in a fight. But in Andre's arms, I can be soft.

He lowers me to the bed and covers us with a blanket. He kisses my chest and buries his head in my breasts, his ear to my beating heart. I run my fingers through his thick caramel hair and hug him closer.

"Isabelle?"

"Yes?"

"Let's save them. Every last one of the Huguenots." He looks up, flashing me a sleepy smile.

"I've never wanted anything more."

CHAPTER TWENTY-EIGHT

The dwindling fire crackles in the cool morning. I close the window, my body still burning from my night with Andre. Sheet soft around my naked body, I watch him sleep. I touch his temple softly with my fingertips and trace his jaw and lips. After all this time, to touch him like this feels triumphant.

His sleepy eyes crack open, looking up at me with a smile. He holds my hand, kisses my wrist, and pulls me back to bed. I lie my body close to his and savor his warmth against my cool skin, as if I can't get close enough. He lingers his lips on my neck with a drowsy groan.

"I want a cottage like this someday," I say.

"Then we shall have it."

Worry pushes its way to the surface. I ignored it last night, but in the bright light of morning, I can't avoid my concern. "What now, Andre? After we save them and arrive in Geneva?"

He leans against his elbow, hand supporting his cheek. "What do you want to happen?"

"I want to save more Huguenots—both of us, together."

His hand still rests on my waist, but his gaze drops from mine. "Elizabeth."

"I know. You need to return to Quebec to be with her."

"I hoped we would set sail for home after this, with Henri and Charlotte." He pulls his hand from me and rubs his face. "But you couldn't live a quiet life in Quebec. That's not who you are."

"I can't save them unless I'm in France." My chest aches and I grow lightheaded.

"It's all right." He pulls me to his chest and wraps his arm around my back, softly kissing my forehead. "Let's help this group to Geneva, and then we'll figure out what's next for us."

I lift my head and hold back tears. "There will be an us?"

"Forever and always, there will be an us."

I kiss him eagerly, press my body to his, and feel every second of this moment with him. I push the future away by sliding his hand between my legs. His touch turns my body tense and hot. With his powerful arms, he rolls me to my back and wraps my leg around his hips. I arch when he presses his fingers onto me. He moves me like he's playing music. Soft and firm, slow and rough, with complete control. I grab the metal scrolls of the headboard and stifle a scream as he takes me fully. Wholly.

"My desire for you only grows each time you touch me," I say. "How do you know exactly what I need?"

"Your body speaks to me. I listen." He kisses my breasts and buries his hand in my curls.

"I should feel exhausted, Andre." I smile and laugh. "But I only feel strong. Like everything has woken up."

His tongue glides up my breastbone and he grabs my face in his hands, kissing me deeply again. "I'm happy to replenish your strength any time madame wishes."

We kiss through smiles. I've never felt playful, not ever. Not until Andre's hands landed on my body.

I nearly demand that he take me again when someone knocks at the door. I must bite my lip to control myself. "Yes?"

"Isabelle," Charlotte says. "I hate to interrupt you. We must leave today."

Andre and I glance at each other, accepting that our time exploring each other in this perfect little cottage has ended.

"We'll be right out," I say.

We dress, and when Andre helps me with my stay, I watch his eyes. Back in Quebec, I never returned his gaze when he stared at me with longing. But now, I'm free to explore the desires of my heart. I pull him in for a kiss and he presses me against the door, hand behind my head. We enjoy a deep, passionate kiss, his hand firmly on my hip and grabbing at my skirt.

"This journey will not be easy," he says.

"Journeys never are." I bring his lips to mine gently, to taste him. To remember his softness.

Out in the bright sun, the group waits for us under the shade of an oak. Madame has prepared breakfast.

"Did something happen?" I ask Charlotte.

"A friend owns a hotel in Macon," madame says. "She sent a letter this morning, and it seems two men are traveling south, hunting for Protestants. She has delayed them by one day to allow word to reach me."

"We need to move. Now," I say.

"I'll gather some food for your journey," madame says.

Andre turns to me. "You think it could be them?"

"I have no doubt James and LaMarche are after us."

"Is it the documents they want?" Andre places his hand to his stomach where they're securely fastened with cloth. "Won't James just tell LaMarche where the money is?"

"The documents show proof of their lies," I say. "We could go to the king and ruin them. They want blood."

"Yours?" Andre asks.

"Both of us."

I turn to look for Charlotte and find her with Henri, up against the back of the house. Henri glides her hair from her face and kisses her cheek.

Andre whispers, "They're perfect for each other. Wily and secretive but full of heart."

"Yes, they are."

Andre rests his palms on my cheekbones and kisses me softly. The worry over our journey fades when he touches me. Every time he pulls me into his chest, I soften in a way I never have.

"They will find us before we can make it to Geneva," I say.

"I won't let them hurt anyone," he says. "I know you won't either."

"Naira taught me everything I need to know. I'm ready."

Charlotte and Henri amble toward us, holding hands. "Is something wrong?" she asks.

"Nothing to worry about," I say.

"Don't lie to me." She pulls her shoulders back. "How am I to help if you keep sheltering me from the truth?"

Henri smiles. "I don't care about the truth. But if I finally get my chance to pay the Catholics back for my treatment, then point the way."

"I believe James and LaMarche are after us. They'll find us before we can get this family to Geneva."

"Leave them here," Henri says. "They're with Huguenots. They'll be safe."

"They aren't safe anywhere in France," I say.

Madame returns with a sack of dried meats and hard cheese, and a jug of wine. "What about you, Madame?" Charlotte asks. "Aren't you tempted to flee with us? Start a new life in Geneva where you can sleep without fear?"

"I will die here, at my farmhouse," she says. "Under my trees and on my soil."

Andre sneaks a glance toward me. "And a lovely farmhouse it is."

"You must be on your way." She walks to the family and helps them prepare for the journey.

Andre and I turn to each other. "James won't stop until he hunts me down," I say.

"Let him fatigue himself with the hunt." He kisses the back of my hands.

I want to stay here and breathe for a while, but I know I can't, not with James so close. I say goodbye to the perfect French cottage I'll never see again. A dirt road leads east, toward gentle hills that glow gold and emerald green. My new and old family beside me, I let my heart settle around my choices and accept the reckoning I know I cannot outrun.

Four hours. That's all we're able to manage as Josephine fatigues easily and her parents complain of aching knees. We find an abandoned stone house with no doors or windows, but at least we'll be out of sight. We decide to sleep during the day and travel at night and ration our food, knowing it might take weeks to reach Geneva.

As the sun disappears into night, I stand watch outside the building, waiting for the cover of darkness to protect us. Leaned against the stone wall, I take a deep breath of the balmy evening, thinking of the freezing nights my mother and I walked after our exile from La Rochelle.

"You really think they'll come for us?" Charlotte leans against the wall next to me.

"James won't release me," I say. "I know he won't."

"He has his little wench, Antoinette, and money and power with LaMarche. Why would he go through all this?"

"He still believes I'm his."

"Even after you poisoned him and stole his documents?"

"Especially after that." I lean my head back to the cool stones and release a long exhale. "James will spend his life fighting himself, trying to prove his worth to the world. Breaking me has become sport for him—the ultimate test of manhood."

"Andre sees you as the warrior you are. So do I, and so does Henri." She places her hand on my shoulder. "I wonder if you do."

Her eyes glisten like crystals in the moonlight. "I feel like a warrior who has not yet tasted victory," I say. "I need to see these Huguenots cross the path to a new home."

"Much like Henri needs to watch Catholics bleed," she says. "I may be young, but I know that trying to heal the past will never work. I can't bring back Clémentine or Henri's father or your parents."

I swallow against the tightness in my throat. "You are quite wise, Charlotte."

"I still wish to fight, just for the future, not the past." She squeezes my hand and smiles. "I'll gather the group."

Everyone enters the shadows of midnight, eyes wide and shining, the Perrins huddled together with the four of us surrounding them, protecting them. We begin another trek on another road, every step that much closer to freedom.

Josephine has yet to speak. I walk with her, my arm close to hers. "Are you frightened?" I ask.

She nods yes. "I just want to go home."

I hate to be the one to crush her world, but I have no choice. "You'll never see Paris again."

She stares at her feet as she walks, choking back tears.

Andre leads the way and I stay behind, hearing a gallop in the distance. I turn and examine the blackness, but I see no movement. I listen, as Naira taught me, but the galloping fades to the quiet of our footsteps.

Madame Perrin trips and tumbles to the ground. I rush to help. "Do your legs hurt?"

"Yes. I'm sorry, Isabelle."

"It's all right. We're in this together."

I keep my arm around her waist, lifting the weight off her painful leg. Every rustle grabs my attention as I search the black night for any sign of eyes.

We walk this way for hours, me on alert, my arms aching from carrying Madame Perrin, and Josephine in and out of tears. "Just leave us," Josephine begs, but I ignore her and keep walking.

By the time morning arrives, fatigue envelops us. We collapse under an oak tree with its far-reaching branches that shade us from the sharp sun. Henri buries his head in his arms, not yet recovered from the poison. Charlotte hands him the wine.

I stare behind us, convinced I sense something.

"What is it?" Andre whispers.

"They're close."

"How do you know? I don't see anything."

"I can feel it," I say. When Naira told me to listen, I didn't understand. I was using my ears. Now it's clear I'm to use my senses—my mind and my heart. "I hear them."

He uses the back of his fingers to pull my usual curl from my face. "I'm ready to fight," he says.

"We should be prepared. How can we do it out here alone?"

He looks to the bright sun with squinted eyes. "Fallen branches. I can shape spears. We need to find shelter against this heat."

"The temperature will drop once we climb the mountains. We need to push them, Andre. I'm not sure they can do it."

"Like you said, if we have to carry them on our backs, we won't leave anyone behind."

I place my hand on his cheek. "You never try to hold me back. Thank you."

He leans forward, pressing his hand to mine. "And why would I want to restrain you? I need you, Isabelle. The whole you or nothing at all." He kisses me, soft and steady. "And the whole you is as tough a woman as I have ever met."

"It's time to move."

The group grumbles when I tell them to keep moving, but Charlotte stands next to me. "We can do this."

Josephine drags herself to standing. "I'm not sure my parents can walk much farther."

"They'll have to," I say. "And you will need to make sure of it."

We walk at a painfully slow pace, taking turns helping the Perrins. Henri pushes through fatigue and extreme weakness.

Andre sharpens sticks as we walk, handing one to each of us as he finishes the sharp points. We pass through a clearing, far too open and exposed. I scan the trees, watching the clouds descend around us, darkening but doing little to diminish the sweltering heat.

A flash of movement catches my eye. I turn, arms out, my breathing rapid.

"What is it?" Andre asks.

"I saw something."

"I see farmhouses up ahead," he says. "Let's find shelter in one for the afternoon and we can continue again at night."

"Andre, what if they're here?"

"They very well might be. But we have no choice but to carry on."

We arrive in a cluster of small farming homes. Andre asks if we may take shelter in a barn for the afternoon until the sun goes down. A man nods and shows us to a storage barn at the edge of the houses.

Everyone takes a spot on the ground, lying back and letting their bodies rest. I kneel in front of Henri and Charlotte. "Are you prepared to fight? If not, you may want to take another path to Geneva."

Henri holds my hand. "Remember when we saw slaves at the dock in La Rochelle?"

I cringe at the thought. "That memory is burned into me."

"Shackled and terrified," he says. "That will be us if we don't fight to stop it."

Charlotte rests her hand on ours. "I'm ready for anything."

I force a smile, worried about putting them in harm's way. I don't know who LaMarche might bring and what they would do if they found us.

The farmer was nice enough to replenish our wine, so I take a large gulp and walk to the tree line to watch the hills. I see nothing, I hear nothing, but still tension coils inside me.

"They're too smart to be in plain sight." Andre says.

"I know. But I can't just sit and wait."

Andre leans me against the rough bark of a red oak, slides his hand around my waist, and presses his lips to mine. I run my fingers through his hair and down his neck.

"My only regret of this adventure is not enough time alone with you." He kisses the top of my breasts as my knees soften.

"We must steal every moment we can," I say through heavy breaths. I lift his shirt and crawl my hands up his chest. "What happens when they find us?"

"Shh." He pulls back to look at me. "We'll figure it out. But right now, I want you."

He leads me into a copse of trees, shaded and clustered close. He lays me down and kisses me hungrily.

He lifts my skirts, hand trailing along my leg, teasing me with his touch. With sudden force, he presses my arms above my head and pushes inside me and I no longer worry about anything. All I can think of is my hunger for him. His body on top of mine, we rock and move together, his lips nearly touching mine but keeping distance enough to stare into my eyes.

He releases my arms, and I reach for his face. When his hand grips my thigh, we find another moment of exhilaration. Breathless, he finishes with a sweet, soft kiss.

He rests against my chest and as my heart settles, I hear something crunch in the distance, like a stick breaking under foot. Andre doesn't move. But I can now listen, and I hear everything.

CHAPTER TWENTY-NINE

Another nighttime walk through the hills. The terrain grows steeper and rockier. The air thins as we climb. Along a stretch of flat earth, my heart rate increases. I search the dark corners of boulders and trees, but still see nothing.

"Isabelle, it's hard to breathe up here," Josephine says.

"I know, but we must keep going." I wrap my arm around Madame Perrin and drag her along the rocky earth.

"Please, stop." Her knees give way.

"You don't understand. We don't have time."

"Why must we hurry?" Josephine asks. "Can't we rest a bit longer?"

Charlotte and Henri lean against each other, eyes heavy and shoulders slumped. The Perrins look at me as if I'm their torturer, not their savior. Against my judgment, I nod. "Fine. A few minutes."

Five heavy bodies collapse to the ground. Andre whispers in my ear, "You look worried."

"I am." I look at our weak and tired group, and worry crawls up my spine like a shiver.

"Naira would tell you to listen to nature," Andre says.

"Don't you feel it?"

"Yes," he says.

Taught by the Huron, we've both understood that our connection to the earth and wind and trees runs deep—if you're willing to listen.

"Everyone up," Andre says. "It's time to move."

They grumble and weep but drag themselves up.

As the group scrabbles over uneven ground, my arms grow cold. I turn back to hear galloping—the fast beat of horse hooves thumping from the darkness. I steady my feet and yell. "Scatter!"

From the black appears a horse. His long face rises and falls as he gallops toward us. The Perrins stumble behind me with grunts and screams. The horse approaches and a man's arm takes shape. From his hand, a whip dangles in the breeze.

Something grabs me from behind, drags me out of the horse's path. I throw my weight forward, hurling whoever is on me to the ground. Andre lifts his head.

"I'm so sorry," I say.

Screams. I turn to see the man on the horse galloping past the group, whipping them all on the backs. They fall to the ground, their screams piercing the night. I lift my skirts and run to them, but something trips me. I land hard on the ground and gasp for breath.

Hands grip my dress. They grab my arms and drag me toward the trees. I can't get my footing. It's dark and I'm disoriented. A familiar smell.

James.

I grab the flesh of his forearms in my fingers and twist until he screams. He yells and releases me, but only long enough to find my footing and face him. He lunges for me, but I throw my palm to his nose.

I hear running and stupidly turn around. "Andre?"

James wraps his arms around my waist. I kick and throw my head, but he clears my throws. "Stop, Isabelle!"

"Get off me!" I bite his wrist. He screams but only tightens his grip harder.

"Stop fighting! I won't hurt you."

"I don't believe you." I jab my heel into his shin, and he throws his body over mine, pressing me to the dirt. He leans to my ear. "Stop. LaMarche wants to hurt you. I came to stop him."

"Lies." I keep thrusting and kicking, but he seems to sense my every move.

His lips press to my ear. "I love you."

"No, you don't."

Screams again in the distance. Andre appears, runs toward us with eyes shining in the dark. Just as he nears, LaMarche appears from the dark and strikes Andre's temple with the handle of his whip. Andre falls to the ground with a grunt.

I wait for movement. "Andre?"

James yanks me to standing. LaMarche saunters over, twirling his whip in circles.

"Stay there, LaMarche," James says, his arms tight around my chest.

LaMarche laughs. "Shall I send a stake straight through this man's chest?" He whips Andre's back and I wince at the familiar sound I've heard in my dreams for years.

Andre grunts and forces himself to stand. He spits, presumably full of blood. Andre steadies himself and launches a punch straight into LaMarche's face.

I land my elbow hard into James's side and slam my heel onto his foot. He grabs my arm when I try to run away. I stare back at him, wishing I didn't have to do this. But then I hear the awful thwack of a whip that sends me to a place of rage. I knee James in the center of his damaged hip. The hip that never fully healed from being shattered in the war. The torture he endured because he protected me, and his father sent him to fight as punishment.

James crumbles to the ground, and I want to scream. "I don't want to hurt you."

I run to Andre as he and LaMarche exchange blows. James catches my ankle and I hit the ground with a thud. The hard earth knocks the breath from my chest.

I blink to focus and hear screaming. Three men appear from the trees. They have our group by the arms, by the hair, Josephine by her ankle. Henri is too weak to fight, but he tries. LaMarche takes one final harsh blow to Andre's cheek where he thuds to the ground, unmoving.

My breath cycles in and out, my heart thumping against a rock under my ribs.

LaMarche nears, his boots crushing rocks underneath. I push myself up, but he slams his foot over my hand. I hear a bone crack and blinding pain overtakes me. Unable to speak or move, I look at the men LaMarche hired to abduct us, holding us prisoner—all except one.

No Charlotte.

I almost smile knowing she's hiding, waiting for her move. Then James grabs hold of my ankles and yanks me back. Something slams into my head, and everything goes black.

 * * *

Wetness soaks my lips.

Is it water? Blood? I part my mouth feebly and taste wine on my tongue. I blink my eyes open, but quickly shut them again. Blurry darkness is all I see. I remind myself to stay calm, to keep breathing.

Thumping returns to my head, crawling through the numbness and coaxing me back to consciousness. I manage to grunt and blink again as shadows come into focus. We're in a barn. We must be near a village. A fire crackles in the center of the dirt.

My hand pounds with pain and I remember my broken bones. I groan, trying to wiggle the last two fingers, but the pain is too intense. A hand appears with wine again to my mouth. I turn to see James.

"Drink it."

"I would rather die."

"Stop being so stubborn, Isabelle." He slams the jug to the ground, wine sloshing over his hands. "I'm here to take you home."

"I'm not going anywhere with you." My voice trembles.

"You are my wife," he says through a tightened jaw. I want to scream at him that I cancelled our contract and I'm free of him. But I don't say a word. Not yet.

They've tied Josephine to her parents, their backs against each other. Henri is tied to the wall, whip marks swollen and red across his bare back. Andre is in the corner, crumpled and bloody, his hands tied at his waist. His eye is swollen, and his lip busted, blood dried on his chin.

Control yourself, I think. Naira told me about captors. How they use family to manipulate you. The room comes into focus now. Hunting storage. Muskets, rifles, butchering knives, and even bow and arrow. A table against the wall, presumably used for butchering, is stained burgundy with bits of dried raw meat on the legs.

"You would let him hurt me?" I ask James, my eyes set on LaMarche.

"No. Even though you poisoned me."

I pull my hand to my chest, my arm shaking from the pain. "It was sleeping powder."

LaMarche steps closer and I look up at him, my jaw tight. "I don't understand the hold you have over Monsieur Beaumont." He sighs. "We did our best to save him from you, but…" He throws his hands up. "One cannot fully rid himself of the demons that live deep inside."

James clears his throat and looks down at the ground like a shamed child.

"What do you want from us?" I ask.

He kneels face to face with me. "You know what I want. The documents." He pulls a blade from his holster. "And I want you to pay for what you did to me back in Paris."

James pushes him in the center of the chest. "You promised you wouldn't hurt her."

He looks down at me with a sneer. "I've broken her hand and punched her hard enough to go unconscious. *Now* you ask that I don't hurt her?"

"Just give him the documents, Isabelle," James says. "You can all go free."

One look at LaMarche's face tells me that none of us are going free. "You believed him when he said that?" I ask James.

"He wanted the scrolls, and I wanted you."

I push with my good hand, noting a sore flank where I landed on a rock. With a grimace, I lumber up and lean against the barn wall. "How could you want me after all this?"

He leans into my ear. "I saw you with *him*. In the field. You were making me pay for my indiscretions. I promise you, it worked. It nearly killed me to watch you with him."

Sick bastard.

LaMarche saunters over to Andre, guarded by two of his men. I watch closely, noting the Perrins as they tremble.

LaMarche grabs his whip. He first smiles at me, then lashes Andre's legs. I don't scream like he wants me to. Andre's legs recoil, but when he catches his breath, he twists to the side and spits blood. He looks up at LaMarche. "Coward."

LaMarche winds his arm for another lash, splitting Andre's sleeve and exposing raw, bloody flesh. I step forward. "Stop."

LaMarche turns to face me, but my eyes stay on Andre as he lifts the front of his shirt to reveal a bare chest. No documents. Andre shakes his head left to right slowly.

One of LaMarche's men lights a homemade torch in the fire. He holds the blazing cloth to Josephine's feet until she screams. I lunge toward her, but LaMarche steps in front of me. "Where are they?"

"I don't know. Now stop!"

Josephine screams loud and frantic. Flashes of blood splatter into my memory as they drip down limestone walls, and I must remind myself that I am not dreaming. This is real. LaMarche lifts his hand, and the man pulls the torch away. Josephine stomps her foot in the dirt as it smokes from the toe of her boot. She rocks and whimpers.

As I watch LaMarche pace, I note a shadow behind a barrel. One eye appears from the darkness. Standing behind a post, at last, is Charlotte, rifle at her side. She slipped in and lifted a gun from the wall without being noticed. Smart girl.

"Who is next?" LaMarche asks. He turns in a circle and stares at Henri's bare back. "This pig needs another lesson."

I smell the searing flesh of Henri's father when they burned him at the stake. How his hair released a scent of sulfur as it went up in flames.

I grit my teeth and grab James's shirt with my good hand. Ball it in my fist and beg him. "Make it stop. I will go with you. Just please, make it stop."

He looks at LaMarche. "Let them free."

"No," he says.

"I'll make good on my promise. You helped me get her back, so I'll tell you where the money is."

LaMarche steps closer, whip dragging at his feet. "Well, then?"

"In a chest in Antoinette's apartment. She had the money all along."

LaMarche snarls. "You stupid fool!" He balls his fists. "Antoinette left Paris and took everything with her. I don't know where she went."

James moves near my shoulder, but LaMarche pushes him back. "You make him remember a time long gone. A time when his family lived as heathens. Dirty, filthy, lying Protestants."

"Your own daughter lied to you. She betrayed you both." I grin, withholding a laugh.

LaMarche slaps my cheek. A sharp edge of my tooth cuts into my tongue. It makes me think of our friend Etienne. Before they severed his tongue, he screamed loud enough for Henri and me to hear. His words float back to me like a fog. *You may take my body, but my mind remains free.*

The day I watched him dragged through the streets, I knew my life would never be the same. My branding is seared into my memory. Far worse than the white-hot iron blackening my skin was watching my mother scream. Knowing we were all powerless.

LaMarche slaps me again on the other cheek.

Naira. I float away from the torment of my memories to see her shining black eyes. She smiles at me and bows her head. *Step one, master your mind. Step two, master your body.*

Another slap, and another. The sting reminds me that even with a broken hand and blurred vision, I am still stronger than him. I will never be powerless again.

A smile forms when I narrow my eyes at LaMarche, and it enrages him.

LaMarche breathes a long sigh onto my cheek. "It was me who rammed the blade through your father's stomach. I watched him fall to the ground and beg for mercy." He releases a slow, controlled breath. "I smiled as he took his last breath."

I close my eyes and swallow the bitter taste in my mouth. I lean my head back and sigh, then slowly track my eyes down past Charlotte as I lower my vision to the ground. She's poised, ready to shoot.

Chills climb through my body as realization hits. "He fought you for what you did to my mother. It wasn't about his ships at all."

"That day, I got a taste of Protestant blood. And it left me thirsty for more."

"And that is why, Monsieur LaMarche, you will burn in the fiery pits of hell." I look straight into his eyes. "I've seen it in my dreams. The devil will pull you from earth and set your black soul ablaze." Disgust boils through him.

"Isabelle, stop." James says.

"No, I will not stop. This man raised a wicked daughter. He kills and tortures and makes our Huguenot lives miserable. He steals children and imprisons innocents. He deserves the eternity of torture God will surely shackle him with." I raise my voice, nearly shouting. "God will rain fury down you and you will see the faces of those you killed. Burned flesh and sliced faces. The screams of shackled women will pierce your ears until you can no longer stand it and you will stab yourself over and over until your eyes bleed your soul clean."

LaMarche reaches for his knife and charges toward me. I sense James wants to stop him, so I elbow him in the face to force him back, then I reach for LaMarche's blade, slam my arm into his elbow and twist the blade from his hand.

As he reaches back, his anger slowing his reactions, I flip the handle and land the knife deep in his chest. LaMarche stumbles back and stares at me, too stunned to move. His men run toward me, but Charlotte shoots from the corner, a bullet landing in the back of one's head. Andre kicks the legs out from another and reaches for a spear, shoving it through another's hand. The man writhes but Andre rolls him into the fire, his hand still speared.

James grabs me from behind. Charlotte shoots again, but misses the third man, who pounces on Andre. Instead of fighting James off me, I lean back and use him as a fulcrum as he pulls me toward the door. I arch my back and slam my feet into the third man's ribs. He doubles over but reaches for a knife. Charlotte runs toward him with an ax, landing straight in the man's fleshy neck.

Andre cuts the ropes binding Henri to the rafter and Charlotte rushes to release the Perrins while one of LaMarche's men burns bright red in the fire. I look around, but LaMarche has disappeared. Slipped out of the barn during the fight.

James drags me outside, but I throw the back of my head into his face.

He releases me, hand to his bleeding nose. "Dammit, Isabelle. Where did you learn all this?"

"Naira." I catch my breath, looking in every direction for LaMarche. "She taught me to fight. To listen."

I realize we're on a rocky ledge, the hunting lodge on the only flat section of earth.

"I'm not here to hurt you," he says. "When a street beggar found me and told me he helped you escape the city, I knew this was my last chance. I'm here to save you from LaMarche and bring you home."

"You aren't listening. James, I am no longer your wife." I let my words settle into him. "I wrote to the notary to break our marriage contract."

Blood dribbles down his chin, but he doesn't wipe it away. "You finally did it. You broke free of me."

"I tried to love you, James. I did. After everything you did to save me. I felt I owed you to try."

His chin crumples as it only does when he holds back tears. "Is this because of Antoinette?"

"No. You bedded her because I couldn't make you happy."

Footsteps. Many of them. I turn to see my forged family surround me, each with a weapon pointed at James. Charlotte and Henri with rifles, Andre with an ax, and even Monsieur Perrin with a scythe.

James pauses and looks around at all the people here to protect me. He steps slower, but stops when Andre steps forward, ax raised in the air. "We could have had a wonderful life, Isabelle," James says. He ignores the group and focuses on me. "But you never let go of your Huguenot past. You never fully let me save you."

"I didn't need to be saved."

Charlotte walks to me, hands me a bow and arrow, and nods.

"You want to be with..." He barely flicks his eyes toward Andre. "You want to be a Protestant."

"Yes, James." Bow in my left hand, arrow in my right, I feel, and I listen. "I want you to let me go."

He opens his mouth to speak but without a second thought, I position the bow, use my strong fingers to pull back the arrow against the crushing pain in my other two. I exhale, and I release my grip.

The arrow flies just past James, nearly grazing his ear, and lands in the neck of LaMarche who stands still in the dark shadows, rifle pointed at the back of James's head. LaMarche stumbles forward into the moonlight, hand trying to catch the pooling blood, but it gushes too fast. He looks at his hand, then at me. He tries to speak, but blood gargles in his throat and pours out of his mouth.

I drop the bow and arrow and walk to him. "I've never killed anyone before," I say. "But the world is better without you." I lift my skirts and kick his stomach hard enough to throw him back. He stumbles and loses his footing, falling backward off the rocky edge as the arrow drains the life from him. His soul will land where it belongs, in the dark, sharp, pit of sin.

I turn back to my family, raise one hand to indicate that they can lower their weapons. James stares at me, tears glistening in his eyes. "I should have seen it. You were using me. For secrets. I thought you loved me, that you simply needed me to try harder." He steps closer. "To be stronger. But you were living another life the entire time."

"So were you." I exhale and place my hand on his chest. "Go find Antoinette. She has your money."

"I wanted to force you to be my future. Now I realize I can't force you into anything." He looks Andre straight in the eyes. "I relent."

He nods, mustering what strength he has left.

"What about the documents?" I ask.

"Keep them. They're no use to me anymore. I have no interest in the slave trade… or imprisoning Huguenots."

As he walks away, I allow myself to exhale. James was part of my past, my step into womanhood. His lies taught me to be strong, to fight for truth. He brought me here, to this moment.

Without a word, we gather the weapons and return them to the hunting lodge. They aren't ours, and we won't need them where we're headed.

We climb the craggy hillside, stumble over rocks and through grassy fields, past clear streams and down into a valley. We are broken, burned, bruised. We are thirsty and exhausted, but we have each other.

The valley welcomes us, a peaceful cluster of whitewashed cabins with painted doors. A man approaches, walking stick in hand. He smiles widely. "Helvetia. You are safe."

Henri holds Charlotte and Monsieur Perrin wraps his arms around his family. Andre kisses my cheek. We stare at the village silently as Charlotte reaches into her skirt. She pulls out her tiny Geneva Bible. In the morning light, she holds it out to the man, who smiles and nods. "You are welcome here."

Sunlight pours from the sky, reflecting off the winding river that glistens blue and silver through the valley. Green hills surround the tiny town and the warm amber sun lights our way down the path to freedom. We take our first steps into our new life, where Protestantism may be practiced in the light of day, without consequence. Where temples still stand, and Bibles aren't hidden or burned. Where our scars are welcomed as symbols of our fight.

Where love lights the way.

FIVE YEARS LATER

Our home is a stone cottage. Two bedrooms and a kitchen, a cozy fireplace. Toys fill Elizabeth's bedroom. Andre sculpts animals out of wood and Elizabeth delights in creating worlds of fairies and toadstools and every wooden creature her father can create.

Andre has only sculpted one creature for me—a wolf. Tall legs with painted fur the same color as my hair. Eyes the color of sunlit forest moss. She stands at my windowsill where I glimpse her every morning when I wake. My nightmares have stopped. I often think of Naira and hear her whisper to me. *Dreams are the language of the soul.*

Now my sleep matches my awake.

This cool spring morning, Andre and I hold Elizabeth's hands as we walk home from church. Here in Geneva, we do not pray in the dark or in the forests. We attend service in a simple stone temple in the center of town where we sing freely in French, our voices loud and unrestrained. No more whispers. No more shadows.

"Isabelle," Elizabeth asks.

"Yes, darling?"

"Can you take me mushroom hunting again?"

"You enjoy the hills, do you?"

"Very much." She swings her hands forward and back with ours. "Papa says you know things."

I smile at Andre, whose eyes still light when he looks at me. "Does he now?"

"He says you're a fighter, just like Naira. I can't remember her, but I think I miss her."

"We all miss her," I say. "But everything she taught is still with us." I bend down to look into her deep brown eyes. "Do you miss Canada?"

"I don't remember much, but Papa is happy here, and so am I."

Andre bends down and lifts her in his arms. He kisses her on her cheek. "My little mushroom."

"I'm not a mushroom!"

He tickles her and her laughter turns my heart into a sweet ache. Once we arrive home and warm ourselves by the fire, a knock rattles the door. Elizabeth can hardly contain her excitement at seeing the Reynards. She loves playing with their daughter Clémentine.

We welcome them inside and the girls run off to Elizabeth's room to play.

"We didn't see you at church," I say.

Charlotte checks to ensure the door is closed. "We have news."

When Andre left Geneva, it took him ten months to return. Forced to stay in Quebec through the winter, he prepared Elizabeth for the journey, and I traversed the trails through France and Helvetia. Huguenot trails of those exiled, fleeing in secret, desperate for someone to guide them. I learned the terrain, sharpened my hunting and fighting skills, and Charlotte and I escorted dozens of families to their new homes. She has continued to learn the art of poisons, though thankfully has had no use for them here.

Monsieur Perrin works as a clockmaker and Josephine often watches the children while we help Huguenots escape their homeland. Henri works as a silversmith, but takes trips to France alone, feeding his burning hunger for Catholic retribution. He steals, mostly, though I doubt he stops there.

News means Henri has discovered something on his travels.

"The army wants to institute a new program," Henri says. "Billet soldiers in Huguenot homes. Allow them to torture families to force conversion."

The old, familiar anger pushes its way through the cracks of my peaceful exterior. "They're always finding new ways to torture."

"They'll brutalize women in every way imaginable. They'll beat the fathers and make them watch. Every awful thing you can imagine will come true," Henri says.

Charlotte balls a linen towel in her fist, wrapping it around her hand so tight that her fingers turn pale. I place my hand on her shoulder. "We are safe."

"But they aren't," she says.

"We have time. We'll make a plan."

Henri kisses Charlotte. He flashes her his usual devious smile. "We aren't done fighting, my love. We are simply getting started."

Andre pulls me to the window, glides his hands through my hair. "I promised you we would save everyone we could. I meant that."

"We have Elizabeth to think about." Without the tea from Quebec, I still never did carry a child, a surprise that has felt just right. "It's not like five years ago. We're a family now."

"You best serve our family by being true to your purpose."

I wrap my hands around his neck. His touch still weakens me. "The first thing you said to me the morning after we wed was 'I promise to love you forever.'"

"And I will." He kisses me softly as his hand glides along my collarbone. "I also promised to fight by your side."

"Does this mean we're heading back to France?"

His smile lights up as his copper eyes reflect the sunlight. "It means Henri is right. We're just getting started."

I wrap my arms around him and stare at the windowsill. My wolf stares back at me, her green eyes nudging me toward my pack. As if Naira smiles from the other side of the world.

When I close my eyes and listen, I feel it.

Naira was right. The quieter we become, the more we can hear. And my heart now guides me, my family by my side.

It is time to defy the Crown.

THE END

ACKNOWLEDGEMENTS

I'm extremely grateful to be able to tell this second installment of Isabelle's journey. My daughters are descended from at least thirty-three Daughters of the King, and I've been intrigued by their stories from the moment I first read about them. I wanted to explore incredible young women from our past and this series allows me to shine a light on heroines often overlooked in our history books.

I'm always hungry for more action-adventure stories with fierce female energy. The driving force behind the Defying the Crown series is to show young women that they are unstoppable and that their stories matter.

Thank you to Black Rose Writing for seeing the potential in this series and trusting me to continue Isabelle's historical adventure. This writer journey would not be possible without my critique partners and author friends whom I learn from every day. Lisa, Naomi, and Brigette, I'm so grateful for your friendship and incredible insight. Jen and Sayword, your writing skills are unmatched, and I'm so lucky to have you both in my life. To my mentor Irene, your teaching skills are a gift. The Women's Fiction Writers Association with its endless well of support and community has played such an important role in my growth as a writer.

As always, I give endless thanks to my husband Mike who supports my obsessive need to tell stories and always encourages my dreams. To my two daughters who keep me striving to be the best mom and give me a reason to never give up. To my stepdaughter Chelsea for her support, and my sister Heather for always being my person.

I'm grateful to every reader who has taken this journey with me. As I prepare for book three in this historical series, I will continue to strive for a wild and exciting adventure that will leave you hopeful for the future.

ABOUT THE AUTHOR

Kerry Chaput is an award-winning historical fiction author. She believes in the power of stories that highlight young women and found families. Born and raised in California, she now lives in the beautiful Pacific Northwest, where she can be found on hiking trails and in coffee shops.

Connect with her at www.kerrywrites.com.

NOTE FROM THE AUTHOR

Word-of-mouth is crucial for any author to succeed. If you enjoyed *Daughter of the Shadows*, please leave a review online—anywhere you are able. Even if it's just a sentence or two. It would make all the difference and would be very much appreciated.

Thanks!
Kerry Chaput

We hope you enjoyed reading this title from:

BLACK ROSE
writing™

www.blackrosewriting.com

Subscribe to our mailing list – *The Rosevine* – and receive
FREE books, daily deals, and stay current with news about
upcoming releases and our hottest authors.
Scan the QR code below to sign up.

Already a subscriber? Please accept a sincere thank you for
being a fan of Black Rose Writing authors.

View other Black Rose Writing titles at
www.blackrosewriting.com/books and use promo code
PRINT to receive a **20% discount** when purchasing.

CPSIA information can be obtained
at www.ICGtesting.com
Printed in the USA
LVHW090918270123
737749LV00001B/1

9 781685 131678